THIS IS NOT A
F*CKING ROMANCE

EVIE SNOW

EXILE
PUBLISHING

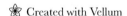

The Rules

Rule 0: Follow the Rules or be banned.

Rule 1: Any more than three spiked items of clothing are banned outside of ~~Goth Night~~. (See Rule 10. Thanks, Kevin).

Rule 2: No throwing dice in anger—on Board Game Night or any other night. (This means you, Kevin).

Rule 3: No raining on anyone's parade.

Rule 4: No long tails on Furry Night.

Rule 5: No bitching on Drag Poetry Night unless you're the bitch onstage.

. . .

Rule 6: No contradicting Candy.

Rule 7: No one other than Candy is allowed behind the bar (unless invited).

Rule 8: No complaining about Barney's singing on Karaoke Night.

Rule 9: Candy's love life is off limits.

Rule 10: Goth Night is henceforth known as Prancing Rainbow Pony Appreciation Night. No arguments. (This means you, Kevin).

Rule 11: No arguing, strongly "discussing," or fighting in Hard Candy. (Kevin!)

Rule 12: Any song called "I Want Candy" will only be played at Hard Candy when hell freezes over.

The Nights

Monday: Munch Night

Tuesday: Drag Poetry Night

Wednesday: Furry Night

Thursday: ~~Goth Night~~ Prancing Rainbow Pony Appreciation Night

Friday: Geek Speed-Dating Night

Saturday: Karaoke Night

Sunday: Board Game Night

Chapter 1

Candy Blume had run her own bar for long enough to recognize trouble, and the skinny bleached blond who'd just walked into Hard Candy set off a whole bunch of alarm bells.

For one thing, he was trying too hard. People who came to her bar at five thirty p.m. on a Monday dressed up like an extra for *Mad Max: Fury Road* were *definitely* not acquainted with the rules Candy had posted on the door of the neon-pink TARDIS dominating one wall of her bar. Rule One clearly stated that any more than three spiked items of clothing were banned outside of Goth Night.

And it wasn't Goth Night.

It was never Goth Night thanks to Kevin, who was currently sitting with his posse in a back booth arguing over whether or not a black dragon could wipe out an entire Dungeons & Dragons party in one go.

Candy refocused on the newcomer. There was something about him that was making her feel squirrely, but she couldn't pinpoint the cause.

He was short—a couple of inches taller than her five feet nothing—and although he had a cocky, buzz-cut prettiness, he was definitely not comfortable in that outfit. His fake leather biker boots could've been pulled from a budget stripper's prop cupboard and his spiked belt made his stonewash jeans hang off his hips like a five-year-old's when wearing his dad's tool belt.

And then there was the jewelry.

Candy wasn't averse to a bunch of jewelry. In fact, she was currently wearing enough rings to level half a college football team, but this guy was wearing three spiked dog collars all stacked on top of each other. He'd also decked himself out with spiked armbands, wristbands and—if Candy wasn't mistaken—a fake eyebrow piercing. And it was all topped off by an exaggerated, crotch-first swagger that risked dislocating his hips.

This was a soft and squishy person trying to appear tough, and Candy had learned a long time ago that squishy things got squashed.

She suppressed a sigh. She was going to have to be nice. She didn't want to be nice. Nice wasn't her thing. She left that for the nice people.

She pulled a glass from the rack behind the bar and spritzed herself a Coke. She hadn't turned the music up yet because the patrons present were here for the conversation— or, more to the point, a verbal skirmish over a dragon's killing capabilities.

"Can I help you?" she asked when the guy reached the bar.

Spike Boy froze, his wide-eyed expression confirming her suspicions before he turned up the attitude. "You talkin' to me?"

The De Niro tough-guy act would've been perfect if his voice hadn't broken on the last word.

Candy raised her glass to her lips, making eye contact as she took her time drinking half its contents. She put the glass down. "Yep. I asked if I could help you. Can I get you anything?"

"Yeah, you can. I'm here to ask you something." Spike Boy tried to regain his earlier bravado, but he couldn't hide a trace of underlying vulnerability, the kind Candy associated with people like her best friend Sophie, who was way too nice for her own good. Candy's impression was validated when the guy flinched at a particularly loud bellow from the back of the room, which was followed by a plastic percussive noise Candy knew all too well.

"Kevin! What's Rule Two?" Candy yelled without breaking eye contact with the newcomer.

"No throwing dice in anger. But I'm not angry. I'm *mildly* irritated," Kevin said in a long-suffering grumble.

"Mildly irritated is what I'm gonna be on your ass if you don't pipe down. I'm hearing raised voices and dice being thrown aggressively, so here's how it's gonna go. It's my bar, so the damn dragon doesn't kill anyone. It flies over your little dwarves, elves and whatever-the-hell else, blows them a raspberry, then flutters off to file a tax return on all its gold like a proper dragon citizen. Got it? Or you're out."

There was a grumble of protest, quickly smothered as someone wisely put their hand over Kevin's mouth.

"I'm *so* glad we can all agree. And you—" Candy snapped her fingers to get Spike Boy's attention since he was now staring at Kevin's booth like a toddler gawping at bears in a zoo. "You wanted to ask me something?"

"Are you . . . are you Candy Blume?" He smoothed his hand over his hair in what would have been a casual gesture if he hadn't forgotten he was wearing a wristband with quarter-inch spikes on it.

Alarm bells picked up in Candy's head again. She'd heard that question a lot over the past two years, usually from debt collectors wanting to pick her bones for money her ex-husband owed them. Spike Boy didn't look like a debt collector, but neither had the last two leeches, whose fake gold chains had made them look like the rejected extras from

Straight Outta Compton. She slipped a hand below the bar to touch the baseball bat she kept within easy reach. After the last time her ex-husband had paid her a visit and broken her arm in some messed-up effort to convince her to stay with him, she'd decided the time to be caught unawares was over.

"Yeah, I'm Candy Blume," she said. "Who wants to know?" If this guy wanted to do this conversation in clichés, so could she. With more attitude. While asleep.

His Adam's apple bobbed as he swallowed. "I'm Matthew . . . Matty." He thrust his hand across the bar. After a few moments Candy let go of the bat. She made a point of gripping his hand firmly before she picked up her glass of Coke to take another sip.

"Hi, Matty. How can I help you?"

Matty Last-Name-Still-Unknown glanced around as if taking in his surroundings for the first time: the zinc bar, the steampunk copper coffee machine, the antique beer taps, the giant cogwork sculpture hanging over the back booths and the giant cast-iron chandelier overhead. He focused for a long moment on the prominent portraits of Johnny Rotten and Patti Smith in their cogwork frames next to the shelves of spirits, then turned his attention back to Candy, who, as was customary, had done up her heart-shaped face in Gothic makeup to match her black-on-black clothing. She'd used extra liner this morning, liking how it made her look a little like Kayako Saeki, the vengeful ghost from *The Grudge*. Sometimes a woman had to paint on the confidence she wanted to feel.

As his eyes reached the top of her head, Candy noted he'd used a whole lot of too-pale concealer to cover up acne across his cheekbones and on his chin. Oh, this guy was so squishy he should come with a warning.

"Gwen didn't tell me that you had a shaved head," he said after an awkward silence.

Candy gave him her best fierce scowl. "Gwen?"

"My sister. She went to high school with you."

"Ah." Candy's Spidey senses tingled even more. High school had not been a high point in her life. She'd been reminded as much last night when some idiot had tagged her in an old picture on Instagram of her standing next to her old locker and scowling at her nemesis, popular pretty-boy cliché Trent Green. Trent had been making fun of her hair, which she'd worn over one half of her face because her love of Japanese horror movies was long and studied. The idiot who'd tagged her had hash-tagged the image #happymemories.

Candy had untagged herself from the picture and then reached for the hair clippers. Minutes later the bathroom floor had been littered with the remnants of her signature black waist-length mop. Sometimes you had to cut the past off.

Running a hand over her short-shaved hair, she looked at Matty suspiciously. "Gwen who?"

"Smith," Matty said quickly.

"Smith?" Candy swirled the last of the Coke in her glass. "Nope, doesn't ring a bell. That's quite a generic last name you've got there."

"She's three years younger than you."

"That would explain it. So, I'm gonna ask again, how can I help you? Or are you here just to tell me your sister's not up to date on my hairstyle?"

Matty's Adam's apple bobbed again. "It's my twenty-first birthday next week. On Wednesday."

A crack formed in Candy's defenses. "Congratulations," she said.

"And I wanna hold my party here. I was wondering if I could talk to you about that?"

Candy shifted her head side to side to release a little of the tension. So that was it: geeky gay kid about to turn twenty-one hears that some edgy girl his sister went to school with owns a bar and wants to show his friends he's now a big boy with a whole new badass personality. It happened sometimes.

"You want a Coke?" she asked.

"Yeah . . . uh, yes ma'am."

"How many people are we talking here?" Candy asked over the sound of ice cubes clinking into a glass.

Matty shifted his weight, obviously trying to get back some of his previous attitude but not knowing how. "Um, maybe a hundred or so. Maybe more."

"That's a whole lot of people." Candy scanned her bar, doing the math. One hundred college-age newcomers in this small space? They'd drink way too much, there'd be security issues, and, if Matty's outfit was any indication, they'd be trying to live up to their image of Hard Candy by dressing in their Halloween sluttiest. All this meant hard work, likely destruction of property, and the potential alienation of Candy's regulars. Still, most of her Wednesday night crowd *would* be out of town attending Furry Fiesta in Dallas, and if she sent out an email this afternoon, people shouldn't be too put out . . .

She made a snap decision. "You'd have to rent the whole bar."

"Yeah. That's the idea." Matty shrugged as if it were no big deal.

"I'll be carding everyone, and I can spot a fake from a mile away. Anyone who tries that shit on me will be out on their ass within seconds. I don't care if it's a private party or not."

"Yeah. Most—all of my friends—are older than I am. They're cool."

Candy slid the Coke she'd just poured across the bar, noting the way Matty's hand shook as he picked it up. The crack in her tough exterior widened even more.

This guy was just a baby. Sure, he was only nine years younger than Candy, but he was a world younger in experience. If Matty Smith wanted to walk on the wild side for his twenty-first, Candy wasn't going to stop him. And she wasn't going to destroy his illusions by telling him that the wild side in this case was just a lot of happy, friendly geeks who liked to dress up when they weren't working regular jobs.

"Alright, Matty Smith. Let's talk," she said, already doing the math on how much to charge. The number her brain came up with was a nice one. A very nice one. "I don't want to mess around. Are you sure you can afford to rent an entire bar for a night? That's a lot of money. I'll need a fifty-percent deposit and there'll be a minimum drinks charge to make it worth my while."

Matty's chin jutted out. "I know. But my bro can afford it."

Candy tilted her head to the side at this sudden vehemence. Her gut was telling her something still wasn't quite right here, but still . . . money was money and Candy needed a lot of it right now if she was going to do more than just keep Hard Candy open.

"Alright then. Let's work out some numbers, and if they don't make your brother faint, it'll be my pleasure for you to have your birthday party at my bar next Wednesday."

Chapter 2

Trent Green surveyed his specially designed kitchen with the air of an inconvenienced tyrant. He should have been content. He was surrounded by melted chocolate and sponge cake; his patisserie, Dolce Design, had more work than ever; he'd almost gotten the last of his four siblings through high school; and he was running ahead of schedule on today's orders.

Everything would be looking great if it weren't for his kid brother, Matty, who had spent the past twelve years making Trent's life hell. In fact, Matty was one of the reasons Trent had scrawled "What doesn't kill you makes you stronger!" in Magic Marker on the wall above his 3D chocolate printer.

Yeah, the words weren't original, but that didn't mean Trent hadn't earned that motto. His parents should have named him Trent "Adversity Crusher" Green, because then maybe he'd be leading the life he'd imagined for himself at age eighteen: working as an award-winning architect, chilling with his friends on the weekends, and playing in the band he'd formed in high school. Maybe he'd have a wife by now, or at least a girlfriend and time for more than casual sex. Instead he'd been given the middle name "Placido," meaning "serene and peaceful" in his mother's native Italian. It had caught the attention of the irony police and they had come down hard, leaving him solely responsible for three almost-grown sisters and one pain-in-the-ass brother while running a gourmet patisserie that was regularly visited by Austin's high-strung brides-to-be. As Trent's nona had said over breakfast, his life contained so much drama that he should write to the networks about featuring him in a reality show. He was beginning to think she was right.

He hunched his phone between ear and shoulder while checking the consistency of the Ecuadorian single-origin chocolate that was halfway to melting in a double boiler.

"Are you even listening to me?" Matty demanded in his ear.

"I'm listening, but what you're saying isn't making much sense," Trent replied. "You want to hold your twenty-first in a what?"

He could almost hear Matty's eye-roll. "Like I told you, it's a steampunk bar. I've already talked to the owner and negotiated a price—"

"You, negotiated a price? You? Did you promise them one of your kidneys or two? No, wait, let me guess . . . you signed away the house." Trent swirled a spoon around the pot, momentarily distracted by the beauty of the moment when all the chocolate pieces melted down in a rush, transforming into liquid heaven.

"No, I told the bar's owner she could make you her *bitch* because you drive me *insane*. Anyway, like I said, I've arranged a price and I just need you to transfer the deposit. She needs it by tonight so she can let her regulars know the bar will be shut for a private function. I said that wouldn't be a problem." Matty threw the words down like a gauntlet, knowing full well how seriously Trent took commitments made by himself or his family, especially financial ones.

"So are you gonna tell me the number you negotiated?"

Matty did and Trent immediately autopiloted into a short meditation exercise designed to stop his adrenals from exploding. He pictured himself sitting in a safe, quiet space for a couple of seconds while *not* focusing on how much easier it would be if he walked out the door, climbed into his truck and drove far, far away.

Trent's safe place was the rocky outcrop in Garner State Park that he'd climbed two days after his high school graduation. Back then he'd been free to do whatever he wanted; the world had been open to him and he'd been spoiled for choice. It had been the last time he'd felt like that, because one week later . . .

Trent forced himself to refocus on stirring the chocolate, even if it meant doing so more vigorously than needed. As the scent of pure luxury wafted up, he concentrated on that. It was almost perfect consistency. Soon he'd be able to work it with the cream he had already sitting out, turning it into a silky ganache. Everything neat, pliable . . . scientifically calculable. If only his family were this easy.

"You gonna say anything?" Matty demanded.

"That's a lot of money." Trent cursed himself for not giving his brother a budget. What the hell had he been thinking? Yeah, he could afford it, but that didn't mean he wanted to spend that much for a bunch of Matty's friends to get shit-faced. Not when he still had the twins' college tuition looming in the distance.

"Yeah, but you said I could have my party wherever I wanted."

"Why do you wanna have your birthday party in a steampunk bar? I thought you wanted to do something that the whole family could be a part of."

Matty made a noise between an exasperated groan and a sigh. "No, *you* thought I'd want to do something with family . . . and it's not like Nona isn't going to be cooking me a birthday dinner before. This time I want to do something without anyone there who'll make me feel like crap for existing."

Trent spotted that for the grenade it was and sidestepped it. Matty always pulled the guilt-trip card when he was trying to sneak something past Trent. He just had to work out what that thing was.

Trent's parents hadn't exactly been cool with Matty being gay. It had taken them dying for Trent to wise up to how different his childhood had been from Matty's. While he'd been their straight and popular oldest son, Matty had been a weedy, geeky gay kid who was constantly fighting a losing battle to earn their parents' love. And no matter how much Trent had tried to fix the damage his parents had done in the twelve years since they'd died, Matty was still able to turn the guilt screws on Trent for not being there when he was younger. Some days, when Trent was caught unawares, the guilt trips worked; some days, like today, he didn't buy it.

"What the hell is a steampunk bar? What does steam have to do with punk?" he asked as he took the pot off the double boiler and skirted around his patissier, Rakeem, to carry it across the room.

Matty let out a frustrated growl. "Are you an idiot or something? How could you not know what steampunk is? It's punk with, like, steam . . . Victoriana stuff. Like Goth but with more brown leather and cogs. Surely you've been asked to design a steampunk cake before now."

Trent had, but since his little brother was going to bust his balls no matter what, he couldn't resist the urge to do some busting right back. "And what do cogs and steam have to do with you turning twenty-one?" Trent asked as he set the pot of chocolate on a workbench where he'd laid out all the tools and ingredients for this batch of truffles: scrapers and spoons along with tubs of organic Jersey cream and cups of freshly diced macadamia nuts.

"Nothing and everything! This is about me deciding who I

want to be. I'm not a kid and the way you treat me is *so* disrespectful. You were already taking care of the four of us by the time you were my age! *You* didn't have to answer to anyone."

Right. Anyone except Nona, four grieving siblings, all our Irish relatives in Massachusetts, our Italian relatives in New Jersey, and a whole lot of debt collectors. And that's not even counting the fact I was breaking every one of Dad and Mom's rules about how men were supposed to act when I took on running Nona's cake-making business.

Trent swiped the back of his hand over his forehead, catching the way Rakeem's shoulders were shaking with silent laughter. Trent's family dramas were the constant amusement of his kitchen staff.

"Is the person you want to be someone who's studied for their finals so they can earn their business degree with a decent grade point average?"

Trent knew he'd pushed it to far the minute the words left his mouth. The problem was, when it came to Matty, he never got the balance of being a big brother and a father figure right. Trent had tried his best not to ride Matty too hard, but he had so many hopes for his siblings. He wanted them to have high-paying careers in jobs they loved so they never had to repeat his struggles with money. His sister Gwen was well on the way with her medical residency, and the twins, Carlotta and Anna, were headed to college to study law and veterinary science, but Matty had always treated his college education like it was an unpleasant obligation.

"I just want to know you understand that this life isn't going to give you any breaks and that your education is important," Trent said and knew it was the wrong thing yet again when he was met with obstinate silence. He huffed a sigh. "Alright. If this is what you want—a party with your friends and no family interfering—it's what you're gonna get. No strings, no guilt. I get it. But this is your birthday and graduation gift combined. Hear me?"

Matty made a spluttering noise. "You're actually gonna pay for this party? You mean that? *Really* mean that?"

"Yeah. I mean that. The whole thing about turning twenty-one is that you can decide what you want to do. I'm not happy with how expensive this party is, but I respect that I didn't give you a budget, so send me the payment details and I'll take care of it."

"Really? *Really?*"

"Yeah." Trent allowed himself a smile at the incredulity in Matty's voice. "Really. Now get off the phone, asshole. I've got some truffles to make."

"Okay! Great. I'll send through the details now!"

"Yeah, love you too," Trent said to dead air before putting down his phone and staring blankly at the rapidly cooling chocolate before him. He mentally went through his schedule for the rest of the day—if he got these truffles done, finished hand-painting the other, specially commissioned ones for that art gallery opening and dropped by the hardware store for a new seal for the downstairs bathroom tap tomorrow instead of today, he'd have time to check out this bar.

He'd said there wouldn't be any family interfering, and he was a man of his word—there would be absolutely no interfering at the party itself. But that didn't mean he wasn't going to check this place out to make sure it was safe.

Matty might be hard work, but he was Trent's little brother and he loved him. Sometimes.

Chapter 3

By ten p.m., the Dungeons & Dragons game at Hard Candy had been replaced by a bunch of regulars from the local BDSM community having their weekly munch.

As usual, the only sign that this was a group of kinksters was the teddy bear sitting on their table, put there so any nervous newcomers could find them. To anyone else, they were just a bunch of people loudly bickering over which *Star Trek* series was the best.

"Can you tell them to keep it down? I'm trying to work here."

Candy paused in making a cappuccino to study the hulking silhouette of Kevin, who was now sitting in his usual spot at the end of the bar. The light from the chandelier limned his Afro like a halo, fooling one into thinking he was a cuddly black angel in a button-down shirt.

"What's Rule Three?" she demanded.

Kevin looked up from the MacBook he'd been furiously typing on moments before. "This isn't a matter of Rule Three. I'm not raining on anyone's parade. I'm just saying that they need to keep it down in order not to rain on *mine*. I'm trying to create and they're being disrespectful. I'm at a vital moment in my plot."

"What part of you sitting in a bar to write factors into this?" Candy sprinkled a generous amount of cocoa powder over the froth on the coffee and wandered his way, placing the Skeletor mug she kept just for him by his left hand.

"The questionable atmosphere in here is sadly my muse." Kevin gave her a surly scowl before thanking her politely.

"And what plotty rabbit hole has your muse lured you into tonight?" Candy studied her newly painted black fingernails to hide her amusement.

"My hero has just worked out that his nemesis has infiltrated his cerebral cortex, and he's about to learn that he can duplicate himself and shrink down to fight for his own sanity, using his neural pathways as micro teleportation devices."

"Sounds complex."

"It is. It's important I get it right." Kevin went back to furiously typing for a moment and then stopped abruptly, as if remembering something. "I like what you've done with your hair. It suits you. I think I'll base another character on you."

Candy ran a hand over her head, enjoying the feel of the short stubble. "Can you make this one solvent, with an awesome life? And while you're at it, have her not take shit from anyone."

"No, there would be no conflict if she has an awesome life. You'd be better off asking for her to be a chaotic character whose life gets better. And if she didn't take shit from anyone all the time, she'd be unlikeable. She needs to be at least somewhat likeable. And you're likeable when you're not being mean. Sometimes." Kevin went back to typing.

"Gee, thanks," Candy said wryly. "Then start her out all chaotic, but make sure her life's truly amazing by the end." She rapped her knuckles on the bar to get his attention again. "And while you're at it, remember I'm closing early tonight so

I can pretend the real me *has* a life. You've got to wrap up whatever plot you're working on by eleven."

"I'll try," Kevin said with a martyred air. "What time are you opening in the morning?"

"Noon like every other day, but you can come in at ten. Just let yourself in through the back door. Although, I'm gonna need you to walk Barney for me," she said referring to her English bull terrier, who was currently "guarding" the bed in her apartment upstairs instead of snoozing by the base of the coffee machine. Since no hot food was served at Hard Candy—she had a deal with a couple of nearby restaurants for delivery to customers— she usually managed to get away with having Barney in the bar during nighttime business hours. This was mainly because almost everyone loved him, and he spent most of his non-walky hours snoring out of sight of anyone who didn't.

Kevin huffed a sigh. "Alright, just make sure you leave out some poop bags."

"You always say the sweetest things to me." Candy blew Kevin a kiss, waiting as he predictably caught it and put it in his shirt pocket. It was one of the most adorable advertisements for OCD ever.

"Hey Candy, can we get a couple more of those daiquiris?"

Candy turned to see Jake, one of her favorite friendly sadists, standing at the other end of the bar. He was tall, blond and looking hella sexy in a sharp blue suit.

Candy put her hand on her hip. "You got money to pay for 'em, big boy?"

"I got more than that for you." He gave her a grin that would have melted her on the spot if she wasn't completely off men, especially alpha men with a proclivity for spanking. "Love your hair by the way," Jake said. "It makes you look even sexier."

Candy rolled her eyes as she plucked a bottle of Bacardi

off the shelf. She expertly added some crushed ice to a shaker and then followed it with a squeeze of lime, some simple syrup, and the rum. "Is that even possible? I thought I was the sexiest woman alive."

Jake frowned thoughtfully, then raised his voice to be heard over the sound of the shaker. "I didn't think it was possible to enhance perfection, but you've managed it."

"You're only saying that so I don't put strychnine in your cocktails." Candy poured the drinks into two chilled glasses and slid them towards him, collecting his money and putting it in her old-fashioned cash register. "Hey, while you're here sexually harassing me, would you know anyone who wants to do some bar work next Wednesday for a private function? Women preferable. I'll take men, too, but no handsy assholes. We're talking around one hundred college-age kids coming to a twenty-first, and I've got no idea if they're going to be angels or demons from hell."

"Might do. How many bodies do you need?" he said, suddenly all business. Jake was a band manager and knew a lot of out-of-work musicians.

"Around two or three should do it. One on the door, one to help me serve drinks and maybe one spare if I can't talk Kevin into being here." She ignored Kevin's snort.

Jake nodded. "I'm on it. What's the best way for them to get ahold of you? Messaging okay?"

"Yeah, but I'd rather meet them in person. Before Monday preferably."

"Done."

Candy spent a moment watching him return to his table. Since her divorce two years ago she might have decided men weren't worth the energy, but that didn't mean she'd given up looking at them.

Her phone buzzed in her back pocket and she pulled it out to see a message from her ex-mother-in-law.

Candy, we need to talk about Beau. It's urgent. Don't ignore this. Please.

Her entire body tensed.

"Kevin?" she asked.

"Typing."

"Can you man the bar for a couple of minutes?"

"Can it wait?"

"Nope. I've got to make a call and it's gotta be private. It'll only be five minutes. Pretend it's research for that kick-ass character you're gonna base on me."

Kevin frowned. "What about Rule Seven?"

"I'm waiving Rule Seven for now, and I'm also thinking of waiving it next Wednesday for that private party if you're interested in helping out. But you have to act like a proper barman if someone orders something you don't approve of. Not the Drinks Police. Got it?"

His eyes brightened. "Are you giving me the keys to the register?"

Candy reared back. "Not on your *life*. You'll only try and reorganize my cash drawer. And I am definitely not in the mood to be lectured about tidiness. If someone needs change or wants to pay with a card, tell them I'll be back in a minute."

"Okay." Looking long-suffering, Kevin allowed himself to be ushered behind the bar. The minute he got there he started frowning at the shelves that were normally hidden from the customers' view. "You could really organize this place more—"

Candy pulled the key out of the register, jamming it into the front pocket of her jeans. "Don't want to hear it. If there's anything urgent, just knock on the door. And remember, no tidying or sorting *anything*, or there go your coffee privileges and my benevolence in not requiring a minimum drinks order for your D & D games. Don't push me. I'm psychically watching you." Candy pointed two fingers at her eyes and then at him, grabbed her phone, then walked the two steps to her shoebox-sized office and closed the door behind her.

Leaning against it, she finally let the dread she was feeling overwhelm her for one long moment before pulling herself together.

Marlene answered the call straight away, her words coming out in a harried rush. "We need to talk about Beau."

"Yeah, I saw that from your message." Candy glanced around the tiny room, barely seeing the trays of receipts, shelves of files and the ancient PC sitting on the makeshift desk she'd concocted from an old hardwood door and bricks she'd found next to a dumpster. She'd once had a proper desk, but she'd had to sell it to pay off the credit-card debt Beau had racked up to supply his habit. With its crumbling red bricks, the substitute desk actually fit the bar's vibe better than the old one. Candy knew she'd find that funny one day.

"Beau's finally, *finally* agreed to start going to Narcotics Anonymous," Marlene said. Only someone who'd lived with a junkie in their home could understand the relief in her voice.

Candy closed her eyes and let her head fall back against the door. "Good for him."

"And since it's such a huge step I was thinking that it would be great if . . . maybe we could both go to his first meeting. To show our support."

The words hung in the air for a moment. Hurt that Marlene would think she'd even consider this, Candy spoke before she caught herself. "Why should I care, Marlene? He took everything from me. My home, my life savings, most of my friends and a big chunk of my self-respect and dignity. And worse, he exploited Sophie's generosity when she got that job for him on her brother's ranch by trying to rape her and blackmail her for goddamn drug money. And then, after I told him that I was divorcing his ass, he broke my arm. So give me one good reason why I should waste one more minute on him."

"You had some years of happiness. It doesn't serve anyone to pretend otherwise." Marlene's words contained the gentle censure that killed Candy a little bit more every time she heard it. "Just think about it. That's all I'm asking. The meeting is next Wednesday. I'll message you the details and call you again once you've had time to think. Bye now." With that Marlene hung up, leaving the small sense of happiness Candy had built of late lying shattered at her feet.

She swiped the back of her hand over gritty eyes that had been dry of tears for nearly two years—ever since she'd learned that the man she'd once loved more than anything no longer existed. "Fuck."

Chapter 4

Trent stared at the heavy wooden door in front of him, which, with its large bolts, resembled the entrance to a medieval castle or a dungeon. There weren't any signs on the door saying if the place was open, or if it was even a bar. Just the scorched words "Hard Candy."

He checked his phone for the details Matty had messaged through. Yeah, he was in the right place. He just wasn't sure what kind of place this was.

He glanced from side to side, taking in the fifties-themed laundromat to his left. An Elvis track was playing on a juke-box, and the people inside seemed to be having a good time—or as much of a good time as someone could have washing their underwear. On the other side of Hard Candy was a restaurant specializing in Cajun home cooking. If the smell of the food was any indication, it was worth investigating later.

On down the street, Trent could see Sixth Street—the notorious hub of Austin's nightlife—which he'd never really sampled other than the time he'd visited a bunch of bars armed with a fake ID on his eighteenth birthday. Not long afterwards, his parents had died, leaving him working too many jobs with too much responsibility. It was one of the reasons he'd given Gwen and now Matty the chance to have a birthday blowout on their twenty-first. Gwen had asked for a gift card at her favorite bookstore instead of a big party, but Matty wanted this.

Shrugging off a small twinge of self-pity that always came with thoughts of what could have been, he refocused on the bar in front of him. There could be anything behind that closed door, which had him worried. Despite Matty's attitude, Trent's brother had all the survival instincts of a limping chicken buying a package tour of Gator Island.

Out of all his siblings, Matty was the one Trent worried about the most. Matty's unique combination of naiveté and arrogance acted like a red flag to the wrong crowd, and Trent often found himself lying awake at night imagining all the trouble a lippy gay kid could get into if they ended up in the wrong Austin bar, on the wrong Austin street. This was a great town, but that didn't mean there weren't assholes here.

And with Matty wanting to have his party in a bar named Hard Candy . . . well, Trent couldn't be blamed for being concerned. The problem was, Trent's baby brother had already made an agreement with the owner, which meant that unless the place was a strip club owned by the mob or a biker gang, Trent was obliged to pay the deposit. The expensive deposit.

Bracing himself for some seedy dive, Trent pushed open the door and was met with . . .

"The Love Cats" by The Cure?

Feeling disoriented, he took in his surroundings and experienced an old kick of inspiration. Twelve years ago, he'd been completely caught up in the image of himself as an architect, designing unique spaces for people who'd appreciate his talent.

And this place was definitely unique.

The floor was covered in reclaimed boards that had been painted in black enamel except for every tenth board or so, which had been painted a dull gold. The huge cast-iron chandelier hanging from the pressed-tin ceiling should have been overpowering, but it wasn't. Instead it complemented the distressed brown-leather booths, the zinc bar, and what was either a Victorian-era steam engine or a copper coffee machine made up of old-fashioned levers and taps. Even the beer taps looked like antiques, resembling the faucets from a claw-foot tub in some old haunted English mansion.

The entire back wall was taken up by a kinetic sculpture that featured a series of turning cogs backlit in neon blue. And in an odd, whimsical touch, there was an old-fashioned British police box painted bright pink to the side of the discreetly lit room. "TARDIS of the People" was written in scrolled cursive across the top of the door, and below it was a chalkboard bearing a numbered list written in very small print.

There were a bunch of people conversing in the booths next to the backlit sculpture, but far from the gay-bashing rednecks Trent had anticipated, they all looked like regular citizens who'd dropped by after a hard day at the office.

He allowed himself to relax. Yeah, this was cool. It seemed welcoming, non-judgmental, safe . . . Maybe he'd underestimated Matty. *Again, like always*, a small voice echoed in his head, driving home the guilt he always felt when he got it wrong with his little brother.

Who wouldn't want to have a party somewhere like this? It even smelled great. There had to be incense burning somewhere, and the smoky-exotic scent was inviting rather than overpowering.

Trent turned his attention back to the bar, where a hulking barman with an impressive 'fro was studying him with a frown, as if he was ready to pound on anyone who insulted his place. Trent could respect that. A big barman meant security. This guy looked like he could handle himself.

He wandered over and settled on a barstool made from a

repurposed vintage tractor seat. "This is one helluva place, man," he said.

"I like it," the barman replied abruptly.

"I think I might too." Trent studied the shelves of spirits displayed against a bevelled and etched mirror. Anyone who owned a place like this wouldn't want it trashed, which meant they'd probably keep an eye out for drugs or bad behavior. The barman alone looked like he could take care of an army.

"Hey, my kid brother is thinking of having a party here next week and I was wondering how strict you guys are," Trent said.

"There are rules here."

The way the barman spoke implied the rules were strictly enforced.

"That's good, that's really good." Trent reached into his wallet, pulled out a twenty and pushed it across the bar. "Johnnie Walker on the rocks." He tried to keep his voice as casual as possible, not wanting to betray the fact that he hadn't been in a bar in a non-work situation for over three whole years. That last time had been at a bachelor party for a high school buddy.

Trent had left early when it had dawned on him that he couldn't relate to any of his old friends anymore. They'd known him as the prom king headed for college with everything he could ever want, not the substitute father who was wading through neck-high debt while looking after four siblings. While his high school friends had been goofing through their first years of college, Trent had been working three jobs to meet his household's expenses. And when he hadn't been doing that, he'd been struggling to learn how to communicate with the brother and sisters his ultra-traditional parents had taught him were his inferiors.

He wasn't so stupid to think the attitude adjustment wasn't ultimately a good thing, but it also meant he had a whole lot of trouble relating to anyone who'd been a part of his old life.

The lonely realization had only been tempered by the knowledge that one day—maybe once he'd finished paying off the twins' college—he'd be able to work out who he was and get his life back.

Maybe he'd even be able to come somewhere like this without worrying about neglecting his responsibilities. The thought cheered him. The twins would be done with school in four years. Four years wasn't all that long.

The big guy behind the bar looked at the money. "Are you going to want any change?"

A wave of goodwill overtook him. "Nah, man. Keep it all."

"Alright." The barman turned and studied the shelves, readjusting the position of bottles here and there with an air of intense concentration, acting as if he had all the time in the world. It felt like an age, but he eventually reached for a bottle of bourbon, carefully measuring out a single shot over ice cubes before wordlessly sliding it towards Trent.

"Thanks." Trent took the glass, figuring the care in making sure the measure was right was another good sign; the last thing he wanted for Matty's party was a generous barman. Matty had never had a head for booze, and for some reason Trent never understood, his little brother had spent the past three years sucking up to a bunch of UT frat boys and sorority girls. Trent wouldn't trust them not to do something shitty if Matty was out of it. Having almost been one of those frat boys, he knew exactly the type of shit they'd try and pull.

He took a sip of the whiskey, glancing at the group of laughing people at the back of the bar and finally let himself relax. The people in here were a world away from Matty's usual crowd. Hell, those guys even had a teddy bear on their table. No wonder Matty liked it here.

Knowing it'd put him in Matty's good books for the first time in a year, Trent got out his phone and transferred the money for his brother's party on the spot.

Trent barely had a chance to bask in the glow of doing a good deed before someone walked in, the music from the laundromat clashing with The Cure for a few notes before the door slammed shut again.

The newcomer was obviously a regular because she started chattering straight away.

"Hi, y'all! Kevin, you look great. I read your latest book. It was so awesome. I *loved* the ending. It really took me by surprise."

Trent glanced over his shoulder at the familiar voice, his eyes widening as he took in a curvaceous blonde in a neon-blue shift dress and red heels. She had legs that went on forever and waist-length hair that surrounded pretty, girl-next-door features.

Trent knew that face. He remembered that face contorted with angry tears the last time he'd seen it. It wasn't a high point in his past.

"Sophie Grey?" he said, but she didn't hear him. Instead she walked over to the booth housing the group with the teddy bear, her voice the same bubbly rush of words that Trent remembered from high school.

"Hey guys! Oh my God, you all look great! Atsuko, how did your *shibari* workshop go? When was that? Two months ago, right? I would've loved to come, but Ian's not really into being tied up. *I'm* not really into being tied up either, but I'm pretty sure Ian would try it if I ever said the word, just to stop me from bustling around the place all the time."

Sophie laughed, and the sound brought an uneasy smile to Trent's lips even as he tried to work out how he'd manage this situation. He also made a mental note to look up "shibari." Raising three sisters and a little brother right through his twenties had left him feeling completely out of touch with his own generation.

"Hey, you never know, you might like it," replied a woman with a sweet, round face and short wavy hair.

Sophie continued talking. "I might. I mean, I haven't tried it! But Ian's super bossy so that counts, right? Not that you guys need to hear that. Anyway, you know what I'm like—I'll talk to you all night, and I know you're here to catch up and meet new people. If any of you ever want to holiday in Hopeville just give me a yell. It'd be great to show you around."

With a cheerful wave, she turned on her heel and fronted up to the bar, turning a hundred-watt grin on the barman.

"Hey, Kevin, can you pour me a Jack and Coke? I totally need it. I was just at this big, schmoozy charity fundraiser thing Ian's friend Sean organized and I'm *really* craving something to help me unwind. Ian might feel at home with all that money sloshing around but I'm not. I had to drink two glasses of wine just to calm myself down so I didn't talk some billionaire's ears off and scare his checkbook away."

"You're talking a lot now, so I don't think it worked," the barman said.

Sophie tapped her bottom lip with her finger, wrinkling her nose. "You're probably right, but I don't have to worry now that I'm around friends, do I?" She slid her backside onto the barstool three down from Trent, giving the barman an inquiring look. "Where's my girl?"

"On the phone to someone in her office. She said she'd be back in five minutes. She's got the key to the register."

Sophie nodded solemnly. "I thought it was kind of strange, you being behind there. She temporarily breaking Rule Seven?" The way she said it implied that the last two words were capitalized.

"Yeah."

Trent knew he had to make his move now or not at all. He'd known this day would come. In fact, he'd intended for it to happen two years ago at a high school reunion he'd helped organize, but he hadn't been able to attend it due to his sister Anna breaking her arm at cheerleading practice. He'd spent that night in a hospital waiting room, catching most of the pictures of the reunion on Instagram. People had seemed like they were having a good time. Most of them. There'd been one picture of a group of his old friends with Sophie in the background. She and the person she'd come with hadn't been tagged but they'd been instantly recognizable. It had been obvious they'd not been enjoying themselves.

Bracing himself, he cleared his throat. "Sophie? Hey, it's me, Trent Green. How long's it been? Twelve years? It's good to see you."

If he expected a friendly reaction, he didn't get it.

Sophie's head jerked around, her mouth opening in a large O before she reached out and rapped her knuckles on the bar in front of her. The gesture took Trent straight back to high school, when she and her friend would knock on wood whenever he was around as if to ward off the devil. At the time he'd gotten a thrill out of being their big bad wolf, but seeing Sophie do it now gave him a sharp pang in his chest.

When she finally spoke, her tone was urgent. "Trent Green? What are you doing here?! You can't be here! Not here!"

"He walked in five minutes ago. Was I supposed to tell him to go away? Do you want me to make him go away?" the barman asked.

Trent held up his hands. "I can leave if you want. I don't want any trouble. But first I'd like to say that I'm sorry——"

"Does Candy know you're here?" She turned to the barman. "Did Candy let him in here, Kevin?"

Trent's gut lurched as he added two and two together. The bar's name, Sophie's presence . . . "This is Candy Blume's bar? Hard Candy is Candy Blume's place?"

Adrenaline started coursing through his system. He'd known for over a decade that this day was coming. That it needed to come. But he'd always pictured orchestrating it himself, not having it sprung on him when he wasn't prepared.

Sophie stared at him. "You didn't know? How could you not know?! You mean you didn't come here to cause trouble? Because if that's your intention, I'm gonna be the first in line to shoot you, Trent Green." She knocked on the bar again. "And I know a few other people who'd be right behind me. There's no way in hell you're gonna mess with my friend ever again." She jutted her jaw out, managing to look as fierce as a bunny rabbit guarding a carrot patch.

Trent leaned back at the vehemence of her words. "I'm not here to cause problems. I genuinely had no idea this was Candy's place." He saw the disbelief on Sophie's face. "If I'd known, I wouldn't have turned up out of the blue like this, thinking I'd be welcome."

Sophie opened her mouth to say more but was interrupted when someone else spoke first.

"You're not."

Trent swiveled around, saw the woman standing in an open doorway behind the bar, and took a walk straight down memory lane into a brick wall: Candy Blume, twelve years older and with even more attitude than she'd had in high school. Surrounded by thick liner, her almond-shaped eyes flashed pure "fuck you." She was also still whipcord-lean and dressed in black. Tonight it was black jeans and a black lacy camisole.

The short hair was new.

In high school, she'd had long hair that had hung over her face like the scary chicks in *The Ring*. In fact, she still looked like she'd be at home stealing human souls. Her long dagger-shaped earrings looked lethal, and there was enough jewelry on her fingers to function as knuckle dusters, capable of sending whoever she wanted to their maker.

"Candy. Wow. How long's it been?" The minute the words left Trent's mouth he knew they were a mistake. He'd pictured this moment so many times, imagining how he'd handle the

33

situation, what he'd say. He just hadn't imagined it would be like this.

He'd always wondered where Candy had ended up. Rumor had it that she and Beau Lineman had married straight after graduation and that she hadn't even applied to go to college. Trent sometimes wondered if maybe he'd played a part in the latter decision.

Over the years, he'd tried to make contact on social media so that he could arrange to meet her in person and apologize, but all her accounts had been private. And the few times he'd tried to work out how to get ahold of her through old high school friends, he'd always hit a wall. Candy's crowd and Trent's crowd had never been all that friendly, especially after what had gone down at their high school graduation.

She'd turned up dressed like the Bride of Frankenstein to the reunion, no doubt to stick it to him. For the past two years he'd imagined over and over how he would have handled that meeting, how he would have worded the apology, how he'd have fielded Candy's reaction.

"What the fuck are you doing in my bar, Green?" Candy snarled before slicing a hand through the air. "Actually, don't answer that, just get out."

"You heard her. You should leave now," Sophie said with an edge of steely determination. "Do I need to call Ian?" Sophie asked Candy. "He just dropped me here on the way back to our hotel, so he'll only be five minutes away."

Candy gave a sharp shake of her head. The daggers hanging from her ears glinted in the light. "No, he's leaving."

Trent held his hands up in the air. "No need to escalate this. I'm going. I was just here to check your bar out because my brother Matty told me he'd arranged to have his party here."

"That was *your* brother?" Candy's eyes widened, and she began vehemently shaking her head. "No way. There is no way he's having his party here. There is no way I'm going to wait on anyone from your family, you jackass. Now get out!"

"You heard the lady. I'd leave quietly if I were you." This came from a blue-suited blond guy who'd come over to see what the fuss was about.

Trent saw only hostile faces and knew he was beat. As he stood up, frustration at himself and at the situation made his next words come out precisely the wrong way. "I'm going. But I want that refund. Tonight," he said before walking for the door.

"It's coming back to you right now. Asshole!" Candy yelled, and he turned to see her giving him the finger while Sophie regarded him with an expression usually reserved for people who abandon puppies on roadsides.

Feeling like the lowest form of life on the planet, Trent stalked out to the curb where his truck was parked and climbed in, slamming his hands on the steering wheel in frustration. In all the different ways he'd imagined apologizing to Candy over the years, getting thrown out of her bar hadn't been one of them. And he sure as hell wanted to know how his little brother had known that Candy Blume owned a bar less than ten minutes away from Trent's store.

Chapter 5

Candy waited for the door to close before she let her shoulders slump. Her heart was pounding, and Jake, Kevin and Sophie were looking at her like they were expecting her to cry. There was no way in hell that was going to happen.

Thank God Candy had heard Sophie speaking to Trent. It had given her enough time to process the shock before opening the office door. Otherwise, who knows how she would have handled this shitshow?

Trent Green. Just thinking his name made her want to knock on wood, the tradition she and Sophie had started in high school when they'd decided he was the freakin' antichrist. He'd just sabotaged Candy's recitation of Lady Macbeth's soliloquy in their sophomore English class. Despite the attitude she projected, Candy had always been terrified of public speaking, and Trent clearing his throat loudly and fake-coughing through the whole thing had caused her to get the only C she'd ever received.

Trent fucking Green, sitting at her bar looking like the last twelve years had magically not happened for him, unless it meant making him appear even more all-American. His mom had been Italian, and his dad had been of Irish decent—he'd bragged about his heritage enough for everyone to know—but the mixed genes had somehow added up to a freckled face that could have featured in a Norman Rockwell painting, with its curly black hair and bright blue eyes. He was also still dressed like some James Dean wannabe, in a white T-shirt and black jeans. She'd once read that James Dean had been short like Trent too—although he had always towered over her. But who cares? Everyone towered over her, including Sophie, who was visibly holding back an avalanche of words, her lips tightly pressed together.

Before Sophie could verbally unleash, Candy gave her a faint shake of her head. She couldn't do sympathy with witnesses around. Not after the conversation she'd just had with Marlene. Not after she'd found Trent Green sitting in her bar like he owned the place.

Kevin cleared his throat, wiping his hands over his shirt. It was one of the nervous tics Candy had come to know well over the past five years.

"I take it he broke Rule Three?" he asked, referring to the rule that no patron of Hard Candy could rain on anyone else's parade.

Candy nodded, bracing her hands on the bar and locking her elbows. "A million times over. Every damn day of high school." Her voice was husky with restrained emotion; as much as she wanted to rip someone's head off, Kevin didn't deserve it. "Thanks, buddy. I appreciate you minding the bar."

"He gave me twenty dollars for a shot of scotch," Kevin said, already making his way back to the safety of his laptop. "I left it by the register."

"You should have told him that he couldn't drink here unless he signed away his soul to the devil."

Kevin shook his head, his expression pensive. "I'm pretty sure that interaction would only work if I were a succubus, or maybe a greater demon. But I don't really know how—"

Candy pointed to the door. "Begone, foul fiend!"

Only the faint crinkle at the corners of Kevin's eyes showed that his words had been said to ease tension, and not a result of his notoriously pedantic nature. "Tomorrow morning at ten, right?"

"Yeah. Not a second before. I'm gonna need to sleep in after tonight."

Candy watched Kevin leave, then turned to face the guys in the booths, cupping her hands around her mouth so they'd hear her over the Shearwater track currently playing. "Closing time's come early."

There was a good-natured amount of grumbling, but she gave them her patented death glare until they got the hint, even if that hint came with one or two of them blowing her raspberries.

Anyone would think she wasn't as scary as she used to be.

"You okay, sugar?" Jake asked, having stuck around. He put a hand on Sophie's shoulder and gave it a squeeze.

"I'm okay!" Sophie said, channelling a whole lot of fake cheer.

Jake turned to Candy. "And what about you, killer?"

Candy set her jaw. "Do I look like I'm not okay?"

He nodded. "I'll see y'all 'round. Don't do anything I wouldn't."

"I'd get arrested for most of the things you do," Candy marshaled up enough spark to say.

He let out a burst of laughter. "Only if they catch you."

As Jake and the last of his friends walked out the door, Sophie turned to her. "What the hell—" she began, but Candy cut her off.

"I can't right now. Let's pretend it didn't happen for a while, okay?"

Candy didn't mention a part of her distress had come from the conversation she'd just had with Marlene. The last days of Candy's marriage had seen Beau living and working at Lonely Creek, Sophie's family ranch in Hopeville. Rather than being grateful for the job, Beau had exploited Sophie's good nature by getting high and assaulting her.

Sophie had never held what Beau had done against Candy, but Candy couldn't forgive herself for not spotting the signs of his drug addiction earlier. If Candy had, she might have prevented his implosion from affecting those around her. Instead she'd kept her head in the sand, wanting to play happy family, and Sophie had gotten hurt. There was no way in hell she was going to let a man mess with any of her friends ever again. And, thankfully, Sophie now had a big tough Brit who loved her and could make sure no one took advantage of her good nature.

Sophie huffed out a breath. "I'd ask if you need a hug, but you're gonna say no."

"If you hug me I'm going to cry, and you know every time I cry a pixie kicks the bucket. It's like witchcraft." Candy patted her friend's hand. "Come on, let me refund The Prick's money," she said, referring to the name they'd given Trent years ago, "and then we can clean up and go upstairs. Barney's gonna be so excited to see you. You know how he gets when you drop by."

Candy felt a wave of relief when the warring emotions on Sophie's face finally settled into a rueful grin.

"Slave master." Sophie grabbed some spray disinfectant and a cloth and started wiping down tables with the muscle memory that came from spending a big chunk of her after-hours time at Hard Candy before she'd relocated to her father's ranch.

"You said it." Candy retrieved her phone from her back pocket and took care of Trent's refund before beginning to tidy up. "While we're working, why don't you tell me how many big swinging dicks were at this function you attended tonight," she said to Sophie.

"You mean besides Ian's?" Sophie gave Candy a wicked grin over her shoulder.

Candy rolled her eyes. "I don't need to know. I mean, with that bald head, he kind of *looks* like a giant—"

"—a giant, *handsome* whatever it was that you were gonna say, right?" Sophie brought over a glass Candy had missed earlier. "Can I tell you my good news now, or do you want me to save it?"

Candy's brows raised. "Spill. You look like you've got ants in your pants all of a sudden."

Sophie bit her lip and then held up her left hand.

It took Candy a couple of seconds to focus. "Is that what I think it is? Or has an iceberg swum all the way down to Texas and attached itself to your finger?"

"It is!" Sophie was practically vibrating with excitement as she fluttered her fingers, causing the massive diamond on her ring finger to catch the light from the chandelier. "He proposed! I mean, he would have earlier, but I wouldn't let him. Not until we were sure he wasn't gonna be bored living in Hopeville and running some small-town newspaper instead of *The London Voice*. But he hasn't gotten bored, and I couldn't love him more. And you would not *believe* the engagement gift he got me! He's bought this gorgeous old house on the edge of town, and he told me tonight that he's arranged for Dad and Hank to move our things from our cabin while we're here in Austin. They were all in on it! I'm so happy, I could burst. The only thing that prevented me calling and telling you earlier was that I knew you'd be too busy for us to celebrate."

Candy saw the joy in her best friend's face and squashed all the roiling emotions she suddenly felt deep, deep down. "Come here." She held out her arms, then was almost knocked off her feet when Sophie pulled her into a hug so tight it squished the breath from her body.

"You're gonna be my maid of honor, aren't you?" Sophie asked, her voice cracking.

Candy squeezed her back fiercely. "Hell yes. Someone's gotta make sure you get married right. The groom needs to know that if he doesn't treat you like a queen, he's gonna have to answer to me."

Sophie laughed, pulling back to look at Candy. Her eyes were shiny with happy tears. "I love your hair, by the way. If you want to keep it like that for the wedding, you go girl. You feel like you've gotten rid of all the bad stuff with it?"

Candy's eyes burned. She'd be crying now if she could. Sophie got her so well.

"Yeah," she lied. "Come on, I'll do the rest of the cleaning in the morning. Let's go upstairs so we can share the news with Barney."

She turned off the lights and the rotating cog sculpture on the back wall before leading Sophie through a concealed door at the back of the barroom. Beyond that, a short hallway led to the building's exit, downstairs to the keg room, or upstairs to the cozy studio apartment Candy had lived in ever since she'd lost everything she owned other than the bar and Barney.

As Candy put her hand on the door of her home, she made a promise to herself that if Trent Green ever tried to set foot in her life again, he'd leave on a stretcher.

Chapter 6

As Trent headed for his family's Rollingwood home, he tried to dredge up as many memories as he could from high school that included Candy Blume. There were a lot of them, and almost all of them left him with the ashy taste of shame in his mouth.

He remembered the first time he'd ever seen Candy, slumped down at her desk at the back of math class the first day of freshman year. She'd had her hair over her face and had been wearing black lacy gloves with the fingers cut out, her nails painted black. He'd joked that she'd gotten the date for Halloween wrong, and she'd given him the finger and told him to go fuck himself.

He would have let that go and left her alone, but then he'd learned that Candy was smart. Really smart, and real competition when it came to being top of the class. And Trent had to be the top of his class. There was no negotiation. He was Donovan Green's son and Donovan Green's kid had to be brainy like his dad.

Trent had loved his father like the earth loved the sun, but he'd always known his dad's love was one hundred percent dependant on Trent making him proud. Donovan

Green was the self-professed "smartest businessman in Austin," running an investment firm that lent big money to big real estate. He'd demanded that his oldest son be a mirror of his success, so Trent had to be the smartest kid in school. Trent's father made fun of anyone who threatened his dominance, so Trent did too. It was that simple. And later, when Matty had started to grow up, Trent had seen what could happen to a son who wouldn't, or couldn't, mirror Donovan Green in every way.

Trent remembered the first time he'd seen his dad making fun of Matty for playing with some of Gwen's old dolls. Trent had been thirteen, Matty had been four, but Trent still remembered seeing the shame on Matty's face and feeling a gut-level terror that his dad would make fun of him too. After he'd tried to defend his little brother, thirteen-year-old Trent had learned the hard way that mirroring his dad was the only way to survive unscathed.

An elderly lady driving a Benz swerved into his lane and Trent slammed on the brakes, automatically reaching out to stop a box of truffles from sliding off the passenger seat.

It was a long-standing tradition that Trent always made a couple of extra ones for his nona whenever he was trying a new batch. God knew she deserved them. At age eighty-two, she should be putting her feet up, but no matter how much Trent told her that he could handle things now, she still worked too hard.

He pulled into the driveway of his family's McMansion a couple of minutes later, turning off the truck and resting his forehead on the steering wheel for a moment before collecting the truffles and slowly walking to an ornate front door with a bunch of carved gargoyles looming over it—the epitome of the house's whole hacienda-meets-Gothic style. The door needed refinishing because Trent's dad had skimped on the quality of the timber, but Trent couldn't bring himself to spend the money. Instead, he was waiting until he had the time to install a simpler door that wouldn't make him cringe every time he walked through it.

Trent's parents had loved this place, with Trent's dad frequently expounding on how important it was for a man to have a castle over which he could be king. And then he had taken Trent's mom out on a boat on Lake Travis for their twentieth wedding anniversary and they'd never come back.

Trent remembered the day he'd found the scrawled note from his dad sitting on the dash of the Porsche he'd gotten for his sixteenth birthday. It'd told him to look after "The Castle." There'd been no mention of Trent's siblings or how to make ends meet after the lawyers had turned up and revealed that his dad's entire image had been built on bluster, bullshit and the kind of creative bookkeeping that could get a person locked in the slammer for years. The police had said Trent's parents' deaths had been an accident, and his father had frequently left him notes telling him what to do, but deep down a part of Trent suspected that there was more to the story than the police knew. Knowing he'd never be able to prove anything, he'd just gotten on with life, accepting that the person on which he'd modeled his entire identity had been a bully, a liar and a fraud.

The Porsche was long gone now, along with his dad's Maybach, jet skis, the expensive kitchen gadgets and his mother's jewelry. They'd all been sold to pay off debt. It had taken every ounce of Trent's intelligence to work out how to keep this house so his family could stay together, and more importantly, how to build relationships with siblings he'd largely ignored since childhood. Some days, when Matty, Gwen, Carlotta or Anna did well in school, or told him they loved him, Trent felt like he'd succeeded. On others, he felt like he'd lost the race before it even started.

As Trent pushed open the front door, he was greeted with a cacophony that confirmed his day would not be looking up any time soon.

It took him a minute to identify the voices echoing through the two-story living area. Matty was having a fight with Carlotta in one of the bedrooms beyond the upstairs balcony, their bellows only partially drowned out by the angsty electronica blaring from Matty's bedroom.

A spray of profanity echoed through the house.

"Hey!" Trent yelled, skirting around the gilt and brocade furniture his parents had bought when he was a kid to walk to the middle of the living room. "Are we all trying to go deaf or something?"

His answer was one slammed door and the music being turned up even louder, the bass beating a dull vibration through the walls and floor.

"Matty stole my new black boots and totally screwed up the heels! And he's saying he doesn't have to pay me back!" Carlotta yelled, appearing just beyond the gold-painted balcony railings. Her long blond hair looked like it had been pulled recently and her delicate features—identical to her much quieter sister Anna's—were screwed up in a pout.

Trent had heard this all way too many times before. "Yeah, yeah, I get it. If he stole them, then he should make some kind of reparation, but for Christ's sake put on some shorts or something so I don't have to see your underwear. Are you trying to scar me for life?" Trent held a hand over his eyes so he couldn't see through the railings and up her long Ramones T-shirt. Jesus Christ, some days . . .

"You hear that? Trent said you have to pay me back!" Carlotta yelled at Matty.

"You're such a liar. I didn't steal *anything*. I thought they were Anna's and she said I could borrow them!" Matty shrieked. "It's not my fault you bought cheap boots. Don't be such a lying bitch."

"Who are you calling a bitch, you elephant-footed *thief*!?"

"Hey! Hey, both of you!" Trent yelled over them. "Respect everyone else's right to peace and quiet or you're out of here."

His words were the right ones, but even he could hear his heart wasn't in them. Still, he was gratified when the music was turned down, even if he could still hear the argument going on in hissed undertones.

At least they were being kind of quiet.

Huffing out a breath, he walked across the room to the door leading to the kitchen. Everything else—including working out how Matty had known about the history between Trent and Candy—could wait for now. He had an important tradition to take care of.

Chapter 7

Half an hour after closing the bar, Candy was sprawled on her stomach across her bed, watching as Sophie cheerfully chopped up chicken with a wicked-looking cleaver. With her neon-blue dress—which clashed prettily with the cupboards Candy had painted crimson—her friend looked like an advertisement for the perfect sixties housewife.

The red cupboards, along with the dark-green walls and the eclectic thrift-store décor had been inspired by Candy's secret love of the French movie *Amelie*, even though she told anyone who asked that she'd gotten the idea from *The Addams Family*.

"Are we going to talk about what just happened at least once?" Sophie asked. Candy's dog, Barney, sat by her feet on the green paisley linoleum, wearing the adoring expression of an eternal canine optimist. The sound of his tail happily thumping on the floor accompanied the Charlotte Gainsbourg song playing on Candy's old turntable.

"Eeesh. Do we have to?" Candy groaned, burying her face in the fluffy black cushion she'd propped herself up on.

Since Candy's studio apartment would charitably be described as "cozy," the only seating options were Candy's double bed, a tattered armchair upholstered in burgundy velvet, or the two vintage Naugahyde kitchen chairs in mismatching red tucked under a small, spindle-legged table. And since Sophie was a much better cook and had insisted on making something to eat that didn't involve opening a Cup Noodle, Candy was letting her guard down. With Sophie she could admit that her feet were killing her from standing up all day; she could admit she wasn't invincible.

"I think we should go over it at least once to get it out of the way," Sophie said.

"We got it out of the way. It's out of the way. We don't need to talk about anything to do with Trent Green ever again. He's been banished. I'm not even gonna knock on wood anymore when I say his name. That's how little I care about him from this day forward." Candy's words were muffled by the cushion, but Barney seemed to understand them because he trotted over and jumped onto the bed, lumping seventy pounds of pure muscle over the small of her back. "You're not helping, boy." Candy flailed backwards to slap at Barney's rump, but her efforts were ignored. Instead the dog started talking to her in his deep-throated whine.

"You tell her, Barney," Sophie said over the sound of renewed chopping.

"You don't tell me squat." Candy levered herself up and twisted her head around to meet her dog's kind, tiny, triangular eyes. "You're my dog, you're supposed to be telling her there's an *omerta* on everything that happened in high school. You've seen *The Godfather*. You know what happens if you squeal. Your big goofball head's gonna be at the end of my bed."

Barney gave her a sharky smile and wagged his tail. Candy didn't even want to think of what all the white hair coming off him was doing to her black clothes.

Sophie frowned. "The mafia code of silence? Anyway, it

doesn't count. At least you can tell me what Trent meant about his brother having his party at Hard Candy."

"Yeah, alright." Candy shared the story of Matty coming to the bar that morning.

Sophie made a thoughtful noise as she set the cleaver down in the sink. "That's really weird. I mean, not the bit about Trent Green's little brother being gay, but why your bar? And why did Matty try and hide his last name but mentioned that his sister knew you?" She flicked her hair over her shoulder, frowning. "I kind of remember Gwen Green. She's around my size but shorter, with black curly hair. I think I tutored her in math once while I was volunteering with that academic extension program Mrs. Brandt was running."

"Yeah?" Candy propped herself up on her elbows. "If she was anything like her brother, I don't want to know."

"From memory, she was kinda geeky and nice. So nothing like him. But this brother, Matty . . . I'm wondering what his deal is. It doesn't make sense that he'd want to hold his party in your bar if he knew anything about your history with Trent. Unless he's up to something . . . or maybe rebelling. It can't be easy having Trent Green breathing down your neck, especially if you're even a little different."

"You're telling me." Candy scowled.

Sophie opened an overhead cupboard, standing on her tiptoes and peering in. "Do you have any cumin? Or ground coriander? I could turn this chicken into a curry."

"I have sriracha chili sauce. Maybe some ketchup . . . potentially some barbecue sauce if the packets that came with the takeout last week are still in there," Candy said. "If you mix them all together they might be nice."

Sophie made a rude noise. "No wonder you stay so skinny. You live on ketchup."

"And fries. Gotta have fries with that ketchup." Candy grunted as she finally succeeded in shoving Barney off her. He promptly rolled onto his back and she gave his pink tummy an absentminded pat as she swung her legs off the bed. "And maybe there's some ranch dressing in the fridge door. I was planning on having it with the chicken as a salad."

"A salad that's just chicken and ranch dressing? You know, between your dad's Chinese ancestry and your mom's German relatives, there's an ancestor crying ghostly tears."

Candy shrugged. "You know Mom's even worse at cooking than me, and Grandma Tang cooks for Dad in Hong Kong, so it's not like I ever had anyone to teach me."

"Doesn't your grandma always send you recipes?"

"Yeah, but she keeps assuming that I know stuff. The last one told me to measure the amount of water to use when I cook rice with my thumb. She says the water's supposed to be up to the knuckle. But whose knuckle? I tried. It didn't work, which means I'm destined to be as bad as Mom in the kitchen."

Sophie closed the cupboard and opened the fridge. "I still have nightmares about that time your mom served up those meatballs that were raw in the middle. Remember how she insisted meatballs are always supposed to be rare?"

"You think that was a one-off? Why do you think I stick mainly to processed food that can't kill me?"

"I'm beginning to see your logic. Hey, I think there might be a mistake. Are these *vegetables*?"

Candy rolled her eyes. "Are they brightly colored and soaked in vitamins?"

Sophie pulled out a bunch of carrots and a head of broccoli with the air of an explorer discovering a whole new civilization. "They're not even limp! This is amazing!"

"Anyone would think I have crap eating habits."

"Anyone would think that you're trying to pretend you don't," Sophie said.

"Listen, sister, I like food as much as anyone."

"But you can't be bothered making it yourself and you're too busy saving money to eat out most days. Which is why the only thing you have in your cupboards is ramen," Sophie said while rummaging in a drawer and pulling out a vegetable peeler. "You know the thing that gets me?"

"No, but I'm sure you're gonna tell me."

"It was the way Trent acted before you came out of your office. He seemed surprised to see me, like he had *no* idea that it was your bar. And then, when you kicked him out, he seemed hurt. After everything he did in school, you'd expect him to come up with something sarcastic to say about you, or even about the bar. But there was nothing. He just left."

Candy looked down at her lap. She was still trying to think of what to say when Sophie spoke again.

"I mean, maybe he came to apologize? Maybe he already knew it was your bar but was pretending he didn't so he could . . . No, that doesn't make sense either, because then why would his brother have booked the party? None of this makes sense. And why would his little brother have known Hard Candy is yours if Trent doesn't?"

"No idea and I don't care," Candy said. "He had his chance to grovel when we went to that stupid high school reunion he organized two years ago."

Sophie started furiously dicing carrots. "Yeah, and then he didn't even come! Remember that red dress I wore? I swear that thing was so tight it left a permanent imprint on my stomach."

Candy's mouth cocked up at the corner. "But your boobs looked great."

Sophie laughed. "That's what Ian told me. I was wearing that stupid dress when I met him, remember? And you were wearing the full Bride of Frankenstein thing. And the whole night was awful! That crappy honky-tonk! And me congratulating Gillian Pickering on being pregnant when she wasn't. Oh, and the hangover the next day after we came back here and got drunk. It was *horrible*."

"Yeah, it was awful." Candy plucked at a loose thread on

the black and burgundy patchwork bedspread her mom had gifted her when she'd moved into this place after her divorce.

"Do you think there's any way—like, *any* way—Trent might actually be feeling bad about how mean he was to you in school?" Sophie asked and then waved a hand. "Hold it, how could he not? I mean, let's forget about that horrible thing at graduation—"

"Yeah, let's," Candy said, not wanting to remember the one time she'd ever cried in public. Trent and his idiot friends had catcalled her when she'd walked up to accept the academic achievement award she'd spent her entire school career working towards. It had been one of the few times her dad had been able to afford to fly to the States and Trent had ruined it.

"But what about all those other times? Was there ever a time you managed to walk down the hall without him giving you hell?"

Candy shook her head. "Nope, not one."

"And yeah, you managed to hold your own, but surely he knew how crappy he was being."

"Surely."

Sophie's head shot up, her face flooding with remorse. "I'm talking too much and it's making you sad. Why didn't you tell me to shut up?"

"Because I didn't need to." Candy climbed off the bed and walked the short distance to the kitchen, wrapping her arms around Sophie's waist from behind. "And a woman has to give her kitchen slave a bit of a leash, otherwise she might stop cooking."

Sophie's body shook with laughter. "That's totally not gonna happen. I was too nervous to eat tonight, so I'm too hungry not to cook. And I *really* don't want your improvised sriracha and ranch dressing chicken."

"If you keep criticizing my kitchen skills, I'm not gonna offer you anything to drink." Candy stepped back, just managing to open the fridge door with the two of them in the kitchen. "What time do you have to be back at the hotel?"

"I told Ian not to wait up," Sophie said. "So if you're thinking of turning that tonic water in your fridge into a magical gin-soaked drink, feel free."

"Already on it. And while I'm at it, tell me what y'all have got planned for this wedding of yours. You're not gonna make me up like Asian Barbie, are you? Because if you are, I'm gonna have to slit my wrists right now and bleed out on the floor. And you know Barney's not gonna like that. Although, I'd wear pink if you wanted me to. You know I would," she amended.

Sophie shook her head. "No, too messy. Besides, being accused of involuntary manslaughter via pink bridesmaid dress would put a crimp on my honeymoon plans." She turned around, bracing herself against the kitchen counter as she looked Candy up and down. "How do you feel about something in red that's a little bit classy and a whole lot sexy?"

Candy laughed. "You mean like that dress you wore to our high school reunion? Because I hate to break it to you, but I'd need a whole lot of padding in the chest area. Not that I don't have a whole lot of drag queens I can call on for advice if you want me to pad this body out. In fact, they're probably more experienced at wearing a bra than I am!"

Sophie's laughter filled the room. "Don't tempt me! I'd love to see you in a pair of huge fake drag-boobs because I know you'd secretly love trying them on."

"Damn straight."

"Every wedding should have huge fake drag-boobs!"

"I sense a tradition coming on."

Sophie pumped her fist. "Right on! We're genius trailblazing women. We don't follow traditions, we make them! Now bring on the drag-boobs!"

Chapter 8

"Nona? You in here?" Trent walked into the kitchen and closed the heavy living room door behind him, breathing a sigh of relief as the sound of his siblings' fighting was reduced to a dull background hum.

Unlike the chaos that frequently permeated the rest of the house, this big airy room with its pink marble counters and terracotta pots of fragrant herbs was peaceful—or at least peaceful enough for Trent's nona to have fallen asleep in a rocking chair placed in front of the open French doors that led to the garden. Her short white hair was ruffled from the cool breeze, and her reading glasses had fallen into her lap. She was wearing her usual navy pants and her favorite yellow shirt dotted with white and green daisies. Without the animation of being awake, the shirt's vivid colors washed out her olive skin.

As always lately, Trent was struck by the lines her face had acquired since she'd taken on the burden of helping him raise their family.

"Hey." Trent crouched by her side, touching her on the shoulder.

She opened eyes that were the same warm brown as Trent's mom's had been. They crinkled at the corners with her smile. "Hello, honey. You're home late. There's some spaghetti in the refrigerator. Want me to heat it up for you?"

"No, no," Trent said in a hurry. "I brought you these."

He held out the box and she took it, weighing it in her hands, suddenly all business.

"What have we got today?"

"Those truffles the gallery commissioned. You know, the ones that were meant to look like Murano glass? I did up a couple extra for you."

He waited, his stomach knotting as she opened the box, making a pleased humming noise at the gold tissue paper Trent had used for presentation.

She selected a painstakingly decorated truffle, fumbling for her glasses before inspecting it. "Hand-painted? Using those new brushes you were so excited about getting last month?"

"Uh-huh." Trent walked over to the percolator where there was a half-warm jug of coffee and poured himself a cup.

She closed her eyes as she took a bite, swishing its flavor around her mouth like the connoisseur she was. "It's good. The texture's right and I like this new batch of chocolate you're working with. Single-origin?"

"Yeah. Ecuador."

"Hmm. It's almost as good as that batch you used from Cameroon a while ago." She swallowed, nodding as her eyes snapped open. "It was maybe a little too—"

"Much peppermint?" Trent cut in. "I was thinking that at first, but then I figured this was gonna be for a function where everyone would be drinking champagne, so their taste buds would be numbed, you know?"

That earned him an admonishing frown. "I was going to say maybe a little too indulgent for me this time of night. You're too hard on yourself."

Trent ran a hand over his hair to cover up a spark of embarrassment. "Only when it counts. And you know I value your opinion. It was your business first."

She gave him an arch look over her glasses. "My store sold birthday cakes for neighborhood christenings and birthdays. You're the one who turned it into the fancypants business it is today. Just one of your cakes earns as much as I used to in an entire year."

Trent waved off her words, not wanting to think about money right now. He spent almost all this time thinking about money, trying to work out how to pay for everyone's college degrees and health insurance, how to make sure he kept this house maintained when all the ostentatious add-ons his dad required had begun to fall into disrepair. The roof had sprung so many leaks lately, Trent swore he'd memorized every individual imported Italian tile, and he'd have to do something about the finish on the fancy marble floor in the living room, which was beginning to look scuffed and scratched. And then there was the maintenance on the expensive European air-conditioning system. Just the thought of how much it was all going to cost was giving Trent a headache. In fact, lately he thought about money so damn much that he swore his brain had dollar signs burned into it.

"Thanks for taking care of things tonight," he said, forcing himself to focus on his nona.

His nona shrugged. "It wasn't a problem. Although Carlotta and Matty need a kick in the pants." She huffed a sigh. "They take after your father with their tempers. I heard a couple of four-letter words earlier that I'd rather my grandchildren not know."

"So did I. I'll deal with it later, but with the twins being eighteen and Matty almost twenty-one I've got to handle it differently, you know? They're grown up and I've gotta respect that."

He opened the fridge, saw the pot of spaghetti in a rich tomato sauce and closed the door again. He always told her not to bother cooking for the family, but she always did anyway. He knew he should eat, but after the run-in with

Candy Blume he wasn't so hungry. In fact, the thought of what had gone down with Candy left him feeling slightly queasy. "Hey, do you know what Gwen's up to?" he asked.

"She said she was going to try and get some sleep, although I doubt that's working with all the yelling. Take her some food if you go talk to her. She's like you. She doesn't eat enough."

"Okay. Why don't you get some sleep?"

Trent's nona pushed herself out of her chair. "I might do that. You're a good boy."

Trent felt a sharp pain in his chest at her words, but he forced a smile. "You say that to all the guys. Sweet dreams."

He walked over and gave her a kiss on the top of her head, momentarily comforted by the scent of her floral shampoo. After she left the kitchen for her downstairs bedroom, he quickly heated up the leftover spaghetti, shredding some basil on top and grating some parmesan before plating a bowl and grabbing some cutlery.

Trent skirted around a basket of dirty laundry sitting at the top of the stairs on his way up. He'd asked the twins to wash it this morning, but as usual they'd forgotten; anyone who said two minds were better than one had never known Trent's sisters. Carlotta—the more political of the two—had probably spent her after-school hours writing a think piece for one of her activist groups, and Anna would have taken off to the animal shelter to volunteer. And now that they were home for the night, they'd both no doubt claim they were too tired to do their chores. Trent was proud of both of his sisters for already thinking about their future careers, but sometimes he wished they understood helping around the house was a part of being a fully functioning adult.

Feeling the tension building at the base of his neck—Carlotta and Matty were still arguing—Trent rapped his knuckles on Gwen's door. A sleepy voice told him to come in.

"Hey. Thought you might appreciate this," he said as he

let himself into Gwen's simply decorated room. He handed her the bowl of pasta before taking his usual seat on the floor with his back against her closed bedroom door.

"Oh thanks." Gwen was curled up on top of her bed wearing an oversized white T-shirt and plaid pajama pants. Her black hair, curly like Trent's, was messily plaited over her shoulder. "Tough day?" she asked, trying a bite of pasta and giving him an appreciative nod. As always there was a book on her lap, although this one didn't look like a medical textbook.

"Yeah. I see you're studying hard."

With a sunny smile, she raised the book so he could see the half-naked dude on the cover. "It qualifies as anatomy study. In fact, it's the study of multiple anatomies in many different unusual poses and positions, which I'm sure you don't wanna know about, so I won't tell you."

Trent rubbed his eyes. "Thank you from the bottom of my heart for being my only considerate sister."

"Can I have that in writing?"

"Yeah, the minute I get the energy to hold a pen." Trent glanced around the room, silently marveling at the piles of books on every surface. At twenty-six, Gwen was halfway through a medical residency at the Dell Seton Medical Center and, when she wasn't sleeping, spent most of her downtime reading. "Can I talk to you about something?"

"Hmm." She swallowed a mouthful of pasta. "What's up?"

He spread his legs out in front of him, ignoring Carlotta's muffled voice as she told Matty to do something anatomically impossible with his head and his ass. "I ran into Candy Blume today. Matty arranged for his twenty-first to be at Candy's bar without me knowing it was hers, and I stopped by to check it out." He tried to say the words casually but couldn't quite pull it off. "And . . . she wasn't too happy to see me. In fact . . ." He picked up a book, saw the genome sequence on the cover and set it down again. "She cussed me out and told me to leave."

Gwen set the bowl of pasta aside. "How you doin' with that?"

"Not too good." Trent looked down at his hands. "I tried to talk to her and apologize, but she didn't give me a chance."

Gwen was silent for a moment before sighing. "Yeah? Well, you knew this was coming one day."

Trent glanced up and saw the compassion that helped his sister excel in medicine. "I need you to tell it to me straight. Am I really different now than I was before? Because seeing how angry she still is . . . that's bad. Really bad." He ran a hand over his eyes. "Maybe it's just because I haven't slept lately, but it feels like I've been hit with a shovel."

"You want to talk to *me* about not getting any sleep?" Gwen's laid-back demeanor shifted to show a spark of the Green family feistiness. "You're actually talking to someone doing their medical residency about how little sleep *you* get? Did you *actually* do that?"

Trent gave her a reluctant half-smile. "Wouldn't dream of it. So help me out here. Have I changed?"

She picked up her bowl and munched on a mouthful of pasta before talking. "You're a completely different person now, and the best sign of that is that you're here asking me that question. I know this wouldn't make sense to someone who hasn't been through what we have—or who didn't know how religious Mom was and how chauvinistic Dad was. I mean, I loved them and miss them and everything, but . . ."

"But?"

"But we both know they spoiled you to the point of almost turning you into a sociopath." She held up her hand when Trent winced. "I'm not saying you didn't learn to be a decent human being after they died, because you did. The way you tried so hard, organizing all that family therapy, being there for all our school things, working all those extra jobs until you could get enough money to turn Nona's cake shop into what it is today . . . it's really admirable. Especially since you couldn't have picked a job that was more of a rebellion against what they taught us about men in the kitchen. And it was worth it, because your cakes are amazing. But Candy Blume doesn't know any of that, and if she did, she wouldn't care. To her, you're the chauvinist asshole who made her life hell in high school. I'm not surprised she's still angry."

Trent felt like every good thing he'd ever thought about himself was being torn down all over again. The first time had been when his parents had died. And now there was this . . .

A question he'd never brought himself to ask sprung to his lips. "Do you think . . . do you think Candy might've thought that I was picking on her because she's Chinese?"

Gwen winced. "Were you?"

"No!" Trent scrubbed his hands over his face, letting out a humourless laugh. "You'd think that would've come into it because of how Dad was, but it was only because she beat me in almost every test, every assignment, every essay. She was just so damn smart. And weird. That Goth thing? I didn't know what to do with it. I was spooked by a woman wearing black, can you believe it?" he said in disgust.

"Yeah, because I spent my entire childhood having to wear stuff that was considered 'ladylike.'" Gwen rolled her eyes. "I had so many dresses. Pink dresses. I miss Mom and Dad a lot sometimes, but the twins don't know how lucky they were to miss out on a lot of their old-fashioned ideas. But anyway, there's no way Candy would know any of this. It's not like you were holding up a sign saying 'I'm making your life hell because my dad won't love me unless I get better grades than you.'"

Trent let his head thunk back against the wall. "I should have fixed this before now. I've got to make this right."

"Yeah, you should have. And if I know anything about the person you've become, you will," Gwen said quietly. "If you could convince me to forgive you for being such a douchebag, you can convince anyone. I can't believe I like you now, but I do. It helps that you started bringing me food whenever you wanted to talk. Your cooking's gotten a lot better. You might want to think about opening some girly bullshit patisserie where no real man would be seen dead." She impersonated their dad's bluster, then gave him a cheeky smile to take the bite out of her words.

"You always give the best advice," Trent said with heartfelt sarcasm before giving in and laughing.

Gwen's smile dimmed. "While we're having this deep and meaningful conversation, I guess there's something you should know."

He looked at her sharply. "What?"

"Matty came to me two weeks ago after you two had that fight. You know, about him—"

"Turning up for work at Dolce Design stinking of booze and weed and scaring off the customers? Yeah, I remember."

"Well, I didn't know that's what he'd done. All I saw was him crying and saying you'd called him a bunch of names. Most of them sounding like the stuff Dad used to say to him."

"I can just guess what those names were." Trent squeezed his eyes shut at the memory of some of the stuff his dad had yelled at Matty over the years. "You know I wouldn't say any of that stuff, ever. And I never have. I don't know why he always goes to a dark place whenever he's in a corner. That was Dad, it's not me, and even at my worst, it never was me."

Gwen pressed her lips together. "I don't know how to help him either, or why he always goes there. And normally I'd have seen right through it as the usual crap he pulls, but he was pretty hysterical. So thinking it'd cheer him up to hear some of your dirty laundry, I told him—"

"About me and Candy Blume," Trent finished before groaning.

"Yeah. Thinking about it now, it was a weird thing to do,

but he caught me off guard and she was in my thoughts after I saw her in a picture on Facebook the other night. I'm sorry, bro. I should have known he was doing his usual thing of accusing you of being like Dad so he could get his way. I had no idea he'd go and—"

"Book his birthday party at a bar owned by someone who hates my guts?" Trent let out a humorless laugh. "I've spent years trying to get in contact with her, and I still never found out she owned a bar." He massaged his temples. "Or did you know about it and tell him?"

Gwen grimaced. "I've known for years."

"How'd you find out?"

She shrugged. "People talk. And I know a bunch of people you don't. Remember, you were one of the cool kids while I was one of the geeks that even the geeks thought were uncool. I figured that if Candy wanted to see you again, she'd let you know. Call it female solidarity. I love you, but I'm totally on her side when it comes to this. I'm just sorry I mentioned the bar to Matty. If I'd known he was gonna pull something like this . . . actually I'm too tired to think of what I would've done, but it would have required surgery to undo."

"You've got to give it to him, because now he's gonna act like I'm the bad guy when I bring it up. And to top it off, he's gotten Candy caught in the crossfire by promising her a bunch of money that she's had no choice but to return. I would've done the same in her shoes. I would've thrown the cash register at my head, too."

"Nooo, you would've done something far more devious than that. I just can't think of it right now. My brain's fried." Gwen yawned. "You'll make it right, don't worry. That teenage douchebag grew up to be a fine, honorable man who I'm proud to call my brother."

Trent studied her face. "Is that sarcasm?"

She wrinkled her nose. "Yeah, a little, but I still mean every word. Now let me digest this pasta in peace. I'm doing my first ever appendectomy tomorrow and if you don't go away, I'm gonna tell you all the gory details."

"Yeah, sure." Trent got to his feet. "Thanks, sis. Love you."

"Yeah. Love you too. Sorry about causing the drama." Gwen handed him her empty bowl and gave him a smile.

"Don't do it again." Trent gave her a faux glare before leaving the room to her relieved laughter. He closed her door behind him, his brain already strategizing.

An apology to Candy Blume had been a long time coming. It was gonna happen as soon as he could come up with a plan.

Chapter 9

Candy woke up to the sound of snoring. She groaned, flopped a hand over her eyes, then yelped when her rings hit her in the face. She hadn't taken off her jewelry last night and from the feel of it—she did a small wriggle under the covers—yeah, she was still wearing her jeans and a thong that was attempting to meld with her anatomy for maximum discomfort.

She lifted her hand and opened her eyes a fraction, feeling the grit of yesterday's makeup. Eeesh. She'd have to deal with that soon too.

"Barney, you're worse than sharing a bed with a man," she muttered to the dog hogging ninety percent of the bed. Barney's ear twitched but he kept on snoring. Through her open windows, Candy could also hear the laundromat jukebox playing James Brown and the sound of people wandering down the street. In the distance a police siren wailed.

She sat up, automatically raising a hand to push her hair behind her ears before remembering she'd shaved it off. She picked up her phone from her bedside table. "It's almost ten! You're a crap alarm clock, Barney. Aren't you supposed to wake me up so you can go to the bathroom or something?"

she said and then remembered he probably hadn't needed to go because he'd come outside with her to say goodbye to Sophie at four.

Stripping her camisole off over her head and unzipping her jeans before jumping out of bed, Candy ran to the tiny bathroom abutting the kitchen and turned on the shower so the water could heat up. Then she hurried to the kitchen and started brewing a fresh pot of coffee.

It took less than five minutes for her to shower, but it took another fifteen to get her makeup right. She went with her usual black eyeliner and mascara, but decided on some crimson lipstick—if she cursed at anyone today, they'd be able to lip-read the words even if they were too stupid to hear them.

After swiftly dressing in a black minidress with spaghetti straps and jamming her feet into a pair of scuffed black Doc Martens, she poured coffee into the biggest mug she could find, topped it up with cold water and walked over the to the bed, poking Barney's rump with a long black fingernail. "Wake up."

That earned her a low growl that was purely for show.

"Cut the crap, dog. Kevin's gonna be here soon and you two are gonna go for a walk to get some breakfast. Because you ate the last of your food when you counter-surfed yesterday."

On hearing his three favorite words—"Kevin," "walk," and "breakfast"—Barney sprang into action. He was standing by the front door within seconds, his ears perked up and his tail wagging.

"So great to see how much you love Kevin more than me."

Candy drained her coffee in several big gulps, wincing at it still being too hot. Kevin was going to be at the back door any minute and she had a bunch of admin to do before opening.

Plus, she had to work out how to politely tell Marlene not to push the topic when it came to Beau's NA meeting. Knowing Marlene, yesterday's call would just be the beginning of a campaign to wear Candy down.

While Marlene no doubt saw Beau going to Narcotics Anonymous as a sign that he'd had a "come to Jesus" moment, Candy thought it was a sign that he'd pissed off every dealer in the state and was looking for new ways to hook up. He was twisted up enough inside to only register the word "narcotics" in the name Narcotics Anonymous.

As if sensing the increased tension in the air, Barney made another grumbling noise. Candy walked to the door and gave him a pat on head. "Yeah, you're right. I should just get on with it and think about it later."

The dog yawned, showing off his adorably wonky teeth.

"Exactly." Candy gently slapped him on the butt. "You're gonna be in the bar with me today too, just in case Trent Green shows his face again. The code word is 'prick.' When you hear it, I want you to stop being such a wimp and bite him, got it?"

Barney wagged his tail.

"Great. Now let's get moving. We've got a day to kick in the balls."

"Candy, honey? Can you tell me if I'm uneven? I think my left titty's slipped, but I don't want to draw attention to it if I don't have to."

Candy paused in making a mai tai to glance up at Fantasia, an all-time favorite of the crowd noisily chatting away in the booths while awaiting the beginning of Drag Poetry Night. Fantasia was wearing a rainbow leotard that clung to her statuesque figure. Her glowing brown skin was decorated in more glitter than a kindergartener would use in a year, and her blue Marge Simpson wig was immaculately styled, but she was right—something was a little off . . .

"I don't think it's slipped down, it's gone sideways. Want to step into my office and fix it?" Candy offered.

Fantasia's blue bouffant wavered dangerously. "Hell yes! I'm on in ten and there is no way my words for the people are going to be upstaged by a rogue titty."

"Are your words going to be as derivative as last week? Because if they are, you'll need all the help you can get. Oh, wait, I forgot you were probably lip-synching. Find your writer and fire them." This was from Kevin who was occupying his usual seat at the end of the bar, the screen of his computer illuminating his face as he typed.

"It can speak?" Fantasia gave Candy a wide-eyed look, clutching her chest. "I never would have known after reading its last pop-up book." She leaned towards Kevin. "Do me a favor, sugar, look in your little computer dictionary for some words that rhyme with 'sass-mole' and 'wuck-fit' then apply them to yourself."

"Rule Five!" Candy pointed at the list of rules stuck to the pink TARDIS, which was currently being used as a tiny changing room for the night's performers. "And Seven," she added as an afterthought.

"Yes, *Kevin,* you know the rules. No bitching on Drag Poetry Night unless you're the bitch onstage, and don't you *dare* rain on my parade," Fantasia recounted as she strutted behind the bar, wagging her finger—complete with inch-long blue nails—under Kevin's nose.

"You're raining on my parade with your cross-eyed chest," Kevin shot back. "Isn't learning how to pad yourself one of the most basic things about doing drag?"

"Isn't learning to write one of the most basic things about being a writer? It's a good thing I'm wearing my good shoes, or I'd be using one of them to beat some good ol' ABC into you:

'*Always* Know You *Better* Respect *Creatures* of Pure Perfection.' You're just blinded by the glow of my magnificence." Fantasia fluttered her fingers at her face. "Take it in, honey—it's the only sunlight you've probably had today, and it is going to *burn* you."

"The only magnificence I'm seeing is how magnificently ignorant your audience is for not seeing the hideousness of your costume. The probability of you losing your balance and getting a concussion is much more likely than me being 'burned.'" Kevin raised his fingers in scare quotes. "And if there were a sunscreen to prevent you from happening to me once a week, I would gladly use it."

Fantasia clutched her chest. "You? Use any kind of lotion? Honey, the only lotion you use is at two in the morning when you realize that you still have no one to love you, and—"

Candy clapped her hands together, cutting off the weekly verbal skirmish that was as much a part of Hard Candy as she was. "Someone please remind me what the consequences are for breaking rules? Oh, that's right, you get yourselves kicked out. Follow the rules or flutter away, people."

"I always follow the rules. My rules." Fantasia snatched up a cocktail umbrella and stuck it into the side of Kevin's Afro as she sashayed into Candy's office, slamming the door behind her.

"She thinks she's so hilarious." Kevin plucked the umbrella out of his hair and slid it neatly into his shirt pocket before continuing his typing. He muttered something else, but Candy couldn't hear over the room's chatter and the sound of the night's emcee, Queera Belle, making sure the microphone was working properly. Candy ignored Kevin while she took drink orders from a rowdy bunch of queens who were now whooping for the show to start. At some point they'd kidnapped Candy's dog, and now Barney was wearing an orange feather boa as he sat in their back booth, his sharky smile on show for anyone who gave him a pat.

Barney always loved Drag Poetry Night and had even

been known to howl along if a queen's performance was particularly bad.

Queera Belle flicked a length of platinum hair over her shoulder, pursed her comically over-painted lips and then raised her voice. "Hello, bitches! We'll soon have you in stitches! Welcome to Drag Poetry Night. You have five minutes left to get your orders from Candy Blume, Mistress of Hard Candy, before being treated to a performance by our very own Fantasia, so hurry, children, and get lubricated. You're gonna need it for the *big* show I have planned for you."

Cheers and catcalls sounded as a sequined stampede descended on Candy, and she took orders, made drinks, stuffed money in the cash register and got on with her job. It was only when Fantasia was strutting onto the stage to roaring applause seven minutes later that Candy caught something out the corner of her eyes that didn't quite fit.

Trent Green was leaning on the end of the bar. He was wearing a black suit and there was a big gold box sitting in front of him. He gave her a wave. To Candy, he might as well have taken out the baseball bat she kept under the bar and smacked her upside the head.

Panicked and furious, she looked around to see if anyone was watching. Fantasia's performance had started, so no one would be wanting a drink until the next queen's spot, but that didn't mean people wouldn't notice if she murdered someone. And there was no way she was going to let Trent's presence crack her. She was Candy Blume, Mistress of Hard Candy. She had a goddamn reputation.

"I can ask him to leave if you want." Kevin's words, just audible at this close range, momentarily put a lid on her bubbling fury.

Candy shook her head. "Nope. It's fine. Act like he's not there. He got my attention yesterday. He's not gonna get me to make a scene today. If Trent Green wants to talk to me, he can stay for the entire show." She jerked her head towards the stage where Fantasia was reciting a poem that could be banned in multiple states and would make the rest blush. "A Neanderthal like him won't even last ten minutes with this crowd." With those words she gave Trent one long, lethal glare and then got back to work.

Chapter 10

Trent took one look at the undisguised fury on Candy's face and wondered if this plan had been the right one. Maybe the best thing would be to go now and leave the gift he'd made on the bar. He'd spent hours on it this afternoon, along with the handwritten letter. Not that he expected her to be grateful, or even interested, but it had felt like the right first step in making reparation.

He'd decided to give her the gift in person so she could see he was earnest—and so she'd have the opportunity to vent—but now he was beginning to think he'd epically miscalculated. It was now apparent that the better approach would've been to send the box via courier, thus leaving it up to Candy as to whether or not she wanted to acknowledge she'd received it.

She was looking killer tonight in a little black dress, boots that screamed attitude and those dagger earrings that kept almost skimming the tops of her shoulders. She hadn't cracked a smile since he'd slipped into the bar twenty minutes ago and found that he'd come on something called Drag Poetry Night.

The majority of the people filling the dimly lit booths were dressed in the kind of clothes, hair and makeup that Trent had only ever seen on Barbie dolls. If stepping into a bar last night had taken him outside of his comfort zone, being around a bunch of drag queens hell-bent on delivering some of the filthiest jokes he'd ever heard in his life—funny, but so filthy his ears may have actually reddened—was a whole new world.

"Oh, and what do we have here? I smell straight boy."

Trent realized that the entire room was looking at him as the drag queen who'd just taken the stage strutted over, as if zeroing in on Trent's fear of being singled out in public. He, or she—Trent remembered Matty and his sisters talking about how drag queens generally like to be called "she" when in drag—was done up like a sexy Marge Simpson.

With a gut-sinking feeling, Trent realized that he'd become a part of the show. His palms began to sweat. He'd be a fool not to see the irony in the situation, given the fact he was here to apologize to Candy for singling her out as a target in high school.

"What's your name, honey?" The queen put a hand on Trent's shoulder as the crowd catcalled and clapped.

"Trent," he said as she thrust the microphone in his face.

"Trent," the queen repeated, putting some bass in her voice before turning to the crowd. "Oh my, isn't that an *up*standing name, ladies? Are you an *up*standing man, Trent?"

"Some people would say that." Trent darted a look at Candy and caught her glaring at him with more venom than the world's stores of antivenin could ever counteract.

"And what do you do when you aren't listening to the golden words coming from my luscious lips, Trent?"

"I, uh . . . I own a patisserie. I design gourmet cakes and chocolates."

Trent saw Candy pause in slicing up limes, her face registering a fleeting moment of either genuine surprise or disbelief. Okay, maybe this was a good thing. Maybe it was worth it. He tried a tentative smile for the crowd.

"Mmm, mmm, *mmm.*" The queen smacked her straw-berry-pink lips. "We've got a boy here who likes chocolates! And I do adore chocolate. Especially *white* chocolate." She ran a fingernail down Trent's cheek and the crowd whooped. "Is there chocolate in this box here, straight boy? Why's it wrapped up all pretty?" The queen tapped the gold box sitting in front of Trent and then thrust the mic under his nose again.

Trent swallowed down a huge ball of anxiety. "It's a gift."

"For who? Which of the gorgeous girls in this room is this great *big* package meant for?"

There was laughter all around and a bunch of raised hands before Trent realized the queen was still giving him an expectant look. "Well, who, straight boy? Are you gonna tell us?"

"I'd . . . rather not." Trent realized it was exactly the wrong thing to say.

"Oh, he's shy!" The queen pressed her fingers to her mouth and the crowd made an "aww" sound. She held up a hand to silence them. "Now, let's not scare him away. Hey Trent, why don't you just whisper your secret in my ear—or maybe you can slide on over into my little pink box and we'll talk about it in private."

She gestured to the TARDIS. There was a roar of laughing objections from the crowd.

The queen's mouth curved downwards in a clownish frown. "Looks like you're going to have to tell us all. Spill your secrets. We're all friends here."

Trent glanced at Candy, saw the fury in her expression and realized that not being honest would only make it worse. After all, if he said anyone else's name and they opened the box, they'd see the letter, and worse, they might even try and read it in public. "Candy. I brought them for Candy."

"Candy for Candy Blume, our very own Mistress of Drag Poetry Night! And does Mistress Candy want to open her pretty box to show us what's inside?" There was a suggestive wink and a big laugh before the queen snatched up the box and shoved it across the bar towards Candy.

"Open it, girl!" someone yelled from the audience.

Candy wiped her hands on a dish towel before taking it with the air of someone handling a vial of the bubonic plague. Trent willed her to make eye contact with him so that he could communicate that none of this had been his intent, but she was too busy giving the drag queen death eyes.

"Fantasia. Rule Nine," Candy said in a low, menacing voice, and then suddenly Fantasia was grabbing Trent's hand and dragging him up onto the stage.

"Or maybe some things are better done in private! And I think we should share something *private* with you, Trent, because I'm starting to think you came here for some of *my* chocolate *tonight!* Come with me, I've got a special poem, just for you."

Before Trent knew it, he was sitting in a chair with Fantasia straddling his lap and reciting filthy poetry to him. Trent, who had been on the wrestling team in high school and knew when he was well and truly pinned, had no option but to be a good sport. He only hoped Candy would see this as a sign he'd changed.

Chapter 11

Candy ignored the hollering coming through the closed door of her office and glared at the box she'd placed on her desk.

The damn thing had sat on the bar for three hours while she'd done her best to wait out Trent's presence, but contrary to her expectations, Drag Poetry Night hadn't scared him off. He was still out there, infesting the place. Which meant that she was going to have to open this stupid box so she knew what sick kind of game he was playing. What the hell was his agenda? Why had he come back to her bar after she'd kicked him out and why had he brought her *this*? What was the catch?

She circled her desk, studying the box like a mongoose circling a snake. The thing was about a foot across, gold, and sported a glossy black ribbon.

She took a step forward to pull one end of the ribbon with a jerking motion, then quickly stepped back.

There wasn't an explosion. Okay.

She slid a fingernail underneath the flap, then stepped forward to peer inside.

Wrapped in gold paper was a perfect dark-chocolate replica of the award Candy had accepted for academic excellence at her high school graduation. It was surrounded by little milk chocolate A-plusses in cups of gold tissue, and bordering *those* were cogs of all different sizes made from different types of chocolate.

She stared at the box's contents for a moment, feeling her mind go momentarily blank as a cheer from the crowd filtered through her office door. She then turned her attention to the only other thing in the box: an expensive gold envelope.

She picked it up and saw her name written in calligraphy. The anger that had been building all night transformed into cold fury. Her first impulse was to throw the whole damn thing in the trash without reading it, but no—if she was gonna kill Trent Green in the next twenty minutes, she wanted to do it by choking him on his own words.

Her hands were shaking as she pulled out two thick sheets of paper with dense writing she'd recognize anywhere. There had been plenty of nasty notes written in this tight scrawl slotted into her locker in high school. Most of them had been about her hair looking stupid or her clothes being dumb, and all of them had insulted her intelligence in ways designed to whittle down her self-confidence. There'd been a time when Candy had internalized it all so much that she'd hated herself as much as Trent Green seemed to hate her.

Phrases jumped out at her from the first few paragraphs.

I'm sorry what I did left you so angry even now . . . was young and stupid . . . please know it wasn't racial, was just competitive . . . didn't understand . . . sorry I made you a target to get my dad's approval . . . wanted to make something that represented my desire to give you back the moment I took from you . . .

The paper dropped from Candy's fingers as she hurled the box and everything in it into the trash, then turned on her heel and marched back into the bar. It was nearly one in the morning and the place was now empty except for Fantasia's crew and Trent. He was sitting in their booth right next to Candy's damn dog, who wasn't even attempting to bite his arm off. Instead Barney was giving the man an adoring look, as though Trent had spent the past three hours patting him.

No. No way. She wasn't going to do this. She wasn't going to spend one more minute watching Trent fucking Green sitting in *her* bar with *her* customers like he owned the place, like he had a right to be here just because he'd written some bullshit non-apology and thought it erased everything. No way.

It took everything she had to modulate her voice as she cupped her hands around her mouth and called out, "Hey people. Home time! If you need a cab, let me know, otherwise sort out your rides and skedaddle."

She was met with a round of protests.

"Rule Six." She glared at Fantasia, who was giving her a rebellious look. "You contradict me, I kick your asses out for life."

It was at least twenty minutes before the last of the queens left, waving at Trent and calling out a series of farewells that were far too friendly for Candy's liking.

"You're welcome in my booth any time, honey." This was from Fantasia, who gave Trent an air kiss that he didn't seem to mind at all before she strutted out of the bar with the other queens, giant purses slung over all their shoulders.

And then Candy and Trent were alone.

Chapter 12

"Hey." Trent slid from the booth as Candy's traitorous dog whined. "Can we talk?"

Candy pointed at the door. "You heard me. It's closing time. Get the fuck out of my bar. I told you I didn't want you here last night and nothing's changed my mind. Go."

Trent held up his hands, his expression so earnest Candy wished the bar had a machine gun turret attached to it so she could turn him into little bits. Tiny little minced-up bits.

"I will. I promise. But I'm here because I thought it would be right for you to hear an apology from me in person. I'm sorry for everything, Candy. For everything I ever did to you. I should have apologized sooner, but there were things that happened after graduation that got in the way. But I want you to know that I respect you, and that I think what you've done here, with this bar, is amazing. I always thought you were amazing. And I guess how good you were at everything was exactly what threatened me. It was wrong, but it's the truth, and I'm sorry."

Candy opened her mouth to repeat that she wanted him out, but realized she was on the cusp of screaming, actually screaming, at another human being. Her entire body was shaking as she filled up a glass with Coke, her movements stilted, like all the anger she'd stored for years had solidified in her veins.

Trent seemed to take her silence as his cue to speak. "I know you probably hate my guts—"

She cut him off. "Don't you dare say another word. Not. One. Word."

He nodded slowly, watching her like a lion tamer would regard a lioness who'd already eaten the clowns and still looked hungry.

Candy filled her lungs with air, trying to find the words to say something that would be calm, cutting and that would send him packing. Instead, all that emerged was a voice low and scratchy with emotion. "I read your note, or at least the first few lines, and they were enough."

"I meant every word. I'm sorry, Candy."

"Did I give you permission to speak?" Her words were a whip crack.

He shook his head, and for a moment she thought she saw a spark of the old combative Trent flash in his eyes. It was enough to set her off. Before she knew it, words were pouring out of her, laced in fury with a side order of vitriol.

"What makes you think you have the right to come back in here after I expressly told you not to? What sort of insane arrogance made you think that gifting me with an apology and some pathetic chocolate merit award is going to make all the times you made my life miserable go away? Do you think this makes you a good person? You just turn up, say sorry and hand over some chocolates for making *years* of my life hell?" She smacked her hand down on the bar. "You think I'm gonna give you absolution for being an asshole now? How dare you! I don't owe you any fucking forgiveness and you certainly haven't earned it."

She could see her words had hit their mark when Trent

visibly tensed. "Candy—if you read the letter. I meant every word. I put a lot of thought into what I said and—"

Candy's chest heaved, and for a moment she thought she may have developed the ability to breathe fire. "Really? Aren't you generous. Should I get down on my knees and thank you for spending, what? Five minutes thinking about how your behavior might have affected me? When I've had to live my entire life overcoming the impact of what you did? I made choices because of what you did! I had significant moments in my life *ruined* because of what you did! I had my self-esteem trampled into the ground because of what you did! You having some epiphany because I didn't kiss your ass yesterday doesn't erase all that. It doesn't erase all the name-calling, all the times you made fun of me in class, all the times you laughed my opinions down in front of other people or made fun of what I wore. It doesn't erase the fact that you ruined one of the biggest moments of my life—getting that award at graduation in front of my dad who had flown across the world from Hong Kong. It was the first time I'd seen him in person in so many years—"

Her voice cracked, and she breathed through her nostrils as a wave of emotion swept through her. Oh no. She wasn't going to cry. There was no way. Not when she hadn't cried since her divorce. Not in front of Trent Green.

Unfortunately, Trent took her silence as his cue to talk again. "I get that you're angry and hurt and I know I've badly wronged you," he said in a low, measured voice. "And I want to make it up to you. Any way I can. I don't care what it is. I'll do it. I was young and dumb and wrong, and I'm sorry it's taken me twelve years to offer you this apology, but some things happened in my life and—"

Candy stared at him, incredulous. "Things happened in *your* life?! You're telling me I should care about your life and how hard it's been for *you*?! Let me tell you something. Life's hard. It's fucking hard for everyone, and just because it wasn't *convenient* for you to work out you'd been a prick doesn't mean you shouldn't have before now. And right now? I've got enough in my life that I don't need this shit." She paused, feeling her blood run cold. "Or is that why you're here? Is this some kind of joke? You want to come see how the junkie's ex-wife's life has gone downhill so you can write about it on social media and share it with your idiot friends?"

"Junkie wi—no!" Trent reeled back. "No, it's nothing like that at all. This is a genuine apology, nothing more."

"I'll believe that when I see it. Let me tell you that it's gonna take more than a lame apology and a box of cheap chocolates to get my forgiveness."

Candy saw a flash of anger cross his face and felt a brief rush of satisfaction on calling this right. There *he* was, the old Trent, hiding behind this new shiny facade. She waited, braced for him to call her the "bitch witch" in that sarcastic tone he'd once used, but although she could hear the frustration in his voice when he spoke next, he still didn't snap and show his true colors.

"I hand-made those chocolates. For you. No strings attached. Just a gift. I'm going now. I don't expect anything more. But if you need anything, know I'm only a call away. Call it guilty conscience or whatever you want, but I owe you and I will repay my debt. My number is in the letter I wrote."

Candy looked away. The adrenaline was starting to wear off and her body was telling her it'd had enough. "Leave. Don't come back."

Trent set his shoulders back, his expression going blank. "If that's what you want. But know I meant every word."

Candy gave him a long, hard stare. "Are your feet glued to the floor or something?"

"I'm going." Trent turned to leave just as the bar's door opened and a newcomer walked in.

If anyone had asked Candy this morning who she wanted to see least in the world, her immediate answer would have been "Trent Green." But then, she hadn't factored in her ex-husband going against the restraining order she'd slapped on him almost two years ago.

A Nine Inch Nails song started playing, industrial and gritty, as Candy looked Beau up and down, sick to her stomach over just how *healthy* he seemed, how much he looked like the happy-go-lucky football player she'd fallen in love with thirteen years ago in high school after she'd challenged him to go to prom with her, thinking he'd tell her to go to hell, only for him to accept. It would have been so much easier to see him if he looked as he did last time, his sandy hair stringy, his light-green eyes bloodshot, and his wiry body emaciated and covered in tatty clothes. But the universe wasn't that kind.

Thanks to the care Beau's mom had heaped on him to counteract the effects of the heroin, Beau looked every inch the easygoing charmer Candy had once trusted more than anyone else in the world. He was even wearing the dark-green shirt she'd brought him for his twenty-sixth birthday four years ago. It was too much for her already overwhelmed emotions. This clean-cut Beau didn't mesh with who she knew he really was; the man who'd tried to rape her best friend, who'd betrayed her confidence, stolen all her money, lied to her, cheated on her, and—the final time she'd seen him—given her a broken arm. She had to remember that the person she'd fallen for in high school had died the minute he'd become hooked on prescription painkillers.

She tried to speak but couldn't. It was like her tongue was frozen to the top of her mouth, so instead she reached under the bar and wrapped her fingers around the baseball bat.

From the corner of her eye she caught Trent watching her. From his vantage point between her and Beau, he could see her pulling out the bat.

In a flash, she realized she couldn't let Trent leave yet. Trent might have made her life hell in high school, but he'd never been a physical threat. And with Trent here, Beau wouldn't get violent again.

Gripping the bat at her side, she closed her eyes for a second and pulled herself together like she'd had so many times before.

"What are you doing here, Beau?" she asked.

Beau was obviously taken aback. "You ask me that when Trent Green's standing there? What the hell are you doing here, man?"

At the sound of Beau's question, Barney woke up from where he'd been dozing in the booth, yawning loudly and wagging his tail just to prove how hopeless he'd always been at judging people.

"A better question would be what the hell are *you* doing here? Didn't you read the restraining order?" Candy was proud of the steel in her voice. "And I can have whoever the hell I want in my bar because it's *mine*." She thumped her chest with a clenched fist. "Which means, if I ask Trent to stop by for a drink, that's my prerogative." She caught Trent's surprise and tried to put as much *don't mess with me* into her expression as possible. If he really wanted to work for that apology, he could start now. "Wouldn't you agree, Trent?"

His eyes flickered to the bat in her hand and he nodded. "Yeah. Yeah, definitely." He walked towards Beau, effectively putting himself directly between Candy and her ex-husband. "Long time no see, man. I hear you've not been so well."

Beau gave him an easygoing smile that Candy knew was one hundred percent fake. "I've been sick, but I'll be getting better soon. That's one of the reasons I'm here. I'd like to speak to my wife about some treatment I've got lined up next week and would appreciate some privacy."

"That's *ex*-wife, and I'm not coming," Candy said, feeling sickened that Beau could still put on this charming act after everything he'd done. "I already told your mom that I've got something going on here. Trent's little brother is having his twenty-first birthday party and he's rented the entire bar. Isn't that right, Trent?"

Trent glanced over his shoulder, meeting her eyes. After a moment he nodded slowly. "Yeah. Yeah, he is."

Beau blew out a breath. "That's a shame. You sure you can't get someone else to mind the bar? It would sure mean a lot to me." He looked at Trent. "Your brother would understand if Candy stepped out for an hour or so, right, man?"

"Cut the act, Beau," Candy snarled. "You've said your piece, which is more than you're due, and now you've got one minute to leave before I call the cops." She pulled her phone out of her pocket with her free hand and set it on the bar. She could feel her legs shaking but forced herself to stay calm.

In a weird moment of clarity, she realized that the main thing helping her right now was the way Trent seemed to be going along with her side of things even though Beau was the picture of wronged innocence. It wasn't logical or rational, but it was enough for her to keep it together.

Chapter 13

Trent felt like someone had put him through a spin cycle.

He wasn't a man who'd ever taken criticism lightly, and letting Candy say her piece hadn't been easy. The remaining fragments of the arrogant kid who'd been Donovan Green's son—who'd been trained not to take any woman telling him what to do—had wanted to lash back, but Trent had held it together, taking the verbal beating he'd deserved without reacting. But he was sure as hell finding it hard not to react to this current situation, especially since he'd seen Candy pull that baseball bat out from under the bar. Even in the dim lighting, he could see how her fingers clenched around it, her knuckles white. She sure as hell wouldn't admit it, but her legs were visibly shaking.

This woman was one of the strongest, take-no-prisoners females he'd ever known, and right now she was terrified.

The last time Trent had seen Beau Lineman, Beau had been standing amongst a group of his friends at their high school graduation with his arm wrapped around Candy's shoulders. Everyone had loved this guy. He'd been attractive, he'd been likeable, and he'd gotten along with everyone. Sure, Beau hadn't been all that smart, but he'd been a good guy. But something had obviously gone wrong, otherwise Candy wouldn't be holding the bat, she wouldn't be threatening to call the cops, and she sure as hell wouldn't have lied about wanting Trent around.

"Beau, I'm warning you, get going or I'll make that call. Trent and I have plans and they don't include you," Candy's voice sliced through the tension.

Beau looked at Trent with obvious confusion. "Alright, I'll go. But I don't get it, babe. You hate this guy. Why'd you have him around after everything he did to you?" He gave Trent a conciliatory smile. "No offense, man, but it's the truth. The way you treated her in high school was rank."

"People change. I learned that the hard way with you," Candy said.

Trent heard the faint quiver in her voice and decided that was his cue to step in. She could be pissed at him later, but he'd be damned if he'd let this go on any further.

"It might be time for you to leave," he said calmly to Beau.

"You're telling *me* to leave?" Beau asked incredulously.

"Yeah. The lady asked you to, so it's time to go." Trent looked Beau straight in the eye. He wasn't a big guy, but neither was Beau, and they'd both played enough ball in school for Beau to know Trent could handle himself.

The muscles around Beau's eyes tightened, and Trent saw the anger before it was covered up.

Beau gave him a rueful smile. "I get it. She's told you some things and they've colored your opinion of me. Just know this woman sometimes imagines things. You probably don't know it, but she's damn good at making up stories."

"*I* make up stories?!"

Beau gave her a long-suffering look. "Candy, I understand why you might feel angry right now, but I want you to know I'm doing this for you. All of it. I won't let you down."

"Get out, Beau. Just get out."

"Get out, man." Trent took a step forward.

"Fine. Later." Beau opened the door, pausing to glance over his shoulder. "Grow your hair back, babe, you look like a dude."

The door slammed shut leaving behind a vibe that was full of strange undercurrents edged in dirty glitter.

"Slide that deadbolt across," Candy said.

Trent did as she asked. "You got a key for these other locks?"

She set the baseball bat down on the bar. "I'll take care of that later."

"Isn't this place a little small to be practicing your swing?" Trent asked to break the tension.

"Not if I'm aiming at someone's head. You're lucky I didn't use it on you." The words didn't have the bite Candy probably intended. She must have known it too, because she swiftly began to collect glasses from the booths at the back of the room.

Trent watched her, replaying what had just happened. The key thing was that she wasn't kicking him out anymore. In fact, she'd locked him in here with her. He didn't know what the hell that meant. All he knew was that he had to do something to get rid of this excess energy or he'd be in trouble soon. He'd always had a quick temper, but had learned to manage it over the years by distracting himself the minute his fuse was lit. And seeing Candy's fear of Beau had been the equivalent of lighting a match with a blowtorch. If there were ever a time Trent needed a distraction, it was now. He had a bunch of questions, but he'd be a fool to think they'd be welcome.

He looked around. "Need help tidying up?"

Candy's head jerked up and he caught a flash of surprise before she shrugged. "Don't break anything."

Figuring that was a yes, Trent picked up a couple of glasses from a nearby table and leaned over the bar, placing them by the sink. Since Candy didn't tell him to stop, he kept going. "Have you got something to wipe the surfaces down with?"

"Here," Candy said, setting out a couple of cloths and some surface spray on the bar. She was stacking a dishwasher now, every line of her body taut as a bowstring.

It suddenly dawned on Trent that the music was still playing—some crooning old- school trip-hop number that sounded like the singer was trying to make suicidal thoughts sexy.

He started wiping down tables and soon realized why he'd been handed more than one cloth. A room full of drag queens shed a whole lot of glitter.

"You got a broom?" he asked.

Candy came around the bar with a broom and dustpan, handing them to him before unlocking a supply closet near the bathroom door to retrieve a bucket, mop and a caddy of cleaning supplies. He started sweeping while she took the bucket into the bathrooms. She reappeared a while later with it full of water. The sharp scent of disinfectant filled the space, overriding the subtle remnants of the incense she'd burnt earlier.

"Use this once you've finished sweeping," she ordered, handing him the mop.

"So, do they shed once or twice a year?" Trent asked, indicating the sparkling pile at his feet.

"All the time as far as I can figure."

He gave her a small smile. "I guess I've got the job?"

"You're free labor."

Despite Candy's ballsy words, Trent was suddenly struck by how much smaller she was than him. Why had he never noticed that before? In a flash he realized it was because he'd never really looked at her. Oh sure, he'd always been *aware* of her in school, but mainly as a challenge. He'd never looked past her tough-girl aura. But she not only barely came up to his chin, he was pretty sure he'd lifted bags of chocolate buttons heavier than her.

He had the sudden urge to share the realization, but knew if he did, she'd probably take out his kneecaps with her baseball bat.

"Make sure you clean under the tables too, so you catch any sequins. Barney sometimes licks the floor if people spill drinks and I don't want him getting sick," Candy said.

Trent glanced at the dog who was curled up in a booth nearby, eyes closed but with one ear cocked. The feather boa was still wrapped around his neck. "Sequins? You sure you shouldn't be running a Drag Dog Night?"

"No one upstages my dog, so no," Candy said before she headed back to the bathrooms.

"Want me to clean those?" he called out.

"Nope." The door slammed shut.

Trent was finishing mopping the floor when Candy came back. In the faint blue light emanating from the kinetic cog sculpture, her tightly drawn face looked dangerous, witchy and sexy as hell.

This inner steel she possessed had been something he hadn't understood or respected as a kid, but as an adult, all he felt was awe. To project so much attitude after confronting both her high school nemesis and her junkie ex-husband in one night was something to be admired.

She took a seat in the booth next to her dog and crossed her arms over her chest as she looked Trent up and down.

Suddenly, he was gripped by anxiety. He knew he was in shape, but what was she seeing? He'd worn a suit tonight, wanting to show her he was serious about his apology, but right now it felt constrictive and awkward. He didn't buy clothes all that often, but he liked simple, good-quality stuff: white or black T-shirts, blue jeans and, if it was cold, a black leather jacket. He thought of them as timeless, but maybe they were out of date. He sure as hell didn't have time to work out what was fashionable. He barely had time to breathe. Was she gonna start making fun him like he'd once made fun of her?

"Your brother knew about me, about this bar," she said. "How come you didn't?"

Trent wrung the mop out one last time. "You really want to hear it? Because it's not a straightforward answer."

"Yeah, why not? After what you just saw, I need you to air some of your dirty laundry to even up the balance. Spill your guts, Green. Tell me how your life is just as messed up as mine."

"Yeah, okay. Just wait a minute." Trent took the mop bucket into the bathrooms and carefully emptied it without mussing Candy's hard work. He returned to see that she was sitting in the same place, although this time she had a glass of Coke in front of her.

"I'm listening," she said.

Trent blew out a breath. "You got any coffee here?"

"Behind the bar. A jug of filter for people who don't like the good stuff. Pour it yourself."

"Thanks."

After some exploring, Trent managed to find a mug and pour himself a coffee. He looked around for somewhere to sit that wouldn't crowd her and settled for one of the barstools.

"Start talking."

He took a sip of the coffee. It was tepid, but better than nothing, and he needed caffeine to clear his head from the two drinks Fantasia had bought him for playing along with the show. "How much do you know about me? My family?"

"Nothing, other than that you're Irish-Italian and have a sister named Gwen who knew enough to tell your brother about me, but didn't know enough to know I'd shaved my head." Candy ran a hand over her head. Trent was tempted to say how much it suited her, but then realized he didn't have a death wish.

Instead he nodded. "Alright. Well, not long after graduation—"

"Which we will not talk about. And we will *definitely* not talk about that bullshit chocolate award you gave me tonight, because even thinking of it right now is getting my temper back up."

Trent ignored the spark of hurt and frustration that sprung from her not getting what he'd been trying to do, instead continuing, "A week after graduation, my parents died in a boating accident." He cleared his throat in the ensuing silence. "I've got three younger sisters and a brother. Matthew. Matty," he corrected. "Gwen was almost fifteen when it happened, Matty was nine, and then there are the twins, Carlotta and Anna. They were six. I was left as their guardian. Our other relatives weren't so well-off they could do more than worry, so my nona—Mom's mom—moved in to help. I had to learn how to be a parent overnight. It wasn't easy. Before then, I'd pretty much had everything done for me because I was a boy and I was the oldest, and then suddenly I'm having to learn how to use the washing machine and how to make sure my brother and sisters were fed and clothed." Trent looked at his hands resting on his thighs, fighting the urge to shift on his barstool to ease the tension in his body. "And suddenly I was having to learn how to do a whole lot of jobs my parents had seen as 'women's work,' while the whole time my dad's voice was in my head calling me a pansy and a freak. So, I worked a bunch of jobs to save up enough money to keep our house and to turn Nona's suburban cake store into a business that could pay the bills. I've called it Dolce Design. And . . . that's pretty much it."

"Aren't you the holy fucking Mother Theresa," Candy said, but there was none of the earlier ire behind her words. "What does this have to do with your brother's party?"

"I'm getting there. When Dad and Mom died, I was left head of the family, and it's been my job ever since to get my brother and sisters through school, through college . . . Anyway, it hasn't been easy, and it hasn't been made any easier by the fact that Matty and I lock horns every time we're in the same room." Trent looked down at his coffee cup, remembering the fight that'd spurred Matty into turning up at Hard Candy. "We were never close. Mom was a strict Catholic who used to lay it on pretty thick about how being gay was bad, and Dad was even worse. Much worse."

"And you?"

Trent shrugged. "I should have stood up for him more. But at the time, I was so focused on protecting myself from getting on Dad's bad side that I didn't really see how bad it was. I made sure no one messed with Matty, but other than that, I mostly ignored him. My sister Gwen used to call me the 'golden child,' which should give you the picture."

"Unsurprising, given how much of a douche you were in high school." Candy waved a hand. "Continue with your tale of woe."

Trent had to take a moment to regain his place in the story. "Yeah, well, anyway, Mom and Dad died and I had to work out how to be a good human being. I did everything I could to build relationships with my sisters and Matty, and it worked for the girls, mostly, but Matty . . . it's like a part of him froze at the angry stage of grief and never moved on. One minute he was this sweet kid who used to dress up in the girls' clothes and sneak their dolls into his room, and the next minute he decided I was just another version of Dad out to make his life miserable. No matter what I've done to convince him otherwise, he still sees me as a carbon copy."

Candy snorted. "I'm sure you've given him reason to think that. You with a gay little brother? I can just imagine how you reacted to all those times he wanted to play dolls with you."

Trent quashed his immediate impulse to bite back. "I'm gonna let that dig slide because you're right, at least partly. Knowing me as you did, you might think I would've bullied him, but I never judged him for being gay, and he came out of the closet pretty much the minute he popped out of Mom. But I could've been a better brother. I could've stood up for him more when Mom and Dad laid into him, but I didn't. And I think that's where Matty's coming from. It's been over twelve years since I started changing myself for the better, but he still doesn't trust me."

"I'm liking him more already," Candy said wryly.

Trent shook his head tiredly. "Yeah? Right now, you can have him, because I'm at a loss of what else I can do to show him I care. We tried family therapy. I've supported him in everything he's wanted to do, turning up to every one of his theater productions. I gave him a job at my store. I've paid for his college degree," Trent said as a chilled-out instrumental guitar track started playing. If this were a movie, the mood in the room should have changed, but Trent felt just as in the spotlight as before, and the edge of self-pity in his own voice was making him uncomfortable.

Candy gave him a bored look. "This pity party is tiring. Make it more interesting, Green."

"Why?"

"Because hearing that you're miserable is making me happier."

He studied her face, looking for any kind of vindictiveness, but only saw faint traces of exhaustion covered up by a whole lot of sass. He shrugged. "Alright. A couple of weeks ago we had a fight because Matty came to work still drunk and stoned from the night before. I came down on him hard—probably way harder than I should have." Trent grimaced at the memory. "I said a couple of things I shouldn't have about his level of maturity—"

"Now, that's surprising." Candy yawned.

"And he went home and told Gwen I'd called him a bunch of names that I'd never say to him in a million years. Unfortunately Gwen didn't see through his bullshit this time, and for some reason thought it'd be a good idea to tell him about how I treated you in school."

That earned him a derisive snort from Candy.

Trent kept going anyway, because this was no doubt going to be the only chance he'd ever get to explain himself. "So not knowing any of this, I came to an agreement with Matty over his twenty-first, telling him he could have a party wherever he wanted as long as he organized it himself like an adult. I guess I was thinking that if I gave him responsibility, he'd see where I was coming from, but now I think all I was doing was rewarding him for bad behavior."

"And he behaved badly by picking my bar to stick it to you?" Candy's mouth curved into a cat-like smile. "Got to hand it to him, he got you good."

Trent nodded. "That's exactly what I said. The only problem was that he got you too. I'm sorry about that."

The room fell silent apart from the sound of Candy's dog snoring, the music and the faint whirr of the cog sculpture.

"Why weren't you at that stupid high school reunion you organized two years ago?" Candy asked abruptly.

"My sister broke her arm an hour before it started. If it's any consolation, I'd planned on using the opportunity to apologize to you then. Thinking about it, I could have found you earlier to apologize in private, but in my head, it felt like the right setting, you know?"

She gave a disbelieving snort. "You arranged the reunion at a honky-tonk. What about me says 'honky-tonk'?"

"Honestly? I had no idea what I was doing; I barely get time to watch TV at night. Someone recommended a bar they liked and I went with it," Trent answered honestly.

"It was a crap venue."

"Yeah. I get how you'd see that. Especially seeing how great this one is." Trent looked around him, marveling at how truly cool the place was.

"And I wouldn't have accepted your apology. I would've told you where to stick it. In front of everyone."

"That's why you turned up? I wondered."

"Yeah. I figured we had unfinished business." Candy nibbled on a long black fingernail while giving him a glare that dared him to say anything.

Silence descended between them as Trent shifted on his barstool and Candy settled more comfortably in her booth across the room.

"So, did you mean it about Matty's party earlier? Is it back on again?" Trent decided to cut to the chase. "Because it's unfair you shouldn't get that money just because you hate me."

Candy tilted her head to the side, holding his gaze for a long moment. "It'll be twenty percent more. Asshole tax," she said, her expression patently saying she didn't expect Trent to agree.

"Ten," Trent countered, reaching over the bar to set his coffee cup in the sink. "I'm feeling guilty, but I'm not an idiot. I know the quote you gave Matty was high because you wanted to make sure he was serious." He saw Candy's surprise and knew he'd been right.

She slid from the booth, brushing her hands over her dress. "Yeah, alright. Your brother can have his party. But I want the deposit back in my account by noon tomorrow with the ten percent extra on top."

"Done. Thanks, Candy."

She stretched one arm across her body, before stretching the other. "You're *really* boring me now. It's time for you to leave. And by the way, this isn't your fucking absolution, Trent Green. Mopping a floor and telling a sob story doesn't get you forgiveness. So don't get any ideas. I still hate you."

"I'm okay with that. I just want you to know that I don't hate you. I never did," Trent said before walking for the door.

There was a moment there when he thought he saw shock

on Candy's face, but he didn't do a double take. Instead he unlocked the door and walked out onto the street.

If he scanned the area to make sure Beau Lineman wasn't still hanging around, he told himself it was what anyone in his shoes would do, and not because seeing Candy's legs shaking had made him feel a protectiveness that stayed with him for days.

Chapter 14

Four days later, Candy parked her twenty-year-old white Corolla on the curb in front of her mom's house. She climbed out and held the door, waiting for Barney to jump out. The dog obediently sat by her feet, looking at her expectantly.

Candy bent down and gripped his head gently between her hands, looking into his kind little eyes. "Here's the deal, boy—when I give you the hint, start foaming at the mouth and pretend you've got rabies. It's gonna be the only way we'll get away with our sanity intact."

Barney just wagged his tail, while Candy wondered if she'd made a major mistake by coming here this morning. It had been one thing to decide to ask her mom for advice when Candy had been in her own cozy apartment; it was another to be confronted with the reality of what visiting her mom actually meant.

Candy straightened and took in the fifties bungalow before her, located in a suburb that Austin's hipsters had yet to get around to gentrifying. The coat of lurid pink paint that had been slapped over its peeling boards was a result of her mom's current obsession with the women's movement. While the rest of the feminists in the world—Candy, her friends and allies included—had focused on working towards change in their workplaces and homes, Pam Blume had decided to take things one step further. Instead of registering to vote, she'd made the more dramatic gesture of painting her house pink.

Candy still had nightmares about how much arguing it had taken to convince her mom that her neighbors might not appreciate having "Pussy House" scrawled on the wall next to the porch. Her mom's argument was that painting the house was a much grander statement than just knitting a pussy hat. Candy had only changed her mom's mind after saying she wouldn't bail her out of jail if she ended up assaulting some guy who'd turned up thinking there was a new brothel in town.

Pam Blume was—and always had been—one of the most naïve women Candy had ever met. For as long as Candy had been alive, her mom had been on a never-ending quest to find herself through new hobbies, whether it be macramé or nude modeling for a local art school. And each time Pam found a new thing, she embraced it with fleeting evangelical zeal before fluttering on to the next thing. The only thing she'd truly stuck with was being a mom—although her embrace of every parenting fad known to man had seen Candy leaving home the minute she'd graduated.

Candy loved her mom fiercely in a conflicted and complex way that she'd never be able to describe to someone in a million years, but if she hadn't been made to watch her own birth video on her twelfth birthday, she wouldn't believe they were genetically related.

She crammed that particular traumatic memory deep, deep down and walked past the four other cars parked on the overgrown lawn in between garden beds filled with the products of last year's obsession with Wicca and herbalism. Each car's bumper was covered in stickers indicating that this was an open-minded bunch of women—very open-minded if the noises filtering from the house were any indication. Luckily, the neighborhood had grown immune to weird sounds coming from the Blume place.

"Don't jump to conclusions. It might be a movie or something. Or maybe even some weird music. She wouldn't have *actually* opened a brothel," Candy said to Barney as they walked up to the front door.

She rang the doorbell. Candy hadn't spent the first eighteen years of her life in this house without learning to warn her mom that she was home.

No one came to the door, but Candy could hear a suspicious wailing noise.

A loud wailing noise.

"Strike me dead now." Candy muttered to the big blue sky before pushing the door open. "Mom?"

The wailing got even louder. And it wasn't one person, it was multiple. Multiple women making noises like—

"Fuck my life." Candy walked down the hall and saw that the closed living room door had a sign that said "Goddesses Awakening." It may as well have been a sock over the door handle.

"There's no way any goddess lurking around the stratosphere would be able to sleep through this," she muttered to Barney, who was more concerned with trotting into her mom's cheerful blue and yellow kitchen, where he took up his usual station in front of the refrigerator, his expression hopeful.

Candy followed and closed the kitchen door behind her, although it did little to muffle the sounds. "You've got no hope, boy—she's on that bean-only diet, remember? The best you'll get is a tofu treat." She checked in the fridge anyway and spotted a note stuck to the door with a rainbow magnet.

If my goddesses are still AWAKENING when you arrive, make yourself a sandwich with the soybean bread I made. Barney's water bowl is in the dishwasher. Mom.

Candy's loud sigh was drowned out by a particularly loud wail.

Thinking this was his cue to join in, Barney pointed his nose to the ceiling and let out a howl.

"Oh Jesus," Candy muttered. "Barney. I think it's probably better you go play in the yard. You're too young to be exposed to whatever this is."

She quickly located his water bowl, filled it up and put it outside the back door while Barney did a lap of the yard, sniffing at the new smells and reintroducing himself through the fence to the next-door neighbor's friendly pit bull.

Candy spent a minute watching him, debating whether or not they'd be able to sneak back to her car and go home. No, she needed to talk to someone, especially given how many messages she'd received from Beau's mom. As expected, Marlene was proving persistent, and Candy needed someone to tell her she wasn't a bad person for not wanting to go to Beau's meeting. Normally Candy would run this by her dad, but with the time difference between Hong Kong and Austin, their work schedules had gotten in the way, and there was no way she'd tell him about all this in an email. And as much as Candy wanted to share this with Sophie, she couldn't—or more to the point *wouldn't*. Not after everything Beau had put Sophie through. And given how happy Sophie was over getting engaged? Definitely nope.

So Candy's only other option was her mom, who was a good choice on paper given Pam's share of addict partners. Sure, most of them had been addicted to pot, bad hemp trousers and—in one off-the-wall case—collecting Beanie Babies, but addiction was addiction, wasn't it?

The wailing picked up in frequency and Candy settled for shoving in her earbuds, selecting a metal playlist and turning it up loud. She then raided the fridge and made herself an organic, gluten-free, salt-free, sugar-free, and flavor-free soybean bread and hummus sandwich. It tasted like Silly Putty.

Even maxing out her phone's volume failed to completely dull the noise. Candy was pretty sure the screamer was Terry, her mom's next-door neighbor and friendly pit bull owner. Candy *really* didn't want to think about a woman who'd once babysat her awakening her inner goddess in any way that didn't involve nice quiet prayer with all her clothes on. Maybe in a church somewhere far away. With soundproofing.

If this whole thing—whatever it was—went on for any longer than ten minutes more, she'd have more than enough reason to leave without hurting her mom's feelings.

Almost nine minutes later, one of her earbuds was plucked from her ears and her nose was assaulted by an overpowering scent of geranium essential oil.

Candy glanced up to see her mom standing behind her, looking for all the world like a manic, plus-sized Martha Stewart in a bright pink kimono that had the word "Goddess" haphazardly embroidered over the chest. Embroidery had been one of Pam Blume's earlier obsessions, kicking in around Candy's eighth birthday. After over twenty years of practice, Pam's lack of skills would make the average sewing circle wail and gnash their teeth.

"Hi, honeybee! I see you've made yourself a sandwich," Pam said, starting to bustle around the kitchen, turning on the kettle and rummaging in the fridge to pull out a big bowl of bean dip along with what were either homemade bean-related crackers or the soles of some old shoes. "Why don't y'all make us some peppermint tea while I see everyone out and have a shower? I have *so* much to tell you."

She gave Candy the same mania-tinged smile that always accompanied a new obsession and bustled back down the hall, her voice filtering back to the kitchen. "Whew, all that divine energy floating around sure takes it out of a person, doesn't it? Why don't y'all have a little something to eat so your energy is restored before you go? I've got some refried beans here with some broad-bean crackers. Homemade, so they're extra healthy. Tiffany, can you open a window? It sure is stuffy in here."

Pam's words were met with a round of murmurs and the sound of one woman—who Candy now positively identified as her former babysitter—saying she'd never had her energy floated so good. Candy hoped no one would want to come down to the kitchen to say hi before they left. She only relaxed when she heard her mom send the last of them off.

Twenty minutes later Pam floated back into the kitchen wearing a loose red homespun dress, her shoulder-length hair damp. She pointedly looked from Candy to the kettle. "You haven't made the tea yet?"

Candy looked at her blankly. "Uh, no. Sorry I got distracted with being scarred for life."

Pam kept talking as if she hadn't heard her. "I like what you've done with your hair. I always told you that having it hanging over your forehead blocked your third eye. But I've gotta say, honey, if you'd wanted to give yourself clear energy channels without cutting it, you could have just dyed it in line with your aura. I just did a course about aura optimization and I've learned so much! Ever since I bleached my hair to this gorgeous golden color, I'm in tune with all kinds of energies I never knew existed before!"

"I'll remember that for next time," Candy said, deadpan. "Mind telling me what y'all were doing in there? Without giving me any details that aren't G-rated," she added to be on the safe side.

Pam waved a hand in the air while pouring boiling water into two misshapen hand-thrown mugs, a product of yet another obsession from ten years ago. "Remember that expert in healing sexual energy that I told you about a few months ago? The one visiting from New York?"

"No, I must've bleached it from my brain straight after,"

Candy said, resting her head in her hands. Maybe she could escape by saying she had sad poisoning due to accidentally stirring a spoonful of negative vibes into her morning coffee. This had been such a bad idea.

"I did her course! It was amazing! And now I'm a qualified Goddess Awakening practitioner, which means I can run my own circles."

Candy's head jerked up as her suspicions became solid. "Circles of what?"

"Circles of women who are learning to awaken their goddesses!" Pam brought the mugs to the table and set one in front of Candy with a heavy thunk. The strong scent of peppermint wafted through the air. "It's one of the greatest feelings of empowerment you'll ever experience. That moment when you're surrounded by a circle of women, all learning how to masturbate proper-*mph!*"

Candy held her hand firmly over her mom's mouth. "And this is where you need to stop talking. Boundaries, Mom. Remember that talk we had after you handed out flyers inviting our neighbors to come celebrate me getting my period? And that time when I was twelve and you convinced me that telling my crush that I was sexually attracted to him was a female-positive move? And all those years you didn't let me shave my pits or use deodorant because you'd decided I was single-handedly killing the ozone layer? *This* is in the same category. Understand?" She cautiously took her hand away.

Pam shook Candy's words off like they'd never been said, her eyes alight with fervor. "I really think you should do it. It would be so *healing* after what happened with Beau."

"Can we talk about something else?" Candy spared a thought for Sophie, who'd always had a tough time with her own mom, a staunchly conservative and overprotective woman who'd probably only ever had sex twice in order to conceive her children. While she'd commiserated with Sophie aloud over the years, Candy had secretly envied her. Sometimes Candy worried that her mom's mind was so open that all the common sense had fallen out.

Pam looked mildly hurt. "Well, sure, honey. But I thought you would want to support me in this. It's feminist, it's positive, and it's making me a lot of money. I'm charging six hundred dollars a head for a morning of positive goddess awakening, and that's no small change. I mean, I do have some expenses. There's the orgasmic wand vibrators . . . and the electricity bill because I got the ones you plug into a power socket. Oh, and I had to have an electrician come by and put in more plugs. I also installed solar panels, so they're carbon-neutral orgasms. That's important. Plus I kind of needed the extra power. The first circle we tried with eight women turning their vibrators on all at once overloaded the fuse box, so it wasn't too safe . . . and the smell was *very* unpleasant. Burning plastic and electrical wires really interfered with the vibe. Oh, that's funny. *Vibe!* Did you hear that?" Pam let out a hearty laugh.

Candy cursed her overly active imagination for trying to picture a vibrator so powerful that eight of them could fry a fuse box. Buckets of brain bleach were going to be needed at this rate. "Can we start this conversation again? I actually have something important I'd like to ask your advice on. And I'm talking mom advice. As in, not-inappropriate-for-a-mother-and-daughter-with-good-boundaries advice. Just plain ol' boring mom advice. It's about Beau."

In the blink of an eye Pam changed gears. "Oh? I'm all ears, honey. Just let me center myself."

Pam closed her eyes while Candy took another bite out of the sandwich she'd been listlessly eating. It still tasted like Silly Putty.

Pam's eyes popped wide open and she reached over and put a hand on Candy's shoulder. "Tell me about it."

Feeling like she might be doing the stupidest thing since she'd agreed to let her mom do a spiritual "cleanse" on her apartment only to find out later it involved nudity, Candy did. It took Candy a number of tries because Pam kept interrupting, but she finally got out all the pertinent details.

"So, I guess what I'm asking, is if you have any advice for how to handle Marlene so I don't feel so guilty," she said before picking up her cup of peppermint tea and trying it. She set it back down with a grimace. She should have brought some Coke along; she knew she had what some people would term an addiction, but hey, it was her crutch and she could lean on it all she wanted as long as it wasn't hurting anyone.

She looked up when Pam didn't answer. Her stomach lurched as she catalogued a whole lot of warning signs that this was about to go *very* wrong. Pam was wearing a smile so sharky it rivaled Barney's on a happy day.

Candy held up her hands. "Oh no! No you don't! Whatever you're about to say, think first. I said I needed *mom* advice, not one of your crazy ideas. Got it? Mom?! Are you listening to me?"

"It worked!" The words shot out of Pam's mouth. "Oh my gawd! It worked, honey!" Pam jumped out of her chair and sped around the table gripping Candy's head to her stomach in a hug.

"*Mph*," Candy said, trying to inhale and not succeeding.

"Gaia's healing energies have finally left their mark! Remember how you said that remote healing course was a waste of money? Well, here's the proof it works! I've been sending my healing energies to that boy ever since your divorce." Pam let Candy go and started pacing the kitchen, her entire body vibrating with excitement. "Obviously it's not a complete healing, but it's a start. It's all about the positive energy." She retook her seat across from Candy, reaching across the table and grabbing Candy's hands in a tight grip, her eyes televangelist-shiny. "Maybe if we both direct some strong healing energy towards him, right here, right now, it will give Beau that extra push he needs to make it to that meeting. I had no idea my powers had become so strong!"

Candy jerked her hands back and thunked her head down on the table. "Please tell me you haven't made this all about you?"

"About me? Oh no! How could it be about me?" Pam asked. "This is about my love and caring for the universe and it repaying me by helping Beau. And as for Marlene, she'll need some healing energy too. It can't be easy for her, having her son being so sick. If I channel some of this amazing power towards her, she'll know she's not alone." Pam paused, giving Candy a censorious frown. "After all, someone should be emotionally supporting her."

Candy pushed her chair back, cursing herself for feeling even the slightest twinge of disappointment. How had she thought this was going to go any other way? "I tell you what, why don't you do that now? I've got to head out. I've got some grocery shopping to do." She didn't, but it was either lie or say something she'd regret later.

Pam's mouth dropped open. "You're going now?! But honey, we've got so much work to do! Maybe if you thought more positively about this, you'd see that this isn't something to avoid, this is something to *embrace*. You're being given a chance to take part in Beau proving to you that he can be a better man!"

"But he's not my responsibility anymore. I don't have to take part in anything." *Do I?* a voice asked in the back of Candy's mind, and she decided she'd had enough. The insanity was already setting in. "Thanks so much for listening, but I've got to go."

"Alright, but when you next see Beau or Marlene, make sure you let them know that some of the changes in their lives are a result of the positive energy I've been sending," Pam said before her expression changed again to one of round-eyed concern. "That's what you want, isn't it? For everyone to be happy and okay?"

"Yeah. Yeah, that's what I want. Thanks for the sandwich and I hope this new thing you're doing with the women and the vibrators works out for you." Candy gave her mom a hug, which was exuberantly returned, before she collected an oblivious Barney and dragged him back to the car.

Chapter 15

Sunday morning, Trent woke up early, filled with determination. The sun was shining through his curtains, he'd gotten his first decent night's sleep in over a week, and the rest had given him clarity. While the old Trent would have believed he was owed Candy's forgiveness, nowadays he knew better. She didn't owe him anything, and she obviously had enough on her plate in dealing with Beau Lineman.

Galvanized, he jumped out of bed, quickly dressed and headed out for his usual morning run, soaking up the stillness of the neighborhood punctuated by birdsong and the odd dog barking. After waving to a few of his early-rising neighbors, Trent impulsively stopped by a grocery store, buying blueberries and the makings for waffles before returning home.

An hour later, he was beating the egg whites when Matty stumbled through the kitchen door wearing a pair of black boxer briefs and a grey Adidas T-shirt. Matty's face had the puffiness of someone who'd been drinking heavily the night before, and Trent had to bite his tongue. There was no way in hell he was going to reward Matty with the fight he seemed to want.

"Hey," Matty said, yawning and scratching his belly. "Have you made coffee?"

Trent spared him a glance. "Nope. Make it yourself."

Matty shrugged, walking to the fridge and getting out some juice he drank straight from the bottle while challenging Trent out the corner of his eye. But Trent just turned off the mixer and began to fold the egg whites into the batter as Matty took a seat on a stool at the breakfast bar, deliberately making the legs scrape loudly over the tiles as he pulled it out.

"Gwen said you went and checked out Hard Candy," Matty said, giving Trent the same look he'd once pulled at ten after being caught deliberately keying Trent's truck in retaliation for Trent ordering him go to church with the rest of the family for Christmas mass. Trent still remembered the frustration he'd felt trying to get it through to Matty that the church thing was so they all had something to anchor them, not about the religion their mother had been so fixated on. In the end, Matty had gotten his way and they hadn't gone, but Trent had made damn sure his brother's pocket money went towards fixing his truck for the next three months. It was a pity that episode hadn't cured Matty of acting out, because at ten years old the behaviour had been understandable; at twenty-one it was unacceptable.

Trent checked that the waffle iron was heated up properly, feeling his temper begin to boil. "Yeah, I did."

"Did you meet the owner?"

Trent poured the first lot of batter into the waffle iron and secured it shut before answering. "Yeah. I met her."

Matty leaned forward. "And?"

He shrugged. "Her place is amazing. I can see why you'd want your party there. It's cool."

Matty stared at him. "You didn't recognize her?"

Trent took his time collecting the blueberries and whipped cream from the fridge before speaking. "Who?"

"The owner!"

He feigned mild surprise. "What about her?"

Matty slapped his hands down on the counter, the noise echoing around the room. "Don't act like you don't know what I'm talking about. Did. You. Recognize. Her?"

"Candy? Yeah, sure. I went to high school with her." The waffle iron beeped, and Trent flipped the two waffles onto a plate.

"And what happened?"

Trent finally rested his hands on the countertop and looked Matty straight in the eyes, allowing a hint of anger to creep into his voice. "What happened was two adults having a conversation and coming to an agreement over how much your party is gonna cost. What did you think was gonna happen?"

Matty was the first one to look away. "Is my party still on?"

Trent topped the waffles with berries and cream before sprinkling on a little powdered sugar. "Why wouldn't it be?"

He could feel Matty's frustration filling the room, but his brother just took another swig out of the juice bottle. "You gonna give me the day off from work on Wednesday?"

Trent had been expecting this question. "Nope."

Matty thumped the counter. "Come on, man! It's my twenty-first birthday! You owe it to me."

Trent shook his head, fighting disappointment over the entitlement he heard in those words. "When you asked for a job at Dolce Design, I told you that you'd have to be treated like any other employee. As your boss, I owe you a proper wage. I owe you safe working conditions, and I owe you the right to expect praise when it's due and feedback when you need to fix things." He ignored the cuss word Matty said under his breath and continued speaking. "The rule at Dolce Design is that unless it's an illness, unforeseen situation, or family emergency, employees have to request time off with a week's notice so I can get someone else to fill their shift. You've known your birthdate your whole life, and you haven't given me a week's notice. Since I haven't got anyone lined up to fill in for you, I can't give you the time off. Suck it up." Trent placed the plate of waffles on the tray he'd prepared, which also contained a pot of hot chocolate and a floral china teacup.

"That's not fair!"

Trent raised a brow. "You're getting the party you wanted. You're getting treated like an adult. That sounds fair to me."

Matty stood up so quickly that his stool hit the floor with a crash. "Don't use that 'I'm better than you' voice! You're just like Dad! All I want is to not need to turn up at eight in the morning to work at some stupid cake store on my birthday."

The muscles in Trent's jaw twitched. "No, Dad would never have given you a birthday party in the first place that didn't involve all eyes being on him, so bringing him into this isn't gonna get you anywhere. In the real world, people don't always get what they want."

"Yeah, I'm living proof!"

"And that cake store is the thing that's paid for your education and the clothes you're wearing. It also pays you a damn good wage, one most people would be happy for. What you're being right now is an entitled, self-righteous brat. You can do better than this. You're a better person than this. So be that person."

"Don't pull that holier-than-thou crap on me!"

"I'm just explaining to you how it is. Speaking of your birthday, Nona wants to make dinner for you before you head out to the bar."

"I don't have to do anything I don't wanna do." Matty's mouth curved into a pout that sent Trent's blood pressure skyrocketing.

"No," Trent said roughly, "you don't. But I'd encourage you to think of why you wouldn't want to share a meal and some cake with the people who love you and care for you more than anyone else in the world." With those words, he picked up the tray and headed for his nona's bedroom.

After taking a couple of seconds to calm himself down, he nudged open her bedroom door with his shoulder. She was still curled up under the covers, but Trent knew she'd be wide awake within a matter of minutes.

He set the tray on her bedside table.

"Was that you and Matty I heard in the kitchen?" she asked, sitting up as he pulled open her curtains.

"Yeah." Trent took a seat on the side of her bed, handing her the pair of glasses sitting next to a well-worn paperback on the side table. "Did he wake you up when he came in last night?"

She put the glasses on and smoothed the covers over her lap. "You know I don't hear a thing once I close my eyes at night. Did you two argue? Gwen told me about the little game Matty's playing with you and the girl from the bar."

Trent shook his head. "No argument. He wants one, but I'm not willing to give it to him. He needs to learn he can't always get the upper hand by goading other people into starting a fight. He's acting like the world owes him everything."

Nona's mouth curved into a soft, playful smile. "Like someone I used to know."

"Yeah, but if I learned how to function like a decent human being, so can he." He poured the hot chocolate, enjoying the aroma and the ritual. "I put cinnamon and a little rosewater in this because we're out of nutmeg. You okay with that?"

"You're the expert." She clasped the delicate teacup in two hands, inhaling as she held it under her nose. "He's got your father's temper. So do you. It's good to see you holding on to yours more."

"I'm trying. Want me to leave you so you can eat your breakfast in peace?"

"Maybe." She gazed out the window at the bird feeder Trent had set up for her last Christmas. It was currently occupied by a pair of spherical doves. Trent made a mental note to hide their seed better; his nona either had a thing for round birds, or just forgot how little they needed. Maybe he could get Anna to ask at the animal shelter if there was such a thing as low-calorie bird food.

"You'll be making Matty's birthday cake for our family dinner on Wednesday, won't you? It would be a nice gesture," his nona said.

Trent rubbed his hands over his face. "I sure as hell don't want to."

"You're going to." It was an order rather than a statement.

He nodded. "Yep, I'm going to. But if I shove some of it in his face when he starts something, you can't fault me."

His nona laughed. "I won't fault you, but I'll make you clean it up. Now let me eat these waffles in peace so I've got the energy to put up with you all one more day."

"Sure thing." Giving her a kiss on the forehead, Trent left the room, sending a silent prayer to the man upstairs that Matty wouldn't pull anything this week. Trent had handled the situation okay so far, but knowing his baby brother, he couldn't let down his guard. Not one bit.

Chapter 16

The morning of Matty's birthday, Trent went over the day's contingency plans while he drove through the streets of Downtown Austin so early that the street-sweepers were still cleaning up from the night before.

He felt a prickle of anxiety at all the ways Matty could mess up this party at Hard Candy. A few years ago, Trent would have called this kind of thinking paranoid, but lately Matty had been selecting the nuclear option when it came to pressing Trent's buttons. The only thing keeping Trent calm was the knowledge that Matty generally didn't spread his bad attitude any further than their family.

Trent pulled into his parking space behind the store, waving to the owner of the bakery next door, Luis, who was standing on the back stoop of his kitchen and enjoying an early-morning smoke. Heavily tattooed from the top of his shaved head to his feet, the man resembled—and was —an ex-felon, but nowadays he was stand-up guy who made the best bread Trent had ever tasted. Some days Trent and Luis sat on the back step of Luis's bakery and shared a beer while musing about how they'd ended up loving jobs their fathers would have scorned. At least Trent hadn't had to go to jail like Luis had before he'd worked out that his dad's idea of being a man hadn't been a great one.

"Hey man, you're here early, even for you." Luis plucked the hand-rolled cigarette from the corner of his mouth, cupping it in the palm of his hand.

"Yeah, it's Matty's birthday today and I've gotta get the cake done before he comes in," Trent said.

Luis whistled before raising the cigarette to his lips to blow a smoke ring into the air. "You might have a problem with your top-secret operation, my man. I think Matty's already here. Or at least he was."

Trent blinked. "What do you mean?"

"Back door of your kitchen was open when I got here at four and the lights were on. Didn't think anything of it because I heard his voice. He was talkin' to some guy."

"Oh yeah?" Trent looked at the rear door of Dolce Design, which was covered in faded pink and orange butterflies. Matty and the twins had helped him paint when he'd moved the store downtown ten years ago. "Did you hear him leave?"

Luis shook his head. "Nope. Anyway, I've gotta get back to work. Good luck." Nodding to Trent, he dropped his cigarette into the bucket of sand he kept by the door and walked back into the bakery.

Trent stared blankly after him for a minute, wondering what he meant, before trying the door handle of Dolce Design. It was unlocked. Bracing himself, he stepped inside.

"What the *hell* happened here?!"

His outraged words echoed off the walls as he took in the mess around him. Either someone had deliberately trashed the place, or a small, localized tornado had touched ground in his kitchen. Trent barely had time to absorb the level of destruction before he realized one of the refrigerator doors had been left ajar and was beeping in protest. He hurried to it, barely catching himself from falling after slipping on the spilled macadamia nuts littering the floor.

Curse words littered the air as he checked the bottles of milk and pots of cream. They were lukewarm. Worse, the Saran Wrap on the bowl of buttercream icing meant for Matty's cake had been removed. There were two spoons sticking out of it.

Slamming the fridge door shut, Trent hurried to check his 3D chocolate printer, the most expensive thing in the kitchen. Someone had tried to use the machine to make a series of love hearts, but had used caramel instead of chocolate. Even without taking it apart, he knew it would be so gummed up it would take him hours to clean, which meant he wouldn't be able to meet the day's orders. Which meant he'd be letting clients down.

Above the machine, the last word of Trent's motto had been scribbled out so that it now read "What doesn't kill you makes you a sanctimonious asshole."

"Matty!" he bellowed, looking around before realizing that his brother must be in the front of the store. Just the thought of what damage Matty could do there had Trent speeding up to a run.

He pushed the door open with so much force that it slammed against the wall, startling the two people sprawled on the cherry-red art deco sofa in the middle of the room.

Trent processed the half-empty bottle of Jack Daniels next to the couch, the bowls of melted chocolate on the floor and the paper truffle wrappers littering almost every surface.

And in the middle of all the chaos was his brother, lying next to an unfamiliar guy who was dead to the world.

Matty sat up, looking at Trent blearily. "Hey, bro. You're not supposed to be here yet." His words were slurred and there was a ring of chocolate around his mouth, making him look five years old.

"Cut the bullshit. What the hell do you think you're doing

here?" Trent's hands clenched at his side. Of all the things he'd imagined Matty pulling today, he'd never pictured this.

"Iss my birthday." Matty beamed.

The other guy, a long-haired chubby dude with light brown skin, opened his eyes a fraction. He was wearing a flannel shirt and baggy jeans covered with chocolate stains. "Whas goin' on?"

"Nothin'. Go back to sleep." Matty patted him clumsily on the chest before he waved a hand to airily encompass the store. "Sorry 'bout the mess. But I wanted to show . . . uh, what's your name again?" He poked the guy in the ribs.

"Brian." The word was a mumble.

"*Brian.*" Matty nodded. "I wanted to show Brian the store since it's my birthday and I had to come here for *work* instead of *partying.*" He said the words carefully and looked proud he'd gotten them out right. "But we're tired now, so let me sleep."

It was Matty's sing-song voice that truly set Trent off. It was the one Matty used every time he'd come up with a scheme to rile Trent up, and in a flash, Trent realized this was just another game. The trashed store, his chocolate printer, bringing some guy here . . . this wasn't just Matty being immature and stupid. This entire thing had been planned.

"You can wake the hell up now." Trent picked up the bottle of booze. It was three-quarters full and he'd put money on Matty's hook-up having drunk most of that. In fact, he'd bet all his savings that his brother had only drunk just enough to act convincingly intoxicated. "What did I tell you about drinking and coming to work? Do you want to be fired? Because that's what's about to happen."

Matty's eyes snapped open again and this time he looked a hell of lot more awake. "What?"

Trent stared him down. "The mess you've made here is gonna cost me a fortune. You've come into my store after hours with a stranger—"

"Brian's not a stranger! I met him last night and he's *nice.*

Nicer than *you are*." Matty shot to his feet, scattering the truffle wrappers in his lap across the floor.

"Nice doesn't come into it!" Trent stepped forward. "I'm doing the only thing I can do given the situation. I gave you an ultimatum about coming to work drunk and what do you do? Less than two weeks later you get shitfaced and wreck the place—on your birthday, of all days."

"Yeah. On my birthday. So you can't do anything. I know your rule. No being mean to people on their birthdays," Matty shot back, his lips curving in a smug smile.

The temptation to give Matty the ass-kicking of his life had never been greater. "Yeah? Well, since this is your twenty-first and you're supposed to be an adult, I'm gonna have to give you some adult consequences. I went out of my way to overlook the shit you tried to pull with Candy, and I've not reacted when you've pressed my buttons this last week, but you wouldn't let this lie. You're fired."

Matty physically recoiled, his mouth forming an O of shock as Trent's words finally sunk in. "You're actually doing it? Actually *firing me*?! On my birthday? You're firing me on my *birthday*?!"

"Yes! Fuck, Matty, you had one thing to do today, just one. All you had to do was not screw up so badly that we fought." Trent grabbed his phone. "I'm getting you an Uber and you're going home. You've really disappointed me. If you're trying to be an embarrassment to this family, you're succeeding."

The words came out before Trent could catch them, and for a moment, Matty's face looked like a hurt nine-year-old's again. Then it was replaced by an angry mask.

"Fuck you. I'll get home myself." Matty grabbed at the sleeping guy's hand. "Come on, Brian, we're going."

The guy barely moved. "What? Where?"

"My place."

"There is no way in hell he's going to our house if you've

only known him one day. Nona and the twins are there," Trent interjected.

"What? So now you're accusing me of trying to take a serial killer home?!" Matty's words were edged in hysterical fury.

"No, I'm accusing you of being irresponsible and of not respecting other people's property!" Trent rammed his phone in his pocket with enough force to shove his jeans down his hips. He saw a car pull up through the store's front windows. Stalking to the front door, he unlocked it and called out to the driver, who confirmed it was the car Trent had ordered. He turned back to Matty. "That's your ride, so get in the car, go home, and get your head on straight enough so that you don't upset Nona tonight at dinner. For once in your life, act your age."

"Fuck you." Matty turned and looked at the sleeping guy on the couch. "Brian, you didn't answer me. Are you coming?"

"No . . . sleeping." Brian curled up onto his side and burrowed his head into his hands.

"Then fuck you too." Leveling a scorching glare at Trent, Matty walked out the door in bare feet, giving Trent the finger through the store's window before climbing into the car.

"And happy birthday to you too," Trent muttered.

"What?" Brian asked.

"Nothing." Trent turned on him, realizing that this was the next situation he'd have to deal with. This guy was on the chunky side, too heavy for Trent to heave out the door and into a ride without assistance. "Where do you live, man?"

"Austin."

"Where in Austin?"

Trent's question was met with a long, loud snore.

"That's a great fuckin' help." Trent took in the state of the store, shaking his head. This place had to be spotless by nine. Plus he had to confirm whether or not his 3D printer was ruined . . . and then there was the shitshow that was no doubt gonna happen at home the minute Matty got there.

He messaged Gwen, apprising her of the situation and asking her to let him know when Matty arrived—he might want to kill his little brother, but he sure as hell didn't want anyone else to—and then messaged his other employees to see if anyone could come in on short notice. He didn't expect to get lucky.

The guy on the couch began snoring evenly, and after glowering at him for a few seconds, Trent left him there. He didn't have the time.

Trent was only halfway through cleaning up the kitchen when he heard a groan. He walked to the front of the store and found Brian sitting up, holding his head in the universal language of pain.

"You gonna puke?" Trent asked.

"No, but I feel like hell. Where am I?"

"My store. My little brother brought you here sometime last night and you trashed the place."

Brian's face screwed up in distress as he looked at the truffle wrappers Trent had yet to pick up. "Oh man, I remember meeting up with this guy—I think it might have been your brother—in a bar. He kept buying me shots and then . . . I can't remember. I'm sorry. For whatever I did. I'm not a drinker normally."

"You should be sorry. This is nothing compared to my kitchen. The minute you can stand up without puking, I want you gone," Trent said curtly, walking back into the kitchen.

About ten minutes later Brian appeared in the kitchen doorway, his eyes wide. "Whoa."

"Did I just hear you telling me you were leaving?" Trent said over the sound of running water as he painstakingly tried to de-caramel the inner parts of his 3D chocolate printer.

Brian held up his hands. "I can if you want, sir, but . . .

can I help? With anything? I feel really bad. I mean *really* bad. This is *definitely* not something I do. This is so *not* me."

Trent looked Brian up and down, finally seeing past the chocolate stains and the five o'clock shadow. This guy had creases in the front of his jeans, like he ironed them. It was impressive that they were still there after he'd spent the night on the couch.

"How old are you?"

"Nineteen, sir."

Trent paused in trying to remove caramel from the inside of a nozzle. He was running against the clock. The day was gonna be hell without an extra person to take care of the front of the store. Brian might be covered in chocolate, but an apron would hide most of it . . . "Where'd you meet my brother?"

"Online. We met in that bar last night, and like I said, he bought me a bunch of shots because I'm underage." Brian studied his feet like he was the only teenager in the whole of Austin who'd never gotten drunk before. "And then he brought me here. He said it was his birthday. If I knew we were gonna make this mess I wouldn't have, but he seemed really nice and kind of lonely." He focused on something over Trent's shoulder. "We didn't do anything in there, you know, other than eating a whole lot of those chocolates, which were really great . . ."

Trent leveled him with a steady look, and Brian looked at his feet.

"He tried to show me how everything worked. Not his, uh, thing. The chocolate. I really liked it—not his thing, the chocolate—and . . . I'm digging myself into a great big hole, aren't I?"

"What do you do, Brian?" Trent asked, feeling old. Really old. When he'd been nineteen he'd been working three jobs and grieving for his parents, not being conned into getting trashed by a scheming twenty-one-year-old.

"I'm studying nursing at UT. First year . . . sir."

"Yeah? My sister's a med student. You get good grades?"

Brian blinked. "Above average. But what——"

"Any criminal convictions?"

The other man studied his white sneakers. There was a glob of what looked like caramel on his left toe. "Once, for shoplifting when I was nine." The way Brian's shoulders slumped told Trent that he still probably asked for forgiveness in his prayers every night.

"What'd you take?"

"Batteries for my Xbox controller. My parents made me take them back to the store and the guy there pressed charges."

"You stolen any batteries since?"

"No sir."

"Do you have a part-time job?"

Brian's confusion was almost palpable. "I normally wait tables, but I'm in between jobs since the café I worked for had to shut down——"

"Take this," Trent interrupted. He reached into the medicine cabinet over the sink and threw Brian a box of Panadol. "Glasses are in the cupboard near you. Once you've taken one of those, take one of those scrapers and start scraping chocolate off workstations. Dump it in the trashcan over there. And once you've done *that*, I need the dishwasher emptied and loaded up again, then I need the floor mopped until it shines. If you do a good job and I decide I like you, you can work the register every Wednesday from nine to one. It's my full-time employee's morning off and I'd want to see you acting with the manners and professionalism of someone working in a high-end cake store, dealing with very stressed-out people who are planning big events. Could you do that?"

"What?" Brian stared at Trent in confusion. "Shouldn't I be cleaning all this for free since I helped make this mess?"

Trent's mouth curved in a humorless smile. "I think

working around the smell of food all morning with a hangover is gonna be payback enough. I don't have any more time for small talk. If you want to try out for the job, get to work. Otherwise, go home."

Ignoring Brian's shock, Trent checked his phone to see if Matty had made it home. Sure enough, there were a number of messages from Gwen that made it clear Matty had arrived and was putting on an Oscar-winning performance.

He's here. He's hugging the toilet bowl and cussing you out like a sailor.

Firing him on his birthday? Way to go, bro.

Okay, reading between the lines now, I get why you fired him but make the damn cake. Nona's expecting it. And btw, I don't think he's even drunk, but I'm not gonna tell him I know it. That toilet bowl is all the company he deserves right now.

"You look like you need this."

Trent turned around to see his newest employee holding a clean coffee cup in one hand and the jug from the percolator in the other.

"Thanks. But I don't think the coffee's gonna help," Trent said, pocketing his phone.

"At least you don't have a hangover."

"Yeah, I do. It turned twenty-one today and is determined to kill me," Trent said, taking the coffee pot and the mug. Holding them, he stared blankly out the window of his store, wondering what the hell he'd done wrong for it all to have to come to this.

Chapter 17

Trent's nona stood in the middle of the kitchen channelling a Sicilian general as she half-successfully gave orders to her granddaughters. Gwen was stirring something on the stove, but Carlotta was talking on her phone and Anna was sitting in the rocking chair by the French doors with a guinea pig in her lap.

"Anna, go put the guinea pig away. It doesn't belong in the kitchen. Carlotta, I need you to put your phone down and help me with the orange salad. And you—" She brandished the wooden spoon in her hand at Trent, who'd just walked into the kitchen with Matty's birthday cake. "Did you do a good job with his cake?"

"Good enough." Trent set the box down in the middle of the large marble-topped table that took up a chunk of the far end of the room. It had been a long day, spent scrambling to meet work orders with half his kitchen supplies ruined and his chocolate printer needing repairs.

"What did you make?" Anna asked from the rocking chair. Still wearing her animal-shelter uniform of blue polo and tan chinos, she was flicking the end of her long plait across the nose of the long-haired white guinea pig sitting on her lap.

"A cake. If that thing gets on the table and eats any of it, I'm gonna be cooking some Peruvian roast guinea pig for our entree tonight."

Anna rolled her eyes at the familiar threat. "You wouldn't dare. Anyway, can you hold Pebbles while I give him his antibiotics? Everyone else is busy and Matty's still sulking upstairs."

Trent groaned. "I've kind of had a big day and wanted to wind down for a while so I wouldn't try kill Matty over dinner. Can't someone else do it? Gwen? Carlotta?"

"I'm stirring things," Gwen said.

"And I'm cutting oranges." Carlotta snatched up one of the three oranges their nona had just placed in front of her, tossing it into the air.

He blew out a breath, seeing Anna's expectant smile. "Alright, where are its drugs?"

"Just here on the chair by my leg. All I need you to do is syringe the liquid into his mouth while I hold him still." Anna raised the guinea pig to her face and nuzzled the top of his head with her nose. "Hey, little guy. Just one more day and you're gonna go back to the center so they can find a nice family to adopt you."

"Or he'll find a nice chef who wants to roast him good. Guinea pigs are the food of the future. They're small, nutritious, and larger animals take up too many of the world's resources," Carlotta said from where she was now haphazardly slicing up oranges while Nona and Gwen discussed whether or not the risotto was done.

"She's not gonna eat you, she's just faking it," Anna said to the small creature as Trent picked up the syringe.

"You got him?" Trent asked. "Because I don't want to spend another night trying to get a rodent out from under the fridge."

"I've got him." Anna maneuvered the little animal into

place. "Here. Just open your mouth little buddy and . . . go, Trent!"

Trent squirted the liquid into the little fuzzball's mouth, half smiling at its indignant squeak. "That thing's almost as loud as you used to be when I made you eat your greens."

Anna just rolled her eyes at him and stood up. "I'm gonna put him in his cage and take a shower before dinner. Want me to tell Matty to come down too?"

"Yes," Nona said as she began to count out knives and forks, setting them on the kitchen counter. "But if he won't, Trent will go up and ask him." She gave Trent a censorious look over her glasses. "You fought with him on his birthday."

"No, he *fired* him on his birthday." Carlotta said with a fierce scowl. She'd always been protective of Matty.

"I did," Trent said simply, meeting her glare head-on. "And you would have done it too in my position. He trashed my store. I had no choice."

"There's always a choice. And you know how hard birthdays are in this family. You could have waited 'til tomorrow to fire him."

Trent jammed a hand through his hair. "Yeah. I could have, but I didn't. Are we gonna do this right now, Carlotta? You and me? Because it's not going to make Matty's birthday dinner any nicer."

Carlotta looked like she was going to argue before Nona stepped in, putting a hand on Carlotta's shoulder.

Trent's nona gave him a stern look over her glasses. "No more fighting. Go freshen up. Dinner will be ready in ten minutes. It should give you enough time to calm down so we can have a nice family dinner to celebrate Matty's birthday."

Trent bit back the words on the tip of his tongue, knowing they wouldn't help the situation. "I'll be down in a minute."

He'd just reached the upstairs landing when he heard Matty loudly saying the cake Trent had made for him—a simple chocolate cake with each and every topping Matty had ever professed to love—was an insult.

Stifling a curse, Trent walked into his bedroom and resisted slamming the door. Then he walked over to his bed and collapsed face down before yelling into his pillow for a solid minute. He then calmly stood up, got changed and headed downstairs.

He managed to keep his cool through dinner even though Matty spent most of it glaring at him across the table. The other part he spent telling Carlotta how depressed he'd been all day. Instead of taking the bait, Trent focused on talking to Anna about her volunteer work at the animal shelter and to Gwen about her first appendectomy being a success.

Nona had presided over everything, wearing a determined, benevolent smile at the head of the table. But the peace and quiet all went wrong when she stood up and got Matty's cake so everyone could sing "Happy Birthday."

After Matty half-heartedly blew out the candles, she gave him a gentle smile. "Happy birthday, Matty. We all love you. We are so proud you're now a grown man who will go on to do good things like your brother and sister here." She looked at Gwen and Trent with pride before turning back to Matty, whose expression was—if anything—even sulkier than before. "I'm proud of you and wish your parents could be here to see the person you've become. I know you've made me proud. You've made your brother proud—"

Her words were drowned out by Matty's enraged shriek as Matty scooped up a chunk of birthday cake and threw it straight at Trent before following that up with two more cake missiles, one of which hit Trent's nona in the face.

The room fell into a stunned silence as Matty stood stock-still, looking in horror at what he'd just done. "I-I'm . . . Nona, I didn't mean to—"

"Get out, Matty, and don't come back until you can act

like an adult," Trent said, his voice deadly calm as he looked first at his brother's sickly-pale face and then at his nona, who was now swiping chocolate icing off her cheeks. "Go to your party before I say something I'm going to regret."

Chapter 18

Sophie Grey was rarely speechless, so Candy had good reason to wince when the other end of the phone went silent. Knowing she couldn't put the conversation off any longer, she'd called Sophie after prepping the bar for Matty Green's party. It would be unforgivable to tell Sophie she'd gone ahead with this thing for Trent Green's brother *after* it happened.

Candy's whole body relaxed when Sophie drew in the audible breath that signaled an oncoming barrage of words.

"If I understand you correctly, not only did you change your mind, you actually let Trent Green come back to your bar, where he hung out with Fantasia and her friends, and then you let him help you clean up after? And even more confusing, you didn't call me straight afterwards to tell me what had happened, which is telling me there's more going on, which is *also* telling me I need to climb in my car right now and drive to Austin."

Candy pressed her lips together after hearing the hurt in Sophie's voice. "I know I'm a bitch for not telling you, but there's a lot going on."

"Like?"

"Like my mom starting up a carbon-neutral masturbation

circle, inviting half the street and charging them six hundred dollars each."

There was a choking noise at the other end of the phone. "Make sure I'm not drinking anything before you spring something like that on me! I just got coffee all down my shirt. And this is a new shirt, and it's white. Your mom's doing *what?*!"

"You heard me." Candy used the time waiting for Sophie's shrieks of laughter to die down to nod at Raven, who was trying to let Candy know he was leaving. A skinnier, balder Ed Sheeran, Raven was one of Candy's regulars who hadn't gotten the message about the bar being closed for a private function. Candy had pacified him by making him a coffee on the house and letting him bitch at Kevin over the renaming of Goth Night to Prancing Rainbow Pony Appreciation Night. Raven didn't intend to embrace forgiveness any time soon.

Sophie finally finished howling, the peals of laughter becoming giggling hiccups. "Oh my god! And I thought that time she was training as a hypnotist to revert people back to their past lives as mermaids was weird. Are you worried about her getting in trouble with the police again? Is what she's doing even legal?"

"I don't know." Candy inspected her nails. "But since Mom's seen half the coochies on her street by now, I don't think any of the neighbors are gonna report her."

"Even the one who used to babysit you? Isn't she quite conservative?"

"She's apparently loosened up a whole lot lately, because on Saturday I learned that she's a screamer."

Sophie burst into another bout of laughter. "That's so wrong! I can't wait to tell Ian about this."

"You do that. Just make sure he lists Mom's contact details and the price she charges if he puts all this in his newspaper."

"Ha! He would, too," Sophie said. "But enough about all that. Explain to me what's going on with you and Trent? Do I need to worry about you? More importantly, do I need to borrow Dad's shotgun and drive over there?"

"Nope," Candy said emphatically. "After Matty Green's party tonight I'm never going to see Trent or any member of his family again."

"But why did you agree to it in the first place?" Sophie asked.

"Because I'm charging him a fortune."

"But you were charging him a fortune the other night and you cancelled it."

Candy was mentally racing to come up with a reason that didn't include telling Sophie about her troubles with Beau and his mom when Matty Green walked into the bar an hour early, looking like his dog had just died.

"Hey, I've gotta go. I might have a drama on my hands," Candy said in a low voice.

"Normal drama, or drama I need to know about?" Sophie's suspicion was palpable.

"I'll tell you about it once I know what's going on. Love you."

"Love you too. And I want answers, or I am definitely coming to slap them out of you. This conversation isn't over."

"Come to see me anyway. You know I like it rough." Candy smiled at Sophie's laughter before ending the call to greet Matty. He was showing none of his last visit's bravado. While he was wearing a skimpy black tank and some jeans that were tight enough for everyone to see that he dressed left, his dime-store eyeliner and downturned mouth were one hundred percent sad clown. Candy didn't have to spot Matty's bloodshot eyes to know he'd been crying. She'd run a bar long enough to recognize an emotional wreck at thirty paces.

"You're an hour early, birthday boy. It's just me and Kevin here at the moment." She put her phone away as she spoke.

"Hey." Matty took a seat on the same stool his brother had occupied a week before. "Do you mind?"

Candy shrugged. "It's your birthday."

Matty looked at Kevin, who was sitting in his usual spot at the far end of the bar, typing industriously. "Is that Kevin?"

Kevin glanced up from his screen. "If you're referring to me, yes, I'm Kevin."

"I didn't mean to be rude." Matty looked like he was going to burst into tears any minute.

"Ignore him. He's got his period. Can I get you a drink?"

"Yeah. Bourbon, please."

"Any particular kind?"

Matty waved a hand listlessly through the air. "Any. I don't care how it comes."

"Okay."

Candy selected a bottle of Wild Turkey and poured him a half-shot over ice. She wasn't about to see him drunk before his party even started. For one thing, Trent might take it as a deliberate act on Candy's part, and the last thing Candy needed was more drama in that department.

Kevin, speaking in his patented "talking to the ignoramuses" voice, broke through her thoughts.

"I think you'll find that medical research has proven men do have hormonal mood swings, but to say I'm having my period is implying that having a period would be emasculating, which I know is not in line with any rational ideological perspective. Menstruation is merely a biological function. A biological function should not be deemed diminishing to one's gender."

Both Candy and Matty turned to look at him.

"Did he just say that?" Matty asked.

"Yeah. I find that he talks as long as I give him coffee," Candy said. "Although if you keep referring to Kevin like he's not in the room, I won't be held responsible for his actions. He bites."

"Are you aware of how much bacteria lives on human skin?" Kevin's face was a picture of disgust.

"He bites after swabbing you with Purell," Candy amended, setting Matty's drink in front of him. "Matty, meet Kevin. Kevin, be nice to Matty. He's had a hard day."

"How did you know?" Matty sat back on his stool in a way that told Candy the half-shot sitting in front of him wouldn't be the first. She made a mental note to do a whole lot more drink-watering tonight. Since Trent had paid for unlimited bottom-shelf drinks, she wouldn't be cheating anyone.

"I'm psychic. It's hereditary. My mom once did a favor for a wise Chinese sage and he gave her the gift of me."

There was a grunt from Kevin. "I've met your mom, remember?"

"You telling me that my father, the great Johnny Tang, isn't sage-like, and that he didn't give her a gift?" Candy raised a brow. "Am I not the greatest gift of all?"

"No comment."

"Since when do *you* have nothing to say?"

"Since you talked me into playing bartender tonight for no money."

"It's a great research opportunity, remember? You said 'Candy, I don't have enough conflict in my current novel,' and I said, 'Kevin, why don't you work behind my bar at a twenty-first birthday party?' and you said, 'If I have to.'"

Matty—who'd been following the conversation like a spectator at a ping-pong tournament—spoke to Kevin. "You're a writer?"

"Yeah." Kevin went back to typing. "And I have work to do." He paused a moment, as if remembering something. "Happy birthday."

Matty threw the rest of his drink back with one gulp. "Thanks. Although it hasn't been all too happy so far. My brother's an idiot."

"That's old news, tell me something new," Candy said with more bite than she intended and then felt guilty about speaking bad about Trent behind his back for reasons she really didn't want to interrogate. She put it down to anxiety over not going to Beau's NA meeting tonight. She knew from experience that Marlene wouldn't take Candy's absence lightly, and there was a chance Beau would break the restraining order again. It was enough to make her feel queasy.

Matty continued talking as if he hadn't heard her. "Can you believe he *fired* me? Actually fired me on my birthday?"

"Oh yeah?" Candy asked, intrigued now despite herself. The old Trent would definitely do something like that, but something wasn't ringing true here. And the fact she was thinking that at all meant that Beau's visit the other night had definitely rattled her. Trent might have helped her clean a bar for an hour, but that only meant that he'd graduated from bottom-feeder to pond scum.

"Yeah. It's not like I really did anything. Just tried to make myself a birthday cake." Matty's bottom lip jutted out.

"Yeah?" Candy asked.

"He's never liked me. He hates me like my parents did. He just does a better job of hiding it." Matty looked down at his hands and Candy noticed how chewed his nails were. "No matter what I do, he's always disappointed."

Candy studied him for a long moment, her pity-party barometer beginning to chime. "That's life, I guess. But it's your party tonight and your brother's not here, so you might as well enjoy yourself to spite him."

The minute she said the words, she realized how stupid they were. She just hoped Matty Green wasn't about to trash her bar and say she'd given him permission.

Matty's head jerked up. "You think me having fun tonight would make him regret it?"

"Fun within reason," Candy amended. "Why don't you chill out here, get your head straight, and maybe talk to Kevin like he's a person for a while before everyone shows up."

"Okay. I'll do that." Matty set his shoulders before sliding off his seat and walking towards Kevin with an exaggerated saunter.

Candy was saved from having to acknowledge Kevin's glare by the arrival of the two temps she'd hired for the night. Jake had lined her up with good people. Taneesha was a drummer and CrossFit enthusiast with a fierce scowl that hid the softness of a kitten. The other bouncer was Blake, a hulking bass player with an impressive ginger monobrow and the overall sweetness that sometimes came with large men.

After talking to them for less than a minute, Candy's worries about how the night would go started to subside. She saw that Matty was now sitting next to Kevin, awkwardly attempting to spark up a conversation, and she relaxed even more.

Yeah, tonight should go well, and then afterwards Trent Green and his family would be gone from her life. All she had to do was get through the next four hours.

Chapter 19

"We're gonna need more Bacardi," Kevin yelled over the roar of people talking and the thump of the industrial club playlist Candy had put on after asking Matty Green what music he preferred.

Candy started pouring a glass of Bud Light. "In the crate at your feet. To the left. And take your time. These guys are getting drunk way too quickly."

Candy's unease had come back the minute the first of Matty's friends had arrived. For one thing, Matty didn't seem to know many of them. For another, he'd become hyper-animated after visiting the bathrooms with a woman who was either a Kardashian pretending to be emo, or an emo pretending to be plastic. Candy could spot someone high on coke, and Matty Green was showing all the signs.

Since the bathroom visit, he'd been talking with too much animation and generally being a pantomime of someone having a good time. And that wouldn't be so noticeable if it wasn't blatantly obvious that the people around him weren't interested. In fact, it was like no one besides Emo Kardashian actually knew this was Matty's party, or even knew *him*. Which was weird and kind of sad.

Candy scanned the packed room, noting that both Taneesha and Blake were earning every cent of their paycheck tonight. Half the room seemed to think this was a dungeon sex party and the other half were acting like they were in a mosh pit.

"Have you seen Matty?" she asked Kevin.

"No." He shook his head before leaning across the bar to better hear what Bondage Jessica Rabbit was trying to order.

Candy waved Blake over. "Have you seen the birthday boy?"

Blake ignored a guy who was either humping his leg or trying to squeeze up to the bar. "Was he the dude who was here when we came in?"

"Yeah." Candy handed the beer to a woman wearing a Morticia Addams dress with a vee-cut neckline that went down to her navel.

"I thought I saw him by that pink thing over there. He was with that skinny guy that Taneesha was having trouble with earlier." Blake jerked his thumb over his shoulder at the TARDIS.

"What was this skinny guy doing?" Candy yelled over the sound of Jessica Rabbit shrieking at Kevin for putting lime in her mojito.

Blake grimaced. "He was feeling up a bunch of people who didn't want to be touched. I think I saw him going in there a few minutes ago when Taneesha was taking care of that idiot trying to crowd-surf."

That was enough for Candy. She put her hand of Kevin's shoulder. "Cover for me."

It took her at least five minutes to elbow her way through the throng. On her way, she managed to catch Taneesha's eye so the woman was at her heels when she flung open the TARDIS door and took in the scene inside

It was immediately obvious that things were not okay. Matty Green was slumped on the floor of the tiny space, completely out of it, while a budget Marilyn Manson was standing between his splayed legs and hastily trying to button up his pants.

Candy turned to Taneesha. "You fine with throwing this asshole into the street using maximum force, preferably making sure he walks funny for a week?"

"Sure am." Taneesha gave the skinny guy a glare that said she hadn't forgotten dealing with him earlier.

Candy moved out of the way long enough for Taneesha to drag him off as he shrieked like a banshee, and then she stepped inside the TARDIS, closing the door. The single light-bulb overhead swung for a moment, casting weird shadows in the small space.

"Hey, birthday boy. You okay?" She crouched down in the vee of Matty's bunched-up knees, taking in Matty's damp, downturned mouth and smudged eyeliner.

Matty's eyes opened for a moment, then closed again. "No."

Candy gripped his shoulder hard enough to get his attention. "Did he do anything to you? Anything at all that we need to have him killed for?"

"No . . . He didn't do anything—much." Matty shook his head slowly. "It's not important."

"Yeah, it is. What do you mean by *much?*" Candy said, while already scanning him for signs that he'd been messed with.

"Exac—cly what I mean. I'm *fine.*"

"Okay then. If you say you're fine, I'll believe you. So why don't we—"

"Nothing's fine!"

Candy barely had warning before Matty's face crumpled and he started ugly crying, his eyes screwed up and nose running all over the place.

Candy's entire body stiffened. "You mean he did do something to you. Do we need to call the cops? Or do you need medical help? Talk to me, Matty."

"Yes! Call the cops. My brother's a dick and they need to *know*. He fired me! On my birthday! He hates me so bad. He pretends he likes me, but he hates me so much he wants me to *die*!"

"Jesus H. Christ," Candy muttered, her hackles lowering as she worked out that Matty was at least visibly fine. "Okay, your brother fired you, your drugs aren't working, and some asshole was just about to assault you. You're having a bad day and I'm sorry about that, but unless you want every single person in this bar filming you when you come out of this box looking like your dog just died, you're gonna have to pull yourself together. Hear me? I've been watching these people and they are definitely not your friends. I don't know what your story is, but now isn't the time to go into it. I can kick everyone out if you want, but it's your party, so I need to hear it from you."

"I don't want to do anything! I'm too sad!" Matty wailed.

"You and everyone else," Candy muttered, knowing there was no way in hell sympathy was going to work in the face of this much self-pity. "And that's how life rolls, but I need you to stand up—"

"I can't do anything! I should just *die* here. I'm so *un*happy."

Candy stood up, torn between frustration, sympathy and humor over the way his bottom lip was sticking out like a little boy's. "Come on." She pulled out the clean cloth tucked into the back pocket of her jeans and held it out. "Wipe your face."

"I can't!" Matty hunched over. "I want to stay *sad*. If I'm sad then he'll feel guilty, and he *needs* to feel guilty. He needs to understand what it's like to hold all this *sadness* inside me all the time, to know what I know. He needs to feel it! They *hated* me and they *loved* him. They thought I was so ugly, so *embar-*

rassing, and they wanted me to be different but I couldn't. And they're dead and they all know it's my fault. I'm different and I can't change and they all hate me for it!"

His shoulders started shaking with fresh tears. This felt more serious to Candy and so she reached down and put a hand on Matty's shoulder. People didn't cry like this unless there was a genuine problem.

"Hey, I know what it's like to be different and like no one can relate. I feel for you, but this isn't the place to explore those feelings. Those people out there don't care, and you're setting yourself up for a whole lot of disappointment if you think they do. Why don't we go to my office where it's safe and—"

Matty's head shot up, the genuine emotion from seconds ago replaced again by substance-fueled belligerence. "I don't have to go anywhere I don't want to! You can't tell me what to do! I can stay here if I want as long as I want. I want my tears to stain my face forever!"

Lord save her from people on drugs. The minute she got out of here she was going to find that Kardashian look-alike dealer and throw her out the door head first. "Okay, I get it, and I'm not trying to act like what you're feeling right now isn't real. It's definitely your party and you can cry if you want to—"

"Yes! I can cry *forever!*"

"—but I can tell you right now that stepping out there crying isn't going to help you with those assholes out there *or* your brother, since he has no idea you're sitting in here and not having a good time drinking his money."

"Yes it will! If I'm sad enough, he'll know! And then he'll know what it's like to be *me.*" Matty hunched down even further, crossing his arms over his chest and giving Candy a water-logged glare.

Candy rolled her eyes as the drama hit Mach 5 levels. Now she knew Matty was fine, her patience was wearing thin, especially since she was very aware Kevin was manning the bar alone. "No, it's not. I know you've had the twenty-first of shitness so far, but if you don't get your butt off the floor of my TARDIS, it's gonna get even shitter. You want that?"

"No!"

"Then wipe the snot off your face and stand up like a grown-ass man." Candy injected enough iron into her tone to get a reaction. It just wasn't the reaction she was hoping for.

"I don't have to do anything you tell me to do! You're just as bad as he is. You hate me too!" Matty shot back, crossing his arms over his chest.

"Lord, save me," Candy muttered under her breath as a knock sounded on the door.

"You need any help in there, babe?" Taneesha asked.

"Sure do." Candy opened the door and stepped out, leaving Matty inside. "The birthday boy is officially, sad, sulking and belligerent."

"At least he's not assaulted and on his way to the emergency room," Taneesha growled. "How can I help?"

If Candy were the kind of person to hug people impulsively, the moment would be now. She settled for giving Taneesha a squeeze of thanks on her brawny arm. "I don't want anyone taking advantage of the situation. He's on a huge comedown from whatever he's on and doesn't want to come out, and I don't want anyone going in there with him."

Taneesha frowned. "You want me to carry him out so we can put him somewhere safe until closing time? Because I can. He's little."

Candy looked around the heaving bar, scowling as she was elbowed by a woman wearing a too-tight catsuit. "He's better off in there, because none of his so-called friends are watching his back. I wouldn't put it past any of these assholes not to take a picture of him looking like shit and post it online. Just make sure he stays undisturbed while I see about getting him some water. He's gonna need it, or all he's gonna remember of his twenty-first is the hangover."

Taneesha shook her head. "It's a shame. This could've been a great party if he'd invited different people."

"You said it."

They shared a look before Candy wound her way back through the throng while trying to remember why this was supposed to be better than going to her ex-husband's NA meeting. On one hand, there was dealing with a man who'd lied to her for years and cost her almost everything she loved; on the other, there was dealing with a hundred college kids pretending they were BDSM superstars. What she wouldn't give for Jake to be here right now, explaining to all these idiots what BDSM really was. Not that she really knew herself, but the image was entertaining her enough to lighten her mood.

She skirted around a Dwayne Johnson wannabe blocking her way. He was wearing a three-inch-wide spiked dog collar around his overly muscled neck and was having a hard time moving his head. The spikes were way too long, and she knew he hadn't been wearing that thing when he'd walked in. She didn't even want to *think* about where he'd been hiding it under that slinky black top and those leather hot pants.

She tapped him on the shoulder. "Hey. You were told the rules at the start of the night. No spikes. Ditch the collar now."

He'd obviously had a few too many because he swayed at her words. "It's not hurting anyone. And the sign on that thing over there says I can wear three spiked things."

Candy had to give him credit for at least being able to read the Rules on the TARDIS. "It does. But I told everyone at the beginning of this party that no spikes were allowed tonight. Hand it over, bud, or you're out."

"I'm not givin' you anything."

"Yeah, you are. You're giving me a ton of satisfaction." Candy waved at Blake, who had just finished busting a bunch of Corpse Brides trying to climb up and dance on the bar for the fifth time that night. "Kick this idiot out," she yelled.

The guy only managed to get out half a protest before Blake put a hand on his shoulder and hustled him to the door.

"These are the most obnoxious people I have ever encountered!" Kevin yelled as Candy slipped back behind the bar.

"Only an hour to go. I'd shut this down right now, but I'm worried they'll trash the place," she said.

"It can't come soon enough," Kevin grumbled. "I'm feeling distinctly uninspired."

Candy looked across the room at the TARDIS where Matty was still hiding. "Tell me about it," she muttered, fighting the feeling that she still had a long way to go before this night was over.

Chapter 20

Trent was staring blankly at an episode of *Orange Is the New Black*, pretending that he wasn't waiting up for Matty, when his phone rang. He glanced at the screen, seeing an unfamiliar number.

"Trent Green speaking."

"You mean, Trent Green driving in and picking up his brother." Candy's tone was ice-pick sharp.

Trent didn't need to be a genius to add two and two together. He rested his head against the back of the couch and stared up at the living room's vaulted ceiling, wishing for a moment that it would come crashing down on him, just for a little bit, so he could get some rest from all this drama in a nice ICU ward. "What's he done?"

"You want the list?"

"Yeah, why not? Better hearing about it from you first." Trent got up, collected his keys and walked for the door.

"Well, topping that list is getting shitfaced by snorting, smoking or huffing something that I wasn't selling. Also inviting a whole lot of people who didn't know him—including a creep who tried to take advantage of him."

"Who tried to take advantage of him? He okay?" Trent

demanded as his body rewired itself for war. He'd just hit the ignition to his truck when Candy spoke again.

"Taken care of. Settle down. That's why I hired Taneesha here, who is getting a great big bonus from you for babysitting and ball-breaking tonight." The phone was muffled for a moment, but Trent could still hear Candy's voice. "Thanks, guys. Yeah, I'll take it from here. Big, bad brother's on the way . . . Don't thank me. You earned that bonus—tonight was hell with a capital H. Yeah, Kevin, I owe you, buddy. I'll even let you organize the cash register one day when I think I can bear it . . . Serious. Where was I?" Candy asked as Trent ground his back teeth.

"You talking to me now?" Trent asked as he kicked his truck into gear, tires screeching as he reversed out of the driveway.

"Yeah. Where was I?" Candy said. "Oh yeah, other than inviting a bunch of idiots, he was almost sexually assaulted. I meant it, you really owe Taneesha that extra fifty I just gave her for almost snapping that creep's dick off. And then Matty stayed holed up in the TARDIS until about an hour ago, when he dodged both my bouncers and went missing—"

"Sexually assaulted?! Missing? What do you mean? Where is he?" Trent steered the truck around a series of slower cars.

"Calm down, Liam Neeson, this isn't *Taken*. Matty didn't seem to even know what the creep had been about to do, and he's safe now. Anyway, I don't have time to go into it. Just be walking through the door in the next ten minutes or your brother is toast."

The call was hung up and Trent was left cursing and speeding down the expressway as fast as he could without putting every cop in Texas on his tail.

Twenty minutes later Trent stormed through the front door of Hard Candy armed for bear.

"Where is he?" he asked, homing in on Candy, who'd been walking across the room with a plastic crate full of glasses in her hands. She hadn't shut off the music yet, but it was turned down, a low beat filling the room.

She didn't bother looking at him, just kept walking, every muscle in her arms defined from managing the crate's heavy weight. "He's sleeping off the booze and whatever the hell else he's on in my bed. We made sure to turn him on his side, but if he pukes, you're gonna hear about it."

"Did someone hurt him? Did the creep you mentioned do anything?"

"Other than corner him in the TARDIS, I don't think so. It was more what we stopped from happening. And as I said, that asshole isn't gonna be doing anything like that anytime soon after what Taneesha did to him. So calm down. I just need you to take your brother home."

His desire to make sure his little brother was safe and unharmed transformed into anger over Matty behaving irresponsibly for the third time in one day. "Okay, where's your bedroom?"

"Upstairs. He managed to creep up there when Taneesha thought he was in the bathroom. I should charge you a penalty for the worry he's caused me tonight." The last words were a growl as Candy heaved the crate up onto the bar. "I've got enough on my hands without having to deal with cleaning up this mess."

Trent finally registered the state the bar was in. There were glasses everywhere and not all of them were upright or in one piece. The floor was covered in so much spilled drink that the dry spots looked like little isolated islands.

"Matty's friends did this?"

Candy glowered at him before placing her hands on her lower back and rolling her neck from side to side. "From what I saw, the word 'friend' doesn't apply. As far as I could work out, your brother just put a public post on social media. The only person who seemed to know him was the woman who gave him his drugs. In short, your brother doesn't have any friends, or if he does, I didn't see any tonight. If I weren't so exhausted, I'd find it sad, Green, really sad."

The words caused Trent to feel guilty, which made him feel even angrier. He risked walking further into the bar, grimacing when his shoes stuck to the floor with each step. "What'd they do? Pour their drinks straight onto the floor?"

Candy rolled her eyes. "And everything else. By the end we were watering the drinks down almost ninety percent, and none of them noticed because they were all so high off their own goddamn supply. I don't like hard drugs in my bar, Green, and that's precisely what I had tonight. Your cover charge didn't cover me having to put up with high idiots."

Trent closed his eyes tightly for a minute. He knew Matty wasn't a saint, but hearing it from Candy's mouth was another matter entirely. "Take me to him. Please."

"Alright, but I'm warning you, if you say *one* smart-ass thing about my apartment, I'm throwing you out a window."

Candy led Trent to a door near the cogwork sculpture. A glass had been jammed behind one of the cogs, making it move funny. He plucked it out, promising himself that he'd fix the warped cog for her somehow.

"You gonna take care of this mess on your own?" he asked, already knowing the answer. He'd followed her into a short hallway, and as the door closed behind him, the music from the bar was all but silenced.

"Yep."

He followed her up a narrow set of stairs that ended in a bright red door. "Don't you have anyone who comes in to clean for you?" he asked.

Candy paused with her hand on the door handle, giving him a look that said his brain might be visibly leaking from his ears. "You ever see anyone else here in the times you've been here?"

"Just you and a whole lot of attitude."

"Then it's just me and my fucking attitude."

"So you're cleaning all that up tonight?"

"Well, I had a blow-out scheduled and maybe a fitting for my ball gown, but since Prince Charming didn't turn up, I might as well date a mop and bucket."

Candy pushed the door open, revealing a small apartment that was as eccentric as its owner. She turned and jabbed a finger in Trent's chest.

"One sarcastic word about my home and I'm gonna be kicking you back down those stairs and throwing your brother behind you. If I could heave him out myself, there's no way you'd be stepping through this door."

"Noted." He followed her into the middle of the room, immediately spotting Matty curled up in Candy's bed covered in a patchwork bedspread. Candy's dog was lying next to him, wagging his tail. Trent spared Barney a glance before refocusing on Matty. "He been like that the whole time?"

Candy put her hands on her hips, studying Matty with a blank expression. "He's drooling more than before, but this is the general theme. And I'm talking about your brother, not my dog."

Trent studied Matty's face, feeling the painful mix of anger, frustration and pain. Guilt was there too. He'd truly failed as a father figure if it had come to this.

From what Trent could see, Matty was wearing a different outfit than what he'd worn to the family dinner, which was unsurprising given his earlier cake-throwing tantrum. Trent had understood why Matty might have mixed feelings about their nona's speech, but he couldn't forgive the cake thrown at her face. And this is where they'd ended up.

"That your bed?" Trent asked, knowing it was a dumb question but needing to say something to relieve the tension inside him.

"You see any other bed?"

Trent looked around, realizing just how small this place was. A tiny kitchen with red cupboards was off to the side, and he could see a matchbox-sized bathroom through an open door. "Alright, let me get him out of here," he said. "Matty." He nudged his brother's shoulder and didn't get a response.

"Tried that. He's out of it, dude."

"Okay." Trent pulled the bedspread back, grunting as he hoisted Matty into his arms. He was a dead weight. "Hold the door open for me."

Candy did. "Watch his head."

"I'm on it."

"Bye, Green."

"Thanks, Candy." Trent looked over his shoulder as he walked out the door, catching a flash of unmistakeable exhaustion on Candy's face. "I appreciate this."

She fluttered her fingers at him. "Go."

Hiking Matty more securely into his arms, Trent made his way through the bar out to his truck.

Chapter 21

"Wake up, dog. If I'm not sleeping tonight, neither are you."

Candy gave Barney a poke in the rump with her foot after she finished loading the final set of unbroken glasses into dishwasher.

Barney—who'd come downstairs when she'd locked the door behind Trent and Matty and settled into his usual hidey-hole under the bar—wagged his tail at her once before curling into an even tighter ball.

"You know you're supposed to be one of the most active breeds in the book, right? Anyone looking at you right now would think you're a snoring potato with legs. At least give me some sympathy. It's not like I'll be sleeping any time soon." Candy picked up a bucket containing the last of the broken glass she'd been able to pick up by hand and took it outside to drop in the recycling.

She'd just returned to grimace at how much work she still had to do before bedtime when someone pounded on the bar's front door.

She froze on the spot, panic stabbing through her. Beau. It couldn't be anyone else. She hadn't gone to his meeting tonight and he wanted revenge.

"We're closed!" she yelled, loud enough that her throat hurt.

The knock started up again and this time Candy ignored it, forcing herself to remember that there was a solid door and a bunch of locks between him and her. She'd locked the back door when she'd come in just now, hadn't she? She froze for a split second, before mobilizing, slipping on the drink-splattered floor as she ran to the back door, securing all four of the locks.

She was berating herself for her own stupidity in leaving it unlocked when her phone rang. She pulled it out, saw Trent's name and answered. "What do you want?"

"Let me in. I'm outside."

"What?!"

"I'm standing outside. Open the door and let me in."

Candy's panic morphed into outrage as she marched to the front door. On the other side of all those locks was Trent, holding a red toolbox in one hand and a pizza box in the other. He had a backpack slung over his shoulder.

"Is this like *The Exorcist?*" Candy asked. "Because I thought I banished you an hour ago."

Trent shrugged. "Yeah, but I came back. Can I come in?"

The scent of peperoni and melted cheese radiating from the pizza box caused Candy's stomach to rumble. "Why?"

"So I can put this pizza down somewhere and then get a start on cleaning up the rest of this mess. See it as a way of me repaying you for saving my brother tonight, nothing more. So if you're about to protest, cut the crap and let me help. Please. I'm guessing you haven't had a chance to eat much tonight, and I sure as hell haven't since Matty threw his damn birthday cake all over me at dinner."

It was the genuine "please" and the lines of exhaustion around Trent's eyes that did it. The vulnerability was so unexpected that it took Candy off guard.

"Yeah?" She searched for some of the acrimony she'd felt

the week before, or even that morning, and realized she was tapped out. "Fuck it. Come in." She stepped aside. "Don't you have to go to work in the morning?"

He set the pizza box on the bar before placing his toolbox and backpack next to it. "Yeah. I start at eight, often earlier. Every day except for Sundays."

"So why are you here?" she asked as she relocked the door.

"Because it's the right thing to do."

She saw the muscles bunching in his jaw and the lines deepen around his eyes. She then realized he was wearing a black T-shirt instead of the white one he'd turned up in earlier. His hair was damp, too, the short curls slicked back, making him look more like a fifties heartthrob than ever. It dawned on her that other than the suit he'd worn the night of his chocolate apology, he'd gone for the James Dean thing every time. Hadn't the man had time to shop for a new style in the past twelve years? Not that the look didn't suit him. She refocused on the T-shirt.

"He throw up in your car?" she asked, going for a safe guess.

"Nope. He threw up on me."

"Huh," Candy said. "You probably deserved it. He said you fired him on his birthday."

He nodded, his expression impassive. "Yeah."

"Dick move." Candy retrieved the now-empty bucket she'd used to collect the broken glass and took it to the sink behind the bar, rinsing it before pouring in a generous amount of Lysol and filling it up again. It was going to take gallons of disinfectant to get this place back in order. And that wasn't even taking the bathrooms into account.

She looked up when Trent didn't defend himself, and for a moment she saw a flash of exhaustion that echoed hers lately. She glanced at the stuff he'd brought. "I get the suck-up-to-me pizza, but what's with the backpack?"

He followed her gaze. "Since your bed probably isn't the most inviting place after my drunk brother passed out in it, I brought some clean sheets so you can get a decent night's sleep while I clean up."

Candy blinked. "You brought me *bedding*?"

He gave her a challenging look. "Yeah. Unless you've got a thing for drool, or have time to visit that laundromat next door tonight."

"And you don't think I have a spare set?" Candy didn't, but she wasn't going to tell him that.

"I just thought it was the right thing to do."

She turned the tap off before standing back and massaging her temples. "And the toolbox? Is that to make me a whole new bed to go with the sheets?"

"Nope. It's so I can fix that busted cog over there." Trent pointed to the wall sculpture and Candy let out a noise that was more growl than a curse. One of the cogs was clearly bent out of shape.

"How the *hell* did that happen?"

"Someone jammed a glass behind it. I took it out earlier."

She hurried over to turn off the sculpture and inspect the damage, running her fingers over the edges of the broken cog. "Now I'm really mad."

"It's bent, but as far as I can see, I should be able to get it back into shape. Just let me clean this place first and then I'll get to it."

She turned on her heel, looking him up and down. "You expect me leave you alone in *my* bar while I'm asleep upstairs? Somehow trusting that *you* will do a good enough job not to leave me with a total mess tomorrow? You? One of the two men in my life who have made it truly crap?"

"Yeah," Trent drawled. "Sounds about right."

The room fell into a silence only broken by Barney's snores and the muted beat of the music.

"Like hell. There is no *way* I'm going to trust you alone in my bar," Candy said finally.

Trent shrugged. "Fine, then I'll get to work while you eat some pizza before it gets cold. The night's not gettin' any younger. It's got extra pepperoni because I figured you'd be a carnivore from the chunks you've taken out of me this past week." Trent walked past her, leaning across the bar to pick up the bucket from the sink and snag a roll of paper towels.

Normally Candy would protest, but after the week she'd just had, she was out of fight. And she was only checking out his backside as he walked away because her brain currently didn't have the capacity to remind her that this was the enemy. He had a nice ass. A nice back and shoulders too. But his ass, now that was something . . .

Barney let out a snort, snapping her out of what was obviously sleep-and-sex deprived insanity to open the pizza box. The minute the delicious smell of pepperoni and cheese hit her nose, her mouth started watering. "I'm too tired and hungry to fight you."

"Not surprised." There was a tinkling sound as Trent swiped down a table covered in shards that had been too small for her to easily pick up by hand. "Are those trash bags by the beer taps?"

"Yeah." Candy threw the roll at him with her free hand, taking a bite of pizza and closing her eyes at how great it tasted. After a sudden silence, her eyes snapped open to find Trent looking at her. "What?" she asked before finishing off the pizza slice in a few huge bites.

"Did you eat that, or evaporate it?"

"Why are you talking and not guilt-cleaning? Get to work." Candy took a seat on a barstool and reached for another slice.

Trent's mouth cocked at the corner in a half-smile. "Yes ma'am."

Chapter 22

Aware of Candy watching him as he worked, Trent was careful not to miss any sliver of broken glass or sticky puddle of spilled liquor. After working in kitchens his entire adult life, Trent knew how to get things done efficiently and done right.

"Do you want some of this pizza or not?" Candy asked.

Trent glanced at the open box. It had been an extra-large and there were only three slices left. "Where the hell did you put all that? Have you got hollow legs?"

"Keep insulting me and I won't leave you any."

"You're still hungry?"

"Maybe."

"Then eat the rest." Trent had barely said the words before Candy pounced on the last three pieces. As he worked, he watched with growing incredulity.

She'd always been skinny—or maybe a better term was "lean"—but looking at her now, he could see that there were shadows under her cheekbones that had never been there before, and that her arms and legs didn't have an ounce of fat on them, just wiry muscle. With that shaved head, and in that short black dress and chunky boots, she was a cross between waif and warrior woman, and damned if he didn't suddenly find her the sexiest woman he'd ever seen. Maybe it was the fact she personified the kind of independence he could only dream of, or maybe it was because her killer sexuality was entirely unselfconscious. Plus, she already expected the worst of him, so he didn't have to be anyone other than who he was . . .

"Any reason you're staring at me?" Candy asked before swiping the back of her hand over her mouth.

"Just admiring your ability to clear away a pizza in the time it took me to wipe down a few tables."

"You're obviously not working fast enough."

Trent let out a short burst of laughter. "You ever let up? Or is that mouth of yours permanently switched on?"

"That ego of yours ever take a holiday?"

"Only when I'm asleep. And I'm *damn* good-looking when I sleep. Smart, too." Trent looked around at what he had yet to do, feeling his mood lighten. "Let me guess, the inside of that pink phone-box thing needs hosing down."

Candy closed the pizza box. "The TARDIS? Yep. Your brother camped out in there for half the night."

Making a mental note to later read "The Rules" posted on its door, Trent peered inside. "He hung out in *here*?"

"Don't worry, big brother. We made sure there wasn't anything breakable in there to damage himself with."

Trent closed his eyes for a moment, trying to stay calm despite the thought of Matty self-harming either intentionally or accidentally. "I don't get it. He's hell-bent on self-destruction and I seem to be the trigger. It's like just knowing I'm alive is enough to set him off."

"I know the feeling."

"Yeah, but you've got good reason," Trent said before grabbing a bottle of disinfectant and spraying the hell out of the TARDIS before stepping inside to wipe it down. "I bullied the hell out of you. I might not have been a good brother before Mom and Dad died, but I've tried damn hard since. I even read books about how to be a substitute parent—"

"You can read?!"

"Yeah. Even the big words."

"Like 'fuck-up'?"

"Like 'sarcasm.'"

"Good Lord, you must have gotten into the advanced class."

Trent stepped out of the TARDIS and saw that despite Candy's words, her expression didn't contain any bloodlust.

He started wiping down the phone box door. "Sure did. But it didn't do me any good. Because somewhere along the way, I've messed up. He hates me."

The room fell silent again except for the music and Trent finished cleaning out the inside. When he emerged, he found Candy wearing a fierce frown.

"Just wondering . . ." she said. "You know, because it's my damn bar and I can ask whatever I like, and because I heard your brother say a few things that made me think there are some big issues you people need to talk about . . ."

"What?" he asked, bracing himself for Candy to go for his throat. He deserved it.

"Have you asked him *why* he's got all those ideas in his head about you hating him, instead of doing all this 'I'm such a hero and he doesn't appreciate me' navel-gazing?"

Trent scowled. "You accusing me of prioritizing self-pity over my brother's mental health?"

She gave him a one-shoulder shrug. "Maybe. Are you? I'm not your shrink and it's not my job to fix your problems—or any woman's by the way, just in case you're going around moaning to every human you meet who has boobs." She paused. "Maybe that's why you got on so well with the queens the other night . . . No, knowing Fantasia, she was probably telling *you* about *her* life."

"Yeah, but hers at least involves what sounds like a healthy sex life." Trent's face flushed as the words slipped out. He waited for Candy to go in for the kill, but instead she just rolled her eyes.

"Antonio—that's Fantasia's boy name—is currently sleeping with at least three people who don't know about each other and who would rip his tightly tucked balls off if they found out. If you think that's a healthy sex life, you are even more deluded than you first appear."

Trent let out a short bark of surprised laughter. "I may be. From what I heard, he does like to live on the edge."

"Are you saying cleaning my bar isn't the challenge of a lifetime? Because last I saw, the men's restroom could make any grown man scream."

Trent nodded solemnly. "You might be right there. You *are* offering me a chance to live on the wild side."

"And I'm not even charging you for the privilege . . . more than I already have for Matty's party." Candy sauntered around the bar and poured herself a Coke. "You want a coffee?"

Trent blinked, trying to keep up with the conversation. "You're offering to make me a coffee?"

"How'd you have it?"

"An espresso if you're using your fancy machine."

Candy selected a small espresso cup from the shelf. "I've got to check your brother's idiot friends didn't do any damage to it sometime. Might as well be now," she said as she began turning levers and dials.

Trent suddenly found a lump forming in his throat. Other than his nona, and maybe Gwen, he couldn't remember the last time someone had done something nice for him when it didn't involve guilt, expectation or some other difficult emotion. Candy had so many reasons to be screaming at him right now, but here she was, making him a coffee.

"Thanks, Candy." At any other time, Trent would feel embarrassed over the emotion that crept into his tone. "That you're letting me help you like this . . . that you're listening to me. It means a lot. You're a good person. Thank you."

A flash of something crossed Candy's face before she covered it up with a scowl, her dagger earrings casting stark shadows against her cheekbones. "Less talk, more work, Green. You think I've got time to listen to you when I could be sleeping?" She paused. "And on that note, I think I'm gonna take you up on your crazy offer and get some sleep. But if this place isn't clean when I come down in the morning, I'm gonna come after you with my baseball bat. Hear me?"

"Yes ma'am." Trent gave her a salute, his mouth twitching when her fierce glare was ruined by a yawn.

"Your espresso's here on the bar. I'll be upstairs if you need anything. And you better not need anything, because I'll be sleeping." With those words she snatched up the backpack he'd brought and strutted off to her upstairs apartment.

It took Trent a while to realize he was grinning.

Chapter 23

You're a good person.

Candy replayed Trent's words as she looked down at one of the booths at the back of the bar, a booth where the man in question was curled up asleep. He was too big for the short seat, so his feet were hanging over the end, and his hands were cupped under his cheek, making him seem acutely vulnerable.

That made her insides feel strange, so Candy searched the room for something to chew him out over once he woke up. But the bar was spotless, the sculpture's cog fixed, and the bottles perfectly aligned with their labels facing out. On top of that, the place smelled great, not just of disinfectant but of the incense Candy liked to burn.

Working on a hunch, she walked over and checked the shelves below the bar where it was usually stored. "Sonovabitch," she said under her breath as she took in the neatness before her. Trent had committed acts of organization that would make Kevin cry happy tears.

This wasn't the Trent Green she remembered.

She'd set her alarm to get in a three-hour nap, planning to come down and clean up the mess if Trent had decided to leave. But he hadn't. It was six in the morning and for some reason he was still here. Moreover, he'd cleaned and tidied, fixed her sculpture and put out the trash.

And he'd brought her fresh sheets that smelled like vanilla.

She darted a glance to where Trent was snuffling. Why the hell did a straight man get to have eyelashes that long? She knew she should wake him, but he was snoring in a low and steady way that told her he'd been sleeping just as little as her lately.

There was no way she wanted to talk to him when she was feeling so off-center, so she went back upstairs to get Barney. And if she spent a couple of minutes finding a blanket to cover Trent up with, she told herself it was only because she didn't want him catching pneumonia from the bar's air-conditioning. Not because Trent had called her a nice person.

There was no way Candy's self-esteem had sunk so low that she'd get a boost from something her arch nemesis had said. No way.

When Candy stepped out onto the sidewalk with Barney at her side, she started to relax; no one who could make her life miserable was awake. Being outside helped as well.

She loved Austin. She especially loved it first thing in the morning when night owls like herself passed the baton to the early risers: the bakers, the street-sweepers, the doctors and nurses who worked the night shift at the nearby hospital. She recognized many of them from those times when she couldn't sleep after work and walked the streets with Barney until she'd solved whatever problem was bugging her.

But walking alone wouldn't cut it today. This thing with Trent was too complicated and Candy needed backup.

"Hello!" Sophie answered Candy's call with the perkiness of someone who'd been a morning person since birth. "Is the world ending? Because I don't think you've called me this early since that time your mom overdosed on vitamin pills while trying that crazy cleanse diet."

Candy recalled how panicked her twelve-year-old self

had been on waking up early to find her mom throwing up in the bathroom, surrounded by vitamin C bottles. "I forgot about that. Ugh, she didn't leave the bathroom for two whole days."

"I remember it as being great, because we had a sleepover at my house and you got to see what it was like to live with the absolute *opposite* of your mom. Remember how mine had a meltdown when she found out you didn't bring three pairs of socks for each day?" Sophie's laughter was cut off when there was the murmur of a male voice in the background. "It's Candy," she said.

"Tell your big bad Brit I'll make up for the early call later." Candy tugged at Barney's leash when he veered towards the garbage men doing their rounds. They called out a greeting and got a friendly howl in return.

"If that's what it takes to get you to visit, then feel guilty, *really* guilty," Sophie said cheerfully. "But for now, why don't you come with me to my new front porch and take in the view? It's beautiful this morning. Can you hear those birds? They're happy birds because this is an *amazing* house."

Candy smiled despite her inner turmoil, picturing Sophie on a porch looking out over some quaint street in her little Texas town. Candy loved visiting Hopeville. In the middle of Texas Hill Country's wineries and lavender farms, it was so far apart from Candy's usual world it might as well be another planet, but the people there had always welcomed her. "So you really like it? You're not just putting on some show to make that man of yours happy for swinging his giant bank account around?"

"I love it! I can't wait for you to see it. But we'll talk about that once you cut the crap and tell me what's going on."

"Trent Green"

"Trent Green what?" Sophie's voice sharpened.

"He's still in my bar."

"Why?"

Candy groaned. "Couldn't you just talk at me for ten minutes or something?"

"Nope. I'm too busy working out how quickly I can get to Austin to help get rid of the body."

"Hate to break it to you, but he's still breathing."

"Then you didn't hit him hard enough."

"I didn't hit him at all. That's the problem. Wait a second."

Candy paused in front of Betty Sue's 24-Hour Diner and handed Barney's leash to the man sitting on the pavement by the door. "What'll you have this morning, Elmar?" she asked.

"A stack of pancakes and double the maple syrup." Elmar grinned, giving Barney a pat on his head and getting a doggy kiss on his cheek for his efforts. "Hey, man, you're lookin' good," he said to the dog.

Candy left Elmar and Barney to catch up and pushed open the diner's door. "We're getting breakfast," she said to Sophie.

"I worked that out. Is Elmar feeling better after that thing last month?"

"Yeah. We all talked him into going to the free clinic and they gave him some antibiotics." Candy walked up to the counter and put in an order for three stacks of pancakes with extra maple syrup to go, then took a seat in a booth, closing her eyes. "God, this is so *tiring*."

"Candy Blume, if you don't tell me what the hell is going on, I'm gonna drive over there and shoot *you!*"

"Sorry. I'm calling for some advice. Trent's in my bar because he's being nice, and I don't know what to do about it."

"Nice? How?" If suspicion were a solid thing, Sophie's words contained enough to fill a dumpster.

Candy summarized the situation. "What do you think his deal is? Is this some weird long-game prank that I need to get my head around? Or do you think he's genuinely changed and

I should stop threatening to cut off his private parts? I'm saying that as a woman whose ex-husband had to completely transform into a rapey, drug-addicted asshole before she'd admit that *he'd* changed." Bringing up Beau in a conversation with Sophie left Candy feeling anxious, but she was running on minimal sleep and the words slipped out.

"Want me to call the Austin Police Department about a woman violently beating herself up because of other people's stupidity?" Sophie asked.

"Nope. Just help me get some perspective on how to handle Green."

Sophie made a humming noise. "I don't know. My first response would be to shoot him while he's asleep—"

Candy let out a burst of laughter; as far as she knew, Sophie had never fired a gun in her life. "How many times have you threatened to shoot someone this morning? You're supposed to be the nice one!"

"I am, until someone messes with my best friend—then I'm one hundred percent Old Testament justice. I'm not objective on this issue. In fact, if I'm really honest, just the thought of Trent being within one mile of you makes me want to kill him."

"Yeah, I understand that. And my problem is that I'm *not* feeling that way. He's being nice to me and it's making me feel weird. So help me out."

"I honestly don't know what else to say." Sophie made a frustrated noise. "Why don't I put you on to Ian? Because he's giving me a look that says I'm totally sucking at helping you. He's come out to the porch and since I've had you on speaker, he might have heard some of it. Hope you don't mind."

Candy ran a hand over her head. "Can you hear me, Ian?"

"I can," Ian said in his clipped British baritone.

"Lay it on me, big guy."

"While I understand my charming fiancée's feelings"—

there was a snort from Sophie—"I don't see any harm in taking the man at his word as long as he's proving useful to you. If he wants to be your personal slave to assuage a guilty conscience, then let him. You get a free cleaner and free meals. But the minute he tries to make you feel obliged to forgive him or even be kind to him against your will, use some of those tricks I showed you with that baseball bat to break every single one of his bones."

"Starting with his dick," Sophie cut in.

"You *are* bloodthirsty in the morning," Ian said to his fiancé before speaking to Candy again. "Am I making sense?"

Candy smiled at the sound of Sophie huffing in the background. "You are."

"Great. If you'll excuse me, now that I won't be providing an alibi for my fiancé murdering someone, I'm going back to bed."

"Did that help?" Sophie asked a few seconds later.

"It did . . . I think. Thanks," Candy said as her order came up.

"Do you want me to come to Austin for some moral support? It wouldn't be a problem."

"No, but I promise I'll come see you soon. Somehow," Candy said, paying for her food and walking for the door.

"You'd better. Love you. And keep yourself safe, okay? And I don't just mean physically. Your heart's been through too much lately, and it should be treated with love and respect. Hear me? Self-lovin' all the way, baby."

Candy laughed. "Sounds like my kind of advice. Love you. Bye." She ended the call before giving Elmar his breakfast and collecting Barney.

As she walked back to Hard Candy, she spared a glance at the sky, which was a brilliant blue. The trees lining the street were waving their branches and the smell of the pancakes and the promise of coffee buoyed her spirits. Maybe she really was overthinking this. After all, once she kicked Trent out this morning, there'd be no reason to see him ever again, and then she could get back to dealing with all her usual problems.

Barney nudged the bag holding the pancakes with his nose.

Candy patted him on the top of his head. "Keep dreaming, buddy."

Chapter 24

Trent was having a weird dream where he was standing on the gangplank of a pirate ship with hungry sharks circling below. He could feel their panting breath on his skin, could hear them making whining noises at the thought of crunching him into little pieces.

There was no way he'd be able to get out of this situation without getting chewed up, but maybe if he sacrificed a limb, he could distract them enough to get away. But was an arm or a leg the better offering? He was a pirate, so a hook wouldn't be too weird, but a peg leg would work better because he needed his hands for his job. And there was that order of hazelnuts he had to chase down, otherwise he wouldn't get the truffles done by Friday. *And* he had to work out what the heck to do about Matty . . . and those sharks had really hot breath. Hot breath that smelled like dog breath . . .

Sharks had dog breath. Who knew?

"Wake up, Green, you're talking in your sleep."

Trent's eyes snapped open, and his head jerked back when all he saw was teeth.

"Barney, get away from there, he doesn't want to make friends with you."

Trent sat up abruptly, his head rebounding off something soft, his legs falling off the plank—no, booth—as his brain added everything up: the daylight filtering through the bar's open front door, the scent of incense, and the sound of music filtering in from the laundromat. Last but not least was Candy Blume, standing in front of her coffee machine. She was wearing a red camisole, black jeans and huge hoop earrings that made her resemble a lady pirate straight out of his dream. How could two circles of metal make a woman look so killer sexy? And if he was seeing Candy Blume first thing in the morning, was he even awake?

"Am I still dreaming?"

She stopped doing whatever she was doing, her brows raised. "Do I look like the woman of your dreams?"

"Kinda." Trent rubbed his eyes. "I was having a nightmare actually. About sharks."

"I'll take that as a compliment," she said, turning dials and operating levers until the savory aroma of fresh coffee filled the room.

Trent straightened, fumbling in his pocket for his phone. "What time is it?"

"Settle down, dude. It's seven. You're not late for work."

As if sensing Trent's panic, Barney hiked himself up onto his back legs and placed a paw on Trent's lap, which drew Trent's attention to the fluffy red blanket covering him. "Did you do this?"

"What?"

"Cover me with a blanket."

"Didn't want you dying of hypothermia. Speaking of the cold, you better eat your pancakes before they get cold."

Trent frowned at her. "Pancakes?"

"Wow, you've turned into a parrot in your sleep." Candy set a small espresso cup on the bar before grabbing a larger mug and going back to work at the machine.

He ran a hand over his face, feeling the stubble, then stood up and stretched, catching the blanket before it fell to the floor. "I was dreaming of pirates."

"I don't really have time to listen to your messed-up fantasies."

"Sharks were trying to eat me."

"So you said. Now that sounds like a dream I'd like to see." Candy finished making herself a coffee, then reached into a paper bag to produce two takeout boxes and some plastic forks. She set one box next to the espresso cup before opening the other.

Trent stared at her. "You got me pancakes?"

"My mom taught me that it isn't polite to eat in front of someone without offering them food. Unless it's three a.m. guilt pizza." She took the lid off her pancakes, squeezing a packet of maple syrup over them before attacking the food with the same gusto she'd shown earlier with the pizza. "Plus," she said, speaking between mouthfuls, "I've poisoned your food with something that'll kill you a couple of hours from now, so it will never be linked back to me."

Barney head-butted Trent's thigh. He glanced down to see the dog's adoring expression and wagging tail. "I think your dog is angling for some of mine."

"He can angle all he wants—you're not gonna give him any, on pain of death. He's already had breakfast. Eat up, Green." Candy put down her fork to gulp a mouthful of coffee before attacking her food again.

Trent bridged the distance to the bar with Barney close on his heels. He watched Candy with amazement. "Do you always attack your food like it's going to run away?"

Her mouth curved for a flicker of a second; it was either amusement or a facial tic. Trent couldn't be sure.

"In my experience, that is always a possibility when it comes to my mom's cooking. Bless her heart."

He picked up the espresso, slugging it back and feeling the caffeine switching on his neurons before he started on the pancakes. "That's good coffee. And these smell great. Are they from Betty Sue's?"

She looked momentarily surprised. "Yeah. And you better eat up because I want you out of here as soon as possible. I don't even know why you stayed."

Unfazed, Trent took a bite of his breakfast, feeling his body sighing with happiness. "You didn't leave me a key to lock up. I didn't want to leave the door open. Especially after what happened the other night with Beau."

He glanced up when she didn't say anything. She was looking at him like he was a jack-in-the-box, and she was just waiting for the unwelcome surprise. In the end she gave him a curt nod.

"Thanks."

"You're welcome."

"Hurry up with the eating. I've got work to do, and that poison I put in your food's gonna kick in soon. I don't want your corpse on my hands."

"Gee, that's the nicest thing I think you've ever said to me." Trent gave Candy a grin that only widened when she snorted, collected the last of her pancakes and walked away to do something in the office behind her bar.

Chapter 25

Candy had fully intended to work her butt off once Trent left, but after eating the rest of her breakfast and inspecting the bar again, she realized that everything was in order for her to go back to bed for a while. Besides, maybe more sleep would help her sort out her emotions.

Yawning, she locked up again, leaving the deadbolt on the back door undone and a note for Kevin in case he came in early. Then she wandered upstairs with Barney before falling face first on the bed.

The last image that crossed her mind before sleep overtook her was Trent's smile when she'd brought him the pancakes. She didn't think she'd ever seen anyone that happy about her bringing them food, ever. And for a woman who routinely served people in a bar, that was saying something . . .

She was jerked from a deep, dreamless sleep when Barney started growling, low and continuously. He'd only ever made that noise once, when someone had tried to grab Candy during one of their pre-dawn walks. That growl said there was an imminent threat somewhere nearby.

She bolted upright. "Barney?"

He was standing in front of the door, his hair bristling, his teeth bared.

Candy's ears strained to hear what was setting him off. All she could hear was music from the laundromat and a woman trying to reason with a crying toddler out on the street. "What's wrong, boy?"

He suddenly let loose with a volley of vicious barks and charged at the door.

Someone was in the bar. Someone who wasn't a friend.

Climbing out of bed carefully so as not to make the floorboards creak too much, Candy snatched up her phone and then scanned the apartment for something to use as a weapon. Hard Candy had been broken into twice before, but she hadn't been living above the bar then. She hadn't been alone with only Barney to guard her.

Footfalls creaked on the stairs. Barney let out another series of vicious barks as his claws scraped the door, intent on telling anyone out there that he meant business, but they kept coming. Which meant they weren't scared of a seventy-pound bull terrier who sounded ready for murder. Which meant they were either psycho or had a gun.

Bolting into action, Candy sprinted across the room and grabbed the cleaver still sitting in the draining rack, channeling all the strength in her body into her voice.

"I don't know who the hell you are, but if you even try and come in here, my dog's gonna rip you to shreds and I'm gonna chop you into tiny little bits. So get the fuck out of my place!" she screamed.

"Candy? It's me. I need you to call off Barney and open the door."

The words were like a punch to the sternum. "Marlene?"

Barney stopped barking, looking at Candy with a confused whine.

"Yes. Open the door. I need to talk to you."

Candy's fingers tightened convulsively on the cleaver when

she registered the over-emotional note to her ex-mother-in-law's voice. "Is Beau out there with you?"

"No."

"Are you lying?"

"No, I'm not lying. Open the door." The door rattled as Marlene tried the handle. Luckily, Candy had locked it on autopilot. She mustn't have been that studious checking the lock on the back door . . . no, she was *sure* she'd locked it. The deadbolt might not be engaged but the other lock was. Definitely.

"I need you to go back downstairs. I'll come down in a minute." Candy rested a hand on Barney's head when he trotted over, still whining as if asking her what was going on.

"Okay. But my shift starts in thirty minutes, so you need to come down straight away. We need to have a conversation."

"I'll be down in a minute, Marlene." Candy held her breath, waiting, then exhaled when there was the unmistakeable sound of footsteps going back down the stairs.

She set the cleaver down with a clatter and then ran to the window by her bed, scanning the street for Beau. Then she checked the bathroom window overlooking the small parking lot behind the bar. There was Marlene's car, but no Beau. Finally, she opened the door a crack, listening to the sound of Marlene moving around the bar, trying to hear if there was a second set of footsteps.

Candy crouched down in front of Barney, taking his head in her hands. "I want you to stick to me like glue, boy. If we don't do this, she won't leave us alone." Giving the dog a quick hug, she quickly descended the stairs, immediately seeing the open door leading to the parking lot.

Marlene had turned all the lights on, and something about that felt wrong all the way down to the pit of Candy's stomach. As did the way Marlene was fussing around behind the bar, pouring herself a cup of filter coffee.

Marlene was wearing a pair of faded green coveralls,

which meant she hadn't lied when she said she was headed to a shift at the computer parts factory she'd worked at for over thirty years. Her dyed red hair had grown out at the roots, showing at least an inch of grey, and her ashen face had acquired even more worry lines. She'd lost a lot of weight too. Marlene had always been fine-boned, but now she was skeletal. In a weird flash, Candy saw Beau as some kind of twisted Dorian Grey, his mom the painting that showed all the signs of his sin.

Barney nudged Candy's thigh with his nose and she finally found her voice. "What are you doing here, Marlene, and how did you get in? I locked the door."

Marlene spun around, spilling the cup of coffee in her shaking hands. "You gave me a key! Remember?"

Candy stared at her in disbelief, cursing the debt that had prevented her from changing the locks. "Yeah, I did. Around eight years ago. But I remember you giving that back after the divorce."

Marlene gave a jerky shrug. "I had one copied. Just in case, you know . . . in case I needed to talk to you."

Candy's fingers curled into fists. "Does Beau have one? Don't lie to me."

"No. Beau doesn't have one." Seeing the way Marlene was fighting tears left Candy's body breaking out in a sweat. *Please don't let her start crying.* Candy could do anger any day. She understood that emotion and could give it as good as she got it, but a crying man or woman? She was lost. Always had been. Especially when that crying woman was Marlene.

"I want you to give me the copy you made now." Candy held out a hand.

Marlene shook her head. "Not until you hear me out. I needed to talk to you."

Candy chose her words carefully, even as everything inside her was screaming for her to find a way to escape this situation. "I really don't think we have anything to talk about. We said it all when Beau and I divorced. Both you and I agreed that we'd work out how to pick up the pieces and move on. I'm doing that. I wish you would too—"

Marlene set her coffee down abruptly, and the familiar tremor from her anti-anxiety medication caused the liquid to slosh over the sides. "Beau didn't go to that meeting last night. I'm blaming you."

Candy swallowed, the sound far too loud for her liking. She moistened her lips. "Yeah. Well, he's a grown man, Marlene, and if he's going to veer off the road to recovery just because one of his victims isn't going to bend over backwards for him, he isn't going to get better anytime soon."

"You married him! 'Til death do us part, Candy. You're still alive and he needs your help! I can't help him anymore. I have no money, I have—I have nothing left. That leaves you. You need to step up and suck it up and *do this*. Because I c-can't." Marlene's voice wobbled as she stared at Candy with a horrible intensity that made Candy's insides clench up into a tiny ball.

"Marlene, I admire you for what you've taken on, but I don't have a part to play in what happens next. He bled me dry years ago. We're divorced. I've put a restraining order on him for assault, which means that I can't go to his meetings without messing with it."

"You *abandoned* him. He was sick and you abandoned him in his time of need. Even worse, you ignored how sick he'd been for *years*. Yours vows were 'in sickness and in health' and you failed him."

"That's not how this works." Candy felt a lump form in her throat.

"It's precisely how it works." Marlene swept her arms through the air, knocking the mug over, not seeming to notice the coffee pooling on the bar and dripping to the floor. "Do the math, Candy. My boy is healthy and fine when he leaves my house at eighteen to marry you, and now he's an addict.

That didn't happen on my watch. It happened on *yours.*" Tears started to roll down Marlene's face, running along the worn grooves in her cheeks. "You were like a daughter to me and then you left us. I loaned you the down payment on this bar and gave you my house to live in for two years when you first got married . . . I was always here for you, but when I need you, you're not there for me. Beau needs you. *We* need you, but you've abandoned us. It's selfish and I expect b-better of you."

Candy dug her nails into her palms, doing everything she could to not physically recoil. Was she responsible for Beau's addiction? Was it something she'd done? He'd gotten hooked on painkillers after getting injured while working on an offshore oil rig, and had moved on to heroin. But if she hadn't been so busy working to pay for his ongoing medical bills, could she have prevented the transition from recovering patient to junkie? Had she given too little? Had she needed too much?

"I get that you're upset," she said when her throat loosened. "I'm grateful for what you've done for me in the past, especially helping out when I needed money to set up the bar. But I paid that loan back years ago, with interest, and—"

"We're *family*. You can't take that back," Marlene's reedy voice cut in. "And right now, you need to support your *family*. Beau's promised me he'll go to the next meeting if you're there. It's Tuesday next week. I need you to go. I *need* this. I've never really asked a favor of you, God help me, but I'm doing it now. I'm begging you, Candy. Come to the meeting. Help Beau get better. Help *my son* get better."

Candy was already shaking her head. "I can't."

"You will. You have to. Because I know you're a good person and this is what good people do when they're needed," Marlene said, before focusing on the overturned coffee mug as if only seeing it for the first time. "Oh, look at that. I'm sorry. I'll just get a cloth and—"

"Leave it. I'll take care of it. Why don't you go? You'll be late for your shift," Candy said in a husky voice.

"I—okay, that's what I'll do." Marlene nodded as if to herself. "I didn't come here wanting to make a scene. But the past two years have been so hard and the money . . . There's nothing left but debt and—"

"I get it," Candy said softly. "He's your son."

Marlene wiped the back of her hand over her eyes. "He is, and I don't know what else to do. He's taking my things and selling them for drugs, and if things get any worse, I'll lose the house to pay off the credit cards he keeps getting. I need you, Candy. I know what he did to you was bad. But I need your help. Help *me*. Please?"

Candy barely had time to react as Marlene hurried across the room to wrap her arms around Candy, holding on to her like a drowning woman. Candy tried to pull back as gently as she could, but Marlene wouldn't let her. She just stood there frozen as Marlene's tears soaked the side of her neck.

"I'll . . . I'll see you next Tuesday. Bye," Marlene said, pulling back and hugging herself while not meeting Candy's eyes. Then she left Candy standing in the middle of her bar, feeling like she'd need to shower for a week to slough this horrible, tar-like guilt from her skin.

She only remembered an hour later that Marlene hadn't given her the key.

Chapter 26

She'd covered him with a blanket and brought him pancakes.

Trent was still thinking about that as Rakeem and his other patissier, Janine, arrived at work, laughing over something Luis had said out in the parking lot. He thought about it even more while he painstakingly decorated the three red velvet cakes Rakeem had made the afternoon before, first coating each tier in creamy white chocolate before adding in a spray of individually painted chocolate roses, violets and carnations. It wasn't Trent's usual style of decoration, but his job was to please, and after carefully studying the design he and the bride had agreed on, he was proud of what he'd done. Luckily this particular job hadn't required him to the use the 3D chocolate printer, because the replacement parts wouldn't be arriving until tomorrow morning.

That thought led him to thinking about what he was going to do about Matty, who was still at home sleeping off a hangover for the ages. When Matty was feeling better, they'd talk. A lot. But for now . . .

She'd covered him with a blanket and had brought him pancakes.

"Trent? You okay, man?"

He blinked, snapping out of his thoughts at Rakeem's

voice. "What's up?" he asked, stepping out of Janine's way as she walked past him to the storage cupboard. As always Janine was wearing over-ear headphones that were vibrating from the volume of her music. She had medical tape on her shoulder, which probably meant she'd added to her already extensive collection of tattoos.

"You were talkin' to yourself," Rakeem said, shaking his head in amusement.

"Oh yeah?"

"Yeah. And Taryn just messaged to say there's a lady out front who wants to talk to you."

Trent frowned. "Why didn't Taryn come get me?"

"Because apparently this lady is talkin' so fast, all she could do was send me a message. I just put my ear to the door and, whew, that woman sure can talk."

Trent felt a faint twinge of unease. "Was the lady doing the talking a blonde? About my height?"

"Yeah. You know her?"

"I might." Trent looked at the cake before him. "I'll deal with her. I need this boxed up so I can drop it around to the venue before six. You able to do that for me?"

"Sure thing." Rakeem gave the cake an affectionate smile. "It looks like something my grandma would love. From this angle, it kind of reminds me of a church—"

"Hat?" Trent finished and they both laughed. "Yeah, I was thinking the same thing. And if I'm honest, the one my nona has sitting on a shelf in her closet was a part of the inspiration. I've never seen her wear it though."

"My grandma has one she wears every Sunday. Mind if I take a picture for her before I box it?" Rakeem asked. Trent was secretive about his clients' cakes being made public before their big day.

"As long as it goes to your grandma and nowhere else," Trent said as his phone buzzed. "If I'm not back in thirty minutes, send in a search party."

He forced a grin, then pushed the heavy storefront door open to be greeted with a wall of Sophie Grey's chatter, which abruptly halted the minute she spotted him over Taryn's shoulder.

"Trent Green, I want to speak with you. Now." Sophie was wearing a bright green shirt, white shorts and a pair of bright blue cowboy boots, but from her tone and stance, she could have been a gunslinger getting ready for a lead-filled high-noon discussion.

"Hi, Sophie. Taryn, you're due to take a break, aren't you?" Trent asked, noting that his most unflappable employee's composure was crumbling. Although there wasn't a hair out of place when it came to Taryn's impeccable Grace Kelly-meets-Halle Berry look, there was a wildness in her eyes that said she'd been through some shit in the past few minutes.

"Yes. I—Yes. Thanks. Nice talking to you, ma'am. I'll leave you in Trent's hands." It said a lot that Taryn didn't even stop to collect her purse from behind the truffle counter before she slipped through the door to the kitchen. There was a quick burst of Rakeem's laughter before the door clicked shut and Sophie and Trent were alone.

Trent looked at Sophie warily, knowing the words were coming the minute she got over glaring at him. He just had to work out how to handle the situation and—

"Give me one reason why I shouldn't shoot you right now, Trent Green," Sophie said, putting her hands on her hips. "One reason. And before you get all up in arms saying that I'm threatening you, remember I haven't said I'll *actually* shoot you. I just want a reason *why* I shouldn't."

"It would help if I knew why I need to give you a reason not to shoot me." Trent kept his body language open. If dealing with four younger siblings had taught him anything, it was to try and stay as calm as possible in the face of conflict.

"You're asking me why I'm here?!" Sophie threw her hands up in the air. "The last time I saw you, my best friend told you never to set foot in her bar again. And then she calls me this morning saying that you've been back to her bar at least twice since then. *Twice.* And you've messed with her head enough that now she's wondering whether or not she should trust you. You!"

Trent felt a jolt of hope go through his system. "Let me see if I heard you correctly . . . Candy called you asking whether or not she should trust me?"

Sophie began pacing the floor, going from the truffle counter to the cases of ready-made cakes and back again. "I've got no goddamn idea what you're trying to do, Trent Green, but let me tell you this: if you mess with my friend, even a tiny bit, if you make her doubt herself, if you make her frown once, and Lord help me, if you make her cry, no one's gonna find your body once I'm done with you. Hear me?" She rounded on him, angry red flags flying on her cheeks. "She's come so far after these past two years for you to just waltz on in and ruin it all."

"With Beau being a junkie and the divorce?" Trent asked.

Sophie froze, her eyes narrowing. "What do you know about that?"

"He stopped by the bar one night while I was there and —" Trent saw Sophie's shock and immediately realized he'd put his foot in it. He held his hands up in the air. "Now, I don't want to cause any problems with you and Candy. So before you go off half-cocked—"

"He came to her bar?" Sophie demanded. "What happened? Did he hurt her again, because—"

"Hurt her? He's hurt her before?" Trent felt every muscle in his body coil; it was one thing to suspect, it was another to get verbal confirmation.

"She placed a restraining order on him. He shouldn't have been there. What did he say, Trent? No bullshit. What did he do and say?"

"Something about wanting her to come to a meeting . . . I

can't remember exactly, but he seemed friendly. It was more Candy's reaction that got me thinking something was wrong. One minute she was kicking me out, and the next minute she was saying she wanted me around and telling Beau that she couldn't go to his thing because of Matty's party."

"What thing? What meeting? Did he say anything else?" Sophie demanded.

Trent was about to say something, then paused. "You know what? I'm not comfortable telling you this stuff if Candy hasn't mentioned it already. She might not want it public knowledge." He caught the flash of hurt that crossed Sophie's features. "I didn't mean that the way it came out. I'm trying not to cause trouble. You probably don't believe it, but I've changed a lot since you knew me. So hear me out before you start breathing fire again." Sophie snorted derisively, but Trent kept talking. "I'm sorry for what I did in high school. I'll feel bad about it as long as I live. Candy tore a piece out of me the other night, making it clear how badly I hurt her, and I'm just trying to find a way to make things better."

"You feel guilty," Sophie said shortly.

"I do."

"Yeah?" Sophie chewed on her lip. "So how guilty do you feel?"

"A lot." Trent ran a hand through his hair. "But I'm trying to make it right and—"

"Why have you changed? Because you were bad almost every day on a low-hum awful level, but what you did at graduation was unforgivable. Candy's dad had flown over from Hong Kong to be there. She's only gotten to see him in person three times in her life, and you and your idiot friends ruined one of them."

Trent studied his hands. "Yeah. I did. And I'm going to regret my behavior 'til the day I die. You were right to get up and say what you said that day. You tore up the whole school from that podium and we deserved it. Especially that bit you said about me realizing one day how much of a mistake I was making by trying to look cool instead of being kind."

He looked up when Sophie didn't respond. Instead she was watching the people walking past the store windows, her expression pensive. For Sophie Grey to be this quiet was not a good sign.

"Want a coffee or something?" Trent asked to ease the tension.

"Nope." Sophie suddenly reanimated. "You decorate cakes for a living?"

Trent nodded slowly. "Among other things, yeah."

"I thought you would have ended up a lawyer or a doctor or something."

"An architect actually. But then my parents died straight after graduation and I had to raise my family. Dolce Design was my nona's business."

"Yeah?" Sophie frowned.

"Hey, I know you don't owe it to me, but can you tell me what's goin' on in your head, because it feels like we've changed gears somehow."

Sophie shook her head. "I don't know . . . Just stand warned, Trent. I'm not gonna kick up a fuss because it sounds like you being around is actually helping, but if you hurt her—"

"Yeah, I get it, you'll shoot me."

She jabbed a finger at him. "With both barrels. And if you tell her about this conversation before I do, I'll—"

Trent gave her a wry smile. "Shoot me again?"

"Right on, cowboy." With that Sophie turned on her heel and strutted out the door to a shiny black Mustang parked on the curb.

Chapter 27

Hey, are you okay? Just thinking of what we talked about this morning and want to double check you're doing fine. I can come visit if you need. I'm here for you. Love you forever xxxSophie

Candy reread Sophie's message, ignoring the dull roar of Hard Candy in full swing as she debated what to do. Sophie had sent the message through at five p.m. It was now midnight and Candy had yet to work out what to say.

Inside she felt frozen, like there was this weird cling-film seal over the emotions she'd been holding in since Marlene's morning visit. She just knew that if she put even a little pressure on that seal, it would tear and she'd be swamped. She couldn't handle that right now. So instead of replying to Sophie, she shoved her phone back in her pocket and focused on her job. Sophie would understand. This wasn't something Candy wanted polluting her friend's happiness. She'd deal with it. Later.

"Hey, Candy, we need you to explain to Kevin that two women kissing isn't gonna kill him. The way he's acting, anyone would think he's never had sex before."

Candy blinked at Ashley and Lydia, two regulars who were managing to take up the same barstool. Since it was the night formerly known as Goth Night, they were both dressed in Victoriana mourning splendour, Ashley's silver braids contrasting brilliantly with Lydia's hot-pink crimped do. "What's this about?"

Ashley sipped her chardonnay. "The virgin at the end of the bar was taking offense at us kissing *again*. Y'all gonna tell him off?"

Welcoming this moment of Thursday-night normalcy, Candy looked at Kevin, who, as usual, was hunched over his laptop. "Are you raining on someone's parade *again*?"

"No." Kevin glowered at her before turning his ire on the two women. "I was merely pointing out that such a public display of affection can make others feel awkward."

"You mean someone who is a thirty-year-old prancing ponyboy *virgin*," Ashley shot back.

"That's twenty-seven and I'm not a virgin. Technically. And I resent that name. It wasn't my idea. It was hers." Kevin gave Candy an aggrieved look and then went back to typing.

The two women glanced at each other and then at Candy before breaking into peals of laughter.

"Okay, you two, cut it out. Back booth is free. Smooch all you like there." Candy gave them her best "don't mess with me" glare.

Lydia waggled her empty wineglass in the air. "Can we get another two drinks first?"

"I would like it on the record for the two hundred and forty-seventh time that I've been unfairly maligned and that your juvenile joke should have expired by now," Kevin said as Candy poured another two chardonnays.

Candy gave him a wide-eyed look. "You mean that *wasn't* you I heard complaining about calling it 'Goth Night,' leading to the huge argument that resulted in me having to change the name to 'Prancing Rainbow Pony Appreciation Night'?" She turned to Lydia and Ashley. "Do you think the name's a problem?"

Ashley shrugged. "I don't care what it's called as long as we still get our night." With that, she and Lydia collected their drinks and wove through the crowd of people swaying to an L.A Witch song Candy had recently added to her Thursday-night playlist. With the exception of Kevin and herself, almost everyone was in black and wearing their preferred Goth style, whether that meant Victorian mourning clothes, eighties puffy pirate shirts, nineties industrial leathers, or over-the-face emo bangs.

Candy took care of an order of grasshoppers for a bunch of industrial goths after reminding them of her spiked clothing rule and then wandered to Kevin's end of the bar, embracing the distraction of their usual Thursday-night bickering.

"Anyone ever tell you that you reap what you sow? You needling people and getting all pedantic is *precisely* why the name got changed in the first place."

Kevin glowered at her. "All I said was that there was barely anything in common between eighties romantic goths, nineties industrial goths and the whole Gothic Lolita thing."

Candy pursed her lips. "No, you didn't just say that."

"Okay, if you're going to be pedantic, I said that to reify everything as 'Goth'"—Kevin raised his fingers in scare quotes —"is reductivist and exactly the sort of conforming idiocy that these so-called goths rebel against. It's not my fault the denizens of this bar reduced the entire discussion to a shouting match. In which I didn't join, may I add."

Candy tapped the side of her head. "Did you make up all those big words so you could feel like a better person than me?"

Kevin sniffed. "Most of my terms are from French post-structuralist philosophy, so they might not be in the traditional dictionary, but my point that the term 'Goth' is too general still stands."

"Want me to change the name to 'Kevin's *Spectacular* Prancing Rainbow Pony Appreciation Night'?"

"It's already humiliating enough to be here on Thursdays as it is. This night is ridiculous. Everyone here is pretending they're non-conformist individuals when they all want to be called exactly the same thing! It's incorrect," he said as he went back to typing.

Candy raised a brow. "Is that yet *more* rain I hear on this parade, Professor Pedant? Because I'm gonna need to charge you for an umbrella if this keeps up."

"No rain. Just the truth." Kevin glanced up, his surly expression becoming wooden as he looked over Candy's shoulder. "That guy's back."

Candy's first thought was that it was Beau and she spun around, hand going to her phone, ready to call the cops, but instead she saw Trent Green weaving his way through the bar, his white T-shirt standing out against the sea of black, crimson and the odd smattering of Lolita pink.

"You want me to make him go away?" Kevin asked using exactly the same tone he had the last times he'd asked, which was a worry, because it meant this was turning into something of a tradition.

Candy squashed down the strange warm feeling inspired by Trent's almost-shy smile. She definitely had some form of Stockholm syndrome; a couple of nights of Trent cleaning her floors and she suddenly enjoyed the sight of him. There had to be some kind of medication for this. It probably involved being put into an induced coma.

She cocked her hip as Trent sidled up to the bar and took a seat. He waved at two queens from Drag Poetry Night who were Gothing it up this evening.

"What do you want, Green?" she asked, proud of her take-no-prisoners tone.

"A scotch on the rocks. Hey, man." He waved at Kevin.

Trent shouldn't have looked so good given he must've had less than two hours sleep in the past twenty-four hours. Fantasia had been right: a straight man shouldn't be this pretty.

"I also wanted to give this to you," Trent said, pushing a paper bag towards her.

"What's that?" Candy looked at it suspiciously. "If it's another merit award, I might not be responsible for my actions."

"Is she always this violent?" Trent asked Kevin.

"I've never actually seen physical violence, but I have been threatened with it on many an occasion."

"There's a first time for everything," Candy growled, suddenly enjoying herself. This was easy. She was angry at Trent and he was feeling guilty. Of all the things in her life, it was unbelievable that this was the most straightforward, but it was. "What's in the bag, Green?"

"Penne *arrabiata*. I seem to have made too much, and since the name of the dish translates to 'angry pasta,' it made me think of you."

"You saying I've got a bad attitude? What do you think I am? Some charity case that needs feeding all the time?"

Trent's mouth quirked. "Nope. But you should really do something about your tendency to say such awful things about yourself."

"And do what instead? Say bad things about you?" Candy shot back.

"I'll take a few on the chin. I figure I have 'em coming." Trent gave her a casual shrug.

"If you're not going to eat that, I will," Kevin said.

"I brought enough for two people," Trent replied.

"This kind of sucking up will get you nowhere, Green, and you're not helping Kevin." Candy gave them both a look of feigned disgust as she turned back to taking orders, momentarily grateful her regulars were well trained enough to be unfazed by slow service.

As she worked, she was aware of Trent's presence, her whole body feeling like it was wired up to a power socket. Finally, after fielding the usual complaint from Raven, Kevin's arch nemesis, about the playlist not including enough esoteric German songs about depression, Candy nudged the cash register shut with her hip and wandered down to where Trent and Kevin were now sitting side by side. Candy's stomach rumbled at the smell of food coming from the paper bag. Good food. Which reminded her that she hadn't eaten anything since breakfast other than the comfort donut she'd bought when she'd walked Barney after Marlene's visit.

Damn him!

She used Trent's distraction to really study him. Yeah, he was pretty, but there were black circles under his eyes and lines of exhaustion on his forehead. They should have made him look like crap, but they just added a Marlon Brando moodiness that, in her Stockholm state, her lady hormones were liking. Perhaps this was because she was a healthy thirty-year-old woman whose previous romantic history included marrying a man who'd proven everything she'd believed good about her life was a lie, so it was only natural that she now felt attracted to her high school tormentor. A therapist would probably link it back to Candy's dad (the sane parent) being absent, leaving her to be raised by her mom (the adult teenager). But Candy didn't have the money to pay for therapy and she didn't have the patience to spend any more time dwelling on how she'd gotten this messed up.

"Didn't you get the memo about the dress code, Green?" she asked, interrupting a question Trent was asking Kevin about the rules posted on the Tardis.

Trent looked down at his T-shirt and then around at the people in the bar. "What's the problem?"

"When you read the sign, didn't you see the notice about each night of the week at the bottom?"

"You mean the one saying Thursday night was Pony Night or something?"

Trent scratched his jaw. There was a faint shadow of stubble there and Candy reminded herself that while she found it sexy, it was also prickly. It was bad stubble. Bad, bad stubble, and she shouldn't be thinking about how it would feel to touch.

"I thought that was kinda weird, even for here, but then I saw a bunch of goths, so I figured it's some kind of Goth Night."

"It's never Goth Night." Candy glowered, before snatching up the paper bag and peering at the large Tupperware container inside. She pulled it out and took off the lid. The rich aroma of good Italian food wafted under her nose. Her mouth watered. "This looks homemade."

"Yeah, like I said, there was some left over. Why is it never Goth Night? It looks like a Goth Night to me." Trent scanned the crowd. "And I don't see any prancing ponies."

"Kevin, if you answer that question, you're not getting any of this."

Surprisingly, Kevin was silent, so Candy retrieved two forks, handing Kevin one of them. He took it while still typing with one hand. It was obvious something had inspired him.

"Do you want a fork too?" she asked, raising her brows at Trent.

"Nope. I've already eaten. Help yourself."

Candy speared some pasta and took a bite. It was like her taste buds had thrown a party and invited their friends along. She covered up her groan of happiness with a frown when she realized that Trent was watching her every move. "If you've put poison in this, you've covered it up with flavor." For some reason she felt a small spark of something akin to pleasure when she saw Trent's shoulders relax.

Kevin speared some pasta and managed to get it to his mouth without looking away from his screen. "It's good."

"For a writer, you suck at describing things." Candy took another bite and then went to serve a customer. "Why are you here?" she asked Trent when she came back.

He shrugged. "I figure dealing with how much you dislike me is easier than dealing with my problems at home."

Candy tilted her head. "Is your brother okay?"

Trent rolled his head from side to side, obviously attempting to relieve a whole lot of tension. "If being okay is not leaving your room for an entire day."

Candy speared another forkful of pasta. "He'll have to come out eventually."

He sucked air through his teeth. "You'd think that, but I suspect my nona's slipping him food, so there's a chance he could be in there for a week."

"Has he got an ensuite bathroom?"

Trent nodded, his exasperation clear. "Yeah. He's got my mom and dad's old room, so he's the only one who doesn't have to share the main one downstairs."

"Nice deal," Candy said, popping the pasta in her mouth. "So now that you've gotten rid of all your extra food, what're you still doing here taking up valuable real estate in my bar?"

"Chilling. Maybe hoping to soak up some inspiration for a wedding cake design."

"You're doing a Gothic wedding?" Candy asked.

"Might be."

"Every Gothic wedding I've ever been to involved some-one's mom making the cake." Candy almost added "including mine" but stopped herself, changing the topic. "You gonna eat any more of this, Kevin?"

Kevin looked up from his screen, a forkful of pasta halfway to his mouth. "I might." He looked at Candy. "Although I have already eaten this evening so—"

"So the rest is mine." Candy pulled the container towards her and shoveled in three rapid-fire mouthfuls. "I've got a job to do, Green, so I hope you're getting all the inspiration you need."

With that totally crap exit line, she walked all of two feet away to the beer taps to glower at a bunch of people who'd broken training to not-so-quietly complain about the lack of service. So much for her earlier thoughts about her regulars being sweethearts.

If she kept watch on Trent sitting at the end of the bar, sometimes chatting to Kevin, sometimes chatting to the friends he'd made at Drag Poetry Night, she told herself that "keep your friends close, and your enemies closer" was a cliché for a reason.

Chapter 28

"Are you undead? Because some humans have to sleep."

Trent glanced up from going through his e-mails on his phone to see Candy standing before him. The bar was now empty—Kevin having said goodbye after thanking him for the food—and he and Candy were alone. Trent had figured that as long as he looked busy, she might not kick him out.

"I got a couple of hours before coming here tonight." He'd known when he set out to make dinner for Candy that this moment was the true test of its impact.

"And?" she asked, while doing something complex and loud with the coffee machine. A Grace Jones number was playing, and it struck Trent that this was a perfect moment. Two kick-ass women were making noise.

"And I guess I'm not tired." He looked around the bar. "Hey, there're some stuff still on those tables. Want me to clean 'em for you before I head out?"

Candy paused, her wiry shoulders tensing. "What's the catch?"

"Guess I need some exercise." Trent started tidying up.

"Yeah?"

He could hear the internal fight in that one word and held

his breath as he waited for her to call him on his lie.

"I guess you probably eat a lot of the merchandise if you make chocolate all day," she said finally before going back to fiddling with the machine.

"Not as much as you think. About as much as you drink booze." While Candy was never far away from a glass of Coke, Trent hadn't seen her drink alcohol once.

"I drink. Just not at work." Candy huffed out a sigh, stepping back from the coffee machine before starting to stack the jugs and glasses Trent had lined up on the bar in the dishwasher.

"And you're always at work?" Trent asked.

She didn't look up from what she was doing. "Lately? Yeah."

"You don't have anyone working temp?"

"Can't afford it. And that momentary slip of honesty isn't a cue for you to give me any kind of advice," she said with a fierceness Trent was beginning to recognize as bluster.

"Nothing wrong in being frugal." Trent looked up at the ceiling when he heard a muffled bark. "That Barney?"

Candy's head jerked up. "How do you remember my dog's name?"

"You've mentioned it a couple of times. Plus, it's hard not to know his name when we've shared a booth. He even offered to share his feather boa with me."

Her mouth quirked. "He's such a slut."

"I wasn't going to say anything, because I'm totally slut-positive—"

"Being one yourself?"

"Having the time would be nice," Trent said and then pressed his lips together. "And now it's my turn to have a momentary slip of honesty. Don't use it against me, Blume."

He waited for Candy to say something cutting, but instead she just looked at him strangely until the moment was broken by another bark from upstairs.

"He need walking?" Trent asked.

She nodded. "Yup. He wouldn't come down at eight because he was too cozy on my bed, so he's probably desperate."

"Want me to take him out? Save you the time?" Trent asked. While he had no right to comment, he didn't like the idea of her walking around Downtown Austin after midnight when Beau Lineman was somewhere out there with unfinished business. And that wasn't even taking into account all the other creeps.

He saw the relief on her face before she covered it up. "Why? Don't tell me you stuck around tonight just so you could get time with my dog."

"Might have."

"You *are* a slut."

Trent laughed. "If you bring him down, I'll take him out for a couple of minutes."

Candy nodded, and for some reason he felt like he'd climbed a mountain. "Yeah, alright. But bring him back in one piece and don't let him con anyone from next door into feeding him leftover étoufée. He especially loves anything with a roux in it."

"He's a Cajun dog?" Trent asked.

"He'd like to think he is. But mainly he's just the biggest food scab in Austin," Candy said as she reached the door at the back of the bar before stopping. "There's a coffee next to the machine if you want it. I'll be down with Barney in a minute."

"You made me coffee?" Trent spotted the newly made cappuccino sitting on the bar. There were chocolate sprinkles on top. "Oh, hey, thanks—"

His words were cut off by the sound of the door slamming shut, so there was no one to see him walking over to pick up the coffee, looking at the sprinkles with a bemused smile.

195

Chapter 29

"Did you get the recipe for chicken rice I emailed you? It's easy to make, so I don't want to hear any excuses about you being too busy to cook for yourself. You're always too busy. Your daddy's just as bad. So busy all the time."

Candy leaned back on her usual bench at the dog park, smiling at the screen of her phone as her Grandma Tang went through the usual litany of worries and complaints, all the while bustling around the kitchen of Candy's dad's small Hong Kong apartment. It was nine in the morning in Austin and ten at night in Hong Kong. In the background, Candy could hear her dad telling her grandfather to make sure the door to the balcony was kept closed for the air-conditioning.

"Yeah, but busy is good, right?" she said to her grandma.

"It is, as long as he eats. And as long as *you* eat." Grandma Tang raised her son's phone close to her face and gave Candy a stern frown. "What about that loser ex-husband of yours? He worrying you still?"

Candy forced a smile. "A bit. But he's out of the picture now."

That earned her another Grandma Tang Stare. "And your crazy mummy? What's she doing? Is she still fat?" Since she was speaking in Cantonese, the only word in English was the word "mummy," a holdover from their habit of half-English, half-Cantonese conversation while Candy learned the language.

Candy looked affectionately at her grandma's apple-round features and newly done white perm. "You know I don't like you talking about Mom like that."

Grandma Tang and Candy's mom had never met in person, but that didn't mean they didn't routinely judge the hell out of each other. Although Grandma Tang was more direct about it, where Candy's mom usually hid her judgment by insisting Grandma Tang had great Chinese wisdom inside her somewhere, it just hadn't been found yet.

Grandma Tang snorted. "I call it how I see it. She still doing stupid things?"

"Last I checked, she was working on bringing all the women in her street together socially," Candy said diplomatically.

Her grandma seemed stymied for a moment. "Well, that's okay. At least she's useful for something. She behind your haircut? You look like some kind of gangster woman."

Candy grinned, not feeling upset in the slightest, especially since she knew her grandma was a bona fide ass-kicker who didn't take crap from no man, including Candy's grandpa. "You trying to compliment me? Because Johnny told me you were pretty badass when he was little."

Since Candy and her father had been forced to communicate long-distance Candy's whole life, they'd formed a uniquely strong friendship. Candy had always called her dad 'Johnny'—the English name he's always used when he was younger and playing in punk bands—while he'd nicknamed her 'Patti.' According to family lore, he'd wanted to name her after the singer Patti Smith before Pam had overridden it.

That just earned her a grunt. "I don't talk about that. It

was your grandfather's bad influence. You want to talk to your daddy?"

"Yeah. Please. Love you."

"I'll pass you to him now." Her grandmother handed the phone over.

"Love the new hair, Patti. You okay?"

Candy felt herself relaxing at the sight of her dad's handsome face, complete with multiple piercings in his brows, nose and ears. Since it was nighttime in Hong Kong, and it was his day off from running his bar, he was shirtless, showing off a torso and two sleeves of arm tattoos that were a mixture of beloved punk band logos and beautifully rendered images of animals, fish and people. Over his heart was a stick figure taken from a picture Candy had drawn for his birthday when she was five.

"Thanks. I like it. And I've been better. You got some time to talk?" she asked.

He raised his brows as he walked out of the kitchen and past a series of electric guitars mounted on the wall. As he ducked past Candy's grandfather, who was now snoozing in front of the TV, he asked, "You want advice from the great sage?"

"Who else?" Candy grinned.

"Because my advice is expensive."

Candy laughed. "Is that what you tell all those drunk businessmen who come to your bar?"

"Sometimes, if I know they've got the cash to waste," her dad said as he opened the sliding door that led to a small balcony. It was his only truly private space ever since he'd moved Candy's grandparents in thirteen years ago.

He was an only son, which meant that his parents were his responsibility. He'd never complained, but Candy knew that things couldn't be easy, and on a purely selfish level, she wished he had more time and money at his disposal. They'd only ever been together in person three times in her life; the first when she'd been a baby, the second on her tenth birthday, and the third at her disastrous high school graduation.

"Okay, we can talk now," Johnny said as he closed the sliding door, taking a seat on a plastic chair and putting his feet up on the balcony ledge. His bad-boy image was somehow enhanced by the profusion of lush tropical plants and orchids that Candy's grandfather lovingly cared for. "What's up?"

"A lot."

He gave the heavens a long-suffering look. "Your mom trying to convince the girl scouts to sell pot cookies again?"

"Worse. She's started a sex ring."

Her dad's dark brown eyes were alight with laughter. "Oh? Sounds normal to me for Pam."

"Doesn't it just?" Candy reached out with her spare hand to pat Barney on the head before he trotted off again to greet a friendly Jack Russel terrier. "Yeah, so anyway, I've got a bit of a problem. It's with a guy, and it's complicated."

Suddenly Johnny was all business, the congeniality evaporating to reveal a hard-assed former punk rocker who routinely dealt with drunk businessmen swinging their stock portfolios around every night. "Beau giving you problems again?"

"Some, but I don't want to talk about that, so don't ask. It's about another guy."

His scowl clearly said he didn't like the subject change. "Yeah? Who?"

"Remember that guy from my graduation? The one who made fun of me?"

His scowl intensified. "Yeah. I do. He bothering you?"

Candy shook her head. "No, the opposite actually. He's helping out. I think he feels bad."

She shared what had been going on with Trent, who'd come to her bar three nights in a row now with mouth-watering homemade Italian dishes, then stayed to help clean up and walk Barney before heading home—and only after making sure she'd locked the doors. He'd even been a stand-in date for Geek Speed-Dating Night, pairing up with at least seven different people over two hours and even managing to survive ten minutes with Hard Candy's terminal tough date, Glenda, who always brought along her pet tarantula for good luck. Candy's dad listened, nodding every now and then as the sounds of sirens and honking car horns drifted up from the streets below his apartment.

Finally, Candy finished talking. "Am I nuts in letting him come around? I mean, if you were in my shoes, what would you do? You weren't that popular in high school, right?"

Her dad gave her a wry smile. "No. Everyone here was so boring and all I wanted to do was join a band and play music. They all thought I was stupid and weird."

Candy nodded, loving that he could relate so well to this. "So, okay, imagine there was a mean girl who made your life at school hell. You ever have any of those?"

Her dad ran a hand over the tattoos on his chest, the edges of his mouth tensing. "Yeah. A couple."

"Okay, so imagine one of those girls turned up to your bar wanting to apologize for being a bitch. On top of that, she's bringing you food, helping you clean up, and doesn't seem to want anything in return. Would you still tell her to go to hell because of what she did when you were in school?"

Her dad tugged at one of the rings in his left ear. "That's a tough question."

"Yeah. Which is why I'm talking to you about it."

"Is this woman attractive?"

Candy snorted. "Is that really important?"

He gave her a shrug. "Might be."

"Okay, yeah, let's say she is. And?"

"She rich? Her business doing well?"

Candy rolled her eyes. "Could you sound like a bigger gold-digger?"

Her dad let out a burst of laughter. "Yeah. Want me to try?"

"Answer the question!"

He rocked back on his chair. "Yeah, I'd keep her around, because I think it'd be nice to have some hot girl from high school sucking up to me. But maybe it's different for guys. To have some rich girl who was too cool for me in school begging to be with me now . . ." His eyes took on a far-away look. "Yeah, that sounds pretty cool."

"Yeah. I guess."

"So I'd keep her around. Let her clean my bar, make me some nice food . . . maybe I'd sleep with her too."

"Eeesh."

"Well, I'm a bad boy now. I've got a reputation. Besides, it'd be me in control. Kind of a fantasy, you know?" Johnny momentarily looked pensive, but the effect was ruined by the way his eyes were creasing with laughter. "Hey, thinking about it, do you know any of those women who made fun of me in school? I could sure do with some help in the bar and it gets lonely some nights after work." He let out another booming laugh when Candy told him what he could do with his bar. "Okay, okay, okay! I'll be serious. You like him?"

"He's not repugnant."

"Then keep him around. Make him work for free. Free labor is always good, in more ways than one." Her dad waggled his brows and laughed again when Candy pulled the finger. "You're such a bad daughter, Patti. Disrespecting me like this!"

"You're such a crappy dad, Johnny. Giving me such bad advice." She blew him a kiss. "Anyway, everything going well at your place?" she asked. Her dad's bar was in Kowloon, one of Hong Kong's busiest areas. And much like her, he rarely got a day off, which was why it was so unusual for her to be able to talk to him at home like this. Usually they snatched quick moments when either Candy or he were at work.

He shrugged. "It's okay. One day it'll burn down and I'll get the insurance. What about yours?"

Candy laughed at the familiar response, knowing full well how much her dad loved his place. Same as she loved hers. "Same here. One day I'll set a match to mine. You coming to see me soon?"

He nodded. "Always. You coming to see me soon?"

Inexplicably, Candy's eyes prickled with tears. These were questions she and her dad had been asking each other since her graduation. "Yeah. Always."

"Okay. Good. You eating okay?" he asked in perfect imitation of his mom.

Candy blew her dad a kiss. "As much as you are."

"That's what I thought. Eat better. Love you. Bye, Patti."

"Bye, Johnny. Love you." Candy hung up the call and called out to Barney, who was currently playing tug of war with the Jack Russell. "Hey boy, we're goin' home."

Barney ignored her, intent on tugging the smaller dog the entire length of the park.

"We might get some breakfast waffles."

If it were possible for a dog to fly, Candy's did, right to her side. The Jack Russell collapsed back on its backside.

"You're such a junk-food whore." She scratched him behind the ears. "You think he's gonna come by tonight?"

Barney's doggy grin clearly communicated that he didn't care what Trent did, as long as waffles were in his own imminent future.

Candy sighed, looking up at a big blue sky just visible through the leafy canopy of the giant oak tree in the dog park's center. "Maybe he won't. It's a Sunday. He's probably got better things to do."

Chapter 30

Trent put his elbows on the kitchen counter as he searched through one of his nona's handwritten cookbooks for something to make Candy for Sunday dinner. After taking her the *arrabiata* on Thursday, he'd followed that up with veal *polpette* on Friday—on what had turned out to be a geek speed-dating night—and a rich Sicilian-style *ribollita* on Saturday that Candy had snatched out of his hands before he'd even sat down. That had felt good. As had the way her mouth had quirked in a barely suppressed smile before she told him to go sit in a booth if he wanted to stay clear of what turned out to be a karaoke night to remember.

Before the night was over, he'd ended up on a small stage set up near the TARDIS, belting out his version of Britney Spears's "Hit Me Baby One More Time" after Candy had thrown down the challenge as though knowing he wouldn't do it. Trent had, to a standing ovation and a whole lot of howls from Barney. He'd even let someone put two tiny pigtails in his hair and wrap a borrowed tartan dish towel around his waist. He'd also joined in the good-natured booing when Candy insisted that everyone was only clapping and cheering because they felt sorry for him.

It had felt good, as had the sleep he'd gotten last night and the dream he'd woken up to. Candy Blume naked. Very naked. And doing things to him that he hadn't had the energy or time to fantasize about in a long while. He didn't expect that particular fantasy to be acted out anytime soon, or ever, but he sure as hell enjoyed it.

Each night when he walked into Hard Candy, every muscle and cell in his body tuned into exactly where Candy was and what she was doing. He now had a mental catalogue of all the faint ways she'd shown she was happy to see him, even if she never said as much.

The coffee, especially, was turning into a tradition. After everyone went home, she'd make him a cappuccino and then go get Barney. Trent would walk the dog around Austin's night streets, usually taking a wander down Sixth Street as the last of the bar stragglers headed home and the various bar workers said hi to Barney and asked after Candy as they closed up for the night. He enjoyed the feeling of doing something good for someone. And, if he were honest, he got a kick out of the mutt as well. Who would have known a dog could have so much personality? Which reminded him that it'd be nice to take something for Barney to eat tonight too. Maybe he could stop by a store and get some dog chews.

He turned a page in his nona's cookbook, resting his finger on a recipe for *arancini*, which lead him to thinking about risotto. Maybe he could make a risotto with fresh sugar snap peas and mint from his nona's garden. And maybe he could take Candy some of the leftover salted caramel truffles from yesterday's big order. He hadn't taken her anything from Dolce Design yet, not wanting to remind her of his first botched apology attempt. But he'd worked out she had a sweet tooth from seeing how much caramel syrup she poured into her lattes, so maybe . . .

Yeah. He'd make the risotto and take her something a little special for after.

Although he wouldn't make it until tonight, he headed out to the garden to see if there were enough peas on the neatly ordered vines his nona lovingly tended. He loved the tradition in this: deciding on a dish, gathering the ingredients and making it when the time was right. His work at Dolce Design was his income, his life, but home cooking recharged him and reminded him that things didn't have to be perfect for people to be happy. He was enjoying the anticipation of seeing Candy eat it in a blink then give him that faint nod that meant she'd really enjoyed herself.

He'd discovered his love of cooking after his parents had died. The structure of following a recipe and the gratification of seeing people eat what he'd made had been a vital ego boost at a time when he'd felt like he was failing at everything. In retrospect, it had been one of the first steps he'd made to recreate himself as a better person. And if he'd conveniently forgotten all the times his siblings had turned their noses up at something he'd worked his backside off to make, demanding tater tots or McDonald's, hey, that was his prerogative. They liked his cooking now, which wasn't hard to do because all the recipes he followed were his nona's, and her nona's before that. His nona had even stopped cooking because Trent was willing to make those dishes. He liked that.

After breaking the taboo of being in the kitchen, it had seemed natural to learn how to bake so he could take over his nona's business after she retired. There'd been a steep learning curve, and he'd had to take a hell of a lot of night classes, but he'd learned how to work with chocolate so he could turn his mental designs into something that people wouldn't just want to buy, but something that they'd want to buy for a *lot*.

He spent a couple of minutes in the yard, weeding the garden beds and checking that his nona hadn't snuck behind his back to put more seed in the bird feeders; the local doves were already tubby enough to qualify as mini blimps. Then he wandered back into the kitchen with a handful of freshly picked mint, feeling more chilled-out in this house than he had in weeks.

Maybe everything would work out. Matty would graduate and get over this angry phase, Carlotta and Anna would excel in their chosen courses in the colleges that had accepted them, Gwen would finish her residency without going crazy from sleep deprivation, and Nona would be able to finally relax and realize that she didn't need to worry anymore . . .

"What's that stupid smile on your face for?"

Matty was sitting at the breakfast counter in front of a bowl of cereal, looking for all the world like an insomniac, anemic vampire. His skin was pale, his eyes were bloodshot and red-rimmed, and his whole body—dressed in a wrinkled gray T-shirt and a pair of overpriced black Calvin Klein briefs—was hunched over the bowl like he was scared it was going to be taken away.

Trent walked past him to the sink, collecting a glass and filling it with water before setting the mint sprigs in it so they'd stay fresh.

"You look like hell. You okay?" he asked.

"No."

Trent leaned against the counter. "Yeah?"

"*Yeah?* That all you're gonna say? You're not gonna ask why? You're not gonna say anything else?" Matty spooned in a mouthful of cereal. The hearty crunch of him chewing combined with his morose frown would have struck Trent as comical any other time, but not right now.

"I don't know, Matty, you gonna tell me what you want to hear? Because lately, I feel like you're setting me up for all these tests without telling me the rules just so you can watch me fail."

Matty scooped up another large mouthful of cereal, chewing it slowly, and Trent had to tamp down the urge to tear the spoon from his hand.

"I'm moving out," Matty said finally, setting down his

spoon and bracing his hands on the edge of the counter. "You got anything to say about it?"

It took everything in Trent's body to keep his face impassive. "You're an adult. You got a job to support yourself?"

Matty shrugged. "I'll get a full-time job."

"Yeah? Doing what? Because I didn't think you'd gone in for any interviews yet. And aren't you business majors supposed to do some kind of internship first?"

"Yeah. But I failed my degree, so that's not in the cards now."

The words reverberated like a pistol shot in the quiet room.

"Say that again?" Trent asked in a deadly quiet voice, anger beginning to bubble like lava in his belly.

"I failed."

"How?"

"I just failed. What does it matter? Like you said, I'm an adult now, so it's none of your business."

Trent pinched the bridge of his nose. "No, just wait. What do you mean by *failed*? Does that mean one subject? One semester? One *year*? What does it mean, Matty?"

"It doesn't matter what it means!" Matty's voice cracked.

"Yeah. It does. It sure as hell does, because if you've known for longer than a week you've lied to me," Trent snarled. "We had an agreement. I'd pay for your college and for all your living expenses until you were twenty-one, and all you had to do is *get your goddamn degree* and let me know the *minute* there were any problems so we could work something out! And instead you kept the fact you're failing from me until *after* the school year ends?" He started pacing the kitchen. "Is that what the cake-throwing bullshit was about? You wanted to distract me from the fact I'd paid for an expensive goddamn party for you to celebrate turning twenty-one and graduating—"

"No one asked you to!" Matty threw his hands in the air as

he pushed away from the counter, his stool clattering to the floor.

"Yes, you did! You asked me! You! You asked me when you goddamn *lied* to me and told me that you wanted to celebrate your birthday somewhere special so you could also celebrate the graduation you must've known you wouldn't be having. What kind of idiot do you think I am?" Trent was breathing fire now. "You think I work my ass off for you to pull something like this on me? You think you can use the fact I care for you—although who knows why—to distract from the way you've been behaving like a spoiled brat? You think I'm that much of a pushover?" Trent slammed the flat of his hand down on a countertop. "All you had to do was be honest. *Honest.* You've had everything else handed to you on a fucking plate. Do you know how many people in this country are still paying off student loans? Do you know how many people don't have families who support them getting an education? You think I wanted to work all these years with no social life just to hear crap like this? *What fucking planet do you come from?*"

Trent's chest rose and fell as he vaguely became aware of noises in the rest of the house. They'd no doubt have an audience soon. Fuck, fuck, *fuck!* Why the hell hadn't he called Matty on his behavior earlier? Somewhere along the way, Trent had enabled his little brother to be the inconsiderate asshole Trent had spent his adult life trying not to be.

"Stop making it about you!" Matty yelled back, his voice stringy with anger and tears. "It's always about you. You and that stupid job and your stupid fucking hero complex. No one cares about you! And yeah, I lied to you, because I knew you'd react like this!" Before Trent could stop him, Matty picked up his bowl of cereal and hurled it across the room, the sound of shattering porcelain echoing around the kitchen.

"What the hell did you think that was gonna achieve?!" Trent roared. "Clean that up."

Matty shook his head. "No. You clean it up. You're the one who's so stuck on this house being perfect all the time."

"Clean. It. Up," Trent said, fury lacing his tone.

Matty gave Trent a watery sneer. "I don't have to do anything you tell me."

"Yeah? If you're in this house, you follow the rules, which means you respect everyone else's time and possessions. Clean up the damn mess, Matty, and explain what the hell is going on, or your stuff is gonna be out on the curb by noon."

Trent caught the genuine fear that crossed Matty's face before he covered it up with outrage. "That's bullshit!"

"What's going on here?!" a pajama-clad Gwen demanded as she walked into the kitchen, pillow creases still marking her cheek, her hair tied in a messy braid. "Nona's out in the living room worrying that you're killing each other, and I had to threaten Carlotta with death to keep her from filming. What the hell y'all trying to do to each other?"

Matty rounded on her. "It's him! He's treating me like I'm nine!"

"Because that's how mature you're acting!" Trent yelled back. "How long did you know you were failing college? How long have you been stringing me along while I've supported you, blaming your shitty behavior on exam stress. How long have you been lying to me, Matty?"

"You failed college?" Gwen's question was drowned out by Matty's shriek of "I hate you!"

"Real fucking mature." Trent's lip curled. "What are you hoping to get out of this whole scene? Don't think I don't realize you've set me up here, springing the news on me like you did. What do you want?"

"A reference!" Matty yelled.

Trent stared at him, stunned. He met Gwen's eyes for a moment and saw his sister shaking her head at him, trying to stop him from really losing his cool.

"A reference? What part of pissing me off like this equates to me giving you a reference?"

"You owe me! You fired me the other day for something that happened outside of work hours. You owe me a reference. And that day's pay. I'd turned up to work. You're the one who sent me home—"

Trent felt the thread of his remaining patience snap. "That's it, I've had enough. You're my witness," Trent said to Gwen. "I gave him a chance, I've given him every chance. He turned up to work drunk twice, brought a stranger to the store and trashed it, kept the fact he was failing college from me so I'd keep paying his bills . . ." He looked at Matty. "You're out, Matty, unless you come up with an explanation for your behavior, an apology to me and to every person in this house, and a concrete plan for how you're gonna pass college next semester. And if you can't man up and do that, don't come to me." With that, Trent stalked out of the room.

"Trent? What's happening?" his nona asked as he let the kitchen door slam shut behind him.

"Just me doing what I should have done a long time ago. I've got to head out, but I'll be back later. If Matty gives you an apology, do me a favor and don't let him off the hook easy, okay? Make him understand there are consequences to his actions."

"You know I can't do that." She shook her head. "He's my grandson and this is between you boys—"

"Try, for me. And tell him to call me when he's ready to man up. If he hasn't done that by tonight, I'll be back to clear out his stuff. He's gotta grow up."

With that, Trent collected his wallet and keys, not sure where he was heading yet, just knowing that he couldn't stay to wonder where the hell he'd gone so wrong.

Chapter 31

"I don't think he's coming tonight."

Kevin's voice broke Candy out of her brooding thoughts while the last of her Sunday night crowd filtered out of the bar, many of them holding board game boxes under their arms. Candy was only realizing how much she'd been looking forward to seeing Trent getting his ass beaten on Board Game Night by a bunch of geeks armed with inch-thick rule books.

"He's usually here by eleven thirty and it's almost one," Kevin said.

"Pardon?" Candy finally focused on him. He was busy sorting the pieces from his Starfarers of Catan set back into the box after a particularly epic game with his usual Sunday night posse, who just happened to be the same crew who were still surly for what he'd pulled with the dragon during their last D & D game.

"I said, I don't think Trent is coming tonight."

Candy shrugged. "Like I care."

"Want me to walk Barney?"

She shook her head. "Nope. We went out at midnight and got soaked in the rain. Remember when I asked you to watch the bar while I had a shower and you got all uppity because you were winning your game or something?"

"That's technically not what happened." Kevin put the lid on the box and then carefully placed it in his backpack. "I won't be in tomorrow. I've got some meetings."

"Yeah? Anything important?" Candy asked him.

"I'm not sure."

"Want to talk about it?"

"Not right now. Make sure no one sits in my seat." Kevin ran his hand over his chest in a gesture that gave away his nervousness.

Candy gave him a solemn nod. "Sure, big guy. I'll keep your seat free."

"Thanks. Bye. I'll leave by the back door if that's okay. My car's parked next to yours."

"Sure. Night." Candy huffed out a breath and looked around the bar. She'd already tallied up the cash register. Other than putting out the recycling, cleaning the bathrooms and wiping down the floor and the bar, there wasn't a whole lot to do. And Trent Green hadn't turned up.

She went back to destroying her manicure by nibbling her nails as the playlist looped back to the starting Kendrick Lamar track.

Maybe she could go upstairs and get Barney.

She'd never felt uncomfortable in her own bar, which always seemed more like home than her actual home, even when she and Beau had rented a house in the suburbs. But tonight she felt edgy. Marlene still had a key. Sure, Candy could slide the deadbolt across, but it didn't feel enough.

Thanks to the money from Matty Green's party, she was now debt-free, but she still lacked a financial buffer for any extra expenses. Which meant that she was gonna have to live with the idea that Marlene had a key for at least another month. Which meant that if Marlene flipped out or just got careless and left the key around, Beau could take it. And maybe that deadbolt wasn't as strong as Candy thought . . .

She locked up the front door and made a decision about the back one. Knowing it wasn't exactly rational, Candy hurried to the basement, selected a full keg of Pilsner and manhandled it up the stairs. It took a lot of stops and starts, and just as she got it to the top of the stairs her phone buzzed.

Stomach clenching at the thought of it being Marlene or Beau, Candy looked at the screen. Her entire body slumped with relief when she saw Trent's name.

I'm outside.

You're late, she replied.

I've got cake.

What type?

Chocolate caramel mud cake with extra caramel frosting.

Candy allowed herself a grin as she hurried back through the bar to find Trent standing on the other side of the front door with a shiny red cake box.

"This better be good cake." Candy took the box from him and strode across the room. "You trying to impress me?" she asked, setting the box on the bar before turning to find Trent finishing with the door locks without being asked.

She frowned when she realized something wasn't right. She'd expected a witty comeback, or even the quirked mouth she was beginning to recognize as Trent silently calling her on her bullshit. Instead she got nothing.

"You need me to walk Barney?" he asked.

"Nope. He's already been out."

"You still serving drinks?" he asked, walking across the room.

Candy really looked at him, taking in the creases at the sides of his mouth and the stilted way he was moving. "You okay? Because if you looked any stiffer, you'd be a corpse."

Nope, that didn't get her the mouth quirk thing either. Instead he rubbed his hands over his face, his voice muffled when he spoke. "Then I'd fit in real good on Prancing Pony Night. About that drink . . ."

Candy set the box aside after peeking inside to see a whole lot of cakey heaven. She was pretty sure Trent had made her a cake decorated with little prancing ponies jumping over obstacles made of caramel M&M's. There should be a law restricting something so sinful, and she'd tell him as much the minute she got a smile out of him. This mopey Trent wasn't right. He didn't even match the old Trent from high school. That Trent had sneered and jeered, but he didn't go around acting like his house had just burned down.

"What're you drinking?" she asked.

"I don't care. Something. Whatever you're having. It's my shout."

"I could drink a bourbon and Coke."

"Just pour mine straight." Trent rested his elbows on the bar and held his head in his hands. "A double if you're cool with that. I'll catch an Uber home if I'm not sober when I leave, but I'll give you a hand doing the bathrooms and stuff before I go."

"Magnanimous of you." Candy gave him an arch look. "But unnecessary. I was planning on doing the rest of the cleaning tomorrow morning before I do the accounts."

"You sure?" Trent looked around the bar before focusing on the sign on the TARDIS. "It was Board Game Night tonight, right?"

"Yeah, and you let Kevin down by not coming to see him infuriate everyone by winning."

His mouth quirked at the side, but it still wasn't right. It wasn't a genuine smile. "He tell them all they were doing it wrong?"

"How did you know?" Candy poured herself a single shot of bourbon and added Coke before taking care of Trent's double shot and sliding it across the bar. "I need you to do something as payment before you drink that."

"Yeah?" He straightened up. "What?"

"There's a keg in the hall." She jerked her thumb towards the back of the bar. "I need you to put it in front of the back door." She held up a hand. "No questions or this conversation is over and I'm kicking you out." She paused for dramatic effect. "But the cake stays."

He frowned. "Your back door is your apartment's nearest fire exit."

That gave Candy momentary pause, but she covered it up with attitude. "You telling me how to run my place?"

He shook his head slowly. "No, but I'll charge extra for having to haul you out through a window."

"Dudley Do Right much?"

"Just a fellow business owner who knows a little about safety regulations."

"You gonna do it or leave?" Candy regretted the words when she saw his frown deepen. She didn't want him to go, but she couldn't back down. That wasn't how this worked.

Trent finally nodded. "Give me a minute." He strode to the back hallway. Seconds later, there was a thud of something heavy being set down against the door.

He walked back into the bar just as Candy was lifting the cake he'd made out of the box. She studied it first from one angle, then from another. Yep, it was definitely a prancing pony cake, complete with ponies, M&M obstacles and hand-painted trees. It was possibly the nicest thing anyone had ever made her, and since she wasn't too comfortable with all the warm fuzziness she was feeling right now, she feigned a scowl.

"What's the catch, Green?"

"No catch, unless you count me using you as a guinea pig for testing out the new parts for my 3D chocolate printer," he said, taking his seat again before picking up his drink and throwing back a mouthful.

"I'm not sure I want to eat it. You made it too pretty."

Candy licked some caramel off her finger. "You gonna want a slice?"

"If you're having one."

"You sure are accommodating tonight. Except for being late." Candy ducked below the bar to select two plates and snatch up utensils. "Why were you late?"

"I was moving enough of my little brother's stuff onto the front lawn to show I mean business."

Candy schooled her expression to blandness. "You people sure have strange living arrangements. What'd he do?"

Trent took another slug of his bourbon, almost finishing it off. "Why're you assuming it was Matty and not me?"

"Because your brother's a brat." She took a sip of her drink, enjoying Trent's surprise.

"Yeah?" Trent swirled his almost empty glass around.

"Uh-huh. Which you're probably responsible for somehow if you raised him."

Trent's mouth curved in a faint smile. "You don't give an inch, do you?"

"I call it how I see it." She held up the knife. "I'm warning you, I might be murdering a chocolate pony or two in the next couple of seconds."

His smile became genuine. "Murder away. I've got the design for them saved."

"You made the designs from scratch?" She carefully cut out a chunk of cake, avoiding any pony decapitation despite her threat. She then plated it and slid it towards him.

"It was either that or stay at home and murder Matty. And I hear it's hard to run a cake store from prison."

"Yeah, I can see that." Candy cut herself a generous slice and attacked it, barely muffling a groan when the taste of luxury chocolate hit hungry taste buds. She'd shoveled in another four mouthfuls before she stopped long enough to talk. "What have you put in this thing? Crack?"

Trent paused with his fork halfway to his mouth, snorting. "Did you just compliment me, Blume?"

She forked up another big piece of cake, making sure to get a generous amount of frosting. "You fishing for compliments?"

"Might be."

"Then it's passable."

Trent let out a sharp bark of laughter. "Anyone ever tell you that you're one of a kind?"

"I've been called worse. By you, actually. Almost every day of high school." Candy regretted her words when she saw the laughter leave Trent's eyes. She picked up a tiny chocolate pony and set it on the bar in front of him. "But you're not so bad now. Have a prancing pony."

"Yeah?" Trent asked, his voice softening. "That's good to hear. I like you, Candy. You're a good person. I wish I hadn't been such an idiot in school, because you were, and always have been, one of the most interesting and attractive women I've ever known. You were too different from what I'd been taught women were supposed to be. Too real. Too weird and sexy. But I get it now."

Chapter 32

The music playing in the background drifted to the fore as their eyes met. Candy watched a flush travel up his cheeks.

"I've never been much of a drinker," he said.

She set her fork down. "That's obvious."

"Probably came out different than I meant it."

"How'd you mean it?" Candy swallowed around what was suddenly a bundle of weird, edgy nerves.

"You know, I, ah, think I'll go. I've really liked what we've shared the last few nights. I like helping you and I don't want to ruin it with my big mouth. The cake's all yours. Make sure you lock up after I leave."

"What? You're just gonna say something like that and go?" she demanded, her weird feelings transforming into a welcome ire.

"Yeah. I'm in a strange mood tonight. I'll see you tomorrow. Don't eat all the ponies at once." With those last ridiculous words, Trent stood up and started walking to the door.

Candy picked up her drink, slugging it back before slamming the glass down on the counter. "There is no freakin' way you're getting one over me like this. Stop right there."

Trent paused, turning around. "Why?"

A jolt of sheer power shot through her system at the knowledge that anything she said, anything she did in this moment was her choice and he'd go with it. It wasn't guilt fueling his behavior. It was something else. Trent Green found her sexy. Trent Green wanted her. Trent Green, the last person she'd ever thought would want her physically, had just admitted he did, when her own husband had stopped wanting sex six years into their marriage and hadn't bothered to explain why.

And it was about time all that ended. Right here. *Right now.*

Feeling light-headed and determined at the same time, Candy stalked around the bar. The sensation got sharper the closer she got to Trent. Her body began to feel languid, liquid, like she was a big cat stalking her prey.

His eyes widened, and she had to suppress a smirk. Yeah, she was totally in charge right now. He'd lit the match, but the fire was hers to control. There was a crackle in the air. She knew he felt it.

"Repeat what you said," she said, giving him her best cold-bitch stare as she came to stand only a foot away. "Do it now."

The flush on his cheeks got darker. "I should really go."

"Because you want to?" Candy poked a fingernail into his chest, seeing actual goosebumps travel over his exposed arms in response to the contact.

He swallowed audibly. "No."

She trailed the fingernail downwards, digging it in a tiny bit. "Because you're scared of me?"

"No."

She went lower, at his stomach now, flattening her palm so that the tips of her fingers touched the waistband of his jeans. "Because you don't want me?"

He shook his head slowly. "No."

She moved her hand lower, closing over him, feeling him, gripping him a little tighter than would be comfortable.

"Because you just threw down a challenge. You know that, right?"

She felt the moment he realized this was actually happening, as the hard bulge under her hand twitched. She smirked. "So here's the deal. I want to get off. And you're gonna get me there. You fine with that? Just nod. I don't need to hear you speaking right now unless you've got something vital to say, like that you want this stopped."

She saw his inner self fighting for control until it worked out what was good for it.

Then he nodded slowly.

"Good. Then get on your knees."

She dug her nails in a little more before releasing him, putting her hand on his shoulder and pushing him down. He went easily, still looking straight into her eyes. The powerful feeling inside her intensified. In that moment, she felt like the sexiest woman on the planet. Maybe she'd soaked up some of the energy from the Monday night crowd over the years, because this felt *right*.

"Put your hands on my thighs," she ordered.

He did what she asked, and the contact of his hands on the bare skin just below the hem of her dress caused a ripple of heat to shoot straight to her core. She bit the inside of her lip, not wanting to show him how good this was yet. She wasn't gonna give it away that easy. "Raise my dress and pull my underwear down."

"Yeah?" Trent's voice was husky.

She raised a brow. "You want this to stop?"

"Hell no," he said, his voice prayer-like as he slid his hands up her thighs, up her bare skin, until he reached the fabric of her underwear.

"Stop dawdling. Pull them down."

He did, sliding her underwear down reverentially.

Candy's nipples were so tight they were aching with every breath, every brush of fabric against them, but she wasn't gonna let him know that either. Instead she feigned a yawn, stretching her arms over her head so that her dress hiked up. She saw Trent's eyes dip for a second. "You want that?" she asked.

"Yeah."

She flicked off one ballet flat and raised her leg, sliding it higher and higher, knowing her dress was hiking up, knowing what he'd see. Finally her foot was resting on his shoulder. The strain of the stretch made her feel even more powerful. "You've got five minutes to make me come. Get to work."

She'd barely gotten the words out before Trent's hands gripped her backside and his mouth was right where she needed it, licking, sucking, targeting her clitoris with an intensity that had her head falling back. Her hands gripped his hair, holding him tighter as her panting and his moans filled the air.

The power of it—the knowledge that Trent was just as into this as she was—sent Candy flying way sooner than she would have liked, but he didn't stop. Instead, he shifted his hand, his fingers slowly sliding into her and pumping as he kept up an almost unbearable tongue flicker on her clitoris. The entire lower half of her body was liquid pleasure, building . . . building . . .

"Now!" She barely realized she'd shouted as it washed over her so much more intensely this time. Candy's fingers tightened in Trent's hair before she collapsed against him, her whole body curved over his.

Candy expected Trent to pull back, to demand his due, but instead he started leaving tiny butterfly kisses on her thighs. It took her a while to realize he was saying stuff, and even longer to make sense of his words around the white noise, but finally her brain put it all together.

"You're beautiful. So hot. So good."

It was too much. A wave of emotion came from nowhere. All of a sudden, Candy's eyes stung, her nose felt stuffy, and her chest felt tight. Too tight.

In a swift movement she removed her foot from Trent's shoulder and stumbled backwards, wiping her hands over her face before looking at him.

His mouth was damp, his chin wet from her, and she knew she needed to banish this feeling of vulnerability or else something inside her would break.

She ran a hand over her head, the short spikes of her hair lending her the strength she needed to pull herself together. "You're not bad, Green."

He gave her a hot look as he got to his feet. "Yeah? I try to be good at everything."

She shrugged, putting as much attitude as she could into that one movement, knowing full well she was only wearing one shoe and that her entire body was still shaking. "If I were grading you, I'd give you a B. Try harder next time. Same goes with the cake."

She caught Trent's shock and then saw his mouth curve in a wide smile.

"I'll be seeing you then," he said in a casual voice.

"I don't doubt it. The way you've been hanging around here, I should be charging you rent." She managed to get enough sass into her voice to sound convincing, but knew he'd totally seen through her when he burst into laughter.

"You are one *amazing* piece of work, Candy Blume."

"Don't forget it."

Trent's smile widened as she snatched up her underwear and strutted to the bar to finish her cake. She didn't turn around until she heard him leave, and then she slumped forward, her head in her hands. "Eeesh! Candy, what the *hell* are you doing?"

Chapter 33

"I thought we agreed that it sucked when we didn't talk at least twice a week. And here I am leaving a whole lot of unanswered messages. Anyone would think you're freaking out about having to wear a bridesmaid's dress."

Candy flopped back on her bed, grimacing at the hurt in Sophie's voice. "You angry at me?"

"A little, but only over you making me worry. What have you been doing? And you better make it a good story."

"I might have done the wild thing with Trent in my bar last night. I made him crawl." Candy stretched her free hand above her head, catlike, and grinned at the stunned silence on Sophie's end.

"You *what*?!" Sophie shrieked. "You and Trent Green? You and Trent Green had sex? Like, actual sex? And you're okay with that? Like, actually okay with that?"

Candy felt genuine laughter bubble up. The sound surprised Barney, who was curled up on an armchair after leaving the bed in disgust over Candy tossing and turning all night.

Maybe all the weird, Trent-inspired emotions were worth it if it meant she didn't have to avoid Sophie anymore for fear of letting her problems with Marlene and Beau slip out. The distance between them had been killing her.

"Better than okay," Candy said. "I'm not gonna give you too many details, but I *can* tell you that while I didn't really come into contact with the thing we used to call him, he saw a whole lot of me and I liked it. Actually, that's an understatement. I haven't been done that good for years. Maybe ever. It was all about me for once, and that felt damn good."

There was another stunned silence before Sophie let out a burst of relieved laughter. "I know that voice. It's the one you only use when you've won something. You really did make him crawl, didn't you?"

"Let's just say he spent some time on his knees." Candy rolled onto her stomach, turning the video on so she could look at Sophie's face as her friend drove somewhere. "You gonna judge me?"

Sophie darted a look at her phone screen. "Never. But I might question your sanity. Because I don't want you hurt, and if you remember how he used to be—"

"I actually think he's genuinely changed. And besides, it's not like we feel anything for each other. It's just sex. Plus, I get the satisfaction of knowing he's gonna be walking weird from sexual frustration unless I decide to un-frustrate him. On my terms."

Sophie darted her a piercing look. "And you're definitely okay?"

"Yeah. He started coming to the bar last Thursday, helping me clean and close up, and it's been kind of nice to have someone around, giving me a hand."

Sophie's face contorted into a worried frown. "You've been lonely, haven't you? I knew I should be coming to see you more. And don't tell me no. Because you know I'm right. I've been spending so much time with Ian and—"

"Whoa, pony." Candy sat up. "You haven't done anything wrong, and I'm totally on top of it, okay? But you can do me a favor." She swung her legs off of the bed and walked into the kitchen, stretching some more as she looked out the window at a sunny sky. Yeah, today was gonna be a good one.

"Anything."

"Tell me what's going on with your wedding planning and how I can help. Have you got a date yet? Because I'll have to sort some stuff out with the bar. It won't be a problem. I just have to have a little warning."

Sophie parked and rolled her eyes, then looked directly at her phone. "You'll get plenty of warning because we're not doing it for at least a year. We had a meeting with a wedding planner yesterday, and it turns out that weddings that aren't held in someone's backyard involve a hell of a lot of advance planning. And this is gonna make me sound totally naïve, but I had *no* idea that I'd have to start looking for a wedding dress at least twelve months ahead. Can you believe it?"

Candy shook her head. "Nope."

"Remember how we went shopping for yours? We found so many awesome dresses at those thrift stores. The one you picked in the end was gorgeous—" Sophie stopped talking abruptly. "And that's probably not what you want to be reminded of. Sorry! My big mouth. I'm so caught up thinking about my wedding that I'm not thinking of you. Are you gonna be okay or is it gonna bring up memories?"

Candy peered in the fridge, spotted the leftover prancing pony cake and stuck her finger in the icing before licking it off. "I seem to remember you telling me you were gonna give me a slapping the other day. Want me to do the same to you?"

"If I need it!"

"You don't. I loved my wedding day. I just don't love what the groom turned into. So relax and tell me more." Candy realized she was actually telling the truth. Maybe last night really had been good for her. The memory of Trent calling her beautiful fluttered through her mind and it felt good. Uncomfortable, but good.

Sophie huffed out a relieved sigh. "Okay, so there's the dress, and then there's the guest list, which is gonna be nuts! Ian's gotta give all his friends from the UK plenty of warning so they can schedule their private jets or whatever. And then there's the security, because it turns out that he knows a whole lot of people who the paparazzi would love to get shots of . . . which is kind of ironic, with him being in the media. You know, I didn't understand what I was getting into when I started dating that man. Here I was, thinking he was just this big sexy British guy who made me think of Jane Austen novels, and then I find out he's on a bunch of rich lists and that he could buy my daddy's ranch a couple of thousand times over, which means I might actually *be* in a Jane Austen novel. Sometimes I wonder what the hell he's thinking being with me."

Candy paused in setting some coffee on, her good mood momentarily dipping when she heard the insecurity in Sophie's voice. She definitely hadn't been a good friend of late if Sophie was this worked up.

"Well," she said, "I could give you a nice, reassuring answer about you being the best thing in his life and that he should be thanking his lucky stars every day that you're even letting him breathe in your vicinity . . . but it's really because of your boobs. He's gotten stuck in their gravitational pull and can't get away. So just make sure you get your girls out from time to time and he'll be yours forever."

Sophie laughed, giving Candy a shoulder shimmy that made her chest wobble. "That's what I'm hoping!"

"That's what I *know*. So stop thinking stupid thoughts and remember that man worships you. It's kind of wrong how much he worships you. In fact, I'd keep an eye out for him making any ritual sacrifices in your honor. If he starts eyeing your dad's sheep—" Candy stopped when Sophie's laughter drowned her voice out.

"Okay! I'll stop being stupid," Sophie said. "But back to you. Tell me truthfully. You and Trent. You really okay?"

"Yeah. I'm getting used to him coming around. And I don't even have to pay him minimum wage." Candy nabbed herself another scoop of icing on the end of her finger, licking it off. "And he makes nice food. Anyway, enough about me. What sort of dress made of fairy wings and sparkles are you thinking of wearing to your wedding, Cinderella? And what did this wedding planner say?"

Sophie let out a snort. "I have *no* idea about the dress yet, but she had this idea for the wedding that involves sheep, and y'all are gonna wet your pants laughing after I finish telling you about it. I'm already tempted to use it for Ian's next birthday party instead."

Chapter 34

"You going out again tonight, honey?"

Trent was almost to the front door, about to head to Hard Candy with a box full of food, when he heard his nona's voice behind him.

"What are you doing up so late?" he asked, looking through the dimly lit living room to see her standing in the doorway of her bedroom.

The twins were already in bed, and Gwen was on night shift at the hospital. The silence made Trent aware of how much noise Matty made.

"Do you know where Matty is?" she asked.

Trent felt his gut tighten at the worry in her voice. "No, but I know he's in contact with Anna and Carlotta. I overheard them on the phone after my shower."

"Oh." The room fell into silence. "Because he's not as strong as you are and I worry."

"I know." Trent set the box on the hall table and walked across the room, pulling his nona into his arms and resting his head on the top of her curls. "But it's gonna be okay. I can't protect him anymore. He doesn't want me to. My overprotectiveness has gotten him to where we are now. I've let him get away with too much to make up for how he was treated by Mom and Dad."

"Your father didn't understand him."

Trent shook his head as the feeling in his gut got sharper. "No, he didn't."

"He didn't know what a beautiful boy he had. I used to tell Angela that she had to protect him, but my daughter wasn't strong. She never stood up to your father the way I would have, and her religion got in the way. She was narrow-minded about some things."

"Yeah, I miss her like crazy, but Mom wasn't exactly rational when it came to her faith," Trent said with a sigh that ruffled his nona's hair. He stepped back, his hands on her shoulders, his heart breaking a little over how frail she'd gotten. "But you know this is something I had to do. You understand?"

"I do." She rubbed her fingertips under her eyes, and it was only in that moment Trent realized she'd been crying.

"Hey, what's this?" He wiped away a tear trickling down her cheek with his thumb. This small, amazing woman had been strong enough to overcome the grief of her only daughter's death to help Trent raise her four other grandchildren. She'd cooked, cleaned, helped them deal with their own sadness, and had supported him when he'd needed it most. She'd even trusted him with the business she'd built from the ground up. And he'd never once seen her cry.

But she was crying now. Trent wished in that moment he could teleport Matty here to witness this, but he couldn't, so he settled for trying to cheer his nona up. "He's gonna be fine. I tell you what, if I don't hear from him after a week, I'll track him down to make sure. Okay?"

The relief on her face was heartbreaking. "You'd do that?"

"Yeah. I can't say I'm not gonna kick his ass when I find him, but I'll find him."

"You're a good grandson. Thank you."

"And you're the best. Period. Now go get some beauty sleep and I'll come in with your hot chocolate in the morning."

He was heartened when she got a little iron back in her expression. "I'm not a child, you arrogant boy. You don't have to use that babying tone of voice."

"No, but I sure do like it when you tell me off." Trent kissed her on the forehead. "See you in the morning."

He was halfway to the door when she spoke again. "Who is she, Trent? The woman you're cooking for every night?"

He picked up the box and then turned to give her a smile. "Someone who makes me happy. And I have no idea why, because she'd use me as a doormat first chance she could get."

That earned him a small laugh. "That's nice to hear, honey. You deserve a strong woman." With those words she turned and walked back into her room.

As Trent headed out to his truck, his mood cheered at the thought of seeing Candy again. He'd outdone himself in the kitchen and hoped she'd approve.

He also hoped they'd do more of what she'd let him do to her last night. A hell of a lot more.

"You okay? You seem edgy."

Candy looked away from Hard Candy's closed door and forced herself to focus on Jake, who'd leaned his elbows on the bar, resting his face on his hands.

There were a couple of nervous newcomers tonight at the munch, both women. As always when someone new turned up, the air at the back of the room gained an edge of anticipatory horniness, with a couple of the unattached regulars in the crowd already competing for attention, hoping to score. Normally Candy just got on with her job and ignored any sex-chemistry zinging around—it was something that came with running a busy bar—but tonight was different.

It was eleven thirty. If Trent turned up at the usual time, she had a half hour. Which meant she could maybe snatch a couple of minutes to brush her teeth and check her makeup—

"You didn't even hear me, did you?" Jake asked.

"Yeah I did." Candy ran her hand over her head, feeling the newly shaved stubble. She'd redone it this morning. She wondered if Trent would notice.

"I'll believe you, although your story wouldn't hold up for a second in court." Jake gave her a curious smile. He was dressed, as always, in a suit. Tonight's was charcoal gray and fit so well it had to have been tailored.

"Can I ask you something? Just curious," Candy blurted, then tried to look as uninterested as possible in the answer.

"Yeah?"

"How do you . . . how do you know what to say and do? Do they tell you what they want you to say or do you just do it? And how do you know whether or not they're actually liking it?"

Jake gave her a long, serious look for a minute. "Usually there's a conversation about what they like and about what I like. It's different with each person, but communication, nego-tiation is key. And sometimes I throw that all out the window in favor of winging it, consensually and within reason. How much detail do you want here?"

Candy waved a hand, feeling a flush travel up her face and not liking it. "That's already too much. Forget I asked."

Jake nodded, his expression serious for a few more seconds before his mouth curved into a grin. "I don't believe it. Candy Blume, Mistress of Hard Candy, has got herself a plaything. Who is he?"

Candy tapped her ear. "Sorry, was that someone breaking Rule Nine? Rule Nine that says anyone who pries into my personal life gets kicked out of my bar?"

His grin turned wicked. "Yeah."

"Shouldn't you be whipping someone right now, Bondage Boy?" Candy gave him a glare.

He looked completely unrepentant. "You volunteering? Because that would be some kind of bucket list experience."

"Do you have a death wish?"

He laughed. "No. I'll take a couple of Bacardi and Cokes. How'd the guys I arranged go at the party last week?"

Candy relaxed, giving him a nod. "You did good. If I could afford to hire more people, Taneesha and Blake would be the first ones I'd call." She measured out the Bacardi and spritzed Coke into two glasses before collecting the money and Jake's usual generous tip. "Now go away." She fluttered her fingers at him.

"Yes ma'am." He gave her a salute before sauntering off to join his friends. Distantly Candy heard him say he thought she'd found a man. She knew she should traipse over there and do some Rule Nine enforcing, but she didn't.

Instead she kept herself busy wiping down surfaces that were already clean and sorting bottles that were already organized while keeping one eye on the door at all times.

She'd been intense last night. Maybe it had been too extreme. Maybe she'd been too pushy. Maybe Trent was having second thoughts. They hadn't talked about it, so she had no way of knowing if he was actually going to turn up . . .

The door opened and Trent appeared dressed in his usual white T-shirt and a pair of blue jeans that shouldn't have looked so great. He had a small backpack slung over his shoulder and was holding a medium-sized box.

Candy felt everything inside her start to do a nervous dance. She covered it up with snark. "You're early."

"You're surly." Trent matched her feigned scowl with one of his own, setting the box on the bar.

She looked at it. "That has to be more than one meal. You trying to feed half of Austin?"

"Just you."

He pulled out a blue earthenware baking dish with a domed lid. Suddenly the scent of roast lamb filled the air and Candy's mouth started watering. Especially when she could see there were also four smaller dishes in the box.

"You got somewhere I can heat all this up?" he asked.

Candy gnawed on the inside of her lip, feeling like she was about to take a big step off of a very steep cliff. "There's an oven in my apartment."

Trent's eyes widened. "Yeah?"

She rolled her eyes. "Don't act like this is a big deal. Barney's gonna need a walk too."

"Yeah?" Trent put the dish back in the box. "His lead and stuff upstairs?"

"On a hook behind the door. But you're just heating up food and walking my dog because I'm hungry and can't get away to walk him myself. That's all. Don't get any ideas," she said while her body called her a liar. She might be telling Trent not to have any ideas, but she was definitely getting a couple. Most of them weren't appropriate to be having in public.

His mouth twitched. "Suits me. I came for Barney anyway. He likes it when I visit."

"He likes it when anyone visits."

"You say that, but we've got an understanding."

Candy snorted. "You'll be understanding what it's like to have a seventy-pound dog jumping all over you the minute he smells that food."

"It's nice to know someone appreciates all this food I make you." Trent looked at the crowd in their usual booth at the back. "What night is it? The sign says something about a munch, but I don't see any food."

"Monday night is BDSM night. A munch is what these guys call their get-togethers."

Trent's face showed confusion before he let out a bark of laughter.

"What's so funny?" she asked. "You judging people, Green?"

He shook his head. "Nope. Just laughing at myself. I saw the teddy bear two weeks ago and thought they were just a bunch of nice business people—which I'm sure they are, but sometimes this place takes me by surprise." He ran a hand over his eyes, still grinning as she stared at him. "Alright, alright! I'm gonna go heat this food up. What time you finishing work?"

Candy checked the time on her phone. "In around thirty minutes or so. If you're making food, I'll take care of everything tomorrow morning instead of tonight."

"See you then, Blume. Make sure you knock before entering. I might be indecent." Trent laughed when she gave him the finger.

She waited until he'd disappeared through the door leading to her apartment before she allowed herself a smile.

"So he's the guy? The one you kicked out two weeks ago?" Jake called out.

Candy rounded on Jake's table. "That's it. Rule Nine has officially been broken. You're all banned. Hear me? No more Munch Night unless I hear a damn good reason. And that reason better include an apology with some serious crawling. On your knees."

There was a wail from the regulars as Jake gave Candy a shit-eating grin.

She played to the crowd, turning up her bitch act to twelve as everyone started calling for Jake to apologize, which he did with his usual charm, going on one knee and ordering a round of drinks on him.

After letting him off the hook, Candy got to work serving everyone, relieved that she'd be busy enough until closing to remain distracted from the fact that Trent was in her apartment at this very moment, making her food and being as sexy as hell.

. . .

At closing time Candy waved the last of Jake's crew out the door and then spent a couple of minutes clearing away their glasses and organizing her cash drawer. Then she wandered into her office and sat at her desk. She was dawdling. Her entire body felt weird; it was all turned on, but also nervous and surly that it was due to a man. She didn't like it. So here she was, messing around in her small office, straightening papers that were already straight and checking emails she'd already checked.

She knew Trent had taken Barney for a walk, because she'd heard the happy barks that meant Barney was telling the neighborhood cats to get off his turf. She also knew they had returned, because she could hear Trent's footfalls overhead. He'd wandered over to her bed a couple of times, and each time she'd tensed up, her body zinging with anticipation as she wondered what he was doing up there. Was he as turned on as she was thinking about them having sex? What if he wasn't? What if this was just him being nice? What if—

"Argh! Get your head on straight, woman. It's only food," she muttered to herself. She wondered if she could call Sophie at this hour, but no. That would be stupid. She was a thirty-year-old woman. She should be able to handle a man making her dinner in her apartment. This was no freakin' deal. She was gonna eat his food, then kick him out. She didn't want him expecting anything. She didn't want him thinking that he could just suck up to her and get into her pants. She still had the upper hand . . . plus, she was hungry.

With that thought, she stopped by the bar's restrooms, checked her makeup, brushed her teeth and then marched upstairs, the whole time ignoring the little voice in the back of her head telling her she definitely wanted sex. Lots of sex. With Trent Green.

. . .

Trent heard Candy's feet on the stairs and quickly made sure everything was in place before opening the door. He caught her on the landing, noticing the flash of surprise before she hid it behind bluster.

"What the hell were you doing up here? I could hear you stomping all over the place. And did I tell you that you could mess with my record player?" she demanded as Trent stood aside, letting her walk past him.

"You didn't say I couldn't." He shrugged, doing his damnedest not to let his eyes drift lower than her collarbones. It was difficult. She was wearing a short little black dress and a pair of scuffed Doc Martens that really did it for him. As did the hair. She'd shaved it again and was wearing the dagger earrings he loved so much.

She'd also put on fresh lipstick—its deep crimson was making him think things that shouldn't be contemplated when there were sensitive young minds like Barney's around.

A new Lana Del Rey song started up and momentarily broke the mood. Trent couldn't be sure, but he thought he caught Candy's eyes widening as she focused on the table.

"I thought you were heating up the food, not putting on a show," she said.

Trent closed the door and crossed his arms over his chest. "It's nothing much," he lied. "I'm just civilized and think good food should be presented in a way that does it justice."

She walked over the table Trent had just spent fifteen minutes fussing over, running her fingers over the crisp white tablecloth and studying the black hand-glazed plates that he'd bought a couple of years ago, but had never used for fear his siblings would end up breaking one.

He felt an acute sense of nervous anticipation as he waited for her to say something. He knew he'd made too much food —the dishes on the table looked more like a jigsaw puzzle than the makings for dinner for two. He had at least five comebacks at the ready in case she snarked, but he hoped he'd see some sign at least that she'd like what he'd done. He was also worried he'd gone overboard with the fat black candles he'd placed on the kitchen counters and on the small TV stand by the bed. He'd picked them up from a boutique on the same street as Dolce Design thinking Candy would like the Goth feel. The same went for the black cloth napkins—

"This is nice. Thanks."

Trent blinked. "Pardon?"

Candy turned to fully face him. "Haven't you ever been complimented before?"

"Yeah. Lots. But not by you. What's the catch?"

"You have to feed me."

"Like, literally?" Trent's mouth curved in a smile. "Because you're the last woman I'd expect to tolerate being spoon-fed."

"The idea of you waiting on me hand and foot has its appeal."

He let out a short burst of relieved laughter. "Then I'd consider it. Are you gonna take a seat or are you just gonna stand there?"

"Are you telling me what to do in my own home?"

"Nope. Just asking you a question, because Barney's gonna report us to Animal Cruelty if we don't start eating and paving the way for leftovers." Trent jerked his head at the dog, who'd trotted over to Candy's side and was now letting out a low, persistent whine.

"Don't push it, dog. Go sit on the bed. Now."

The mutt gave her a doggy glower but trotted over to the bed and curled up into a big, grumbling ball on the covers. Candy gave Barney an exasperated look before pulling out a chair and taking a seat.

"What do I do with all this cutlery?" she asked.

"You've never eaten at a fancy place before?" Trent asked, genuinely surprised.

"You judging me?"

Trent took a seat across from her. "Nope. Just surprised. It's another reminder that I don't really know much about you outside of what I knew at school and this bar." Realizing he'd just left the door open for a whole lot of bad memories, Trent quickly started talking. "Are you asking the question because there's no clear line between starters and mains with everything here on the table?"

"Something like that." Her glare dared him to contradict her.

"Alright, so why don't I tell you what we're eating?" He began taking lids off dishes. Fragrant steam wafted into the air. "For starters, we're having this caprese salad with the mozzarella, the tomato and the fresh basil. I also did up this small antipasto plate. The pickled vegetables are homemade, and the prosciutto has been cured naturally without any sulphides in case you're worrying. I wasn't sure what sort of bread you liked, so I brought two kinds, some sourdough and some rye. They come from the amazing bakery next to my store. And for the mains, we'll be having leg of lamb done Italian-style with roast greens and potatoes dauphine on the side. And just in case you don't like the potatoes, this is polenta done up with a homemade stock and some herbs from my nona's garden."

He tried to gauge Candy's reaction, but she was giving him poker face. He cleared his throat.

"And this here is a red wine and porcini mushroom gravy. It's not all that traditional or even a proper recipe, but I was playing around in the kitchen and liked how it tasted. And for dessert I've done up some fresh strawberries in vanilla sugar and I'll serve them with mascarpone and some hazelnut truffles I made at the store today . . . maybe with a little sprig of mint on top. That okay with you?" He paused, trying to read her face again, but came up blank. "Or if you don't like it—"

"It's fine."

"You okay?" He was relieved when she suddenly became animated again.

"Why wouldn't I be?" she asked, picking up a knife and fork.

He shrugged. "Oh, there's the wine too. I guessed you might drink white from what you'd said, but—"

"White's fine."

"I'll just get it out of the fridge."

Trent got up quickly, retrieving the bottle of oaky Napa chardonnay he'd put an embarrassing amount of thought into before snatching up two wineglasses. He came back to the table, pouring them both a small measure. The whole time he could feel her watching him.

"You gonna say anything, Blume, or are you just gonna watch me wait on you?" he asked, and could have shouted "Hallelujah!" when she visibly shook off whatever was going on in her head and relaxed, giving him a sardonic smile.

"If you're offering." She took the glass and raised it to her lips. "I like the idea of you doing things for me, whenever I want you to. It feels good."

"Yeah?" Trent paused, zeroing in on her crimson lipstick. Damn, this woman was sexy. "What kind of things do you want me to do for you?"

Her eyes dropped to his mouth. "You can kiss me."

"Yeah?" Trent raised his glass to his mouth to prevent himself from launching across the table. "Where?"

"Here." She held out her hand, wiggling her fingers playfully, their multiple rings flashing in the candle light.

Trent took it. Kissing the backs of her knuckles, he used a little bit of tongue to see if she'd react, and stifled a smile when she tutted and pulled her hand back.

"What else?" he asked, suddenly nowhere near hungry for food.

"Here." She pushed her chair back and pointed to her neck. She then looked away and muffled what would have

239

passed as a disinterested yawn if it weren't for the crinkling at the corners of her eyes. Her hand was shaking a little too. She was definitely as turned on as he was and he liked that a lot.

"Alright." He walked around the table, anticipation making his voice gravelly. "You want me in front of you or behind you?"

"In front." She looked at him from below her lashes.

"You're gonna have to move your chair back more," Trent said, feeling like he was going to light up like a torch any minute.

She pushed her chair back enough to make room, making eye contact the entire time. Trent was gratified to see goosebumps ripple over her skin.

Trent gripped the chair on either side of her shoulders before leaning forward and kissing the spot on her neck she'd chosen. He darted his tongue out and tasted her skin, feeling her fast-beating pulse. Leaning back, he checked her expression, wanting nothing more than to rip her dress off and bury himself inside her hard and fast.

Despite having red flags on her cheekbones and taking breaths as heavy as his, she was still managing to pull off the ice queen act.

"Push my dress up," she said.

His hands shook as he pushed her legs apart so he could lean in closer. When his thumbs connected with nothing but bare skin at the vee of her thighs he groaned. "You naked under here?"

She gave him another fake yawn, but he caught the way her breath hitched when he moved his fingers. "Touch me."

Trent moved one hand so that his fingers skimmed whisper-soft skin, moistness. "You all bare down there too? You shaved for me?" he asked. She hadn't been bare last night and he'd loved that, but this, knowing that she'd done this for him left him feeling like he'd won the lottery. Candy Blume wanted him. She'd planned to have sex with him tonight. And that, *this*, was more than he'd ever dreamed.

She gave him a cool look. "Are you waiting for an instruction manual?"

Trent didn't waste any time. Within seconds he was running his fingers over petal-soft folds, daring to dip a finger inside, all the while losing himself a little in her eyes.

Chapter 35

Candy didn't know what the hell she was doing, but it felt so good she didn't care. At first she'd told Trent to kiss her, thinking that she'd do some kind of power-play thing, but by now it was obvious he was the one in control. The way his fingers were moving so confidently over her told her he knew it too.

Still, she let him play as she widened her legs, leaning back in the chair and giving in to the sensation for a while.

It felt good—amazing actually—but not right. She wanted more. She wanted this man to know that she was running this show. She wanted to be the best damn lay he'd ever had so he'd remember her forever. Just those thoughts were enough to spike her pleasure. Her hips undulated with the slow movements of his hands until, finally, it was too much.

In one movement, she pulled her dress over her head, getting a kick out of the way Trent's eyes went to her chest. She didn't have a lot there, but it was more than enough to catch his interest.

"Kiss them while you finger-fuck me, slowly," she ordered, purring when he leaned forward, running his tongue over first one nipple, then the other, his fingers still working, his breath hot on her skin.

Candy lost herself for a long few moments, pure sensation overtaking her body. She could feel it building inside her, the pooling heat so pure and good, but it still wasn't enough.

Abruptly she gripped Trent's hand, holding it still. "Take your pants off, Green."

"Yeah?"

His face showed so much need for her that Candy almost tackled him to the floor.

"Yeah, and sit on that chair." She pointed to the chair he'd abandoned, loving how quickly he pulled off his shirt and unbuttoned his fly. He was just pushing his pants down when Candy got up, every nerve ending in her body feeling languid and supple as she reached for a shopping bag that was still sitting by the table from earlier. By the time she'd opened the box of condoms inside and pulled out a packet, Trent was sitting in the chair, naked. He had an athletic build: broad shoulders, a well-put-together torso and a damn fine penis. It was standing up, happy to see her as she walked towards him. She was still wearing her boots and it felt *good*. She was in control. This moment was *hers*.

She ripped the condom packet open with her teeth.

"Hands by your side, holding the chair," she ordered. "And spread your legs."

She waited until he did what she said, and then slid the condom over him in one smooth movement, feeling the jerk of his cock under her fingers, savoring the hiss of his breath.

Straddling him, she pressed her body against his and brought his head forward to her chest so he could worship first one breast and then the other before she lowered herself, positioning him, then sinking deep.

They both groaned.

It stung a little—it had been a long time—but it felt right.

"Make me come," Candy ordered, barely recognizing her own voice. "Hard."

It took a second for her words to register, and then Trent was all over her, his hands raising and lowering her, grinding their pelvises together, both of them moaning at the contact, both of them moving wildly against each other.

Candy was the first to fly, gripping Trent's shoulders and throwing her head back. She felt the moment he came, his shout filling the room, his body shuddering and his fingers digging into her hips.

They collapsed against each other, Candy's fingers in Trent's hair, holding his head to her shoulder while Trent's breath puffed against her skin.

"Well, that sure was one way to do an appetizer." Trent's voice was a sexy-husky exhalation.

"Count it as my contribution to dinner." Candy inhaled the smell of him: soap, warm man and maybe a hint of chocolate. He felt so good inside her, surrounding her, his hands gentling now on her skin.

He laughed. It was a low, happy sound that shook both their bodies. "If that counts as an entrée, I'd give it five stars in any review, Miz Blume."

"Your contribution wasn't too bad either. Four and half stars." She brushed her lips against his cheek, telling herself it wasn't quite a kiss because that would feel too intimate. But he turned his head so that their lips brushed, and that sent a tingle right to her toes.

"What happened to the extra half?" he asked.

"There's always room for improvement." She leaned back, running her nails down his chest with just enough pressure to leave faint marks. "You still gonna feed me dinner? I'm a hungry woman."

"I can tell." He ran his hands up and down her back before gripping her ass. "You're gonna have to get off me first."

She leaned forward, resting her head against his shoulder. "When I say so."

He kissed the skin just above her ear, his lips brushing over the stubble, sending a fresh shiver over her skin. "That's fine with me."

Chapter 36

"So, I barely know anything about you other than the fact you're as sexy as hell and so smart you intimidated the hell out of me when I was younger," Trent said as he served Candy's main course, the spoon hovering over the polenta. "Want some of this?"

"Mm-hmm." Candy gave him a nod while lounging in her chair like a satisfied cat.

She'd just finished off a piece of bread piled high with prosciutto and pickles, and Trent swore he'd never seen one woman eat with so much gusto. This even though his sister Anna held their family's record for the most burritos eaten in one sitting.

Candy had already demolished the first course and it didn't look like she was stopping any time soon. He liked that. He also liked the way she'd come back from the shower wearing that black dress and nothing else. He wanted her out of it again tonight. But for now he wanted to talk.

"You think you have a right to information just because you got in my pants?" She took a bite of the lamb and paused for a moment. "Damn, this is good. You could sell this on street corners by the ounce, Green."

He grinned. "It's all a part of my evil plan."

"To what? Get me hooked so I have to keep coming back for my fix?" Candy paused with the fork halfway to her mouth, and for a minute, Trent swore he saw a flash of panic before she covered it up with resting bitch face. "Because I should have said this earlier, but I'm not looking for anything more than sex and good food. Don't get any ideas."

Trent shrugged, ignoring the faint twinge of hurt that speared right around where his heart was. "Who says I'm looking for more?"

"Just so you know. I've already been down that road once and I lost ten years of my life. I'm not looking to lose any more time."

"Yeah?" Trent sat back and studied her over his glass of wine. "Doesn't look like your time is being lost right now."

"It's the post-sex glow. Reality's always around the corner." Candy speared another mouthful of food, glancing away.

"What does that reality look like for you? Because mine's pretty good right now and that's distracting me from all the bad. Isn't that how it works? You take a little bit of this"—he spooned potatoes onto his plate—"a little bit of that"—he scooped up some lamb and some green beans— "and then you add some really good stuff"—he poured over the gravy —"and it covers up the mediocre bits. Not that I'm saying my cooking is mediocre. But you get what I mean, right?"

Candy swallowed and quickly forked up more food. "Maybe for some people the gravy *isn't* the good stuff. Maybe the gravy taints everything it touches."

Trent was really feeling that twinge in his chest now. "You saying I'm tainting your life? Because I don't have to be here if I'm making you uncomfortable."

He was relieved to see a flash of remorse as she set her knife and fork down. "That's not what I meant. This might be the gravy for you, but I was talking about different gravy— okay, this metaphor is weird. What I'm trying to say is that my reality involves stuff that makes everything else way more complicated, and it means I can't relax. I can't just *be*. I can't just enjoy life, because I know it's always there."

Trent relaxed a fraction. "So tell me, what's the thing getting in your way? I know I wasn't a happy memory, but I'd like to think that's changed lately."

She looked down at her plate. "Maybe. Can we not talk about this thing? Between us. Because the more we talk about it, the more it makes me wonder if I'm doing something really stupid. I'd just rather be stupid for a while without knowing it." She looked up and shocked Trent with a genuine smile.

He recovered his composure, knowing that if he made too much of a big deal out of it, she'd spook. "Alright. So tell me something that makes you happy."

"I'm gonna be Sophie's maid of honor at her wedding in a year or so."

"Yeah? Who's she marrying?" Trent's shoulders relaxed as he scooped up some more potatoes.

"Ian Buchanan. You might have heard of him—he's a hotshot newspaper editor from London who's taken over the paper in Hopeville, Sophie's hometown. You heard of it?"

He nodded. "Yeah. I source some of my ingredients from there. There's this amazing lavender place. So she's settled out in Hopeville? What does she do there?"

"She runs holiday cottages on her dad's ranch. Which is how she met Ian. When they met he was a total asshole, but he saw the light and I think he's gonna be good for her. Or else."

"Yeah? So what's involved in being a maid of honor? I mean, I've made cakes and chocolates for all kinds of weddings over the years, and it's impossible to be half-Italian, half-Irish without having a whole lot of cousins getting married all the time, but I've never been in a wedding party before."

She tilted her head to the side. "Why not? I mean you had

a bunch of friends in school. Surely some of them have gotten married by now. And that big family of yours must have needed your help once or twice."

"Yeah, I usually get asked to do the cakes and chocolates for free." Trent gave her a rueful smile. "And as for friends from school, I've been to one or two of their weddings as a guest, but I don't keep up with most of them anymore. But we're talking about you. What do you think Sophie's gonna expect from you?"

He caught Candy's flash of uncertainty. "I don't know. My own wedding was held in my mom's backyard with Sophie and me wearing a couple of charity-store dresses. It was fun . . . It was a good day."

"It's good you have happy memories."

"I do. Or I did . . ." She fell silent for a moment, before visibly shaking it off. "But I think Sophie's wedding is gonna be in a totally different ballpark. Ian's friends are all super rich, and I know he's gonna want the absolute best for Sophie whether she likes it or not. And while I know Sophie doesn't want me to be perfect, I want to get it right for her, you know? She's getting better about believing in herself, but I know she'll be worrying about talking too much, when as far as I'm concerned, she can talk as much as she damn likes. If anyone judges her, I'll be the first to take 'em out."

Trent laughed at her fierceness. "Settle down, tiger. I'm not gonna be judging her." He tensed, waiting for her to remind him of his behavior in high school, but she didn't. Instead, she leaned back and gave him a belligerent scowl that he was beginning to find pretty cute.

"Damn straight." She picked up a slice of bread, biting into it.

"Hey, I've got a question."

"What?"

"Why didn't you go to college? I mean, you were smart

enough to get any scholarship you wanted, and I always pictured you as a doctor or lawyer, but . . ."

"But I'm running a bar instead? Are you trying to insult me?"

"No! No. I guess I just wondered how you came to be running Hard Candy instead of getting a degree."

She shrugged. "It's not that complex. Beau and I wanted to move out of our moms' houses after we got married and we couldn't afford to do that with me in college. So I figured I'd work for a while, he'd work for a while, and then I'd go to college when we had enough money." She took a sip of her wine. "My dad owns a bar in Hong Kong. It's been in my family for three generations, but Dad made it his when he took it over from Grandad Tang. And I guess I liked the idea of continuing the family tradition over here, since I couldn't afford to go visit him. There was this organization for people with business ideas to get funding, so I applied and got the money. Then I borrowed some from my mother-in-law too, and a bank. And Hard Candy was born." She blew out a breath. "And since then it's become my life."

"You've built a family, haven't you?"

"Yeah. But let's not get too sentimental."

Trent knew her well enough now to know that the crinkle at the edge of her eyes meant she was happy. He took a bite of his potatoes, letting Barney's snores from the bed fill the silence. "So, other than helping out with Sophie's wedding, what do you do for fun? What makes you happy?"

"The usual stuff. Walking Barney. Getting out in the sunshine. Spending time with my friends. That's mainly Sophie outside of the bar. Although, I haven't really seen much of her since the divorce because I've been working all the time. Debt sucks." She looked down at the table.

"I remember what that was like," Trent replied. "But you look like you're keeping it together."

He was rewarded with a pleased look. "Yeah. I am. The money from your brother's party paid off the last of it."

Trent smiled. "Should we toast to that?" He raised his wineglass.

"Why not?"

"To hard work paying off," Trent said. "And to you for kicking the walls down. You're something else, Candy Blume."

"Damn straight." Candy clinked her glass against his, and in that moment Trent felt something shift between them.

"Mind if I ask you a what-if question?" he asked. "It's kind of a stupid thing."

She shrugged. "Yeah, why not?"

"What would you do if you had a million bucks, right now?"

Candy took a sip of her wine, giving him a catlike smile. "You offering to pay me for that huge orgasm you just had? Because you're welcome, and I accept money from all banks, in all currencies."

Trent let out a bark of laughter. "It was something. Would you accept dessert instead?"

"I might. What is it?"

"Orange cake. It's a family recipe and one of the best cakes you'll ever try."

"Oh really? In that case I'll take it. But if you keep paying me in cakes, I'm gonna have to watch my waistline."

Trent felt his internal temperate go up a couple of degrees. "Does that mean you intend on giving me more orgasms?"

She set her wineglass down and stretched her arms languidly over her head. "I might let you have one or two, as long as I'm satisfied with your performance."

"Want to be satisfied now?"

Her gaze turned eagle-sharp. "Why not? We'll call it a pre-dessert appetizer."

Chapter 37

Much later, as early morning noises drifted through Candy's apartment's closed windows and Barney's snores filled the room, Trent studied the ceiling, feeling both wired and more content than he had been in possibly forever.

He was happy. And he had a hunch Candy was too, if the single kiss she'd pressed to his heart after the last time they'd had sex was any indication. The way she was curled around him was pretty nice too. He glanced at her head resting on his shoulder. Who would have known that Candy Blume was a snuggler? And who would have known a couple of weeks ago that he'd find himself here in her bed?

It felt good that she trusted him enough to be with him like this. He didn't want to read a whole lot into it, but he wanted more. He wanted to know more about her. He wanted to spend more time with her. Their different schedules were playing hell with his sleep, but he just didn't care. He'd do whatever he could to keep this going. It felt too good to lose.

"You still awake?" Candy's sleepy murmur snapped him out of his thoughts.

He kissed the top of her head. "Yeah."

"Idiot." She nuzzled her nose against his skin. "Remember

your question, about what I'd do if I had a million bucks? I was just thinking about it."

"Do you often snore while thinking?" Trent asked, earning a half-hearted swat.

"I was thinking that I'd fly to see my dad. I've never been to Hong Kong. That'd be cool. I was dreaming of seeing him and meeting my grandparents for the first time in real life. It'd be nice, you know. To get in touch with my culture. Maybe feel like I belong. Always wanted to know what that felt like."

They fell into silence. Moments later, the sound of Candy's low, deep breathing filled the air, while Trent was left staring at the ceiling again, this time wondering how a few simple words had left him feeling like his heart was too big for his chest.

Candy poked Trent in the ribs. He was sprawled on his back, taking up most of her bed and looking way too hot for seven in the morning. There was a trace of black stubble on his jaw and his already curly hair was boyishly disheveled. She liked that, and right now she couldn't get too worked up analyzing the feeling. Having nine or so spectacular orgasms in the space of twenty-four hours did that to a woman.

He opened his eyes, giving her a slow smile while running a hand over her thigh. "Mornin'. You okay?"

She shrugged. "I might be. Although, if this good mood wears off any time soon, I'll know some of those orgasms you gave me were fake."

Trent's body shook with silent laughter. "Did I just hear you compliment me, Blume? Is that what just happened?"

She ran her finger around his navel a couple of times because it was there and because she wanted to. And then she followed the faint trail of hair from there down to the top of the sheet. "It might have. You gonna take me for breakfast?"

"Hmm." Trent pulled her down against his chest, nuzzling the stubble on her head. "You thinking about food again?"

Candy gave him a bite that caused him to yelp. "If you're making it . . . or buying it."

Trent ran his hands down her back, settling her more comfortably against him. "And what are you gonna give me in return for this feast?"

"The chance to live another day?" Candy nipped him again, this time darting her tongue out to soothe the mark. "So, about breakfast . . . Barney needs to go for another walk sometime soon and I'm in the mood to get out of the bar."

"Interesting terms and conditions. I think we're gonna need some more negotiation." In a quick movement, Trent rolled her over, nuzzling his nose against her collarbone while Candy wiggled to make more room for him, feeling happiness as a radiating thing circulating through her veins. It would wear off soon and things would go weird—they always did—but for now she was going to grasp this thing with both hands.

She poked him in the ribs, causing him to yelp and start laughing. "Start negotiating, Green. Aim for win-win, but if you can't manage that, I better come out on top."

"Yes ma'am."

Chapter 38

Candy and Trent had just walked downstairs, Barney trotting along ahead with his lead in his mouth, when there came a very persistent knock on the bar's back door.

"You got any orders coming in this morning?" Trent asked.

"Nope." Candy gnawed on the inside of her lip while going through a list of who it could be. If Marlene was working her normal shift, she'd still be at work. Kevin wasn't coming in today because of whatever meetings he had, and Sophie always called ahead just in case Candy was sleeping. Which left Beau or—

"Oh no!" She slapped a palm over her face.

"What? What's the problem?" Trent looked at the beer keg Candy had propped against the back door again last night. "Is there something I can help you with?" he asked just as Candy's phone started to buzz. She pulled it out, looked at it and sighed.

"Yep. You can help me lots. Whatever you do, don't accept invitations to anything, okay? I don't know if this current phase she's going through involves men too."

She ignored Trent's confused exclamation and strode to

the door, maneuvering the beer keg to the side, grimly thinking that if there was ever a litmus test for this short-term thing she and Trent had going, it was meeting her mom.

"Hey baby!" Pam exclaimed the minute the door opened.

Candy barely had time to react before she was pulled into a hug that smooshed her face against her mom's shoulder while the familiar scent of liberally applied geranium oil barraged her nostrils. And then just as quickly, Pam let her go to bend down and greet Barney, her green hemp dress pooling on the floor.

"And how's my handsome man? Are you handsome? Yes you are. I brought you some tofu snacks. I soaked them in mushroom stock before I dehydrated them." Pam rustled around in her bright blue handbag for a moment before pulling out a paper bag that smelled like feet and contained something closely resembling a mummified mouse.

Barney snapped the treat up with his usual enthusiasm, but it was all downhill from there. Candy watched him, silently commiserating while Pam looked confused.

"Maybe he's allergic to mushrooms," Pam said. "I've never seen him spit food out before."

"There's a first for everything." Candy knew she had to get this out of the way. "Trent, this is my mom. Mom, this is Trent, and before you ask, yes, he stayed the night, no, he doesn't want his palm read, yes, he and I were just going somewhere, and no, he wasn't a Franciscan monk in a past life."

"Pleased to meet you, ma'am." Trent held out his hand after darting a confused look at Candy.

Candy didn't have time to warn him before Pam threw her arms around Trent and pulled him into a hug that Candy knew from experience was cutting off vital oxygen.

"I'm so happy to meet you!" Pam exclaimed. "It's such a relief to know that Candy is moving on from the negative energy that's been surrounding her lately. I can just feel you are a step towards the positive. You're so *strong* and *virile!*"

"Mmph!"

"Mom, if you don't let him go I'm gonna call emergency services to bring in the jaws of life." Candy rolled her eyes.

Pam let Trent go before shooting Candy an aggrieved look. "You don't need to overreact. I'm a hugger. Always have been." She patted Trent's chest. "You're alright, aren't you, Trent? I put some extra-strong healing into my touch, so if you're feeling that any aches and pains have gone, that's from me."

Candy took in Trent's horrified bemusement and knew she definitely must have done *some* forgiving in the past couple of weeks, because her first impulse was to rescue him.

"You feeling relief from any aches and pains, Green?" she asked.

Pam was wearing the expectant smile she always wore when she wanted someone to tell her that she'd done a good job.

"I might be?" he tried.

Pam rounded on Candy, her eyes shiny with triumph. "See! I told you! These powers of mine are getting so much stronger. You said you were going to breakfast? Why don't I come too? It's gonna have to be somewhere that does brown-only food, but there's that place a block over that's mainly all beans and burgers. I like their beans. Do you like beans, Trent?" Pam held up a hand, turning to Candy. "But we can't go until I've done what I came to do." She took one of Candy's hands, holding it to her generous chest and turning suddenly serious. "I owe you an apology, honey. You came to me asking for advice the other day, and I realized I could have done so much more to support you. I was just distracted from the cosmic energy of all those orgasms and—"

"Excuse me?" Trent interjected.

"Don't ask, and she won't tell," Candy said quickly.

"Mom, you don't need to apologize. I understand that you were distracted, and just in case you're thinking of doing something to make it up to me—"

"I am!" Pam explained. "Which is why I brought along my feng shui book!" Pam fished in the bag slung over her shoulder and produced an intimidatingly thick tome.

"Don't," Candy finished, but she was too late. Pam had let her hand go and had marched past her into Hard Candy.

Candy groaned just as Barney braved the anti-dog treat again. He made a gagging sound and spat it out with a whine.

"Candy?" Trent said, with the air of a man who has *seen* things.

She patted him on the chest. "You can leave if you want. This is gonna get weird."

He glanced over his shoulder when Pam called out something about negative energy needing shifting. "I think it's already gotten weird. That's your *mom?*"

Candy set her shoulders back. "Yup. You have anything to say to me about it?"

He shook his head slowly. "Wouldn't dream of it. It's just that she's—"

"Honey, can you help me?" Pam's voice filtered in from the direction of the bar. "I think we should hang a few of these mirrors I brought around the place so they reflect negative energy out the door. According to the book, there shouldn't be any sharp corners, but there are a whole lot of those in here. So I'm thinking that you can hang some streamers or something to break up the bad stuff."

"She's my mom," Candy finished Trent's sentence, speaking in a low voice. "And if you're gonna stick around, I need you to be respectful. She sometimes has . . . inventive ideas, but she's a good person with a big heart and I don't want her feelings hurt. Barney, you've tried it two times already. Leave the damn tofu alone!" she said when Barney made yet more choking sounds that were soon drowned out by Pam's voice, more strident now.

"And I think we're gonna have to paint this booth thing again. I thought the pink would be better than the blue, but that was all before I got this book; it's saying that pink *isn't* such a good color in a space like this. And we need something to represent fish because they encourage creativity. Maybe I could paint some fish on it, or at least some seaweed, you know? That show, *Doctor Who*, had fish people in it, didn't it? It would still work."

Candy gave Trent one last warning look before she stalked past him. "Mom, leave the damn TARDIS alone. I let you paint it pink before, but the agreement was that you couldn't do anything else."

Candy found Pam standing with her hands on her hips, sucking air through her teeth. "I don't know, honey. Can I at least remove this silly list of rules you've got up here? It's so *negative*."

"Touch those rules and I'm gonna sabotage your new solar panels," Candy said in a low voice.

"But—"

"Step away from the TARDIS, mother, or your new orgasmic business is gonna blow another fuse." Candy ignored the snort of muffled laughter coming from behind her. Obviously Trent had gotten over his shock.

Candy's mom was only momentarily stymied, then her eyes lit on the cogwork sculpture at the back of the room. "And that thing is so *industrial*. There aren't enough curves to counteract the masculine feel. Maybe if we attached a mirror to one of the cogs? It would then rotate, turning any negative energy into positive—like a tap turning on! Or we could change the light behind it to something more tranquil. Don't get me wrong, the blue bulbs create a watery feel, which is what this book says you need, but if they were yellow, it would better reflect the sun's healing powers. And I don't think you've got enough of that in here."

Candy looked up at the ceiling. "Mom! I get that you're trying to make me feel better, but I need you to leave the bar alone. If you wanted to apologize, why didn't you just bring me flowers?" The words escaped before she could stop them.

Pam gave her a disappointed frown. "You know I stopped studying herbalism when I learned that flowers scream when you cut them. I couldn't bring wailing plant corpses into your place. No, I think feng shui is much more positive. If we put a few mirrors here and there, maybe the problems you've been having with Beau and money would just be reflected out of your life. You can't tell me that some of my healing energy hasn't worked, not when I've found you this morning in the company of a man with such positive, *virile* energy. I've been telling you for years that you need to embrace your sexual side—"

"Mom! Boundaries, dammit!" Candy's shout filled the room as she felt a flush of mortification to a degree she hadn't experienced since she was in high school. Except, unlike back then, Trent didn't make fun of her. He came to her rescue.

He cleared his throat. "Ma'am?"

Candy's mom spun around, a small hexagonal mirror gripped in one hand and *Feng Shui for Beginners* in the other. "Call me Pam."

"Pam. I think what you propose is a kind and generous idea"—he ignored Candy's snort— "and I've got a little handyman experience. So why don't you tell me where you think those mirrors should go and leave them with me? I'll take care of it."

Candy's mom gave him a grin that matched the power of the sun. "That sounds like a great idea!" Her expression turned smug. "You should keep this one, honey. He under-stands the important things in life."

"Yeah, I can see that," Candy said wryly.

Trent gave Pam a solemn look that didn't fool Candy one bit. She could see the way his eyes danced with laughter. "And there is nothing I'd love more than you coming to breakfast with us, so we can get to know each other better, ma'am. But Candy kind of made me promise to take her somewhere romantic this morning, it being our first night together . . ."

He left the words hanging as Candy spluttered, wondering if she'd inherited enough of her mom's magical energies to strangle a man with her thoughts.

"Oh, I completely understand!" Pam crossed the room to pull Candy into another unexpected hug. "I *understand.* I knew when I woke up this morning that the universe was telling me that I needed to come see you, baby. I just didn't realize it was to give you my blessing. This man was obviously sent to you at the right time and for that I send my thanks to the Council of Goddesses."

Candy's first impulse was to tell her mom that Trent was the same guy who'd made her miserable in high school, but then she realized that she didn't want to. For one thing, Pam had always argued that Candy needed to wear brighter colors to ward off the attention of the bullies. And for another thing, it would be a bitchy thing to bring up when Trent was going to all this trouble to rescue her. So instead she pulled back and gave her mom a tight smile.

"You couldn't be more right about that. Thanks for visiting, Mom. Why don't y'all just leave your feng shui stuff with Trent and I'll see you later this week."

"Sure thing." Pam bustled over to Trent, handing him the book, the mirrors and a whole lot of instructions. Then, with one last hurt look at Barney, who had decided to sit on his treat so he could pretend it didn't exist, she whisked out the door.

Candy and Trent stood in silence, listening to the sound of Pam's car backfiring a couple of times before she drove away.

"So . . . that was your mom." Trent's mouth twitched.

"She's, ah, interesting. I really felt the energy. In fact, she had a *lot* of energy." His shoulders were shaking now with suppressed mirth.

"Don't you dare!" Candy pointed a finger at him. "No laughing! Just because she's a little different and she thinks that—"

"I have *virile* masculine energy?" Trent asked with raised brows.

Candy burst into a cackling laugh. "Oh Lord. Take me to breakfast, Green. If that didn't scare you off, I think I'll keep you around a little longer. Just to see what she does when she sees you haven't hung up those mirrors."

He put his hands on his hips. "You setting me up, Blume?"

"Hell yes! Because I haven't laughed like that for years." Candy walked forward and impulsively wrapped her arms around his waist. "I'm beginning to think you're good for something."

He kissed her on the forehead. "I try. Now let's get you some food while you're being nice."

Chapter 39

"Want to come hiking with me one day, Blume? I haven't done it for years, and I was thinking I'd like to go on one with you. I figure you'd scare all the critters away with that death glare of yours."

Candy gestured for Trent to hold that thought while she made a couple of martinis for a unicorn and another kind of horse creature who were cheerfully chatting with someone dressed like Sonic the Hedgehog with a tail. The tail was a problem. Since the person was new, Candy would pull them aside and politely explain the no long tail rule later, but until then, she had to trust her Furry Night regulars not to trip over it and hurt themselves.

"When?" Candy asked as she took the unicorn's money and leaned on the bar in front of Trent. He'd come in early tonight, bringing a big dish of lasagne and box of cherries dipped in chocolate. He'd also brought along some coconut truffles for Kevin, who was currently caught up in a conversation with Libby, librarian by day, busty sheep creature by night. She could only communicate through messaging because her costume's headpiece got in the way of real talking, but Kevin was typing replies on his phone with a smile on his face. They were no doubt talking books, because they always talked books.

"We could go for a hike next Sunday morning, maybe?" Trent said, playing with the handle of his coffee cup. "I have the whole day off, and I know you don't open until twelve, so if we left at around seven or so, we could walk for a couple of hours, have brunch somewhere nice, and then I'll bring you back here in time for opening. We could bring Barney too so he can feel like a country dog for a while. He'd probably like to get in touch with his inner man-eating wolf for a few hours." Trent gave Barney an affectionate smile. The dog was curled up under the coffee machine wearing the set of bunny ears someone had given him earlier in the evening.

"Yeah?" Candy nibbled on one of her fingernails. Going out meant something. It felt bigger than spending the last few nights wrapped around Trent in her small bed and grabbing breakfast before Trent left for work. Going for a hike was something couples did. It involved planning. And it meant more complications in her already complicated life.

Beau had his NA meeting tonight and she'd received an avalanche of messages from Marlene, all of which she'd ignored. With Trent here, she was a little less worried about bad things happening if Beau turned up, but she'd be lying if she said she'd gotten much sleep last night. Instead she'd lain curled up against Trent's chest, going through what-if scenarios. The bomb was going to drop tonight, she just didn't know what form it would take. She was dreading the judgement on Trent's face when he realized how complicated her life really was.

"Or we could just hang out here with your crazy crowd like always." Trent looked around with a bemused grin, oblivious to Candy's thoughts. "If anyone had told me a month ago that there were a bunch of people who liked to dress up in fur suits and hang out, I wouldn't have believed them, but now that I'm here and seeing it, it feels normal."

"Normal is relative." Candy relaxed a little. "Most people use themselves as a benchmark for normal, but if they looked at themselves closely, they'd realize they've got a whole lot of weird tics and habits. We all do. The saner people are the ones who accept who they are."

"Is that philosophy I'm hearing?" Trent asked after Candy had taken another order.

"Is that sarcasm I'm hearing?" she asked as she poured a Kahlua for a fluffy green dragon, adding a recyclable straw so they could drink it through the hole in their suit.

"Call it bone-deep surprise."

"Nice to know I keep you on your toes . . . and on your back." They shared a smoldering look before the sound of Candy's name being spoken in a teary, high-pitched voice rang out over the music.

Candy spun around. It wasn't hard to spot Marlene weaving through what was now an audience rather than a group of cheerfully chatting patrons. Candy's mind was already working through the hundred or so strategies she'd devised to deal with a situation like this. The problem was that she couldn't think properly with all the adrenaline telling her to *run*. All she knew was that she had a full bar of people here and that this scene was about to be public.

"What's going on and how can I help?" Trent's voice jarred Candy out of her panicked thought-spiral.

"Beau's mom," Candy said, knowing she should explain, but not knowing what else to say.

"You okay?" Trent asked.

"No. I've just got to *think*," Candy said in a low voice.

Marlene was almost at the bar now. She was wearing faded jeans and a plaid shirt, and her hair was pulled into a tight ponytail that made her face look even more careworn. Her eyes were bloodshot, and Candy recognized all the signs of someone who hadn't slept for a long time. Tired meant unreasonable. Unreasonable meant a scene. If Marlene made a scene, Candy had to come up with a way to make everyone in the room okay with what was happening. She couldn't have *this* messing with her work, her people—

"Can I help you, ma'am?"

Candy watched, stunned, as Trent stood up and put himself between Marlene and Candy.

"No." Marlene clutched her handbag, barely sparing him a glance; her attention was focused solely on Candy, who suddenly felt like throwing up.

Marlene raised a shaking hand, chopping it through the air. "You lied to me! You weren't going to come tonight, were you?"

Candy shook her head, bracing her hands on the bar to stop them shaking. "No, Marlene, I never said I was going to come. I need you to leave."

Marlene reeled back as if Candy's words had physically harmed her. "Not even after I asked you? Not even after I told you what it would mean to *me*? Are you that heartless? Did all those years mean nothing to you?"

In her peripheral vision, Candy could see people fidgeting uncomfortably. This was untenable. Hard Candy was a place where people could escape their everyday problems. Candy had worked for years to get it right; she'd designed the Rules so that everyone could feel safe and protected—protected from something like *this*. And now, the sight of people shifting uncomfortably, some of them starting to take off their costumes and leave, made her feel like angry crying. This was so wrong.

She schooled her voice and expression towards as much calmness as she could. "Marlene, if you have something to say, I'd prefer you say it to me in private. This is not the time or the place."

Marlene made another chopping motion through the air. "Why? So you can brush me off? So you can pretend that *you* didn't cause the troubles I have to live with every day? Seeing how heartless you are right now, how little you care, is finally showing me the real you, Candy Blume. No wonder my son needed to start medicating himself with narcotics! You drove him to it."

"You don't mean that. If you'll just come with me and talk about this—"

Marlene burst into angry tears, her frail body shaking as her words came out too loud, filling up too much of the space around her.

"And you won't come tonight for what? For *what?* This? These people? Beau is going to *die* if you don't support him, and all you can think of is people who wear stupid costumes? Shame on you!"

A flash of pure fury rocketed through Candy's system. She might take crap herself, but never about her people. "Yes, Marlene. I'm thinking of these people because they're my friends and customers. I won't have you shooting off your mouth about them. Now I'm gonna ask you again—please leave before I make you leave."

The bar fell completely quiet except for the incongruously happy playlist Candy had lined up for the night. As Candy took in the discomfort on the faces of her patrons who weren't wearing their headgear, she felt like something had been broken. This felt so, so wrong and it was her fault. She had to make this stop, but she didn't know how—

"Ma'am. Do you need a tissue?" Trent's softly spoken question broke through the silence.

Marlene turned on him, surprise and incredulity warring with anger. "A *tissue?* What? Why?"

Trent reached over the bar and retrieved a tissue from the box by Candy's hip. "Here."

Marlene snatched it out of his hands. Rubbing at her eyes. "Candy, if you don't—"

"Do you need a glass of water too? It looks like you've had

a rough time of it," Trent said gently, overriding whatever Marlene was about to say.

Marlene's face showed real irritation now. "Yes, I have, but I don't have *time* for water. I have twenty minutes to make sure she comes to the meeting. If she doesn't, Beau won't come. He hasn't been home for a week now. No one's seen him or heard from him. I don't know what he's doing or where he is, but I know that if I get her there, he'll see that he's *supported*."

"Excuse me for asking, but how do you know he'll be at this meeting if you haven't seen him for a week? Is he missing? Have you contacted the police?"

Marlene's mouth started to tremble. "The police?"

"If he's been missing. It's probably a good start. Want me to help you call them now?"

Marlene looked at Trent with wild eyes. "Who are you?"

"Just someone who can see you might need some help right now." Trent pulled his phone from his pocket. "Now, if I dial the number, do you want to talk to them? Or do you want to give me details so I can?"

"Details?"

"Yeah. Why don't we go have a talk about this somewhere less noisy?" Trent said, completely ignoring the fact that almost no one was speaking. He stood up and pointed to the bar's entrance. "There's a Cajun place next door where I can buy you a coffee. We'll have enough quiet there to give the police the right details. They might need you to go down the station to fill in some forms too. If he's been missing for a week, you should definitely report it to someone."

Candy saw the minute reality hit Marlene, the minute Marlene started to buckle. Marlene's voice shook as she answered Trent, her voice heartbreakingly small as she wrapped her arms around herself as though to hold it all in. "But I thought that if Candy came, maybe he'd come to the meeting and see her there and—"

"But he's got no way of knowing she'll be there if you

haven't been in contact with him, and I bet there are an awful lot of NA meetings held on different nights in this city. You've got no way of knowing which one he'd go to." Trent's voice contained just enough firmness to sink in. "Now come with me and we'll start seeing about making sure your son is found. I used to know Beau in high school and he was a good man then. And if he's got any of that man still in him, I'm sure he'll realize that it's wrong to worry his mom like this."

Within a matter of seconds Trent was leading Marlene from the bar, sparing a concerned look at Candy, who was unable to do more than give him a short shake of her head to tell him she couldn't take any sympathy right now.

The door closed and someone coughed.

Candy met Kevin's eyes.

"Well, that was awkward," he said. "I'm glad Trent made her leave because that was a definite infraction of Rule Nine."

"Yeah, it was." Candy rallied enough to glare at everyone for appearances. "No talking about my personal life, got it?" She waited for a couple of nods before clapping her hands together. "Great. Now let's get back to being the weirdos we all love to be. Anyone who wants a free drink better get their asses to the bar in the next five minutes."

With that the entire bar erupted in a cheer. Soon, everything was back to normal. Whenever the odd person came up to see if Candy was okay, she'd tell them that if they didn't go back to having a good time she was gonna have to enforce Rule Nine.

And in between serving people, she kept her eye on the door, torn between wanting to go outside to see if Trent was alright, and being too scared at what he'd say when he returned.

Chapter 40

Trent stood outside Hard Candy, listening to the uptempo song coming from the laundromat's jukebox and feeling the weight of everything he'd just learned.

Five hours had passed since he'd left the bar. He'd taken Marlene Lineman to the nearest police station and helped her file a missing persons report because she'd been too shaken up to hold a pen properly. Then he'd driven her home to a tiny run-down house in a suburb he'd never visited. Despite the desperate cleanliness inside, it had smelled of antiseptic and mildew.

He'd always seen what his family had gone through as a struggle, but standing in Marlene's house, seeing the sparse, worn furniture, hearing even a bit of her story, Trent realized how privileged he and his family really was. Yeah, at times he'd felt like he was drowning while working to keep his family's well-furnished house in an upmarket suburb, but he had never been in a situation like Marlene's: working in a factory job with no education, no promotion prospects, no health insurance and no foreseeable means to dig herself out of the hole her son had thrown her into.

When Marlene had first made a scene in the bar, all Trent

had been able to think of was rescuing Candy, but now he got Marlene's desperation. He also got some of Candy's wariness. It hadn't taken much time with Marlene for Trent to get a picture of what Candy's marriage had involved once Beau got himself hooked on drugs. Candy was fiercely loyal to the people she cared about, and just as stubborn as her ex-mother-in-law. She would have done everything she could have to keep Beau afloat, which meant it must have taken something really bad for her to cut him loose. Trent just hoped that Beau had gone somewhere to clean the hell up.

Trent also hoped the money he'd left Marlene for groceries wasn't going to go to Beau's dealer. She hadn't asked for it, but seeing her going through empty cupboards and a bare fridge to offer him something to eat—her southern hospitality working on desperate autopilot—had left Trent feeling like he had no option but to help.

He scanned the street one last time and knocked on Hard Candy's door.

It opened almost immediately. Candy was standing on the other side. The lights had been mostly turned off and her face was in shadow.

"Hey," he said. "You okay?"

She looked away. "Okay enough. I thought you'd gone home. I just got back from walking Barney."

Trent's first response was to say something about whether that was safe with Beau still somewhere out there, but instead he nodded. "Mind if I have a drink?"

"Yeah. Bourbon?"

"Whatever. Just something to take the edge off."

He watched her walk over to the bar, noting her stiff movements and impassive expression; it was the same body language she'd worn when he'd first come here with his mangled apology.

He cleared his throat, hoping to hell he could say the right words this time. "Hey, just in case you think I'm gonna judge you for what happened tonight, I'm not. You're a strong woman and I admire you for how you handled it. You stuck up for your people and you didn't lose control. You're a good person."

He instantly regretted speaking when Candy stopped walking, her back to him. He was about to apologize when he realized her shoulders were shaking.

"Candy? I'm sorry, maybe that wasn't what you wanted to hear. I'd have gotten back sooner if I could have, but things took a while." He quickly closed the distance, putting his hands on her shoulders. "Hey . . ."

He felt, rather than heard, the sob go through her body. He barely had time to react before Candy turned around and slammed herself against his chest, wrapping herself around him as the room was filled with sound of the kind of tears that came from a lot of deep-down hurt.

Tears coming to his own eyes, Trent held her tightly until the storm was over, wondering how such a small body could hold so much sadness without falling completely apart.

"Hey, it's okay. I've got you. I've got you," Trent said over and over again. After what could have been minutes or hours —he didn't know or care—the storm abated from sobs to sniffles, and Candy pulled back enough for him to see her tear-ravaged face.

"Feel better?" he asked, gently swiping at the wetness on her cheek with the back of his hand.

"You tell anyone about this, I'll murder you," she said with a small sobbing hiccup, swiping at her nose and giving him a waterlogged glare as her arms stayed firmly wrapped around him. The strength he saw in her face made him feel like his heart was breaking and being put together all over again.

"Yeah?" he said softly. "No one'd believe me, and isn't there a rule forbidding talking to anyone about your personal life?" He inclined his head towards the TARDIS.

"Rule Nine."

"Yeah, so I wouldn't want to do that. I kind of like it here. I kind of like you." Trent kissed her forehead.

She swiped a hand over her eyes. "You're just being nice to be mean to me. You know I can't handle it."

Trent let out a burst of laugher. "Yeah, I'm the worst—downright evil. In fact, I'm gonna be so mean to you that I'm gonna take you upstairs and we're gonna have a shower together and then we're gonna go to bed. Sound like a masterful evil plan to you?"

She darted a look into his eyes. "Yeah. You're not gonna leave now you've seen me cry? Because I wasn't really crying, it was just water leaking from my eyes. My eyeballs were dry."

There was something in her voice that told him she wasn't just talking about him staying the night. He nodded solemnly. "I hear that a large percentage of this country suffers from eyeball dryness. It's a good thing you were able to fix the problem."

"Damn straight. I'm an independent woman who doesn't need anyone." Her jaw jutted out and Trent had never wanted to kiss a woman more.

"You are, but tonight you're gonna let me take care of you." He ran his hand up and down her back. "And if you want to share a little of what the heck caused this difficulty you've had with eyeball dryness, I'm a good listener."

Chapter 41

"Beau tried to rape Sophie."

Candy said the words as soon as Trent stepped into the shower with her. She was already under the water, sitting on the shower floor with her back against the tiles, watching him undress in the small space with half-closed eyes.

"Yeah?" Trent settled himself on the floor next to her, gesturing for her to sit in the vee of his thighs. It didn't take a lot of convincing before she did.

"She'd gotten him a job working on her brother Hank's ranch. At the time he had me convinced that Marlene was having mental health issues and was racking up a bunch of credit-card debt that he'd had to pay off. We were behind on the rent on our small house, and we saw him taking the job on Sophie's family ranch as a lifeline. I just didn't know that the reason we needed the lifeline was Beau's drug addiction."

"What happened?" Trent asked, already guessing the answer, but not feeling too happy when he heard it.

"One night Beau attacked Sophie, and then he tried to blackmail her afterwards so she wouldn't tell anyone, including me. By the time I found out, his dealer had already turned up and taken almost everything in our house. I had to sell the rest to pay off all the credit-card debt. And then there were the debts that weren't exactly legal. Beau had managed to borrow a whole lot of money from his dealer. I barely managed to stop the guy from taking Barney and all the stuff in the bar." Candy swiped a hand over her eyes. "Hearing what Beau'd done to Sophie destroyed me. She means more to me than anyone other than my dad. I love my mom, I love her so much, and I appreciate everything she did raising me as a single mom when she was only twenty-one, but she's never gotten it. She's always been like that. It's just her way. And I know that she loves me more than anything, but . . . it's complicated."

Trent rested his chin on top of her head. "Yeah, I could see that. Sophie's always been there for you. She's like family without all the drama."

"Yeah. And I was the one who pushed Beau to take that job, stupidly thinking it'd help fix our marriage. He'd been depressed for a while, and we hadn't had sex for a long time . . . I figured that it was my fault at first, but after a while I thought it was because he missed his job on the rigs. I didn't realize that job was behind all our problems. So stupid. I was so stupid. It took me years to work it out." Candy turned her head to meet Trent's gaze. "Can you believe it?"

He kissed her temple. "Yeah. I can. Sometimes when you're working hard, you don't have time to notice all the small things. I've seen it in my own family. Dad did the same thing to us. Left us with a whole lot of debt after managing to hide it from everyone. You can't blame yourself for it."

Candy settled against him more comfortably under the water's spray, her naked body slipping against his. "But you'd blame yourself if you were in my situation."

Trent paused. "Yeah. I would. But that's because I have an overdeveloped sense of responsibility."

Candy let out a short burst of laughter. "That something a shrink told you?"

"Yup." He nodded, smiling. "But that doesn't mean it's not true. Does Sophie blame you for what happened?"

"No."

"Then you shouldn't blame yourself. Sometimes people are just assholes. Take it from someone who used to be one," he said.

"You're not so bad now."

"Was that another compliment?"

He was gratified to feel Candy's body shaking with another burst of laughter. "Maybe."

"No, that's not good enough. I want to know if the hard-ass Candy Blume just outright admitted she complimented me, because this might be the only time ever!"

As Trent said the words he started running his hands over Candy's bare skin, seeking out the bits that he knew were ticklish and copping a feel along the way. It was only when she was howling with laughter and had turned around to straddle him that he stopped.

"Hey," he said as she settled herself down on his lap.

"Hey." She leaned forward for an open-mouthed, toe-curling kiss.

"Want to make out?" he asked, running his hands down to her backside and lifting her enough that she was almost sinking down on top of him, groaning when she did.

"Yeah." She raised herself and sunk down again. "Make me forget everything, Trent."

Pulling her head down for another one of those kisses, his other hand guiding her on him, Trent tried his best to do precisely that.

Chapter 42

Candy was nervous.

She scanned the street as she got out of her car, making sure the window was wound down enough for Barney who was lounging in the back seat. She then took in the designer fashion stores, antique stores, cafés and the gourmet bakery right next to Trent's patisserie. When she studied the front of Trent's shop, her stomach did a flip-flop.

She'd known that Trent's business would be fancy if he'd managed to keep his family's Rollingwood home, but she hadn't expected it to be this fancy. Gold cursive spelled out the store's name across the spotlessly clean windows, and through them she could see beautifully lit displays of cakes and cupcakes that looked too sophisticated to be edible. There was even a sofa in the middle of the store. Who ever heard of a cake store with a sofa? Especially a fancy red one.

She braced herself and pushed the door open.

"Can I help you, ma'am?" asked a tall, slender woman resembling Halle Berry. The woman's makeup was perfect, her hair was pulled back in a slick ponytail, and her crisp white shirt and a dark green pencil skirt looked like something Marlene Dietrich would have felt right at home in.

In that moment, she was acutely aware of her simple black camisole, faded black jeans and worn Doc Martens. She was wearing the dagger earrings she knew Trent liked and had put on some crimson lipstick, too, but right now she felt more like an extra in a B-movie than the Hollywood vamp she'd been going for.

"Is Trent here?" she asked. The woman's name tag said "Taryn."

"Yes, may I ask your name?"

"Tell him it's Candy."

"Alright, just give me a minute."

As Taryn walked through a gold-painted door at the back of the room. Candy wondered what the hell had possessed her to surprise Trent instead of calling and telling him to meet her out front.

She studied the rest of the store to quiet the anxiety, hating that she was feeling this way. There was a display of gold-speckled truffles that seemed more like works of art than edible chocolates, and behind that was a large glass case where a four-tier wedding cake was done up with a profusion of real-istic-looking pink orchids. Trent had made that. He'd said someone had paid a fortune then cancelled at the last minute because the groom had gotten cold feet.

The door behind Candy opened again and Trent walked through. His curly hair boyishly flopped over his forehead and he had a streak of flour on his cheek, but what she noticed the most was his concern. "Candy? Hey, what are you doing here? You okay?"

"Yeah." She shifted from one foot to the other, glancing at Taryn who was now standing by the truffle counter pretending not to be listening. "Do you have some time free?"

He frowned. "Why? Has something happened?"

"No. Just . . . just tell me if you've got some time free, or I'm leaving." She heard the sharpness in her own words and gave him a belligerent scowl. "I'm trying to do something nice to thank you for last night, okay?" She ignored the quickly concealed smile on Taryn's face. "I brought you lunch."

Trent crossed his arms over his chest, his mouth suddenly curving into a wide grin. "Did you make it yourself?"

"Hell no. I bought it, and it was expensive, so you better freakin' enjoy it. I figured we could maybe go eat it down by the river, or in a park or something. So tell me if you're free or Barney's gonna be my date today."

"Give me a minute." Trent opened the door behind him. "Hey, I'm gonna be out for an hour. Call me if you need anything." There was the sound of some guy with a deep voice saying yes.

"You've got an appointment for a wedding cake consultation at one thirty," Taryn said.

Trent pulled out his phone. "It's only twelve."

"I've got to be back at the bar by one thirty anyway. I'm opening late today," Candy said, not giving any hint of how big that decision had been for her.

"For me?" Trent's smile got even wider.

"Yeah. Don't make too big a deal out of it."

Candy turned and stalked towards the door, allowing herself a pleased smile of her own the minute she knew Trent wouldn't see it.

"Are you feeling better today?" Trent asked around forty minutes later. His head was in Candy's lap and he was looking up at her while munching on a blueberry.

"Yeah." She smoothed his hair off his forehead and then flicked him on the nose so he wouldn't think she was getting too sappy. "You? You've been averaging, what? Four hours sleep a night this whole week. You gonna fall into a coma?"

He opened his mouth for another blueberry and Candy dropped one in. "Hmm, probably. I'm gonna need at least one night of solid sleep soon. Otherwise I won't be able to dodge all your verbal bullets."

"Says the man who just got fed." Candy glanced at the demolished remains of the Cajun meal she'd ordered from the restaurant next door to her bar. The blueberries had been an afterthought, after she remembered Trent telling her he liked them.

"Says a man who is very happy right now. You're good for me, Blume. I haven't taken lunch off in years."

"Yeah?" Candy asked, realizing that she hadn't taken time off for years either. She looked around her, really noticing their surroundings. Birds were singing and somewhere nearby a busker was playing a violin. It was a one hundred percent Disney situation. "It's been a while for me too. Working seven days a week, twelve hours a day for the past two years hasn't given me a lot of free time."

"You think that's gonna change any time soon?" Trent asked, tilting his head back to look at her better.

"I'd like it to, but I'm not going to be able to afford to hire someone for at least another year. I need to build up an emergency fund. And being able to afford some kind of health insurance would be nice. At the moment, Barney's got better medical coverage than I do." She threw a blueberry at her dog, who'd been studying their leftovers with avid interest, his body vibrating with excitement. He snapped the berry in the air and then gave Candy an offended look when he realized that she'd fooled him with fruit.

"A year isn't so long." Trent reached up and ran his finger along her jawline. "Do I factor in during that time?"

"You might," she said, feeling a warmth in the place that had opened up last night after she'd offloaded all the hurt.

"Good enough for me."

"I'm gonna expect more food."

"Yeah, that works for me too."

"And no promises," she said. "I can't do those. My life's been too complicated."

Trent nodded. "I get it. I'm the same. I've been a substitute dad for over a decade. This time with you has been the only me time I've had in years. And even then, I know I've got a big fight on my hands when I finally have it out with Matty."

"You heard from him yet?"

Trent's mouth flattened into a line. "Nope. I know he's staying with one of Carlotta's friends and that he's got enough money to live on for at least another few weeks, because Nona admitted she gave him a wad of cash. Which worries me because it means it's gonna take a lot longer for him to wake up and realize that his behavior has consequences. He's a grown man and I want him to learn how to act like it, otherwise this world is gonna chew him up and spit out his bones."

Candy held up another blueberry, dropping it into Trent's mouth when he finally opened up. She spoke as he munched. "That's a really nice talk you gave there. How's your overdeveloped sense of responsibility and side order of guilt coming?"

He swallowed the blueberry. "Not too good. In fact, if it weren't for you distracting me, I probably would have caved a couple of days ago."

"That sounds more like the man I'm getting to know." Candy ran her fingers through his hair. "How did the high school bully turn into such a bleeding-heart softie?"

Trent captured her hand and placed it on his chest. "When he worked out that being a decent human being should come before winning. Besides, lately, this hot lady has shown him how beneficial it is to let her win because it gets her off."

"You saying it doesn't get you off too?" Candy dug her nails into his chest, loving how his pupils dilated.

"This conversation is gonna get us both in a whole lot of

trouble soon," Trent said huskily just as his phone started buzzing in his pocket.

"You gonna answer that?" Candy leaned back on her hands.

Trent screwed up his face. "I don't want to."

"But you're gonna have to?"

"Yeah," he grumbled as he sat up, pulling his phone out of his pocket. "Hey, what's going on?" he asked.

Candy watched his expression change. There was a moment of silence and then muffled words loud enough for Candy to hear someone was either crying or hyperventilating.

"Gwen. Calm down. What's going on? What's happened?"

Candy couldn't hear anything now, but she saw Trent's reaction to whatever he heard. "*He's what?* Where are you? . . . I'm coming. Hold on."

He turned to Candy with wild eyes.

"Matty's just tried to kill himself. I gotta go."

Chapter 43

"Where is he?" Trent burst into the hospital waiting room, coming to a skidding halt in front of Gwen. She was sitting next to Carlotta, who was hunched over holding her head in her hands. His nona and Anna were nowhere in sight.

"They're treating him now," Gwen said in a calm voice that was belied by her tear-streaked face. "Carlotta found him."

"Where? Where'd you find him? At your friend's apartment?" Trent asked Carlotta, touching her shoulder. The apartment was a nice place in a safe part of town, so he'd thought Matty would be fine. It had never occurred to him that Matty would be a danger to himself.

Carlotta looked up, her blond hair stringy and her eyes red-rimmed. "He called me this morning talking funny, so I knew something wasn't right. I tried calling him back and when he didn't answer, I went around to check on him." Carlotta choked up and Gwen reached out to rub her back. "I found him passed out on the floor in a bunch of vomit and called an ambulance. He was all alone and that was your fault! Where have you *been* this week?"

Carlotta's words were like a bludgeon across Trent's already guilt-ridden conscience.

"He needed you and you weren't there for him. You kicked him out and didn't *care* what happened. He almost died because you were so caught up with your new girlfriend that you didn't even think to check he was okay. And now he might die." Carlotta abruptly stood up, her face crumpling. "I'm gonna go find Nona and Anna." She left the waiting room, not sparing Trent another glance.

Trent looked around wildly, Carlotta's words already running on repeat in his head. *His fault, his fault, his fault.* "Which room's he in? I've got to see him."

"You can't." Gwen grabbed Trent's hand as he started to walk away, intent on finding someone to take him to Matty. "The best thing you can do is leave this to the professionals. Trust me."

Everything inside him rejected the fact he couldn't fix this. *He should have been there!* "What did he take? What are they doing to him? You understand this stuff. Is he going to be okay?"

"As far as they could work out, he took a whole lot of Advil with vodka, which could be good and bad. Good because it was the slow-release kind, which means it might not have had enough time to dissolve in his stomach. Bad because if he took the pills before he started drinking, it's the . . ." Gwen's eyes filled with tears. "It's the worst way to go. He'll be facing multiple organ failure. Liver, kidney . . ."

Trent tried to process what he was hearing around the white noise. "Was it planned?" he asked, his voice a husky croak.

Gwen hugged herself as tears started spilling down her cheeks. "Yeah. Probably. Carlotta said there were a bunch of packets sitting in a plastic bag, which means he went out and bought them especially."

Trent spun around looking for something to punch but

only saw a group of exhausted people across the waiting room watching him warily. He covered his face with his hands. "*Fuck!*"

The next few hours were some of the worst in Trent's life. As he sat waiting with his family, he thought that if only he could will it hard enough, his little brother would be okay and they could somehow fix this—*he* could fix this. He went over every confrontation he'd had with Matty since their parents' deaths, trying to work out what he could have done differently, how he could have been a better person so Matty wouldn't have ended up *here*.

"Are you Matthew Green's family?"

Before Trent could focus on the doctor in front of them, Gwen started peppering the doctor with questions about Matty's liver function, talking in a technical language beyond Trent's ability to follow.

"I don't give a shit about the details right now. Is he alive?" he demanded, speaking over Gwen.

The doctor's expression stayed calm. "Yes."

"Is he gonna stay alive?" Trent searched her face.

"Yes, but—"

"Can we see him?"

The doctor shook her head. "Not yet. But we'll let you know when."

She turned back to Gwen to answer the question that Trent had interrupted. He stared at the ceiling, tears leaking out the corners of his eyes as he thanked whoever was watching over Matty for saving him.

He sure as hell didn't know how he was gonna make this right, but he would. His little brother was never gonna feel the need to do something drastic again. Trent would make sure of it.

· · ·

When someone finally came to say they could see Matty, everyone but Trent had gone for something to eat. He quickly messaged them to let them know they could come back, and then hurried after a nurse who showed him to an antiseptic-smelling room.

Trent's first thought was how small his brother looked. And how sick. Matty's olive skin was a washed-out gray, his bleached hair was matted against his head, and there were black circles under his eyes. But the thing that really got Trent was the IV sticking into the back of Matty's hand. Seeing something stuck in his brother like that made Trent feel like howling. This was wrong. So, so wrong.

"Hey." Trent touched Matty's shoulder when he saw Matty's eyelashes flutter.

Matty focused on Trent before he looked away, his eyes welling up. "It didn't work."

Trent felt his chest wrench at the disappointment in those words. "No, and that's a damn good thing too." He sat on the side of the bed and cupped Matty's cheek. "What were you thinking?"

Matty closed his eyes. "I wasn't."

"Why didn't you call me?"

"Because I didn't know if you'd come." Matty's body started shaking as he curled into a ball, his mouth open as he started crying in a way Trent hadn't seen since the day their parents had died. Without hesitation, Trent did just what he'd done the night he'd had to break the horrible news to Matty and the girls. He immediately pulled his little brother into a hug, taking care not to mess with the IV.

"I would have come," he said, holding Matty as tightly as he dared. "Any time, any day. You just had to call me. I don't care what was said before or what was done, I'll always be there for you. You're my brother. I would have come."

"But you don't get it." Matty shook his head against Trent's shoulder. "You don't know what I've done."

"You couldn't have done anything that'd be worth killing yourself for."

"You don't know, you don't know . . . you don't know what I did. And when you find out, you're all gonna hate me. That's why I wanted to do it before you found out." Matty's body was shaking now, his words coming out in gasping breaths.

"Nothing's worth you dying," Trent said in a fierce growl. "Hear me? Nothing. There's nothing you could have done—"

"I killed them. Mom and Dad. I killed them." Matty pulled back enough for Trent to see the heart-wrenching grief beneath all the snot and tears. "I killed them."

Trent felt like his heart was breaking all over again. "They died in a boating accident. You were home with me, remember? There's no way you could have been involved."

"I was! It wasn't an accident. They died because of me. It was my fault!"

"How?" Trent asked, desperately wanting to understand how this idea had been sitting in Matty's head for so long.

"They had to die. Dad told me. They had to die because of me. I was bad and—"

"Bad how?"

"Because I'm gay!" The words punched right through Trent's heart. "The day before they went to the lake, Dad told me that I was sending our entire family to hell for not being like him . . . like *you*. He told me that if anything happened to them before I straightened out, it would be my fault because I'd corrupted them. He said that I'd made God want to single them out for punishment. And they died, so it must be true. I put a curse on them and they died and it was *my* fault."

Trent squeezed his eyes shut as the words echoed around the room, fighting fury at people who'd been dead for twelve years. If his parents' death hadn't been an accident, then his father had deliberately put this idea in Matty's head before they'd left for the lake. But Matty was still talking, his body shaking.

"And I knew that when you all worked out that they died because of me, you'd hate me. You'd hate me so bad, and that made me hate *you* because I can't change. I can't. I couldn't be like you and I hated you for that. They loved you. They didn't love me. So I wanted everyone to see that you were just as messed up as me. I wanted you to screw up, because if you did, maybe I wouldn't be so bad. It wouldn't all be my fault."

Suddenly, every confrontation with his little brother played through Trent's head in a fast-action slide show, but this time, instead of being furious, Trent just felt sadness and an urgency to make this right. He gripped Matty's shoulders. "Matty, I need you to listen to me. Have I ever said anything to you that would make you think that I thought you being gay was a bad thing?"

"No, but—"

Trent kept talking. "You didn't do anything wrong. God made you just the way you are. You hear me? Anything Dad told you came from his own ignorance and because he was fucking up so badly at life that he had to take it out on someone. He was just that kind of man. And Mom was a good woman, but I don't think she took the right lessons from her Bible. You hear me? Ask anyone, ask Nona—she'll tell you, and she believes in God just as much as Mom did. You didn't kill them. They died in a freak accident, and anything they said before they died wasn't about you. It was about them. I need you to tell me you're listening, because this is important. Are you listening to me?"

He saw the faint spark of hope in Matty's eyes as his brother nodded, and he felt like bawling.

"I love you. You've driven me crazy with all the stuff you've pulled over the years, but that's just the small stuff. This is bigger than that. I love you. I'll always love you."

He saw movement out the corner of his eyes and realized that his sisters and his nona were standing near the doorway, all four of them crying. "And Nona and the girls love you too, and we're gonna do whatever it takes to get it through that thick skull of yours."

Matty's body convulsed with fresh tears. "Oh God, I'm so sorry. So sorry."

Trent ran his hand over his brother's hair. "Yeah, we all are. We should have noticed you were hurting like this sooner." Trent gestured for everyone else to come over, meeting Carlotta's eyes for a moment. "But we're here for you now, and by the time we're finished, you're never gonna doubt it again."

Chapter 44

Candy was leaning against the desk in her office, clutching her phone to her ear, listening to Trent's ragged breathing as her own heart pounded in suspense over what kind of news she was about to hear. "You okay?" she asked.

"No. No, I'm not doing that well."

She could hear the exhaustion in his cracking voice. It had been over thirteen hours since he'd heard the news about his brother and Candy had spent the whole time on edge, willing Matty Green to be alright.

"How's Matty?"

"He's . . . they got him in time. My sister found him. He's alright physically—or at least he will be. But mentally . . . some stuff came up and it's gonna take a while to help him sort it out. It was my fault. I should have spotted it sooner. But I didn't, and now I've got to fix this somehow."

"You sure that isn't your overdeveloped sense of responsibility making you feel like you're the reason for all the bad stuff?" she asked in a husky voice.

"Yes . . . and no, it's the truth. I should have seen this. I was selfish and this is where we ended up."

Even as her heart broke for what Matty Green must have

been going through, a tiny part of Candy asked, *What about us?* She squashed it down hard. She was used to this—something bigger than her coming up, someone else needing to come first. When she'd been small, it had been her dad having to leave for Hong Kong when his student visa ran out, and then he hadn't been able to come see her because he had to earn enough money to both pay her child support and support his parents. It had been her mom desperately searching for a new thing every few months as a way to keep herself positive in the face of being a single mother. And then, when Candy had become an adult, it had been Beau and his problems.

She was used to this, and in her heart she knew that she had to come second in this moment too. Still, she couldn't prevent her next words from slipping out, knowing she'd kick herself later for showing so much vulnerability.

"When am I going to see you next?" Candy bit her lip as she waited for Trent to answer and focused on the bulletin board hung next to the door. Amongst yellowed ticket stubs and flyers for various events, there was a picture of her and Sophie, hugging each other. It had been taken on Candy's thirteenth birthday. Candy would do anything to have her friend here right now.

Trent cleared his throat. "I don't know . . . I dropped the ball. It's not you, it was me only thinking of what was going on in my life. You were right when you said I should ask Matty what was going on. And lately I wasn't there to see the signs that Matty was acting out because he was hurting. I was too focused on me."

Candy looked down at her Docs, feeling like a weight had suddenly been dropped on her chest from the sky. She cleared her throat, forcing her voice to be calm. "Did you just give me an 'it's not you, it's me,' Green'? Because if you did, I'm gonna have to come and kick your ass. Although, it sounds like you're doing a lot of that to yourself already."

There was a pause at Trent's end before he spoke again in

a rush. "I'm so tired, I'm not saying the right words. I did say that, but don't take it . . . I'm not saying . . ."

"You're saying that you need to spend time with your family." Candy dug her nails into her palm until it hurt. She'd been through tougher stuff than this. It had only been a few weeks—days even. She hadn't planned this thing between her and Trent, and any fool could see it was obviously not meant to be.

Trent broke the silence. "Yeah. And I don't know how long it's gonna take for Matty to be okay, so . . ."

Candy bit the side of her cheek so hard she tasted blood. "Go help your brother. It's been . . . it's been good getting to know you as a human rather than a teenage asshole."

There was a long pause, and Candy couldn't be sure, but she had a hunch Trent was trying to pull himself together too. Finally he spoke in a low husky voice. "I'm sorry—"

"I don't want to hear it. This isn't a fucking romance, Green. This is real life and real life is complicated. Take care of yourself and your family."

Candy ended the call, keeping her eyes on the photograph of her and Sophie. It was hard to see all the details through the blur of tears, but eventually she pulled herself together enough to pull up Sophie's number on her phone.

Sophie answered immediately. "What's wrong? You never call this late."

Candy opened her mouth to speak but no words would come out. She had to swallow a couple of times just to breathe properly. "Need you."

There was a fumbling noise at the other end, like Sophie was moving quickly. "You at the bar?" she asked sharply.

"Yeah."

"You safe?"

"Yeah. I just . . . I just need to see you."

"Want me to come to you?"

Candy was about to say yes, but then realized that she didn't want that. "No."

"Want to come here? I can be in a car driving in minutes. I'll come pick you up."

"No . . . I can't ask that of you. I feel like I need to get out of here, but I can't close up. It'll let too many people down." Candy swiped at the tears falling down her cheeks. "I haven't closed the bar in years. Not even when Beau broke my arm. Not when it was all going wr-wrong. I can't."

"Yes, you can. And I'm gonna help you. You're crying. You never cry. If you're crying, it means something is broken, and it sounds like you can't fix it on your own. So it's either you come here, or I'm coming to you. Blame it on me. Leave a sign on the door saying 'Bar closed because Sophie said.'"

Candy gave a snort. "No one would believe it! You're a marshmallow."

"So are you. You're just a marshmallow covered in a whole lot of hard candy. Hear what I did there?"

"I'm choosing to ignore it." Candy knew, in that moment, that Sophie was right. She needed Sophie. She needed space. She needed time.

"Bring Barney and come stay for a couple of days," Sophie cajoled. "If it helps, *I* need you right now. I'm beginning to panic over this wedding thing. In fact I'm panicking a lot. In fact, this panic attack I'm having is gonna have me plastered all over the walls if my best friend doesn't come to Hopeville and give me a hug. I need a hug. Come give me a hug."

Candy let out a spluttering laugh. "You finished?"

"Do I need to talk more?"

Candy looked around her office, realizing that for the first time in years that she really didn't want to be here. "No." She drew a shaky breath. "I'll see you in a few hours."

"Wait, are you okay to drive? Because I mean it, Ian and I can drive to Austin right now and—"

"No, I'll come to you. I'll be there in a couple of hours," Candy said, her vision blurred with renewed tears. "See you in a while. Love you."

Candy ended the call and then opened the door into the empty bar to find Barney sitting there, watching her with a worried doggy expression. "Hey, boy," Candy said, crouching down and resting her nose against his. "We're gonna go away for a while."

With that, she went back to her office, sent out an email to all of her regulars and posted a sign on the front door. Then she packed up the few things she and Barney would need, loaded them into the car and headed through the night to Hopeville.

Chapter 45

Candy had barely arrived at Sophie's new house when her car door was yanked open and she was pulled out of the car and into a tight hug. "You okay?"

Candy shook her head against Sophie's shoulder.

"Is it Beau?"

She shook her head again.

"Trent?"

She nodded, trying to speak around the lump in her throat.

"Did he hurt you?" Sophie's tone said she was ready to call a posse and saddle up if Candy even gave a hint of a yes.

Candy shook her head.

Sophie sighed, pulling back and studying Candy's face. "You've had a bad one, haven't you?"

Candy nodded. "Yeah. But I don't think I can talk about it right now. I just need . . . I just needed to get away from everything. Get some perspective. I've been working so hard, it's been so constant, I just don't know anything anymore."

Sophie nodded. "Whatever you want, sweetie. We've got the bed all made up and Ian's gonna take care of Barney tonight because you and I both know he'd steal your dog in a minute."

Candy let out a watery laugh. "I'd like to see him try."

Sophie gave her a smile that didn't erase the worry in her eyes. "I wouldn't. I've got a pretty good idea you'd win, and I like my man in one piece." She released Candy from the hug and took her hand. "Come on. Let's take your stuff inside and get you settled. Just remember you don't have to talk if you don't want to, you hear me? Just let yourself be, get some sleep, and tomorrow is just for you. No one expects a thing. There's no one you have to look after, no rules you need to enforce to make sure everyone's fine. Nothing to clean up. Nothing to worry about."

A wave of emotion swept through Candy's body on hearing those words, and Sophie must have understood because she pulled Candy into another tight hug, not saying anything about the tears that messed up the front of her T-shirt.

"Good morning."

Candy glanced up from her curled-up position on Sophie's porch to see Ian Buchanan standing in the doorway, holding a cup of coffee and looking like he'd stepped out of an action movie with his handsome-but-battered face, bald head, and a whole lot of muscles left over from his time as a bare-knuckle boxer in his youth.

It was around seven in the morning. While Candy had tried to sleep after Sophie had shown her to an airy bedroom, she'd just stared at the ceiling replaying the past few weeks in a continuous loop, wondering why the hell she couldn't stop crying. Finally she'd come out here to enjoy some peace and quiet, marveling at the lack of street noise and the sound of the birds singing their wake-up call, all while a faint warm breeze ruffled the leaves of the two big oak trees in the front yard.

Candy knew Sophie would be up soon, and Candy didn't know what she'd tell her. How could she explain how deep the thing between her and Trent had gotten so quickly—and then how it had gone away just as fast?

"May I join you?" Ian asked.

"Yeah." Candy gestured listlessly to the comfortable wicker chair next to hers. "Sophie still sleeping?"

"Hmm." Ian took a sip of his coffee, gazing out at Barney who was currently snuffling around the flower beds like he'd just discovered heaven. Ian took a seat and stretched his legs out. "It's going to be warm today."

"We're talking about the weather now?" Candy raised a brow but there was no bite in her words. She'd worked out long ago that other than adoring the ground Sophie walked on, she and Ian Buchanan had quite a bit in common, most of it involving their general mistrust of humanity.

Ian shrugged. "Discussing the weather is a British institution. It's a way of saying 'I'm human, you're human, we're all human.' So as a fellow human, allow me some small talk to make you feel comfortable." He patted his leg to get Barney's attention and Candy's dog scampered up to the porch to rest his head on Ian's leg. "You haven't slept a wink yet, have you?" Ian asked while idly scratching Barney behind the ears.

"No." Candy shook her head, surreptitiously swiping at her eyes, which were watering up over such a stupid thing as someone caring if she'd slept.

Ian nodded, his expression bland. "Are you worried about your safety? Is that why you're here?"

"No." Candy plucked at a piece of lint on her pajama shorts, not wanting to make eye contact.

"Has Beau been giving you trouble? And don't even think of shrugging me off like you would Sophie. I'm a journalist and a former shifty bastard—I can spot a misdirection from a mile away."

Ian took another sip of coffee. His body language was still relaxed, but Candy could see the coiled readiness there. She remembered seeing Beau after Ian had gone to work on him two years ago upon learning what Beau had done to Sophie. She didn't doubt Ian would be ready to do it again in a minute.

"Yeah. In a way. But that's not why I'm here."

"So it's this Trent Green character? The one who made your life hell in high school and who owns a patisserie in downtown Austin named Dolce Design. Trent Green who has three sisters, one brother. Lives with his grandmother in Rollingwood. Drives a Toyota Tacoma."

Candy looked at him sharply. "How'd you know all that?"

Ian shrugged as Candy remembered that one of his closest friends owned a security company. "I like to be kept informed when it comes to people who could upset my friends, and I count you as a friend. Did he hurt you?"

Candy drew a shuddering breath. "No. The opposite. But . . . something came up with his family and he's had to put them first." She darted a look at Ian when he didn't say anything. He just gave her the space she needed while he patted Barney.

"And the bar, have you closed it?" he asked.

Candy felt a welcome flash of ire shoot through her. "If you're gonna offer me money—"

"I wouldn't dream of it. I'm just making small talk . . . that thing we British are good at, remember?"

Candy gave him one of her patented death glares. "Slippery son of a bitch."

His mouth curved in a smile that managed to make him appear even more dangerous than usual. "Secretive bitch," he said, then finished his coffee.

Candy let out a surprised burst of laughter.

"That's better." Ian stood up, his gaze piercing. "I'm only going to say this once because sentimental nonsense is not my style, but Sophie loves you and because of that—and because of a couple of other sterling qualities—I like you. I'd like you to know you're welcome to stay here. As long as you want."

Candy swallowed loudly, covering it up with a scowl. "You're right, sentimental nonsense isn't your style."

Ian's laughter echoed over the garden. "I'm kidnapping your dog while I go for a run. I'll leave you to talk to Sophie. She'll be up any minute." He gave Candy a faux-serious frown. "We never had this talk."

Candy shook her head. "Never."

"Good."

Chapter 46

"Why don't you get settled back in and we'll have pizza once it comes? It's good to have you home," Trent said, putting a hand on Matty's shoulder and hating how frail his brother felt.

"Okay." Matty nodded and Trent pushed open the door of Matty's bedroom, his nose wrinkling at the musty smell that came from it being shut up for over a week.

Even taking into account the things Trent had removed when he'd kicked Matty out, his brother's stuff was still all over the place, although it had never really looked like his room. The room was still painted the dark brown their dad had chosen, the carpet was still their mom's favorite olive green, and the bathroom—visible through the ensuite's open door—was done up in an exorbitantly expensive pink marble that hadn't made sense to Trent all those years ago and still didn't today.

Right now, that bathroom represented every flaw in the way his parents had operated. They'd been so worried about appearances that they'd spent a fortune on a room that only they'd see. Seeing all that marble and gilt—chosen for all the wrong reasons—Trent knew he couldn't let Matty sleep in this room anymore.

"Hey, I've got an idea," he said gruffly, placing a hand back on Matty's shoulder to stop him walking by.

"What?" Matty asked as the noise of Carlotta and Anna discussing what kind of pizza to order filtered up from the living room. Gwen had gone back to work—she hadn't been able to take any more time off—but their nona was bustling around in the kitchen, making them all hot chocolate per Trent's request so she'd have a distraction from worrying.

"Why don't we swap rooms?" Trent asked Matty. "We can do it right now. I'll take this one and you take mine. It'll mean you don't get the Liberace bathroom anymore. But on the other hand, it'll mean that you don't have to use the Liberace bathroom anymore," he said, using the name Gwen had given their parent's bathroom ever since she'd seen the HBO movie *Behind the Candelabra*.

Trent didn't add that ever since he and Matty had climbed into Trent's truck to come home, Trent had been getting nightmare images of Matty floating in that ridiculous bathtub, the water bloody—nope, that wasn't a road he was going down. Matty was going to be okay. They were going to sort it out.

"See it as the first step to a fresh start," he said when Matty didn't answer him.

Matty's eyes suddenly sheened over. "I always hated this room, but I thought that somehow, if I was in here, I could be close to them and they'd forgive me."

Trent squeezed Matty's shoulder again before pointedly looking back into the bedroom. "This news is gonna be hard to hear, but I think the only ghosts in here are of your dirty laundry. Honestly, man, it's gonna take me the rest of the night to air the smell of your shorts out of the place."

"Maybe I should leave them here for you to remember me by."

"Maybe I should make you be the one who goes down-stairs to break up the anchovy fight between Carlotta and

Anna," Trent shot back, feeling like he was on a tightrope as he tried to keep things light.

Matty peered over the railing into the living room, where the twins were having their usual shouting match over whether anchovies were a valid topping choice. Trent had a feeling that they were doing it to make Matty feel at home. He had to give it to them—it was kind of working.

"So are you for it?" he asked Matty.

"Yeah," Matty said. "Yeah. I think that'd be cool."

Trent didn't even bother to hide his relief. "Then let's get to work." He walked over to the balcony. "Hey, you two, hurry up and make up your minds on the pizza and then come up here. We're moving Matty into my room and I'm moving into his."

There was a stunned silence. It was Anna who spoke first. "You're giving up the Liberace bathroom?" she asked Matty, pushing up her red-framed glasses.

"Yeah, it's gonna be tough, but I'll be sharing with you guys again."

There was another stunned silence before protests rang through the house, Anna and Carlotta competing with each other to get the most volume—again for Matty's benefit. Trent clapped Matty on the back, praying that the small smile he saw on Matty's face was just a sign of more to come.

"Welcome home, bro. Sweet, sweet, peaceful home."

Later that night, Trent's phone woke him from a deep, dreamless sleep. He sat up, gulping in a too-big breath, his entire body anticipating another emergency that he'd somehow missed.

It took him a few seconds to realize that his phone was still in his jeans' pocket on the other side of the too-big room, and that it had probably been a notification, not a call, because it had only buzzed once.

Sitting up, he switched on the light and was confronted with the brown walls, which felt like they were closing in on him like a vise. He didn't know how Matty had managed to sleep in here for years. It had been less than one night and Trent was already feeling claustrophobic.

The only problem was that he didn't know how he could justify new paint and carpet when he'd be supporting Matty until he got back on his feet.

They had a counseling session booked at the hospital tomorrow, and Trent had lain awake for hours trying to work out how he was going to be able to make sure he was there enough for his brother while also catching up on the orders waiting at the shop, especially the two cakes for high-profile weddings. There was no way he could slip up. When it came to weddings, his reputation was only as good as the last cake.

And somewhere in all of this, he needed to make time for Nona, Gwen, Carlotta and Anna. Because if Matty had been dealing with such a dark secret, what other poisons were lying beneath the surface just waiting to seep out?

And then there was Candy. Just thinking of her, wondering what she was doing right now, and remembering how happy he'd been while Matty was suffering left Trent feeling a pain so sharp, it was like his ribs were breaking, one by one.

He wanted to call her so badly, but he knew he couldn't. If he heard even the smallest bit of sympathy in her voice, he'd crumple, and he didn't deserve sympathy. He didn't deserve her caring for him. He'd thought he'd moved on, become a better man, but the thing with Matty showed that he was just as self-absorbed as ever. Otherwise he would have noticed something was wrong.

That thought spurred him out of bed to check his phone. When he saw a message from Candy, he felt a sting behind his eyes.

Call me when you get the time. I just want to know you're okay. I'm here for you.

Trent knew Candy well enough to know what typing those words had cost. He knew how much of her pride she'd swallowed to send them. And he knew he couldn't reply, because choosing Candy wouldn't leave him with enough time to care for his family.

Setting his phone down on his bedside table, Trent climbed back in bed and pulled the covers tightly around him. Candy would understand. She'd move on. He hoped. Because the thought of her being sad was like acid in an already open wound.

Chapter 47

"I've got a confession to make."

Candy looked at Sophie. They'd just returned from cleaning Sophie's holiday cottages, and Candy was now sitting at Sophie's charmingly battered antique kitchen table as her friend whipped up an omelet for a late breakfast.

"Yeah?" she asked, checking her phone to see if Trent had replied to her message. She knew he'd reply. He couldn't not. It was only a matter of time. Because the thought of him leaving her hanging after she'd sent a message that left her feeling so vulnerable was untenable. Even a "thanks" would be enough to get rid of this terrible feeling that she'd made a needy idiot out of herself. Oh wait—she *had* made a needy idiot out of herself.

Sophie's voice broke through her brooding. "I went to see Trent. After you called that morning to tell me about him hanging around, I got a little gung-ho and drove to Austin to read him the riot act." Sophie set the whisk down. "And he told me about Beau coming around."

Candy stared at her. "And?"

In true Sophie form, an avalanche of words came out, betraying how anxious she'd been. "And I've been feeling bad about going behind your back ever since. I just got so worked up at the thought of you getting hurt again . . ." She looked down at the bowl in front of her. "If you want to chew me out, I completely understand. But I want you to know that you don't ever have to hide anything from me. Ever. You're not a burden, and sharing stuff about Beau won't upset me. Got it? You've been so stubborn for so many years about letting anyone help you, and that's gotta end now. I love you. I'm here to help, and you better damn well get that through your head. This friendship is for *life*." Sophie gave her a fierce look that was still akin to being stared down by a fluffy bunny.

"You're an idiot," Candy said softly. "You've been tearing yourself up over this, haven't you?"

Sophie sniffed. "Yeah. But I love you. And I care. A lot."

"I know you do. And I care about you. I don't want all that stuff with Beau, any of it, to mess with what you have now. Not just for you, but for me. Seeing you happy makes me happy. Hear me?"

Sophie nodded. "If you want to tell me what happened with Trent, I promise I'll listen and not interfere in any way again. I mean, unless you want me to. Because then I'll interfere a lot."

Candy felt some of the ache inside her diminish. "Alright. But I'm gonna need to be fed first. All this emotional crap's too hard on an empty stomach."

Four days later, Candy walked back through the door of her apartment as Barney inspected every surface for any interesting new smells. Finally satisfied things were just how he'd left them, he curled up on the armchair while Candy hugged herself, looking at the bed she'd shared with Trent.

Memories of their time together came back to her in a rush, along with the physical memory of how he'd felt wrapped around her, the scent of his skin, the way he'd rub her back just as she was waking up in the morning . . .

For a fleeting moment, she let it all wash over her. The disappointment. The sadness. The stupid bit of hope that it wasn't over. And then she got on with her day, putting her clothes away, checking that her makeup was sharp, and then heading downstairs to get Hard Candy ready for opening.

She was expecting it to be an interesting day. Firstly, because she never closed the bar, and secondly, because she'd received over twenty messages from Kevin, ranging from concerned to disgruntled to frantic when he'd worked out that his usual writing seat wouldn't be available for days.

There had been no message from Trent.

She'd only checked four times today, each time feeling a horrible spark of disappointment she promised herself would pass.

Allowing herself a moment to sink back into habit, Candy selected a chill playlist, switched all the lights on, turned on the cog sculpture and set up the coffee machine. And then she checked her phone, telling herself it was just to check the time.

It was eleven fifty-nine. If she knew Kevin, he'd be parking in his spot next to her car right now. Yep, there was the sound of Barney's hello bark from upstairs. And then he'd have to walk around his car once to check his tires . . .

She was tempted to dawdle a while to yank Kevin's chain, but the minute she heard the knock on the bar's back door, she opened it.

"Candy—" Beau barely got the word out before Candy slammed the door in his face. When he blocked her, she turned and sprinted back into the bar, intent on grabbing the baseball bat and then locking herself in her office so she could call the cops.

"Candy! Wait! Hear me out!"

She reached the bar, picking up the bat in one swift movement, only to find Beau blocking the way to her office. Heart pounding, she tried to work out if she could run past him and out the back door before he caught her. He wasn't holding a gun. In fact, his hands were currently up in the air like *she* was threatening *him*, but that didn't mean there wasn't a gun stuck down the back of his pants. Every single headline she'd seen about women being killed by their ex-husbands flashed through her mind, and she'd be damned before she became a statistic.

"Get the hell out of here, Beau," she snarled, gripping the bat exactly how Ian Buchanan had shown her, already cataloging Beau's weak points so she could strike if he took one more step. This wouldn't be like the last time he'd caught her alone in this bar, the day after he'd gotten the divorce papers. This time she knew a whole lot more about defending herself.

Beau kept his hands up in the air, taking a step back, his face paling. "Easy now. Just hear me out. I just want a minute of your time and then I'm never gonna come by again. I promise."

"Why should I believe anything you have to say?"

"Because I'm sober. I'm clean. And I want to tell you I'm sorry. For everything."

"Bullshit."

He looked away and Candy tensed, just in case this was an effort to misdirect her attention before he struck. "It's true. I tried to come by yesterday and the day before, but I saw you were closed." He ran a hand through his hair, and Candy saw he'd had it cut. He was skinnier than the last time she'd seen him, and there was something else . . . the cockiness from before wasn't there, or at least it was hiding. And his clothes were wrinkled, like they hadn't been ironed by Marlene.

"I don't care," Candy said. "If I'd been here yesterday I'd have reported you to the cops, just like I'm going to today. Get out of here!"

"I know you've got no reason to care after what I did to

you. But I just want . . . it's a part of recovery for me to apologize to the people I've messed with. And that's what I'm doing. I was telling the truth. I'm clean. I've been clean for two weeks now. I apologized to Mom two days ago and I wanted to apologize to you next."

Beau took a step forward and then stepped quickly back again when Candy raised the bat higher, bracing herself to swing. Ian had taught her the best places to hit in quick succession and she'd already mentally mapped out how it would go. Balls, head or neck. And failing all those, kneecaps and stomach.

"Stay back!" she ordered. "In fact, back away completely. Leave, Beau. I don't need to hear this. I don't want you here. Go!"

Beau nodded slowly, watching the bat, his pale green eyes glassy. "I understand that. But I think it would help you a whole lot to hear what I'm about to say, and I'm willing to risk you smashing my head in if it means I can fix this."

Candy stared at him, incredulously. Maybe her mom's yearly astrology prediction had been finally right, and the planets really were aligned for this to be the year old scores were settled, because first it had been Trent, and now Beau. Except Beau had a hell of a lot more to atone for, and all of it recent.

"What exactly do you think you're gonna fix?" she asked. "You've broken everything so badly, there's nothing left to stick back together."

"I know that. And I don't mean fix *us*. I mean fixing things so you can move on, and so you don't have to worry about me being in your life anymore. I'm sorry, Candy. Genuinely sorry. I'm an addict. I stole your money. I lied to you. I hurt you. I threatened you and I abused your trust. For that, I'm genuinely sorry. I don't expect . . ." Beau looked down at his feet. "I don't expect forgiveness. I just wanted you to hear the words before I leave your life for good."

For a moment, Candy thought she was looking at the real Beau, the one she'd met in high school. But something still wasn't right. The sweatiness, the glassiness in his eyes . . . Something was off.

He continued speaking. "After I came here the other night, I bottomed out. Seeing Trent Green here, thinking you preferred him to me . . . it wasn't rational, but I couldn't handle the idea that I'd ended up being the bad guy."

"That's what it took?" Candy asked. "Why didn't you have your 'come to Jesus' moment after what you did to Sophie? Or after what you did to me when you got those divorce papers, or after the first time you stole something from your *mom?*"

"Yeah, well, it wasn't just that." Beau swallowed audibly. "When I say I bottomed out, I left here thinking I'd get high and come back. But I didn't have any money, so I took Mom's engagement ring when she took it off to do the dishes. I was thinking I'd give it to my dealer—"

"Are you even human right now?" Candy asked incredulously.

"I wasn't at the time. I'm trying to be better now," Beau said, his face flushing. "I didn't get the drugs. The minute the guy saw the ring, he worked out how desperate I was and decided to just take it. They beat me up pretty bad. The first punch snapped me out of it, and I realized what I'd been about to do. After that, all I wanted was to take mom's ring back. But by that time, all I could do was fight for my life. That's when they stabbed me in my gut and left me in an abandoned lot." He reached down and lifted the hem of his T-shirt, showing a long, barely healed scar held together by stitches.

Candy stared at it for a moment. No one could have a wound like that without being in a lot of pain. "Shouldn't there be a bandage or something on that? And shouldn't you still be in hospital?"

"Yeah, and I sure as hell wish I could take some painkillers without getting hooked again, but I thought it'd be better for you to see what happened to me," he said. "It was five hours until someone called an ambulance. That's a lot of time to be lying there, bleeding to death and strung out at the same time. The doctors said the withdrawal should have killed me if being stabbed hadn't. But somehow I survived. I'm alive. And when I woke up in hospital days later, I was on my way to drying out and realizing how badly I'd messed up. I checked straight out of hospital and went to my first meeting that night, even though the pain nearly killed me."

He let his hands drop to his side, his T-shirt still hiked up enough for Candy to see the bottom of that horrible half-healed scar.

She shook her head. "What's this all supposed to mean for me?" she asked finally.

"It means I'm not gonna bother you anymore. I got another job working on the rigs, but this time it'll be in Alaska. My old boss is gonna let me back, so I'll have money to pay you back—"

"I don't want your money. There's no guarantee you won't use it against me later," Candy said sharply.

Beau nodded, a flash of disappointment showing on his face. "Yeah, I thought you'd say that. But I had to try. Anyway. I'll pay Mom back for everything. And I'm leaving Austin." He swiped his hand over his face. "This place isn't good for me. One of my new NA buddies has a brother there with a trailer for rent. I figure it'll be a start somewhere new. Somewhere fresh." He looked up and met her eyes. "Before I go, I just want you to know it was my fault. How it went wrong between us. How I turned out. You didn't do anything wrong other than love me, and I didn't appreciate what I had until it was gone."

"You been listening to country songs lately? 'Cause these sound like lyrics I've heard before," Candy shot back to cover up the turmoil inside her.

Beau shook his head slowly. "Nope. Just wanted to give you my apology. I loved you, Candy. You were the best thing that ever happened to me, and I threw it away. I had you for ten years and didn't see how good it was until it was gone. I'm sorry about that. I'm sorry for hurting you. This is the last you're going to see of me and I wish you a happy life. And if you see Sophie around, tell her I'm sorry for what happened with her too. I'm not gonna try say it in person, because that dude she's with will kill me. But I mean it when I say I regret messing it up with you."

With that Beau turned and stiffly walked out the same way he came, leaving Candy listening to the sound of his car pulling out of the parking lot, the bat still gripped tightly in her hands, her heart still pounding.

Chapter 48

Candy was spritzing herself a Coke with shaking hands when Kevin hurried through the back door of the bar moments later. He was wearing a button-down blue shirt and a harassed frown, but even in her scrambled state, it felt like something wasn't right.

"We need to discuss something," he said.

"Nice to see you too," she said to cover up her relief over him being here. This was her life. This was normal. She slugged back half of the Coke and then walked around the bar to unlock the front door, peeling off the notice she'd posted before leaving for Sophie's.

She could feel Kevin's frustration vibrating through the air. "You okay?" she asked while crumpling the note in one hand.

"Twenty-three messages!" he blurted, his nostrils flaring. "I sent twenty-three messages!"

"You sure it wasn't twenty-four?" Candy asked as she walked back behind the bar to throw the notice in the trash, the familiar banter calming her down like nothing else.

"Would I get a number like that wrong? Twenty-three."

Candy made a production of checking her phone. "Let's see. Yeah. You're probably right—"

"Probably!?"

"But I don't see why you're so upset. I replied to you."

"You replied to one message! And you only said you'd be back today! No explanation, no reassurance that you wouldn't leave again straight after!"

Candy shot Kevin a sharp look. His normally groomed Afro was lopsided, as if he hadn't picked it out after waking up, and she realized that his shirt buttons were crooked. "You're genuinely stressed out, aren't you, big guy?" she asked in a softer voice.

"Yes!" Kevin said. "You being absent raised a lot of worries. Which is why we need to talk." He looked around the room as if checking Candy hadn't sneakily redecorated the place overnight, then homed in on his barstool like it was a long, cool drink of water and he'd been lost in the desert for months.

"About what?"

"This. I've had to resort to a drastic solution to the problem because this situation cannot happen again." Kevin unzipped his backpack with economical movements, pulling out a rolled-up sheet of paper and another pile of official-looking papers. He rolled out the larger sheet across the bar, rubbing one hand over his chest and looking at Candy with a desperate urgency until she walked over.

It was a sheet of grid paper with a sketched layout of the room.

"This is a map of the bar." She ran her finger over the top of a square neatly labeled "Incorrectly Painted TARDIS."

"Yes. I got the dimensions as correct as I could."

"Why's there a compass drawn on the side here?"

"Because it's a map."

"A kraken is eating a sailing ship here in the corner. Why's that there?"

"Because it's a *map*." Kevin was relaxing enough now to

reward her with one of his usual glowers. "That's not important—"

"And why have you written 'Here Be Dragons' in the space where my office is?"

"Because if your bar was a dungeon, you would be the boss everyone fought at the end. The best I can figure is that you'd have at least as many hit points as Smaug—"

"The dragon from *Lord of the Rings?!*" Candy gave him an incredulous look.

"*The Hobbit,* actually, but maybe I should have written 'Desolation of Smaug' there instead." He paused. "In fact, I doubt any party, including dwarves and a halfling with a magical ring would be able to kill you. You're too formidable. So that wouldn't work. 'Here Be Dragons' is the best I can do for now."

"Gee, thanks. What's so important about a map of my bar? Other than offending me," Candy amended while collecting Kevin's Skeletor mug and getting a start on making him a coffee.

"The map is important because I need to be very clear about what I'm proposing."

"Which is what?" Candy frowned in concern when she saw the faint sheen of sweat now dotting his brow.

"Here. Read this." He slid the other sheets of paper towards her and then hunched down on his barstool, his body vibrating with the nervous movement of his knee.

When Candy brought his coffee over, she picked up the paper. "Proposal for a ten-year lease of nine square feet of Hard Candy, encompassing the barstool marked X on map labeled 'Hard Candy,'" she read out loud before glancing at the map. Sure enough, there was an X over the circle representing the stool Kevin usually sat on. She looked back to the document. "And further proposal to lease the booth indicated as 'Y' for three hours every Monday from four p.m. until eight p.m.—" She looked at Kevin. "Your Dungeons & Dragons game?"

He nodded, his body now visibly jiggling in anxiety. "Keep reading."

"The proposed weekly rent on both X and Y is two thousand dollars—" She reared back. "What the hell?!"

"Keep reading."

She shook her head. "I can't, this is——"

"Please. It's important to me."

She gave Kevin a long look, seeing the plea in his expression before she glanced back at the document. "Okay. So you want to pay me two thousand dollars a week, with incremental two-percent increases in rent every year for ten years to accommodate inflation, and in return you want keys to be able to access the bar at any time between the hours of eleven a.m. to one a.m., with the proviso that you walk Barney if necessary. You also want the right to organize my cash drawer once a month, because the current system is untenable." She gave him a glare and then went back to reading. "And you further propose to purchase naming rights over Thursday night for ten thousand dollars, along with paying another two thousand for me to make a rule that no one can argue with you about the name unless they pay an equal sum to a charity of my choice." Candy let out a snort. "You want to pay twelve thousand to rename Prancing Rainbow Pony Appreciation Night?! Now I know you're really talking Monopoly money. Kevin——"

"I'm serious," he interrupted. "The meetings I had last Monday? The reason I wasn't here? I've just been offered a seven-million-dollar development deal to come up with a TV series based loosely on my Cerebellum Trilogy."

Candy stared at him. She didn't know a whole lot about writing, but even she knew that was crazy money. "They're what?!"

Kevin's anxious expression transformed into an offended

one. "If you didn't notice. My books sell in exceptional numbers."

Candy tried to process the amount of money he'd just mentioned and . . . nope. He could have just said he was secretly Batman and had a fetish for parasols with penguins painted on them. "Yeah. I know, but——"

"And I've been on the *New York Times* Bestseller List multiple times, with my last book selling over five million copies. It was bound to attract attention. Additionally, as you know, I've sold a number of screenplays successfully to both DC and Marvel as well as smaller studios, I've been invited to speak on a number of panels at the San Diego Comic Con now for four years. There was that coverage of me in *WIRED* last year when I——"

"Okay! You're a big deal in the world of geekery!" Candy ran a hand over her head, incredulity threatening to swamp her. "I knew you must have been doing well when you bought that Tesla."

"Yes, I am. And the Tesla was only small change given my current net worth," Kevin said, as he finally stopped rubbing his chest. "But the reason I've become a big deal is because I found this place, which has, unfortunately, become my muse. I can't afford to risk being locked out of it again, or for it to change dramatically, erasing whatever witchcraft it has over my ability to write." He paused, giving Candy a pleading look. "Please accept my terms. My attorney wrote the contract and I had her make sure it's fair and in your best interest. You'll also see there is an additional clause for you to offer to sell Hard Candy to me at twenty percent more than market value if you ever decide to give up running the bar."

"But that makes no sense," Candy said, rifling through the documents and seeing that Kevin's attorney had, indeed, written a contract that was skewed ridiculously in her favor. "You could have just asked for a key. We don't need to do all this. It's so much money——"

"I need a guarantee. I can't be locked out from my muse again. Please agree to the contract," Kevin spoke over her.

Candy's protests froze on her lips when she saw the determination and desperation on his face. "You mean this. You actually want to pay me over a hundred thousand dollars a year so that you can sit in this bar."

He nodded. "And write like I always do. Yes. If it helps, the million I'd pay you over ten years is only a small percentage of my current net worth and I anticipate that I'll earn more from royalties, investments and further contracts in that time. So in actuality, it's a miniscule amount. To me. But to you it's a lot. So take it. It would be idiotic of you not to."

Candy's brain was already doing a whole lot of math. "You still have to follow the Rules, including any other ones I create."

He nodded. "I like the Rules."

"And you can't get uppity or act like you're paying me a wage, or that you have any say in the actual running of my bar—not how I arrange my shelves or how I treat my customers. And on that note, you aren't allowed to act like you can tell my customers what to do. You'd be a tenant of your nine square feet of space, nothing more. If I want to hire more staff, I can. If I want time off, I can take it. If I want to hire the bar out for private functions—"

"That is all your prerogative."

"—because I'm not gonna take what you're offering if it's gonna mean I'm stuck working seven days a week, twelve hours a day for the next ten years," Candy said, not quite believing she was having this conversation. Any minute now, she'd wake up, walk downstairs and open the bar. She'd find Kevin at the door and they'd get on with their day as usual.

"I resent you calling me uppity. But this is why I want this contract. And you'll see everything you just mentioned is listed there to your advantage. If you don't have complete dictatorial rule over this bar, the magic might go. That means you hire who you want, you do what you want. As long as this bar is an extension of your vision. That's the thing that must continue." He paused. "With the exception of Thursday night's name. I would like it reinstated to Goth Night as of today."

"Buddy, anyone who pays me that much money can change the name whenever they want," Candy said wryly before reading over the contract again, seeing that what he'd said was true. She ended on the last page, staring at the rent schedule Kevin had written up. It only required her signature and her bank details.

With this money, she'd be able to have a life again. She'd be able to *live* rather than just survive. She'd have time to do all the stuff other people took for granted. *She'd be able to see her dad.*

Little butterflies began to dance in her stomach. Okay, maybe she wouldn't be able to do it immediately—she'd have to wait a couple of months until she'd broken in some new staff and gotten her finances sorted—but soon. She pictured Johnny's face when she told him, and the butterflies put on tap shoes and really went to town. Or better yet, maybe she'd surprise him . . .

And she'd have time to really be there for Sophie in planning the wedding. And maybe, if Trent sorted his life out, she'd have more time for him too. They could go on that hike. They could be together at decent hours rather than making him miss sleep. Maybe she'd even have the time to learn to make Trent a couple of those dishes Grandma Tang was always bugging her to learn. Or, better yet, maybe she could get *him* to learn how to make Grandma Tang's dishes. Yeah, that sounded better. Much better. All he needed to do was message her back.

"Okay, big guy," she said to Kevin who was already holding his *Star Trek: Next Generation* pen out to her with an anxious, expectant air. "You've got yourself a deal."

Chapter 49

"Are you okay, man? You've been standing there for almost an hour."

Trent glanced up from the blank sketchpad where he'd been trying to come up with a design. His horse-loving clients wanted a sculpted wedding cake big enough to feed one hundred guests. It was going to be comprised of two horses running side by side with lifelike chocolate models of the bride and groom standing on the saddles and holding hands. The cake part would be encased within the "skin" covering the horses' bodies, and Trent knew he had to get the supports and the chocolate thickness right to maintain the structural integrity of the piece. But he also had to make sure the horses looked like they could launch themselves off the table at any minute. He'd known this job would be hard when he'd accepted the contract and charged accordingly, and now he had to make sure the design was flawless. If only he could concentrate . . .

"Hey," Rakeem said.

Trent turned to his patissier, who was looking at him with a worried frown. "What? Sorry. Did you say something?"

"I was saying that you've been standing there playing

statue for almost an hour. You need sleep, man. That cake's not due for another two months, so you'll have plenty of time to work on the design so it doesn't fall apart, which won't be an issue because we both know you could design it in your sleep—if you *got* sleep. I'm more worried about *you* falling apart."

"Your faith in me is amazing," Trent shot back.

"My job here is amazing," Rakeem said over the mixer as he expertly cracked a bunch of eggs into the bowl with one hand. "And I want to keep it. Which means my boss has to get enough sleep to keep his shit together. I've got two fast-growing kids who always need new shoes, not to mention this crazy thing called an education. I can't have my boss jeopardizing that by being so tired at work he does something stupid like smothering himself in the refrigerator by accident."

Trent raised his brows, looking at the fridge. "You saying I'm so puny I could fit in that thing?"

"I'm saying you're so tired, you're dumb enough to try. Anyway, Matty's out front, and if you don't go home and get some sleep, I'll tell him to set your grandma on you. I'll take care of making the orders this afternoon."

Trent looked at the whiteboard on the far wall, where all the week's orders were prioritized in the order they needed to get done. He'd already done up a batch of gold dusted truffles for a high-society baby shower this morning and they'd been picked up at two. All that was left was—

"What about putting together the *croque-en-bouche* for the DeLanier wedding?"

"Janine can take care of that with me. She's already done a bunch of them with you supervising. I'll make sure she gets it right." Rakeem jerked his head towards Janine, who was nodding along to whatever she was listening to as she painstakingly piped strawberry macarons onto a tray.

"Yeah, okay. I'll just let Brian know I'm heading home early."

"Already done. You hired a great guy there, by the way. The brides love him. If he keeps attracting new people to this store, you're gonna have to give us all a pay rise."

"Who would've thought that finding him drunk on my couch would be a good thing?" Trent gave Rakeem an exhausted smile. "Okay man. I'll check in with Brian and see if Matty needs anything, then I'm gone."

Trent walked to the front of the store to find Matty on the red sofa looking at his phone. Brian was behind the counter serving a customer who came in at least once a week for a selection of truffles.

Trent had been worried how Matty would take him hiring Brian, but instead of being upset, Matty had become a fixture in the store on his old work day. And whenever he was around Brian, Matty looked so happy that Trent was thinking about giving Brian a pay raise just for that. It had been two months since Matty's suicide attempt, and while Trent still wasn't sleeping, Matty was doing better every day. Matty had even re-enrolled to finish his degree and applied for an internship with a software company. It was enough for Trent to tentatively hope they were over the worst.

"Hey. What's up?" Trent asked, feeling a twinge of panic when he saw that Matty wasn't smiling.

"Hey." Matty darted a look at Brian. "Have you got a minute? There's something we want to talk to you about. We were gonna do it tomorrow, but since there's no one in the store and you're free . . ."

"Yeah?" Trent's palms were beginning to sweat now. "What's up?"

"Promise not to lose your shit first," Matty said.

Trent looked from one man to the other. "Why?"

Matty swallowed, his Adam's apple bobbing. "Because this is gonna be hard for you to hear."

"What is?" Trent immediately took an inventory of Matty's appearance. His face wasn't pale, he didn't look sweaty or sick. In fact, he seemed fine. He was dressed like he'd just come from the gym and he had a backwards baseball cap on his head, but that didn't mean there wasn't some deeper psychological thing going on underneath it all—

"Brian and I are moving in together." Matty paused long enough for those words to find their mark. "I'm moving out. I got a job. It's working for a small software company, helping them with basic stuff to start, but I think I can help them grow their business with what I've learned at college and while working for you. If I get results, it'll mean a good salary."

Trent's brain desperately scrambled to process what he'd just heard. "But what about your degree? The internship you said you'd applied for?"

"I'm still gonna finish my degree. The company's cool with me taking time out for class, and this is better than any internship." Matty stood up. "And I need to leave home. I appreciate what you've done for me, putting up with my bull-shit and everything, but I need you to stop treating me like a kid. Which I'll keep acting like if I'm in your house under your rules—"

"It's our house, Matty. We all own it."

"But you might as well be my dad. Which means while I'm living in that place, you and I won't be able to really get to know each other. It's a weird dynamic. I love you, bro, but I've gotta find my own way." Matty gave Trent a pleading look. "Just because I'm gay doesn't mean you have to protect me from all the assholes in the world. You can't. And I can't be myself unless I can work out who the hell I really am."

Trent felt the words like a punch to his sternum. For a moment all he could hear was the unspoken *I don't need you.*

"What's the deal with you and Brian?" he asked huskily, looking at the man who was shyly studying his fingernails as he pretended that he wasn't a big, conspicuous guy wearing a pastel-pink shirt in the middle of a room full of cakes and chocolates.

"We're friends," Matty said, giving Trent an obstinate look he'd seen on their father's face and on his own in the mirror. It was pure fighting Irish.

Trent huffed out a breath. "Okay, but——"

"I'm letting you know because I love you and respect everything you've done for me. But it's time for me to grow up. You know it. I know it. I need you to let me go so we can all move on. Let me do this without fighting me. Please?"

Trent felt something tighten in his chest, so much so that breathing was suddenly hard. "You sure about this?"

"Yeah."

"What if you get sad again?"

"I'll ask for help." Matty walked forward. "I promise I'll call."

"No bullshit?" Trent asked, his voice cracking as he pulled Matty into a tight hug.

"No bullshit. It's gonna be okay. You got me through it. I'll be fine."

Chapter 50

Later that night, Trent mulled over his conversation with Matty as he furiously worked in the garden, aided by the glow of the fairy lights he'd set up last year for the twins' seventeenth birthday party. It was either this or go to bed, and Trent didn't want to spend another minute in that bedroom. Every time he walked through the door of that marble foolishness called a bathroom, he wished he could go back in time and tell his parents just how much they'd screwed up. He'd tell them that they didn't have all the time in the world. He'd tell them how long it would take their kids to undo the damage they'd wrought.

I don't need you to look after me anymore. Matty's words echoed through Trent's mind as he attacked the weeds with a savagery that involved a lot of seedling casualties, the rich smell of upended soil spreading through the air.

"Can I join you?"

Trent heard his nona's question, but he didn't stop what he was doing. "I'm in a really bad mood and I'd rather be alone right now if that's alright with you. I'll come in soon." He threw the weeds in his hand onto the growing pile and went back to furiously pulling more out.

"I think I'll stay out here." His nona settled on the grass next to him and started pulling weeds at a more sedate pace. "It's an odd time to be gardening, but the older I get, the less sleep I need."

"No, you don't have to do that." Trent put a hand on her shoulder before brushing off the specks of dirt he'd inadvertently smudged on her top.

She looked at him over her reading glasses. "Someone has to do it."

"No, they don't. Or at least you don't right now. Come on. Let's go inside." Trent tried to urge her to her feet, but she remained stubbornly kneeling.

"No, someone has to pull out the weeds. And since I'm here, it might as well be me." She kept plucking away, adding to the pile Trent had already started.

"No, not you."

"Why not me?"

"Because I don't need you to," he said.

"But you used to. After your parents died. Remember, when we had this foolish big house but no money for food?" she asked with a smile. "I fed you all with this garden for nearly two years. We had chickens then. And that rooster that was so *loud*."

Trent's mind flashed on a memory of getting up at three in the morning to go work part-time at a bakery and finding his nona already up, making him breakfast. "Yeah, I do. But I don't need you to work anymore to help us out now. We're all grown up. We can do it on our own."

"How can I be sure of that?" she asked, still busily weeding. "After all, I'm responsible for you all. Anything that happens to us is my fault. I have to keep you all safe."

"That's not how this works anymore, and you know it. You worked yourself into the ground so we'd be able to be independent. You should have some time for you."

"That might be the case for you, but what about Gwen, Matty, the twins?"

"Gwen's doing fine, and you and I both know the twins can't wait to start college in the fall."

"And Matty?"

Trent paused to look at her. In that moment, he knew that Matty had already told her about his decision to move out. "He'll be okay. As long as we deal with the stuff with Mom and Dad as it comes up. I've just got to be vigilant. You don't have worry about any of that."

"But I still do. You say I shouldn't worry. But if I don't make sure everyone's okay all the time, things might not be so good." Trent's nona grimaced, looking up at the fairy lights and a half-moon beyond. "I lay awake at night, thinking of all the things I could do better to make sure everyone's okay, but it's never enough. Never enough."

"That's just crazy talk. Why would you lay awake all night worrying when I'm already doing that—" Trent stopped talking abruptly as the message behind what his nona was saying sunk in. "You're one crafty lady and a damn good liar. You've always been able to sleep through anything."

She gave him a satisfied nod. "You got your brains from my side of the family. And that overinflated sense of responsibility of yours. If you don't let them go, they won't be able to grow up."

Trent let out something that was half laugh, half groan. "Funny, Matty said something like that earlier today."

"He got his brains from my side of the family too."

They fell silent as Trent looked at the huge house his father had built. "I never liked this place." Just saying it out loud left him feeling lighter inside. "I think it's why I wanted to be an architect when I was a kid. I'd daydream about how I would've designed it better. And the longer we've lived in it and the more that goes wrong, the more I realize *anyone* could have designed it better. Dad spent all his money on the flashy stuff and didn't think twice about skimping on the plumbing, and the guttering . . . and a whole lot of other things. This place should be in the dictionary next to the saying 'all style, no substance.'" He looked at his nona, who was watching him with a soft smile. "How will I know they'll be okay? Really okay?"

"Because I said so. And because between me and you, we raised them well. One of the hardest lessons of being a parent is knowing when to let them go. And you've parented these children for most of your adult life. You'll have to let them go."

"How? They still need me. Other than Gwen, none of them have enough money—" He paused as the memory of standing in Marlene Lineman's house and realizing how well-off his family actually was. "You're suggesting I sell the house."

She looked around her. "For all its faults, this place is worth a lot of money. If you managed it right, you'd be able to make sure everyone has a lot to get them started in their adult life. Although, I'd make sure the bulk of it is tied up in ironclad trust funds when it comes to the twins and Matty. At least until they're twenty-five. That way they'll have to learn that money doesn't come without hard work," she said, her eyes twinkling behind her glasses.

Trent drew a deep breath. "But what about the history attached to this place? It's the last we've got of Mom and Dad . . ." He glanced around him, really letting himself acknowledge the sticky, horrible feeling that had been with him for a long time now. "This place really was the worst of them, wasn't it? That's what we've been holding on to. All of us."

His nona stayed silent.

"Do you think the girls feel the same way?"

"I think Gwen does. And as for the twins, they'll adjust. Like Matty, you've spoiled them a little too much, and it would be good for them to live on campus and learn to be independent women. Carlotta especially. She and I had a talk about her blaming you for what happened to Matty. I explained that taking bad feelings out on other people instead of talking sensibly is precisely how people in this family dig themselves into holes they can't climb out of. It didn't work for Matty and it won't work for her." Her face momentarily took on a fierce cast. "She needs to learn—they all do—that you're not a tap to turn on for money, and that your time isn't always theirs. Matty knows it's safe to talk about things if he feels bad now. They can learn too."

"But what if I let them down again? What if Matty—"

"We'll all be there for them, for him. He's a grown man. And you're smothering him. He needs to go out into the world and make the kind of mistakes that will help him grow into the good man you are today."

It took Trent a few seconds to register his nona's words, and then, out of nowhere, his eyes sheened over with tears, his voice coming out raspy. "Am I? Am I really a good man? Because I sure as hell don't feel like it. I mean, I try so hard, but I constantly worry I'm getting it wrong."

His nona put a hand on his shoulder. "Yes. You are. You are a good grandson, a good brother, and you'll be a good husband to some woman one day. If I can talk you into getting rid of this big ugly place and into making more time for yourself." She made to stand up and Trent rushed to help her.

"You really wouldn't miss it? Even with the garden and everything."

"The garden's not too bad, but the rest . . ." She pursed her lips. "Tacky."

Trent laughed. "Yeah, it is."

"Good." She clapped her hands together. "Now come into the house and you can help me discuss this with your brother and sisters. And while you're at it, you can accept Carlotta's apology graciously, because knowing that girl, she won't be giving it that way."

"What about you?" he asked his nona, who was now brushing grass off her cardigan. "You gonna desert me too?"

"And give up all that nice food you make for me?" She looked at him sharply. "Unless you don't want a nosy old lady spoiling plans with that girl you cooked all that food for."

"I've got all the time in the world for nosy old ladies."

She snorted. "Did you just call me old?"

"You said it first. I was only agreeing with you so you didn't feel bad."

That earned him a playful smack on the arm. "And what about that girl?"

"Yeah, about that girl." Trent looked over his nona's head to the house, feeling the slow dawning of what his future could be like if he willingly gave up some of the responsibilities he'd carried around for the past decade. With his share of money from the house, he could put a down payment on a nice little place with a garden for Nona that didn't suck up all his money. He'd have the time to spend on himself, working out who he wanted to be. Maybe the time to talk Candy into giving him another chance . . .

A jolt shot through his system as he pictured what *that* might be like; her giving him hell every night at the bar, seeing him off to work in the mornings, maybe spending a Sunday hiking once she could afford more staff in the bar . . .

"Are you coming inside?" his nona asked.

Trent nodded, before asking the question on the tip of his tongue. "Does the worry ever go away? That they'll be okay? That they'll get hurt? That they'll be sad?"

His nona laughed softly. "Never. It's a curse for life, but that's what loving people is all about."

Chapter 51

Candy was not having a good evening. For one thing, someone had kidnapped her dog. She knew Barney was fine, because this was Hard Candy and it was Drag Poetry Night, but "fine" covered a whole lot of territory.

Fantasia's crew had taken over her office an hour ago when she'd been distracted filling a big order for drinks, saying they needed to prepare for an extra special performance. A while later, Fantasia had come out and coaxed Barney in there with them. Candy knew what that meant. It meant drag dog.

She didn't want to *think* of how much shampooing it would take to remove whatever makeup the queens plastered on him. Sure, she knew they'd make sure none of the products were toxic, but that didn't mean that his white fur wasn't now technicolor.

"How are we *possibly* going to cope when you leave us to those new people you hired? Do any of them even know how to appreciate poetry?!"

Candy stopped glaring at her office door to find Queera Belle leaning on the other side of the packed bar, her face done up like Barbie on acid, her hair huge and blond.

"You don't need to worry about me going on a holiday

next month, because none of you are gonna survive *tonight* if I don't get my dog back. What the hell are they up to in there?"

Queera Belle pursed her cherry-red lips and gave Candy a coy look. "That's for me to know and for you to find out."

"If Fantasia's involved, we're all going to find out. Especially if she's singing," Kevin piped up from his barstool just as Candy's office door opened.

"What was that? My adoring audience is demanding my attention?" Fantasia strutted out and blew a kiss at Kevin, forcing him to catch it and pocket it.

Candy did a double take. The queen was wearing a bright pink wig that was done up in pigtails. She was also wearing the skimpiest gold cheerleading costume Candy had ever seen. Thankfully, there was a skin-toned bodysuit underneath. No one was gonna get their own personal mooning tonight.

"What the hell have you been doing in there?" she asked. "And please tell me you haven't put my dog in a catsuit."

"A dog in a catsuit? You know questions like that are going to tax her intelligence to its limits. I'm guessing taxonomy wasn't her best subject at school," Kevin said while furiously typing, but Candy caught his mouth quirking and knew just how much he was enjoying himself. She wondered how long it was gonna be before Fantasia and Kevin hooked up. Or maybe they'd just be one of history's unrequited love affairs; as a bar owner, she'd seen a whole lot of those.

But she didn't want to dwell on that right now. Because drag queens had kidnapped her dog.

"Can someone turn this fashion fallout's dial down?" Fantasia shot Kevin a dramatic glower. "This negativity is making my wig limp." She wagged a finger at Candy. "And there is no way I'd *ever* put *my* puppy in a pussy suit—I'm insulted you even asked!" She looked at Queera Belle. "We ready?"

Queera Belle nodded. "Yaass, queen." She looked at Kevin. "Are *you* ready?"

Kevin darted a glance at Candy before nodding quickly.

"He's *never* ready," Fantasia said with a sigh.

"Says someone who's running four minutes and thirty seconds behind schedule," Kevin grumbled.

"For what?" Candy asked, looking from Fantasia to Kevin to Queera Belle. "What's going on? And why are Kevin and Barney involved. If whatever you're about to do involves breaking any Rules—"

"Oh, honey," Fantasia gave her a wicked grin, "why break one when we can break them *all?*" She cupped her hands around her mouth, turning to face the regulars packing the bar. "Listen up, people! It's last call before the show starts, so come up to the bar and get some sugar from our very own Candy Blume, Mistress of Drag Poetry Night, before you take your seats. And if you can't find a seat, make a friend and sit on them instead. We've got a *huge* show for you tonight. More massive than I usually give you, because this is a very *special* occasion."

"What occasion? And *what the hell is everyone doing in my office?*" Candy demanded as the crowd started cheering. Both Kevin and Fantasia ignored her, starting another one of their arguments so they could pretend they hadn't heard her. She wanted to institute an epic round of ass-kicking, but then the bar rush started. For the next fifteen minutes she couldn't do more than serve drinks.

By the time Queera Belle was calling for everyone to be in their seat, Fantasia was nowhere in sight and Kevin had gone. In his spot was a large speaker.

Candy did a double take at the speaker, a great big ball of dread forming in her chest as she added this to the list of suspicious activity. Kevin never left his seat during Drag Poetry Night. Even if his bladder was bursting, he'd stay to heckle Fantasia. Something really big— and probably bad —was up.

Just as she was about to put a stop to proceedings and

demand someone tell her what the hell was happening, the music started.

For a moment, Candy couldn't believe what she was hearing, but then, yes, there was no denying it. The song "I Want Candy" by Aaron Carter was being played in her bar, at full volume. And it was coming from the speaker in Kevin's spot, which meant that she couldn't do a thing about it.

"Oh no! There is no freaking way!" Her exclamation was drowned out by a bunch of whoops. "Rule Twelve!" Candy yelled at Queera Belle, who was now standing on the makeshift stage near the TARDIS and getting everyone to clap along. "This song *only* gets played when hell freezes over!"

"Oh really? Well, ladies and gentlemen, isn't it a coincidence that something truly miraculous has just happened?" Queera yelled to the cheering crowd as a procession of queens strutted from Candy's office, all of them wearing witchy makeup, red contact lenses, and devil horns over ice-blue wigs. Their bodies were covered to the thigh in white puffer jackets, but Candy knew near-nudity was coming because they were all wearing sparkling, stoned fishnets.

"Here are our Demonesses of Drag Poetry Night, and don't they look cold? In fact, so cold, I'd say hell *has* frozen over!" Queera Belle gleefully shouted into her microphone as the frozen demon drag queens set themselves up on stage, throwing off their jackets to reveal pale blue bikinis as they lip-synched with the song.

Before Candy could process all this, another whoop came from the crowd, who were pointing to something behind her.

Candy spun around as Fantasia strutted out of her office, leading Barney on a leash. Candy's dog was done up like a polar bear with demon horns. Fantasia gave her a wink and then turned, gesturing over her shoulder for someone else to come out.

Candy did a mental count of queens. The only person

missing was Kevin, but no, she could see him hiding at the back of the room out of her shouting range.

"Let's all hear just how much we want Candy, people! And give us a great big cheer for our newest addition to Drag Poetry Night, Whiiite Chocolaaate!"

Candy stared at the door of her office as a ridiculous thought crossed her mind. She was already shaking her head when another queen emerged from her office, wearing pink pigtails and a cheerleading outfit just like Fantasia's, except the skin tone of the bodysuit underneath was a lot paler.

Queera Belle was now leading the entire bar in the chorus of the song while this new queen walked towards Candy, stumbling momentarily on unfamiliar high heels, her—his— face a picture of both fear and happiness as he held out a huge gold box.

"Oh no." Candy shook her head as every part of her rejected the fact that Trent Green was standing in front of her in drag. "There. Is. No. Way!"

"Yes way, honey! Yes way!" Fantasia yelled before skipping through the crowd to the stage and taking the microphone from Queera Belle. "Can y'all cheer on our latest queen? Because she's got a great big something in her box to give Mistress Candy, and we all know from the last time just how much Mistress Candy *loves* surprises!"

There was another huge cheer as Candy looked into Trent's eyes.

"What the hell are you doing?" she asked incredulously, taking in his face. Whichever queen had done his makeup had gotten his eyelashes wrong, with one hanging sideways and the other heading off for parts unknown. His red lipstick was worse than anything done at a budget *Rocky Horror* production too.

He shrugged. "It's something to do on a Tuesday night. And I'm on a mission."

"To do what?"

"Woo a girl."

The song stopped and Trent turned to look at Kevin, then Fantasia. Suddenly Iggy Pop's "Candy" started playing and the queens did what they did best, putting on a show like no other.

Kevin was still hovering at the back of the room, obviously controlling the playlist on his phone out of shouting range.

"I can't. I can't process this," Candy said.

"Is my makeup that bad?" Trent asked, blowing upwards to make his wonky eyelash flutter.

She let out an involuntary burst of laughter. "Yes! It's awful. What are you doing here?"

"I'm here for you," Trent said, holding out the box just as the entire bar launched into the chorus of the song. "Open it."

"How did you get in here? *When* did you get here?" she yelled over the singing.

Trent looked over his shoulder at Kevin, his pigtails swishing. "Kevin invited me to his part of the bar while you were distracted setting up the stage."

"That traitor!"

"That friend!" Trent yelled back, holding out the box again. "Open it."

Candy looked at the box. "What's in it?"

"Find out," he said.

"White Chocolate, you're in dereliction of your drag duty!" Fantasia yelled from the stage.

"Coming!" Trent yelled back. "I've got some dancing to do to prove how much I want to be in your life. That alright?"

"You're gonna dance? In *those heels?*" Candy looked down at his feet, which were currently squished into a pair of too-small red stilettos.

"Pray for me." He leaned forward and dropped a kiss on her head, probably leaving a huge lipstick print, before he stumbled towards the stage, theatrically giving up on the shoes halfway and handing them to someone.

And then suddenly, Britney Spears was playing and Trent and Fantasia were in perfect sequence, dancing to "Hit Me Baby One More Time" while the frozen demonesses danced backup in the crowd.

Candy caught Trent giving her a wink mid-Britney gyration, and seeing him there, surrounded by her people, accepted and loving it, she felt the awful tension she'd been feeling for months—maybe years and years—dissolve.

Her smile started as a twinge at the corner of her mouth and then grew with each dodgy dance move—with each pigtail flick and hammy flourish to the crowd—until she was laughing out loud, huge gulps of laughter that made her clutch her stomach, her cheeks hurting. When Trent's eyelash finally gave up the ghost and fell onto his cheek, and his wig flicked Fantasia in the mouth and got stuck in her lipstick, it got even funnier. And as Candy laughed, she realized everyone else in the bar was laughing with her.

The song ended, and Candy expected Trent to leave the stage, but instead Nirvana's "Smells Like Teen Spirit" kicked into gear and then the whole bar was dancing with Trent, Fantasia and their demoness crew.

Giving in to the moment, Candy watched, serving drinks when people wanted them, but mainly watching Trent Green making a fool out of himself on the stage.

And it was all for her.

Chapter 52

"So are you finally gonna open it?" Trent asked four hours later. He was the last person sitting in the bar—everyone, including Kevin, having noisily left minutes ago—and although Trent had taken off his wig and had done his best at wiping off a bunch of the makeup, he was still wearing one eyelash and his freshly donned white T-shirt was smudged with the foundation he'd obviously missed on his neck. To Candy, he'd never been sexier.

She looked at the box as she finished locking up her cash register. "I don't know if I want to."

"Is there a reason for that?" he asked.

"I'm worried you're gonna ruin it," she said honestly.

"You mean I didn't already by not talking to you for months?"

"That didn't do a lot to help your cause." She braced her hands on the bar. "But dressing up in drag and serenading me for most of the night has softened me up enough not to kick you out yet. It's hard to hate on a man who'd tuck his junk for you."

Trent winced. "Yeah, when Fantasia and I came up with this idea, I didn't think it'd mean learning how to make my junk invisible. Any man who can do that for a living has huge balls."

"You did the full tuck? The *full* tuck?" Candy asked, incredulous.

He looked sheepish. "Turns out I'm a bit more of a wimp than I thought. They wanted to show me how, but I just opted for the masking tape part of it. Which means I haven't taken the masking tape off yet because I know it's gonna hurt like hell, especially since I didn't get the memo about shaving everything off first."

"Are you scared?" Candy arched a brow, deciding that now was probably not the time to tell him he could have just used a cut-down pair of panty hose. But the queens had to have their fun, she supposed.

"Yeah."

"Good."

He laughed. "I thought you'd say that. If it makes you happy, I know it's gonna be painful."

"Now you're just trying to make me feel sorry for you."

"If it helps."

"It might." She spritzed herself a Coke just for something to do, because suddenly she had butterflies warring in her stomach. The box was still there. She hadn't opened it. She knew she had to. "How's your brother?"

Trent took a sip of his scotch. "He's gonna be okay. We had a lot of stuff to sort out." He set the glass down. "Are you okay? Kevin told me about the deal. You know, it's funny, but I only realized after he told me his last name that Gwen's got all his books. From what Gwen says, he's an amazing writer."

Candy just nodded. She knew Kevin was brilliant at what he did. She'd known for years. "So what now?" she asked, cutting to the chase.

"You open the box."

"But if I do, it means . . . it means something."

"Yeah. It does. But only what you want it to." He finished

his drink and then turned around to glance at Barney, who was still wearing the polar bear suit while sprawled out in the middle of the bar, fast asleep after all the excitement. "Your dog snores louder than anyone I've ever met."

Candy realized the topic change was meant to give her space. Taking a deep breath, she slid a nail under the seal holding the box closed and flicked the lid open like she had on a similar box months ago. Except this time, when she looked inside there was . . . nothing.

"It's empty." She peered inside and then looked at Trent, her brows lowering. "What does this mean?"

"It means whatever you want it to," he said simply. "I figured that instead of guessing the best way to ask your forgiveness, I'd leave it up to you. What do you want?"

Candy stared at him. "I don't get it."

"Knowing how responsible for everyone you've had to be your whole life, I figured no one would've asked you what you want. So I'm asking right now. What do *you* want, Candy Blume?"

Candy shook her head as a faint buzzing noise started in her ears. It wasn't quite panic, but it wasn't quite comfortable either. "I still don't get it. What do you mean? Do you mean world peace? Do you mean——"

"What do *you* want? For you. Not for anyone else. Just for you, Candy Blume. One of the most amazing women I have ever met and someone so strong that I'm in awe of you every second. What do you want?"

Candy bit her lip, anxiety kicking in big time now. She opened her mouth to say something flippant, to brush Trent off, but no sound came out. So she spun away to start tidying the bottles on the shelves behind her, needing to do something to get rid of this awkward, lost feeling.

"What if I tell you something that you can't give me?" she asked. "What if I tell you something and then I don't hear from you for another three months? Or years." She felt tears at the back of her throat, stinging her eyes, but refused to give into them.

"I won't let you down again."

She spun around. "Yes you will. Don't lie. People let people down all the time. They don't mean to. It just happens. You couldn't have predicted your brother trying to kill himself, you couldn't predict—"

"I won't let you down," Trent repeated softly. "I might have to take some time out to help my family, but I won't let you down. If you want this thing to be just tonight and to never see me again, that's okay. If you want it to be more, I'd like that. A lot. But just know, if you ever need me. I'll be there for you."

Candy felt the first tear trickle down her cheek and swiped at it. "I don't want it to just be tonight. I want more. Lots more."

"Yeah?" Trent asked, his own face reflecting the urgency she suddenly felt.

"And I want *you*. I want what we had before, but more. And I never, ever want to hear that playlist played in my bar again. Aaron Carter? What were you thinking?" Candy spluttered, half laughing, half crying as Trent circled the bar to pull her into his arms. "And there's something bigger," she said, the words coming out before her brain could edit them and tell her that she was setting herself up for a big fall.

"Anything," Trent said against her forehead.

"I want you to come to Hong Kong with me next month. If you really want to do this, come with me. You owe my dad an apology for messing with my graduation."

"Yeah. I do."

Trent pulled her tight against him and everything felt so, so right, their bodies slotting together perfectly.

"Plus, I've never left the country before, and I'm really scared of flying. And of disappointing my Chinese relatives. And I don't want to do it all on my own. I mean, I want some time alone with Dad, but he's gonna be working most days and . . . I just want you with me," Candy said in a rush, burying her face against Trent's chest, loving the way he started running his hands over her back. "And I guess if I do anything wrong and you're there, they'll think it's your bad influence and blame you." she added.

"Done. When are we flying?"

"In a month. For two weeks. Can you do it?" Candy pulled back.

He looked thoughtful for a moment. "Yeah. I think I can." His mouth curved into a slow smile. "Is there hiking in Hong Kong?"

Candy squeezed his backside. "If there isn't, we'll come up with something else."

Trent kissed her then, a long, slow kiss that left the blood rushing in Candy's ears after. "Yeah, I think we'll work something out."

"What about your business?"

"I've made a couple of changes lately that mean I've got more time on my hands. What about your business?"

Candy breathed in deep. "I've hired a couple more staff— the guys that helped me out at your brother's party, actually. Kevin's gonna drive them nuts while I'm away, but it's time I let myself live a little more. I've been hiding out here for too long."

"It's not such a bad place to hide."

"I love it, but it's time I got out more."

"I like the idea of you living it up." He waggled his brows at her. "Ever made love to a man who has some gaffer tape that needs removing soon or things are gonna get *really* uncomfortable?"

Candy let out a bubble of laughter. "You gonna let me pull it off?"

Trent's mouth curved into a gentle smile. "For you? Anything."

342

"You know, I think that's the sweetest thing anyone has ever said to me. Are you gonna scream extra loud when I pull off that tape?"

Trent gave her a faux-stern scowl. "Real men don't scream."

"Do they whimper?"

"They might."

"That's good enough for me." She took his hands in hers, leaning forward and kissing him on the lips. "Come on, Green, let's get this show on the road."

Epilogue

Candy studied the map on the screen of her phone as Trent gently pulled her out of the way of the never-ending throng of people soaking up Kowloon's atmosphere. There was a breeze coming off the bay that carried a heady combination of smells, most of them mouth-watering given all the restaurants around. People were speaking in Cantonese and a bunch of other Chinese dialects, as well as a whole lot of languages that Trent didn't recognize.

Trent had never left the States before but for some reason he felt comfortable here. Maybe it was the way the sights and smells of food mixed with the chaos of city noises. It was a barrage to the senses, but it felt good. It felt like he was living.

He grinned, meeting the eyes of an elderly Chinese man sitting in the door of a supermarket. The man nodded at Trent, and Trent nodded at the man. Cross-cultural communication had been achieved. Trent couldn't wait to tell his sisters and his nona about this.

"Have you found it?" he asked Candy.

"It's just down there." Candy frowned at her phone, then pointed at a narrow alley filled with neon signs and lanterns.

He looked down the alley and then at her. "You okay?"

She bit her lip and nodded. "Yeah, I think so. I just . . . it's been so long. What if he's not happy about me surprising him? Maybe I should have called to let him know we were coming. Maybe—"

"Hey." Trent wrapped an arm around her shoulders and kissed the side of her newly shaved head. "Would you be happy if he surprised you at your place?"

He caught the flash of tears in her eyes before she looked away. "Yeah."

"Then pony up, Blume, and get your ass down that alley. You've got a dad to surprise." Trent slapped her on the rump —it was a risk to his life, but he knew she needed the encouragement.

"Fine. But if you spank me again, I'm gonna put some gaffer tape where the sun doesn't shine while you're sleeping tonight."

"Vicious woman," Trent said, following along behind her as she marched forward, checking in with her phone until she stopped abruptly in front of a heavy brushed-metal door. The words "Metal Box" were scored into its surface.

Candy looked at him. "You ready?"

"Always." He stole a kiss before giving her a gentle push in the back.

"Okay, I'm going in."

She pushed the door open and they stepped inside. Trent barely had time to take in the graffiti murals, the guitars on the walls, and the giant framed pictures of Patti Smith and Johnny Rotten—just like Candy's bar—because there was a shout and words bellowed in Cantonese.

"Patti!" someone yelled. And then a guy that looked like a cross between a punk rocker and a Chinese gangster was launching himself over a zinc-topped bar and running through the crowd towards Candy, his heavily pierced face breaking into a massive grin as he swept Candy into his arms and swung her around. His and Candy's laughter filled the air.

Trent watched on, his heart swelling. And in that moment —feeling his own happiness at seeing Candy so happy—he knew that he loved Candy Blume from the bottom of her heavy-soled Doc Martens to the top of her kick-ass shaved head. He loved this woman like the sun. And the minute he got a chance he was gonna tell her.

"Is this the guy?"

Trent snapped out of his thoughts at the sound of Candy's dad now speaking in English. His arm was slung over Candy's shoulders and he was giving Trent a grin.

"Yeah," Candy said.

"So you're the high school bad guy," the guy said, looking Trent up and down, his expression suddenly fierce. "If you ever make my daughter cry again like you did at her graduation I'll make you regret it."

"That would be your right," Trent replied solemnly. "I owe you an apology, sir. I'm sorry for ruining that moment for the two of you. I was young and an idiot. But I'd like to think I'm a different man now."

Candy's dad stared at him for a long moment before his mouth suddenly curved into a wide grin. He slapped Trent on the shoulder before he looked at Candy. "He must have been *really* good at cleaning your bar."

She laughed. "He grew on me."

"He okay at everything else?"

Candy slapped her dad's chest and then took one of Trent's hands in hers. "Yeah."

"You like him a lot?"

Candy looked at Trent. "A lot."

"Like loving and kissing a lot?"

Candy rolled her eyes. "Like loving and kissing a lot."

Trent blinked. "Did you just say you love me?"

"Yeah, and you better say you love me back or my dad will beat you up. Won't you, Dad?"

"Of course!"

Trent took in the two matching scowls and broke into laughter. "Only you would threaten me into admitting I care, Candy Blume."

Candy kept scowling, but he could see the happiness dancing underneath. "So do you love me?"

"Hell yes. I love you, Candy Blume."

"Damn straight." She turned to look at her dad, who was now grinning from ear to ear. "You got anything decent to drink in this place, Johnny?"

"Sure do, Patti."

With that Johnny Tang announced to the whole bar that the next round was on him. The night turned into one big happy blur from there, but the bit Trent loved the most was Candy's smile.

It didn't leave her face once.

The End!

Acknowledgments

Dear Reader, thanks so much for choosing to read Candy and Trent's story. You're obviously awesome.

We love to hear from our readers so feel free to email us at evie@eviesnow.com

Also, a huge thanks to Andrea Robinson for the amazing edits and to Najla Qamber and her team for the brilliant cover.

To all of our amazing friends, thanks so much for the love and support you've given us on this crazy writing journey. We'd love to particularly thank to the glorious Seldon clan for putting up with us, Barbara Winmill, Katie Keith, Rhyll Biest and the ninja gals, Vanessa Stubbs and Jo Clegg. If we've missed anyone, we promise to treat you to high tea the next time we're in your part of the world.

About the Author

Evie Snow is the pen name for a globe-trotting writing team comprising of Georgina (George) Penney and Tony (The Kraken) Johnson.

George does the actual writing and reads far too many books. In the past, she was well on the way to a contemporary history PhD when moving to Saudi Arabia re-introduced her to a love of writing fiction.

Tony manages plot wrangling and is in charge of caffeine distribution. He once spent twenty years working globally as a petroleum engineer and found the oil industry to be far stranger than fiction.

Together, George and Tony have lived in a bunch of countries including Australia, Saudi Arabia, Bahrain, Brunei Darussalam and Scotland. They're currently on a world-traveling adventure, writing books, seeing all the sights, eating all the food and patting as many critters as possible.

For more info about us,
www.eviesnow.net

Also by Evie Snow

Head Over Heels

Mind Games

Stuck On You

Sweet On You

Save Me From Heroes

Ian Buchanan's Very Big Secret

Evangeline's Rest

Fly In Fly Out

Love Imperfection

The Barbershop Girl